LITERARY TREASON

LITERARY TREASON

AUTHORS ON TRIAL IN THE WAKE OF THE SECOND WORLD WAR

Marius Hentea

BLOOMSBURY ACADEMIC
LONDON • NEW YORK • OXFORD • NEW DELHI • SYDNEY

BLOOMSBURY ACADEMIC
Bloomsbury Publishing Plc, 50 Bedford Square, London, WC1B 3DP, UK
Bloomsbury Publishing Inc, 1359 Broadway, New York, NY 10018, USA
Bloomsbury Publishing Ireland, 29 Earlsfort Terrace, Dublin 2, D02 AY28, Ireland

BLOOMSBURY, BLOOMSBURY ACADEMIC and the Diana logo are trademarks of Bloomsbury Publishing Plc

First published in Great Britain 2026

Cover design by Grace Ridge
Cover image: World War Two UK and Commonwealth, Treason Trials, Lord Haw-Haw, London 1946 (Contributor: PA Images via Alamy)

A catalogue record for this book is available from the British Library.

A catalog record for this book is available from the Library of Congress.

ISBN: HB: 978-1-3504-0692-6
PB: 978-1-3504-0691-9
ePDF: 978-1-3504-0693-3
eBook: 978-1-3504-0694-0

Typeset by Newgen KnowledgeWorks Pvt. Ltd., Chennai, India
Printed and bound in Great Britain

For product safety related questions contact productsafety@bloomsbury.com.

To find out more about our authors and books visit www.bloomsbury.com and sign up for our newsletters.

CONTENTS

FIGURES

ACKNOWLEDGMENTS

This book has been long in the making. After having completed a critical biography of Tristan Tzara, I told myself to steer clear of archives for my next book. This book is a result of that unheeded injunction. That it took so long to finish is a direct result of that archival fever, which led me to consult upwards of forty archives in half a dozen countries. All that would not have been possible without generous institutional support and my wife and children putting up with my absence. I would like to thank the Harry Ransom Center, via the Woodward and Bernstein Endowment, for subsidizing a one-month research stay in 2016, the Swedish Research Council for a project research grant (2016-01099-VR), and the Riksbankens Jubileumsfond for a sabbatical grant (SAB23-0029-RJ) that allowed me to finally finish this book and to publish it open access.

A special thank you goes out to the archivists and librarians who went above and beyond in their help and generosity. The Inter-Library Loan team at the University of Gothenburg, too, were fantastic in sourcing difficult-to-find material promptly and efficiently.

This book has also been the result of numerous intellectual exchanges and discussions, from conferences to invited talks. I would like to single out colleagues at the University of Freiburg, the University of Gothenburg, the University of Kyoto, Tulsa University, Mid-Sweden University, and VUB Brussels for their enthusiasm in hosting me. I would also like to thank professional colleagues from the Modernist Studies Association, at whose annual conferences I have presented work in progress from this book or hosted seminars on topics directly aligned to its concerns, as well as colleagues from the Société des Études Modernistes and the Modernist Studies in Asia network. I will not name individuals, for fear of not identifying every single one by name, but everyone who has helped with this book should know how much I value and appreciate the support and ideas I have been so fortunate to receive.

I would like to thank the editorial team at Bloomsbury for their help in this project; from the first pitch to the final product, everything ran like a dream. Infinite patience was shown by my editor, Ben Doyle, in waiting for the final manuscript.

Every effort has been made to receive permissions for material quoted in this book; if an oversight has happened, I would appreciate the chance to correct that for future editions of the book. I would like to thank Finola Graham for permission to publish previously unpublished letters and archival material by Francis Stuart.

Previously unpublished letters and archival material by Dorothy Pound, copyright ©2025 by the Estate of Omar S. Pound. Reprinted by permission of New Directions Publishing Corp., acting as agent. All rights reserved.

Previously unpublished letters and archival material by James Laughlin, copyright ©2025 by Leila Laughlin Javtich, Amelia Laughlin, and Walker Laughlin. Reprinted by permission of New Directions Publishing Corp., acting as agent. All rights reserved.

This book is dedicated to my family—my parents, my sister, my wife, my children. Let me never betray them.

ABBREVIATIONS

AF	Action Française
BBC	British Broadcasting Corporation
BU	British Union
BUF	British Union of Fascists
CDG	Charles de Gaulle
CNE	Comité national des écrivains
CNSAS	Consiliul Național pentru Studierea Arhivelor Securității (Securitate Archive)
DOJ	Department of Justice (USA)
DORA	Defence of the Realm Act
DPP	Director of Public Prosecutions (UK)
DTC	Disciplinary Training Center (Pisa)
EP	Ezra Pound
FBI	Federal Bureau of Investigation
FBP	Francis Biddle Papers (Georgetown)
FCC	Federal Communications Commission
FDR	Franklin Delano Roosevelt
FS	Francis Stuart
G2	Defence Forces Directorate of Intelligence (Ireland)
HC Deb	House of Commons Debates
IEMA	Irish Military Archives
IMEC	Institut Mémoires de l'édition contemporaine (Caen)
INA	Irish National Archives
IRA	Irish Republican Army
IRS	Internal Revenue Service
JCC	Julien Cornell Collection (Swarthmore)
JO	*Journal officiel* (France)
KBP	Katherine Biddle Papers (Georgetown)
LFC	Louis-Ferdinand Céline
LOC	Library of Congress (Washington, D.C.)

MO	*Monitorul oficial* (Romania)
MoI	Ministry of Information (UK)
MP	Member of Parliament (UK)
NAR	National Archives of Romania
NS	Nasjonal Samling
NSL	National Socialist League
NYT	*New York Times*
PCF	French Communist Party
PCR	Romanian Communist Party
PEN	Poet, Novelist, Editor, Playwright Club
PGW	P. G. Wodehouse
P&P	*Ezra Pound's Poetry and Prose: Contributions to Periodicals*
RAF	Royal Air France
RE	Radio Éireann
RM	Reichsmark
RWC	Rebecca West Collection (Tulsa)
RSI	Repubblica Sociale Italiana (Salò Republic)
SRL	*Saturday Review of Literature*
TD	Teachta Dála (Dáil deputy)

INTRODUCTION

The most prominent international association for writers, PEN, knew that its first postwar congress, scheduled for June 1946 in Stockholm, would face some "unusual problems."[1] Some of these were of an organizational nature, such as scheduling travel, deciding keynote speakers, or arranging catering and hotels (especially when a giant agricultural convention was in town). Others were harder to square. PEN had been set up after the First World War as a venue to defend authors and free speech ("an inalienable right of all creative workers … any censorship of literature hinders authors in their work, is treason to the rights of conscience and should be resisted by all authors"), but these ideals sounded sorely out of tune in 1946.[2] The delegates assembled in Stockholm passed a resolution which stated that "those authors who have not been declared … politically reliable should not occupy any function in the public literary or journalistic life of their country." PEN's centers were instructed to circulate blacklists so that writers "judged undesirable" could not "usurp a work or position in a foreign country."[3]

The problem of the relationship between writer and nation, text and politics, was especially loaded in the wake of the Second World War. When E. E. Cummings proclaimed, in November 1945, that "every artist's strictly illimitable country is himself," he was echoing the ideals of the global Republic of Letters in order to defend his close friend, Ezra Pound, from charges of treason.[4] The same spirited exaltation of the artist as above law or politics was also found in Henry De Montherlant's *Le Solstice de Juin* (1941), an unequivocally collaborationist text, extracts of which appeared in the rabidly pro-German *La Gerbe*: "The artist should be, for himself, the center of the world; rejecting … everything that does not concern his creation."[5] While Montherlant had his own reasons to place artists above common morality or law (it was no secret that he longed for the physical love of young boys), the notion that the artist or writer was severed from political responsibility—the linchpin of how the Republic of Letters understood itself as an autonomous social force, the basis upon which modernist autonomy worked as both an aesthetic and social principle—was at no time more fiercely questioned than in 1945. Writers faced a terrible reckoning for the ideas they had expressed during the war, risking not only critical disapproval but jail time and, in some cases, their lives. Yet what does it mean to say that writing could be treason? Had writing gone beyond "mere words" to a kind of action? Was treason the gravest crime when its underlying principle—national belonging—was thought by many to be the root of all the evil that the world had recently experienced? Or were writers bound to follow, as Graham Greene counseled, "the virtue of disloyalty"?[6] These questions are at the heart of this book, which aims to understand how writing and literature came to be conceptualized in the law and literary field during one of the most epochal moments of the twentieth century, the contested "Zero Hour" of 1945.[7]

Scarcely a decade earlier, state power over authors had receded to such a point that "a writer can say almost anything that he wants to in print ... provided he takes trouble not to use certain words"—by which Rebecca West meant salacious, not political, ones.[8] Duties to the state were thoroughly discredited when, ten days after Hitler came to power, the Oxford Union resolved to "under no circumstances fight for its King and country." From one Cambridge an Apostate opined it better to commit treason than betray a friend; from the other, a Harvard law professor dismissed as outdated the idea "that citizenship is a mutual matter in which the citizen must play his part."[9] The outbreak of war exposed such positions as untenable. Intellectuals had to realize, Cyril Connolly warned in May 1940, that "Fascism is against *them*."[10] This fight had to be our fight, Raymond Aron also saw, with the war driving home "the eternal truth that the writer, even one professing solitude and distance, lives in a national community and participates in its fate."[11] To go from that banal truth to being treated as "national goods," as Jean-Paul Sartre bemoaned the status of postwar writers in the age of power politics, both of the reconstructive variety and of the nascent Cold War type, followed in lockstep with the assertion of the state's prerogative to put authors on trial for opinions that in other times would have been a non-matter.[12]

While questions of wartime conduct were ubiquitous—one conservative estimate is that several million individuals were tried, either formally or informally, for collaboration in the postwar period—authors were particularly singled out.[13] If modern literature has long been characterized as the work of "exiles and emigrés," the statelessness of its practitioners and the universality of its forms were no longer calling-cards of prestige but serious violations of increasingly state-bound norms of literary production; if transgression had been the game, the roosting came to be sounded by clerks of the court and secret-service agents. For George Orwell the zeal to hunt down authors for what were euphemistically called "errors of opinion" was vindictive and unseemly. Yet putting authors on trial functioned as a cathartic purge, a way to cleanse the social body of all the felt evils that had invaded or occupied it during the war. In some countries, like France, writers benefited from a long tradition of preeminence, prestige and state patronage; in others, like Norway or Ireland, they had been instrumental in creating a national consciousness and culture. Yet the wide reach and oversized importance of wartime propaganda primed the search for its instigators and conveyors, especially with the legal expansion of treason's reach to include "intellectual" and "propagandist" actions and writings. Writers who were opportunists, seeking out lucre and advantages, were contemptible; writers who never changed course, and thus displayed ideological purity and unbending conviction, were downright dangerous. Against these examples of selling out and fanaticism were tales of writers who courted risks that, in each telling, became ever more inflated. Cashing in worked on both sides. There were not two camps—the collaborator and the resister—but a grey zone in which moral and political negotiations were warily navigated and retrospectively justified. That the truly uncompromising Yogi were few was a truth that did not suit the popular legends (the "myth of the Blitz," the "Vichy syndrome," the "Good War") being built on moral intransigence and clear-cut divisions. In a literary field wracked by petty jealousies and professional angling, postwar purges were useful tools to punish or eliminate rivals. In a time of paper shortages, a competitor going bust or having its stock seized could only be a boon for upstart venues. Finally, punishing an opinion in 1945 did more than look back to the war that had just ended. The specter of a new ideological conflict, this time pitting the West against Soviet communism, turned decisions over past wartime speech into possible frameworks for a future conflict in which the fighting would be cold, not hot, fought through ideas rather than bombs: "In the twentieth century," as *Time* observed in 1946, "treason has become a profession, and its modern form is the betrayal of ideas."[14]

The other reason authors were singled out was more banal: the graphic evidence there in black and white, as good as a signed confession. "The dossier is ready," *Combat* announced: "It is the full print run of *Gringoire*" (an infamous collaborationist paper).[15] Whatever structural factors conditioned a text—the venue soliciting it, editorial interventions, formal censorship requirements, internalized expectations about audience—were too diffuse to be taken into account: the prevailing idea that writing began with a blank page that was filled by the author's own hand had a simplicity to it that made author and text, signature and meaning, inseparable. Considered transparent, free of irony, ambiguity, or context, writing took on a determinative quality when read for collaborationist beliefs. There was no *double jeu* for the word, which meant one thing and one thing only. Then there was the question of where the speech act took place. Publishing in a pro-Nazi print venue or broadcasting on Axis radio came to be considered acts of treason or collaboration regardless of what was said. (Apolitical or escapist content was perhaps worse than straight propaganda by softening the venue—*look, it's not all propaganda*—and thus functioning as a bait-and-switch.) This two-pronged approach to the word—a context-free, overdetermined reading of excerpts and the direct transfer of a venue's politics onto any work appearing in it—simplified the prosecutor's task. Finally, unlike acts behind closed doors, writing created an impression, an imprint; it was a visible and permanent record of the war. The psychological need to break from the past, Mass-Observation co-founder Tom Harrison predicted in early 1944, would lead to the public demanding "to be rid of the primary figures from wartime": this meant not only that heroes like Churchill would be punished at the polls (as he was) but also that those figures who loomed large in the public consciousness, like Lord Haw-Haw, the American-born Irishman broadcasting to Britain from Nazi radio, would be the subjects of wrath.[16]

This book charts the fate of a number of writers and intellectuals who were investigated or tried for treason in the immediate postwar period. Some of the cases are well-known, such as the aborted trial of Ezra Pound, who was found mentally unfit to stand trial and languished for a dozen years in a mental hospital, accumulating honors and disciples, or Robert Brasillach, the bright young thing of French letters, whose execution sparked a broader debate about the purge and laid the foundation for Sartre's theories of the "engaged writer."[17] The most famous of the war renegades, William Joyce, is better known through the myths associated with the "Haw-Haw" label than any solid understanding of his standing as a fascist intellectual and the lengths to which the law's boundaries were stretched at the Old Bailey. Even though much has been written about these figures, the focus has rarely been on the legal machinations and state surveillance operations that translated writings and broadcasts into dangers to the state or a deeper understanding of how these singular cases intersected with wider concerns about propaganda, fascism, and state power. Other cases covered in this book are less well-known, even if the writers in question are not. P. G. Wodehouse, with legions of readers but few in the academy, was never tried for treason, but the investigation into his wartime broadcasting by the British security services resulted in his exile from the country whose national spirit his fiction embodied. Louis-Ferdinand Céline's reputation as an anti-Semite and his standing as one of the leading French writers of the twentieth century have obscured the drawn-out diplomatic wrangling to extradite him back to France to face trial. Knut Hamsun's position as the leading Norwegian writer of his time led the Norwegian state, which was not particularly merciful toward collaborators, to seek an out through a psychological ruling that saved him from certain death, but the full story of his case has rarely been told for English readers. A handful of Romanian journalists found themselves put on collective trial in a people's court, where justice and postwar accounting were driven more by power politics and the Soviet occupation than any native desire to root out fascism. Finally, there was the "moral trial" that Francis Stuart faced; because Ireland was neutral during the war, Stuart's broadcasting from Berlin was not technically treasonous, but it cast a dark shadow over Stuart's later career and was the subject of his most celebrated work, *Black List, Section H.*

Almost all of these cases continue to divide opinion today, but most of these debates remain relatively uninformed about the wider wartime context and lack a solid understanding of the country-specific treason law in place during the postwar period, a lack that this book aims to redress. My main interest is not the politics of Céline and Pound and the like, horrific and contemptible as they were, but rather how postwar legal systems in various countries understood writing, authorship, and texts. I attempt to uncover the various processes and pressures that not only led authors to collaborate but also situate authorship and writing within the shifting sands of the law and oscillating political climates. The treatment of writing and authorship in this period was not uniform, as experiences of the war and occupation varied enormously, legal systems treated treason and free expression differently, and literary fields mobilized in different fashions to the newfound state control over the word. These national dimensions, though, do not tell the full story, as the fate of authors and writing became an international affair through transnational professional bodies like PEN, the renewed global circulation of ideas, and the diffusion of legal norms and precedents.

Words on Trial

Is it possible to commit treason by pen or speech? "Do civilized peoples shoot their poets?"[18] Those questions—couched in older debates about the responsibility of artists and intellectuals and the limits of free expression—were at the heart of the postwar reckoning. Classical liberalism planted its beachhead on the idea that "mere words" could not amount to treason; dissenting speech, the Millian argument went, needed protection.[19] Yet as a spur to expanding speech's protection, the doctrine of "mere words" is double-edged, expanding the ambit of protected speech because "words only" do not rise to the level of an act (Auden 1939: "poetry makes nothing happen"). But even American courts have never shied from criminalizing defamation and "fighting words," banning obscene or lewd expression, and compensating victims of libels. The claim that words and acts were fundamentally distinct seemed indefensible after a long war dominated by propaganda, and even more so for liberals whose reading of contemporary history was that Weimar's original sin was extending free speech to those vowing to destroy democracy. The liberal poet Archibald MacLeish, for one, saw no way to justify anti-Semitic, pro-Axis broadcasts "on any theory of the freedom of the intellectual to speak his mind."[20]

As an ideological conflict, the Second World War continued to be fought long after the bombing had ended and tanks were grounded to a halt. A staggeringly high number of Europeans—around one in every twenty adult males—came to be investigated in the postwar period for treason, war crimes, or collaboration.[21] In Norway over 90,000 criminal trials took place; in the Netherlands 150,000 individuals were detained under suspicion of collaboration or treason, with criminal trials continuing until the early 1950s; in Belgium about 400,000 dossiers were opened; and in Czechoslovakia over 700 individuals were executed (making the postwar purge deadlier than the subsequent four decades of communist rule). If the purges that swept over postwar Europe were justified politically by the desire to root out Nazism, the motivating factor was more elemental: hatred, the desire for vengeance and retribution, the wrath of people who had experienced the war as an exercise in humiliation and degradation and were now living on a "savage continent," to use historian Keith Lowe's term for postwar Europe.[22] Cordell Hull's view that war criminals did not deserve the "luxury of a trial"—give them like for like via mass executions—was widespread. As Dutch psychologist A. M. Meerloo put it, collective hatred was a "contagious" phenomenon that chose a "defenseless scapegoat" as the object of its fury.[23] With their symbolic notoriety authors fit that category perfectly. In France collaboration was retrospectively made into the crime of "national indignity," to be punished by "national degradation" (loss of property and revocation of civil rights). One writer in *L'Humanité* summoned "wild hatred of the enemy" to the order of a "national duty" (a less feverish commentator recalled that the same writer had followed the Comintern line in 1939 by petitioning for an immediate peace with Hitler).[24] This hatred was even given legal form. In Belgium the provisional government granted a blanket amnesty for acts committed in the immediate forty-one days after liberation. The Tribunals established in the Netherlands in 1945 granted the "community of good Dutchmen" the right to judge those who had strayed, even if just in attitude or beliefs; no appeals allowed.[25]

At the heart of the postwar purge was collaboration through the word, either written or over the radio. Scores of writers and intellectuals were tried in criminal courts or investigated by professional boards for their wartime writings. The "moral drama" of these trials captivated postwar publics.[26] Journalists packed courtrooms and members of the public queued up predawn for prized seats. The masters of the show trial, the Soviets, led the way in 1943 by staging a military tribunal in a movie theater.[27] The BBC (British Broadcasting Corporation) floated the idea of broadcasting Lord Haw-Haw's trial live, as if it were a Wembley cup final, but the Home Office was not prepared for such novelty. The verdicts in these trials became affairs of state as hundreds of signatories petitioned presidents and prime ministers to show clemency to writers sentenced to death. But these trials were also tragedies, the law bent out of shape to serve politics or personal grudges. The persistent critique of the International Military Tribunals held at Nuremberg as "victor's justice" was even more pointed when it came to national purge trials. Britain's foremost left-wing publisher, Victor Gollancz, bemoaned "the reversion to a more barbaric concept of justice" as harsh punishments were meted out "after the caricature of a trial which is worse than no trial at all, simply for the offence of having been on the losing side."[28] This was an unpopular opinion, and an unexpected one for a Jew heartbroken at the suffering of his people, but Gollancz found it intolerable for judges to open trials with black cap in hand or for juries to be prescreened for ideological purity. There was a perverse irony in seeing Goebbels's dictum on legal justice—a trial should begin not with some idea of law but with the idea that this man must go—being used against his followers. In Marcel Aymé's play on the postwar purge, *La tête des autres* (1952), the moral is explicit: "Listen, when the courts are compelled by higher reasons to find a guilty party, they always do."[29] The crimes on the dock had not been crimes when they had been committed; the courts were chockful of magistrates, justices and lawyers who had greased the wheels of occupation justice and now proclaimed themselves people's tribunals; it was not a crime that was being punished but an opinion that clear majorities in most occupied countries had subscribed to until the eleventh hour. These were "show trials" to draw out the responsibilities of the pen and convey the right lessons to draw from history.[30] The postwar trials, both domestic and international, were Janus-faced, looking back at the past with an instrumental sense of the future one wished to deliver. Judgment would be passed not just on individual acts but on the whole experience of occupation and war. Paradoxically, this attempt to cleanse or purge the past involved using some of the very same tools from that despised past. The Vichy government had popularized the term "*épuration*" to describe its purge of those who stood in the way of its project of national regeneration. Was it not "Gestapo tactics" to make a crime out of opinion or belief? *Plus ça change*, many muttered.

What was new was the special contempt for writers and intellectuals who had collaborated. Some of that had started during the war, in some cases quietly, as in members of the Norwegian public sending Hamsun's books to his home in such quantities that they had to be dumped to rot in the garden. The establishment of clandestine newspapers and publishers in occupied countries predictably resulted in the targeting of collaborationist authors and the writing up of blacklists. For writers risking torture and death with each column, the zealous collaboration or change-with-the-times justification of other scribblers could only be an affront. The leading resistance group for French writers, the Comité National des Écrivains (CNE), overlooked some dubious ethical stretches (Sartre's plays premiering in Paris, Camus working for a salary at Gallimard, Aragon volumes issued by German-approved publishers) but came down hard on "undesirables" to be tried for treason or banned whenever victory came. At its secret meetings, the topic of conversation was invariably who deserved the rack, transposing the perennial professional jealousy of the overrated and overpaid into a morally self-satisfying form. But given that many of these clandestine writers had been denounced in the collaborationist press, with calls for the German occupiers to round them up, shut them down, silence them forever, there was good reason to fantasize about a cleansed literary field. When these possibilities moved from hushed dreams to possible realities, writers spearheaded the call for purges in the popular press and sat on committees charged with investigating dossiers of wayward confrères. For national governments, writers and intellectuals were safe choices for postwar trials because the evidence against them was easy to assemble and there was an undoubted symbolic value in bringing them to trial. The belief that democracy could be restored if only false opinions were rooted out was an attractive one (if fascism was a noxious set of ideas, all one had to do was eliminate those who held them and ban their circulation; if it was a structural parasite feeding on an unequal social order, good luck). On VE Day, *L'Humanité* noted that victory would not be complete until "all the vestiges of fascism" were destroyed.[31] The thorny problem of the postwar occupation of Germany also pushed for harshness: de-Nazification policies would be severely undermined, one British official noted, if "our own renegades [were] allowed to go unpunished."[32] A cynic could be forgiven for pointing to the severity of how authors were treated. Jean Cocteau was furious that writers of all stripes were overpopulating courtrooms while factory owners and munitions makers got off scot-free. Even publishers, who in France had pre-emptively banded together to appease the new occupiers with a more severe censorship regime than anything the Germans might have contemplated, were relatively untouched by the purge despite their clear complicity (and legal guilt) in distributing noxious texts. For all the talk of national revolutions, the term that resounded was reconstruction, which required bureaucrats and builders. Making an example of writers or turning them into scapegoats (the term appears often enough in the literature about the purge) displeased no one.

The punishment for literary or radio collaboration varied enormously not only across countries but within them. At the wider country level, the biggest difference concerned whether the country had been occupied. Occupation not only created resentment but also spawned opportunities for collaboration. Treason is more a matter of space than of dates: in an unoccupied country, siding with the enemy required personal initiative or ideological commitment, but in occupied countries daily life presented countless occasions for collaboration. "Among those who accuse me today," Montherlant pointedly asked, "in which papers did they write, on what radio did they speak, what job did they hold in October 1941?"[33] Sacha Guitry, whose case dragged on for nearly three years, asked, "Is it 'collaboration' to exercise one's profession under the eye of the occupier during an armistice?"[34] But not all occupations were the same. The German occupations of Denmark or the Channel Islands were light-handed (at least at first), while in France the occupation started off gingerly, with great respect for cultural institutions, which were encouraged to start up again and provided financing to do so, but, as the war dragged on and the resistance picked up, it became brutal. One exception to these broader rules concerns occupations that were so complete, like the one in Poland, that few opportunities for collaboration arose because the vanquished were considered fit only for slave labor. How political figureheads reacted to occupation—whether they re-assembled themselves as quislings to serve the Germans or reconstituted themselves as governments-in-exile to continue the fight from abroad—also impacted how harshly collaboration was judged.

Within countries, the severity of the sentences against collaboration was strongly linked to when the trial took place, the general rule being the earlier the trial, the harsher the punishment.[35] With emotions still running high during the first trials, that harshness was not entirely unexpected. Since the first trials of writers, intellectuals or radio propagandists would set an example for all those to follow, prosecutors brought forward air-tight cases and pushed for the stiffest punishments. Judges who months earlier had applied the laws of the occupier oversaw proceedings with a calculated severity. Juries channeled their repressed fury into the sentences they passed. Over time the need for reconciliation became stronger than the desire for vengeance. Legal norms that had been so badly undermined by the war and politicized, for understandable reasons, in the immediate postwar reasserted themselves. By the summer of 1947, the Lord Chief Justice announced that the season of British renegade trials had run its course. In France a general amnesty passed in 1951 allowed not only collaborators who had managed to escape trial to breathe easy but also reduced prison sentences for those previously convicted. The one exception to this broad rule concerns the United States, where the treason trials of propagandists became more politicized over time. Ezra Pound was let off relatively easily, with the Department of Justice (DOJ) doing little to undermine a questionable psychiatric ruling, while Eva D'Aquino (Tokyo Rose) suffered a miscarriage of justice as wider concerns about loyalty hardened due to Cold War tensions. That case also stood out as an exception when it came to how gender impacted the trials of renegades: as a general rule, women got off more lightly (Susan Hilton told her supposed handler, who turned out to be an undercover MI5 agent, that he risked the hangman's noose for trading state secrets while she would be out of prison in months; she only got a five-year jail term).[36]

Finally, not all authors are equal. While the legal fact in question was a speech act in print or over the radio, the identity of the writer or speaker mattered for its broader meaning, the intentions behind it, and its wider impact. The Director of Public Prosecutions (DPP) candidly admitted that "the notoriety of the suspect" was a key factor in determining whether to lodge a treason charge.[37] The more famous the writer, the more scrutiny, as P. G. Wodehouse found out after a "global howl" erupted for what he considered rather innocuous and humorous radio talks. A "name" not only lent prestige to the enemy but also attracted readers and listeners to propaganda sources. Writers who were considered to possess talent or literary value, who were not hacks grubbily seeking out thirty pieces of silver, were also judged differently. "If he were just a Tom, Dick, or Harry," one observer noted of Pound's troubles, "he'[d] now, probably, be scot free!"[38] Weighing up the sixty-five signatories on a petition to pardon Brasillach, De Gaulle curtly responded, "In letters like in everything else, talent is a title of responsibility."[39] A more talented writer had a greater arsenal of rhetorically persuasive weapons that bored into a reader's soul and beliefs, with greater impact than workmanlike prose, and also was more aware of what words could do. Those with talent had to respect and honor it, and the only master that such talent could serve was the higher calling of art, not a temporal political master. In some exceptional cases, like those of Wodehouse or Hamsun, the writer's fame was so intimately linked to undeniable cultural contributions that prosecution became problematic. What would Norwegian literature be without Knut Hamsun? Who defined Britishness more than P. G. Wodehouse? Could national categories contain Ezra Pound?

Writing, Speaking, Print, Radio

"Propaganda, propaganda, propaganda. All that matters is propaganda": if that was the lesson a young watercolorist took after the failed Munich putsch in 1923, the world two decades later bore every sign of Hitler's obsession when all communication fell under the aegis of propaganda, which "everyone knows ... is a weapon of warfare, just as much as shooting guns is."[40] No one was under any delusion that government ministries and national radio stations churned it out as a matter of course. Even the BBC, which claimed that the best propaganda was the truth, warts and all, was caught out: William Shirer expressed "surprise" to hear London announce Royal Air Force (RAF) sorties over Berlin when there had been "no air-raid alarm. No sound of planes": "they're all lying these days," he concluded.[41] No occupational group was better prepared to draft those lies than writers. If in late August 1939 Graham Greene already heard "the faint susurrus of the intellectuals dashing for ministry posts" (he quickly took one, too), a few years later it was a stampede: "almost every writer, however undesirable his political history or opinions," Orwell noted, "has been sucked in to the various Ministries or the BBC and even those who enter the armed forces tend to find themselves after a while in Public Relations."[42] One ministry that took in writers and publishers by the truckload was the Ministry of Information (MoI), the model for *1984*'s Ministry of Truth, whose Senate House headquarters in Bloomsbury was effectively a writer's salon during the blackout years: Cecil Beaton, Kenneth Clark, Cecil Day-Lewis, Graham Greene, Rosamond Lehmann, and Dylan Thomas worked there, alongside one of the best-connected literary agents in the land, A. D. Peters.[43] In the United States, Archibald MacLeish headed the Office of Facts and Figures (which became the Office of War Information), where he surrounded himself with fellow writers.[44] Publishers heeded FDR's 1942 call that "books are weapons" by forming the Council for Books in Wartime, which ran the Armed Services Editions imprimatur, under which over 100 million books would be published and distributed to soldiers, and then Overseas Editions, which brought American literature to newly liberated peoples (see Figure 0.1).

The corralling of literary talent for propaganda was equally evident for the Axis. German radio beamed with pride when introducing a series of talks by Wodehouse,

Figure 0.1 Ministry of Information "Books and Freedom" exhibition, Charing Cross underground station. Ministry of Information Photo Division Photographer. Imperial War Museum D 1192.

a "world famous author." In occupied countries, every published text had the German censor's seal of approval, which invariably colored how it was read and turned it political regardless of its content. On the radio, the involvement of so many writers in the production of propaganda resulted in cultural programming seemingly peripheral to the war, such as a series on modern poetry that aired on the BBC (targeting Indian listeners, with George Orwell in charge) or talks on modern American poetry on German radio (hosted by Douglas Chandler, AKA "Paul Revere"). In 1941 listeners to Radio Roma could even hear two Japanese Noh plays.[45] Some cultural programming fused fiction with straight political propaganda, such as the German radio production "Visions of Invasion," broadcast on the eve of the Normandy landings, which predicted massive deaths for the Allies and chided the war effort as a Jewish conspiracy.[46]

The novelty of wartime propaganda was the supremacy of radio (see Figure 0.2): "There is no more powerful weapon than the unseen echo that encircles the earth and passes from one point into the hearts of millions," one MP noted in October 1939: "It is a more powerful weapon for the destruction or the raising of man than anything man has yet discovered."[47] Books may well have been touted as "the means whereby civilization may be carried triumphantly forward," as Churchill's blurb on the front cover of John Brophy's *Britain Needs Books* (1941) put it, but they were not, one MoI official noted, "an easy medium of propaganda to handle."[48] If the appetite for reading during the Second World War was high—Cyril Connolly joked that profits could be had by reissuing

Figure 0.2 FDR going on the air, January 11, 1944. Courtesy of Franklin D. Roosevelt Presidential Library & Museum. Public Domain.

old railway timetables—books did not have the same immediacy as radio, which was considered "an agency of incalculable power for controlling the actions of men."[49] In his 1939 essay "The Radio Voice," Theodor Adorno noted how a listener could become a "slave" to radio's "super-voice" since communication tended in only one direction.[50] By the time war broke out the 1936 Convention Concerning the Use of Broadcasting in the Cause of Peace—which banned hostile propaganda targeting another state and implored signatories to respect "truthfulness" in broadcasting—was in tatters. The appeal of radio as a propaganda engine was too strong: "The loud speaker is untiring. It brooks no argument. No one can answer it back … The uncritical masses can be conditioned and hypnotized by the radio when used by unscrupulous propagandists and when no other point of view can obtain expression."[51]

Hitler had proclaimed that victory would come not through tanks or bombers but targeted propaganda that broke the enemy's morale: "The enemy must be demoralized and driven to passivity … Our strategy is to destroy the enemy from within … Mental confusion, contradictory feelings, indecision, panic—these are our weapons."[52] In almost every European country there were fascist movements whose members were amenable to the German message and isolationists who did not think that whatever happened in Bohemia or a Polish corridor merited the mobilization of "our boys." The political and economic chaos in Western democracies after ten years of economic misery added another body of opinion amenable to the Axis message. Radio was also a military weapon. The staged "border incidents" leading to Germany's invasion of Poland were kickstarted by the Schutzstaffel (SS) taking over a Polish radio station and reading out, in Polish, an anti-German message, thus providing cover to the claim that the Poles were openly attacking the Third Reich. The French Resistance effectively began when De Gaulle used the BBC to call upon "all Frenchmen who want to remain free to listen to my voice and follow me."[53] During the radio war, enemy stations were jammed, relay signals bombed, and the very act of listening to foreign programs could lead to detention, arrest, or even death (around 1,500 Germans caught listening to the BBC in the first year of the war were sent to prisons or concentration camps).

It was "something new in the history of the world," Rebecca West observed, for radio to have made treason universal, easy, banal.[54] By war's end, the "radio traitor" was a recognizable category, and in a number of countries renegade broadcasters were lumped together in indictments or in criminal trials—they all committed the same genre of treason. The "short trip into enemy territory" that consisted of listening to enemy radio was immensely popular, the BBC explained, due to the "novel 'thrill' of hearing, from the comfortable security of one's fireside, the voice of one's would-be destroyer."[55] But listening to the enemy also raised mixed feelings, as can be seen in this account by an eighteen-year-old medical student from Edinburgh:

> My first reaction to Lord Haw-Haw was one of derision, but later I began to grow afraid, as there was always some grain of truth in what he said. I doubt whether the public laughs at him as much as the press would have us believe. I know he has quite a great effect on forming my opinion about the war; I should imagine that neutrals will be even more impressed. I think that, although the public as a whole do not admit being affected by his broadcasts, they must be influenced to a certain extent, for even if they listen only for amusement, some of his shafts must go home, and create distrust of our own propaganda machine in their minds.[56]

The prospect of treason (not only Haw-Haw's but also her own) being turned into an entertainment was uppermost in the mind of this respondent for Mass-Observation, herself volunteering to do a new kind of war work—laying bare her thoughts so that the government could have on hand a "war barometer" of belief.[57] Ideas were monitored, tabulated, and manipulated just like coal production or iron ore extraction; in a war that did away with the distinction between civilian and combatant, ideas were weaponized.

Given its status as a "weapon of war," radio fundamentally altered the meaning of the content it delivered. It also turned speech into something else: legally, America's Federal Radio Commission tried to argue that radio speech was not speech itself but its reproduction through electrical means. Less tendentiously, it was clear that the voice and tempo of a radio broadcast impacted how listeners understood it and that radio productions played around with background noise and were edited to transform the content. It goes without saying that technical faults like static or distortion modified reception (even seasoned foreign correspondents in Germany could not easily identify Hitler's voice on the air). P. G. Wodehouse's five talks on German internment camps were meant to be humorous and light-hearted, but their billing on the Deutsche Rundfunk took out the comic sting and led to accusations of collaboration and treason. Wodehouse's defense—"there was not a word in the five talks which could not have been printed in any English paper"—was premised on radio being a neutral transmission device.[58] While in most cases radio broadcasts were "translated" back into textual form in courtrooms—written transcripts were introduced as evidence rather than poor-quality physical recordings—there was a broader awareness that the medium itself was the message. Words broadcast did not float in the ether as free-standing textual productions but were anchored within a wider network of signification. Writers who claimed that they were given freedom of the air or not forced to toe a particular line were cut down to size as dupes. **"THEY MAY HAVE GIVEN YOU THE FREEDOM OF GERMANY,"** the *Daily Mirror* railed all-bold, all-caps against Wodehouse, **"BUT BY GOD THEY WON'T GIVE YOU THE FREEDOM OF THE MICROPHONE."**[59] Seeing radio as a form in its own right put a spotlight on the processes involved in manufacturing the broadcast. The Romantic conception of authorship as originary genius, working alone to produce an individual text, was an inadequate description of the collective labor behind a radio production: "without their active, willing and regular co-operation," MI5 noted of all the underlings, "the actual propaganda programmes would not have been practicable."[60] If it was perhaps disproportionate to sentence the typist of Jean Hérold-Paquis's radio discourses to forced labor for life, it was nonetheless clear that technicians, engineers, typists, translators, and support staff were critical agents in the dissemination of propaganda. Some broadcasters sought cover in this giant operation by offering up a gramophone defense: they had merely read out what others wrote and thus only "lent" their voices to mechanically sound out words: "All my material was prepared for me and I merely had to speak."[61] At the other end of the spectrum, some broadcasters claimed that they had gone on the air only to transmit their own opinions, not state propaganda. In both cases, the massive institutional apparatus behind any radio transmission intensified authorial responsibility by enlarging the active steps and collaboration to go on the air. When Douglas Chandler was tried, the overt acts of treason in the indictment included telephone calls with a radio producer or participation in office meetings, the argument being that every such act confirmed the intent to disseminate traitorous propaganda. As the prosecutors put it, "our case stops when we have proved that Chandler went in and made a recording"—what was actually said was immaterial to the treason committed.[62] The added benefit of the widened scope of the radio production process was that more witnesses could testify to each step in the production and transmission of a program. Finally, the formal differences between radio and print made it possible to cast writers as negligent in their duty to claim property in their own work. The writer-broadcaster was not in control over how material was used, so the modern copyright protections authors enjoyed, and which made writing something precious, personal, and deserving of legal protection, were discarded in the act of broadcasting. (The 1909 Copyright Act stipulated that employees paid a wage could not claim copyright in the final product, which belonged to the firm that paid for their labor: and thus was born corporate authorship in America.) To be able to control the message of a text required supervising how the message was transmitted, but the writer-broadcasters on trial had signed off any control over their production, which was as good as letting treason flourish.

The Enigmas of Treason

From the Greeks on down, it has seemed obvious that no political order can be maintained if treason doth prosper. Because it seems so obvious, there is no grand theory of treason and little in the way of theoretical justification as to why it is the most odious crime. At its simplest, treason is built on the idea that the protection afforded by the state entails a corresponding duty of allegiance on the part of the citizen (or resident alien). The simple equation becomes complicated when its breach is translated into law, though, because treason is not defined by any resulting harm (failed treason is still treason) and the betrayal has, in post-monarchic regimes, a symbolic victim (*who*, concretely, is the nation?). The very idea of allegiance, at least for one British occupying official in Bavaria in 1946, had "become archaic" because the contractual nature of citizenship had been sundered; similarly, one legal scholar tasked by the DOJ to elucidate treason law in 1945 found only a gaping void in what the term might have meant for the Constitutional Convention.[63] Adding to the illiberal thrust of treason is the undoubted moral subjectivism at its basis: privilege one's own. A war with ethnic cleansing at its heart had revealed the barbarism of that idea.

However treason is defined—and this book charts the various ways it was understood in law and the popular imagination during the war and postwar—it is never cut-and-dry. As one saying goes, it is a matter of dates; in another formulation, one man's traitor is another's liberator (reviled here, put on a five-kopeck postage stamp there, as Kim Philby was). In 1945 the problem of determining treason was more than theoretical. Where did a Pole's loyalty lie when two competing governments accused one another of treason? Was Vichy a lawfully constituted state power, voted in by an overwhelming majority of deputies, or a legal void, an abnegation of *la France eternelle*? And what about those brave Germans who actively sought the destruction of their homeland? After Rebecca West's series "The Traitors," drawn from *The Meaning of Treason*, appeared in the *Evening Standard* in late 1947, a German-born Quaker pointedly asked if her disdain for traitors extended to the thousands of German nationals whose "chief allegiance was not to the country whose passports they possessed, but the country which was fighting for freedom."[64] One cannot fault the moral courage of those who defied nominal ties of national belonging for a greater cause, but the doctrine justifying such behavior was the very same one used by writers and intellectuals going over to the other side. If theirs was a misguided sense of what "freedom" fascism offered, they too embraced the view that the age of ideology had supplanted the doctrine of "my country right or wrong." Treason remained—"we have to punish wrong ideas as others punish crimes: with death," the revolutionary remarks in *Darkness at Noon*—but the nation was no longer the North Star.[65]

How treason is marshaled, when, and for what types of crimes, exposes the political beliefs of a given moment and reveals the government's sense of itself and the image it wishes to project to its citizens and the outside world. As "the heaviest and most cumbersome weapon in the fight for political power," a treason charge not only punishes malefactors but also lays down the broad rules of the political field.[66] By drawing out the harm to a broad "we," the state speaks in a collective voice to define the contours of belonging within a community. If law in a democratic state rests upon and creates a kind of popular authorship—for Hobbes, the people have contracted themselves so that "every one [is] the Author" of the sovereign's acts—the import of that is much more direct when the matter concerns defining the community.[67] The shift of allegiance from a royal body to abstractions like the "state" or the "nation" further complicated matters.

Because the traitor exposes the fragility of our communal bonds, daring to make a free choice while we repress any such desires to overthrow the thick web of duties to family, neighbor, lord, king, and nation, the punishment must be harsh: *you shall be drawn upon an Hurdle to the Place of Execution, where you shall be hanged by the Neck, and, being alive, cut down; your Privy Members shall be cut off, and burned before your Face, your Head severed from your Body, and your Body divided into four Quarters, and they to be disposed at the Pleasure of the King; and the Lord have mercy upon your soul* (see Figure 0.3). Yet no treason, no America; no treason, imperialism over the globe; no treason, slave plantations still; no treason, *le roi à Versailles*: the enigma of treason

Figure 0.3 The punishment for traitors including drawing and quartering. Claes Jansz Visscher, *The Execution of the Conspirators in the Gunpowder Plot (Guy Fawkes)*, 1606. © National Portrait Gallery, London.

is that what cannot be tolerated comes to be necessary. It is self-evident that no state can permit treason, as that would threaten its very existence, but it is equally clear that without rebellion, much of the moral progress of humanity would be unthinkable. The great tension in modern political philosophy, from Hobbes onwards, is between the need for obedience and the right to revolt: treason presumes that the state's continuation is a moral good, but long history shows that some, if not most, states violate basic rights and rule not with the consent of the governed but against them. One may commit treason (although it is never phrased that way) because some goods are greater than the state; order may be a precondition of justice, but some orders are so broken that no justice can flow from them. And it is often through words and writing that those broken orders are first identified.[68]

As the structuring principle behind every political order, treason is a valuable lens for understanding how the state portrays itself, how it shows itself to citizens and others, who it claims under its power, and what limits it lays down for political action and speech. Treason is no neutral, value-free crime, applied mechanically: its mobilization puts state power in action and reveals, performatively, how the state interprets its standing and legitimacy. For there to be treason a text must be determined to be seditious, a secret worth protecting, a certain intent driving an act: as social anthropologists Sharika Thiranagama and Tobias Kelly put it, "To make an accusation of treason is to make a claim to power, to try to police the boundaries of permissible politics, and to exert authority in the face of constantly shifting affiliations."[69] For Carl Schmitt, this struggle for power against the "enemy" is the very essence of the political. "Existentially something different and alien," the "enemy" cannot be tolerated, much less within.[70] It is surprising then to consider that treason prosecutions have historically been rare events. For a state to make an open accusation of treason is to admit that opposition to its rule threatens its very essence: rather than flexing power, weakness is admitted. Leaving the matter in the hands of courts creates uncertainty compared to the use of extra-legal liquidations: witnesses are unreliable; the accused has a right to a defense; juries may err. Trials also create martyrs. Yet in the context of 1945, with popular vengeance targeting collaborators threatening to overwhelm the return to order, reverting to the law promised normalcy and a repudiation of the fascist past. Treason prosecutions also defined, after years of upheaval in a war waged on national principles, who belonged. International jurisprudence was, admittedly, moving toward abstractions like "humanity" and "universal human rights," but nationalism did not retreat tidily in what E. H. Carr called "the most nation-conscious of all epochs."[71] Treason cases were integral parts of that national re-awakening.

If "there is no crime which can more excite and agitate the passions of men than treason," as Justice Marshall put it, the contours of treason change over time and are especially ripe for contestation during revolutionary periods, as John Barrell has shown for the 1790s.[72] Wars and states of emergency harden understandings of loyalty because treason is a more acute danger for a state fighting for its existence.[73] In preparation for the coming war, Code 75 of the French penal code expanded treason in 1939 to include "intelligence with the enemy." From its base in London, the Norwegian government-in-exile issued decrees modifying existing understandings of treason. The Dutch cabinet-in-exile issued a special code that retroactively criminalized wartime collaboration and treason in September 1944, with *politieke delinquents* to be tried in special courts or through purge boards. In Great Britain the Treachery Act (1940) introduced an old term to stand in for a new crime that did not differ in any way from treason save for the ease of its prosecution, and in 1945 William Joyce was held outside British jurisdiction until the Treason Act of 1945, which lessened the procedural safeguards afforded to those accused of the crime, came into force. The 1940 Smith Act revivified sedition's ghost in America, and then, in April 1945, with the war coming to a close, the Supreme Court issued *Cramer*, a landmark ruling on the meaning of the Constitution's Treason Clause. More broadly, one of the principal Allied military aims was "the punishment through the channel of organized justice of those guilty and responsible for these crimes" (Declaration of St. James, January 1942). These war criminals would be hunted down "to the uttermost ends of the earth," the Moscow Declaration (November 1943) ominously announced; some armistice agreements, like the one signed with Romania in September 1944, obliged signatories to mete out postwar justice for war criminals (with the Soviets overseeing the process to ensure that the right sentences were reached).[74] A significant expenditure of resources, personnel and energy came to be devoted to these ends, with lists of renegades drawn up, German and Italian archives meticulously examined, and witnesses interrogated—and that was before any trials.

For the renegades charged with treason, the standard reply was that a higher loyalty had guided their actions. Theirs was not treason but rather a fight against those committing it with impunity. Douglas Chandler chose the symbolic figure of Paul Revere to make himself a "messenger" warning the American people about their nefarious leaders; his broadcasts were signed off with a call to "get our country back." It was the "desire for the good of the country on a long view" that animated British fascists to oppose current policy.[75] Misguided loyalty to policies that weakened the nation was the real treason, continued resistance to the new fascist order the real folly. As a legal matter, this defense was groundless, but it had a certain appeal in its revolutionary roots, Thomas Jefferson's distinction between "acts against the *government*, and acts against *oppressions of the government*."[76] Yet drawing the line between "oppression" and the proper exercise of sovereignty is never simple: who makes that determination, and on what basis? For sure, the starting point of democracy is that there will be an opposition, and without granting the opposition the right to oppose, vigorously and with force, the existing power, democracy falls apart. Yet not all oppositions were granted the right to exist. The occupation forces of Germany were instructed to "prohibit the propagation in any form of Nazi, militaristic or pan-German doctrines"; anything discrediting the Allies, such as pointed critiques of racism in America, British imperialism, or Stalinism, were not tolerated.[77] The exceptional determination of the existing state as fundamentally and irrevocably corrupt and oppressive went further than simple opposition; it was, as the courts determined, an act calculated to undermine the state at a time when its very existence was in question.

Book Outline

The moral problems of wartime collaboration and treason were widespread, as the Second World War upended lives and societies across the globe. This book does not cover every single instance of authorial treason or collaboration but narrows in on a select group of case studies that illuminate wider trends in what was a truly global history. One important principle behind the selection of cases was to cover the variety of wartime experiences (as the nature of the wartime experience greatly influenced the course of the postwar legal actions taken against perceived collaborators and traitors), and to that end the book includes cases from occupied (France, Norway, Romania), unoccupied (Great Britain, United States), and also neutral countries (Ireland). The literary standing and historical importance of certain writers—Louis-Ferdinand Céline, Knut Hamsun, Charles Maurras, Ezra Pound, and P. G. Wodehouse—dictated fuller discussions of their cases. Other writers, like Francis Stuart or Robert Brasillach, have not been central to literary studies but their cases illuminated wider issues with the postwar legal reckoning. Other cases, like those in Romania, involve writers largely unknown by most readers. My hope is that the chapters plot out a wide group of representative wartime experiences, with a balanced interplay between wider social and macro forces and the particularities of individual trials.

Chapter 1 looks at wartime treason prosecutions and investigations of writers in the UK, which was never occupied but was under constant attack from aerial bombs and radio waves. The government even passed a series of wartime laws to make it easier to prosecute radio traitors, with one individual particularly singled out, William Joyce, better known as Lord Haw-Haw, the voice of Nazi radio who taunted Britain at the start of the war. Joyce was not an unknown on the British political scene, as during the 1930s he was one of the major writers and public speakers in the fascist media system, but his trial largely overlooked this past in order to focus entirely on his hectoring wartime broadcasts. His treason trial at the Old Bailey exposed the challenges of prosecuting radio traitors but also the political motivations that could lead the state to bypass established legal norms. Politics also influenced the treason investigation into Wodehouse, the most popular British writer of the twentieth century. While his wartime decision to broadcast on Berlin radio led to an outpouring of popular protest, by the time it came to prosecute him, sympathy for Wodehouse (who had been imprisoned by the French) and his establishment credentials let him escape prosecution. In both cases, the much-touted impartiality of British law gave way to the passions of the political moment.

Chapter 2 examines the most high-profile treason prosecution in the postwar, that of American poet Ezra Pound. While most of the American radio renegades were minor writers with lackluster careers, Ezra Pound was a major literary figure who had helped to define modernism. Having spent over two decades in Italy, Pound was a convinced propagandist for the Italian regime who continued broadcasting for the Axis, on both Italian and German radio, until the dying days of the war. Famously interned by the Americans in a "gorilla cage" in Pisa, which gave rise to the *Pisan Cantos*, Pound was repatriated to Washington, D.C., to stand trial for treason in the autumn of 1945. Although keen to defend himself on the grounds of freedom of speech, Pound was ultimately ruled mentally unfit to stand trial, which led to him languishing in a psychiatric hospital for over a dozen years. Pound's "trial" for treason ended up taking place in the press and parlors of postwar America, and in stealth, with Pound anonymously steering a number of little reviews devoted to his pet theories.

Chapter 3 covers the postwar purge of collaborationist writers in France. The French postwar trials are perhaps the best-known of the ones covered in this book, and the ones that had the greatest contemporary resonance, as major figures like Charles Maurras were put in the dock. The chapter covers the wide debates during the Resistance on how to punish collaborators, including the novel crime invented, *indignité nationale*, and the role of professional guilds to mete out justice. The chapter covers a number of individual trials, including those of Georges Suarez, Robert Brasillach, Charles Maurras, and Louis-Ferdinand Céline. There were important international dimensions to these French trials, with the Céline case involving extradition from Denmark and international media attention.

Chapter 4 looks at the postwar trial of Nobel Prize winner Knut Hamsun, one of the defining figures of the nascent Norwegian state and a cultural founder of its modern national self-consciousness. With its king and parliamentary leaders in exile in London during the war, the Norwegian home front was ruled by a puppet regime that eagerly touted Hamsun's unwavering support for its Germanic policies. The legal definition of treason in postwar Norway was a simple test: was the individual a member of Nasjonal Samling (NS), the political party that did Germany's bidding during the war? Even such straightforward tests proved complicated in reality, as Hamsun's case showed: he felt himself to be a member of the NS and agitated for its cause in NS journals like *Fritt Folk*, but he was not a member in the strict formal sense because he never completed the necessary paperwork. Like Ezra Pound, Hamsun was relieved from a criminal trial for treason because of a dubious psychiatric diagnosis of mental incompetence, but he did undergo a civil trial which led to ruinous financial damages. Hamsun ended up having the final word, though, as he wrote a memoir of his imprisonment and trial that struck back at his critics.

Chapter 5 investigates the status of authorship in postwar Romania. Allied to the Axis powers during the war, Romania changed sides at war's end, only to find itself "liberated" by the Red Army. The armistice signed in Moscow made the harsh punishment of "war criminals" an essential task for Bucharest, but the chaos of Romanian politics during the period undermined much progress on that front. It was only after the Soviet Union began to dictate affairs and the Romanian Communist Party (PCR) seized control of the government that the push to criminalize wartime acts became a priority. In May 1945 the second trial of the newly-instituted People's Tribunal concerned a dozen writers and editors who were accused of spouting fascism. This mass trial of the pen—referred to as "the trial of the journalists"—was more about dictating future affairs than punishing past misdeeds: the state used the trial to show that its power over the press and the written word was supreme.

Chapter 6 looks at the thorny case of neutral Ireland, which stayed out of the war despite Allied pressure to join the cause and German threats of occupation. The information blackout put in place by the censor ensured that little public discussion of the war surfaced in the Irish press, but one very prominent Irish writer, the novelist, poet, and ex-Irish Republican Army (IRA) gunrunner Francis Stuart, ended up spending the war years in Berlin. Stuart's weekly radio talks tested the limits of Irish neutrality; even though he was never formally tried for treason, his case put to the test the rights of free expression for authors.

These case studies all show the entanglement of writing with state power in the postwar period, as the conclusion demonstrates.

This book has three wider implications for comparative literary studies that appear, at first sight, retrograde: bringing the state back in, re-inscribing the centrality of the author, and periodizing the immediate postwar. I wish to sketch them briefly here before the chapters more clearly bring out the stakes involved in this larger analysis.

First, on the state. "Bringing the state back in" runs against the current trend of scholarship invested in the supranational, the global, cosmopolitanism, world literature, the unbounded reach of the World Wide Web. The first major pronouncement on the relationship between the State and the arts, Plato's banishment of the poets from the Republic (due to their excessive love of the beautiful rather than the true or good), was so extreme and hammer-like that it has made us wary of any State power over literature or the arts, a view reinforced by the popular narrative of the "Cultural Cold War" (in the West art is free to be critical, while in the East state control chains poets in gulags). Even if literature has long profited from state patronage and in the past few decades has become, like all the arts, partly dependent upon public financing—from occupational designations and special tax regimes, the financing of teaching posts at universities, grants and subsidies from cultural bodies—there is little consideration for how the State conditions writing or how, tellingly, State organs, from courts to security agencies, read and write. When literary scholars study "institutions," the focus is largely on the professoriate, the status of the anthology, or even, in a metaphorical stretch, genres—but rarely mortar-and-stone edifices with officials having the power to issue legally binding directives. Bringing the state and institutions back in is a paradoxical claim when the state has never been "outside" in any formal sense. It is not easy to "see" state control when censorship boards no longer exist and wide latitude is afforded to the written word—if anything, the key issue today is not the state corralling expression but private corporations. That is a mistake, and not just because state actors (China, Russia) have become incredibly skillful in manipulating speech and expression in quasi-public and private venues. On a more fundamental level, no activity, as Howard Becker reminds us, is outside the purview of the state—if anything, the state's choice to not forcibly intervene reveals the relatively low opinion it holds of art or writing. As Becker notes, clearly picking up some lessons from the wider propaganda battles fought during the Second World War, if art results in "mass mobilizations" then the state does intervene—and forcibly.[78] The immediate postwar studied in this book shows the state not as a neutral, disinterested observer, but as a major actor in the literary field, mobilizing the courts and security services to police writing and expression. It also shows that the state is not a monolithic entity, with a continental-sized capital "S," but rather an amalgamation of competing departments, institutions, and entities jockeying for bureaucratic power and advancing the interests of separate fiefdoms.

The second implication of this work is the centrality of the intention-laden author. Legal control over writing is usually channeled through a determination of authorial intention (obscenity is not discovered by marking up explicit passages but considering the purpose of the larger text), and this is especially true for treason, where the judicial determination of an intent to aid and comfort the enemy is the main issue. The material impact of an act is less important in establishing treason than the intent driving it: a radio broadcast that never went on the air, in other words, can be treasonous because of the underlying intent to aid the enemy. Ezra Pound would later defend himself by saying "No treason without intent": he felt that Radio Roma's disclaimer before every one of his signed broadcasts (there were hundreds of anonymous ones, too, which rather undercut this claim) that he was acting in good faith as a freedom-loving American citizen absolved him of any traitorous intent. One of the ironies of the postwar prosecutions of authors was that while prosecutors were assembling evidence on the intent of a text or radio broadcast so as to make the case for treason, literary studies was moving toward the position that authorial intention was unknowable and a distraction. The classic statement of this position, Wimsatt and Beardsley's "The Intentional Fallacy," published in 1946, paved the way for the structuralist liturgy, familiar to anyone who has taken a university-level literature course, to focus on the text and the text alone. "To give a text an Author," as Barthes famously put it, "is to impose a limit on that text, to furnish it with a final signified, to close the writing."[79] That may be, but the political content of a text cannot be separated from the core political beliefs of its author or the prevailing political conditions at the time of its composition. Determining what those might be in the fog of war is no simple matter, as sociologist Howard Woolston noted in 1942, because society ascribes sinister or evil purposes to minority opinions.[80] But dispensing with "intent" or authorship altogether impoverishes our understanding of how cultural fields operate even further, especially when the concrete reality of authorship cost lives.

Finally, this book stakes a claim for the immediate postwar—"the bitter yesterday, the bad to-day, and the hopeless to-morrow," as a Dachau survivor called it—as a period of complex and multiple temporalities in its own right.[81] While the term "postwar" is popular enough in book titles and course syllabi, in most usages it extends out to the late 1960s or early 1970s, to say nothing of the early 2000s, making it a "legacy" and symbolic marker rather than a concrete historical moment. *L'après-guerre* looked backwards to the devastating war that had just ended and forward to an uncertain post-transition order. Postwar thinking was already present during wartime—in October 1939, French literary critic Armand Petitjean began working on an essay entitled "Pour l'après-guerre," and numerous papers and conferences were held during the war years to think about the postwar future—but naturally accelerated after the defeat of Germany and Japan.[82] In the double bind of historical time that seemed intensely of the present but by its nature had to efface that present (just as wars end, so, too, must postwars), authors were confronted with a series of challenges to the free order of aesthetic creation. The very ground they stood on was uncertain, as Tristan Tzara detailed in a controversial lecture at the Sorbonne in 1947:

> Where is the end of this war, this shredded end that prolongs itself in each individual, bringing about new questions and temporary solutions and necessary but makeshift repairs and the crushing weight of pains and destructions and the gravity of wounds that are still raw? There is no war now, but there is no *après-guerre* yet.[83]

As Tzara makes clear, thinking of the immediate postwar as a period in its own right is not without its own problems (when did the war end?; how did the idea of the "postwar" inhere within wartime itself?; when did the postwar itself end?).[84] Yet important literary and critical texts came out of this period (the rise of New Criticism in the academy, Leavis's *The Great Tradition*, Auerbach's *Mimesis*, Sartre's *Qu'est-ce que la littérature?*) and culture was politicized and under strict national pressures. A more sharply defined postwar, beginning with the end of the fighting in Europe in late 1944 and ending with the establishment of a bipolar global order in or around 1949 (the Berlin blockade, the founding of NATO), may be a brief four-year period, but studying it as an entity in its own right is justified by the extraordinary changes in domestic orders and a drastic realignment of international geopolitics, with consequential impacts on authors and the literary field.

Notes

1 Hermon Ould to Tilgit Hammarling, January 30, 1946, in International PEN Misc Archive, Congress Stockholm 1946, Harry Ransom Center (HRC), University of Texas at Austin.
2 Quoted in Rachel Potter, "International PEN and the Republic of Literature," in *Cultural Organizations, Networks and Mediators in Contemporary Ibero-America*, eds. Diana Roig-Sanz and Jaume Subirana (London: Routledge, 2020), 108–26, at 118–19.
3 HRC, International PEN Misc Archive, Congress Stockholm 1946, Resolutions. I treat the postwar PEN conferences at greater length in "Hope for a New World Order: Postwar PEN and the Reconstruction of the Global Republic of Letters," *Comparative Literature* 77.4 (December 2025): 429–52.
4 "The Case for and Against Ezra Pound," *PM*, November 24, 1945, 12–15, 17, at 14. See Pascale Casanova, *The World Republic of Letters*, trans. M. B. Debevoise (Cambridge, MA: Harvard University Press, 2004 [1999]).
5 Henry De Montherlant, *Le Solstice de juin* (Paris: Grasset, 1941), 101–2.
6 Graham Greene to V. S. Pritchett, in *Why Do I Write? An Exchange of Views Between Elizabeth Bowen, Graham Greene, and V. S. Pritchett* (London: Percival Marshall, 1948), 47.
7 The historiography of the "Zero Hero" is contested; see Ian Buruma, *Year Zero: A History of 1945* (New York: Atlantic Books, 2013) and Harald Jähner, *Aftermath: Life in the Fallout of the Third Reich*, trans. Shaun Whiteside (London: W. H. Allen, 2021).
8 Rebecca West, 'The Future of Literature' (1932), Tulsa, Rebecca West Collection (RWC), 31.20.
9 Quoted in Richard W. Flournoy, Jr., "The Proposed Pan American Convention for Preventing Dual Nationality, Drafted at Lima by the American Institute of International Law," *Proceedings*

of the American Society of International Law at Its Annual Meeting (1921–1969) 19 (23–25 April 1925): 69–94, at 80.

10 "Comment," *Horizon* 1.5 (May 1940): 314.

11 Raymond Aron, *La France Libre*, June 15, 1941, in *Chroniques de guerre: La France libre, 1940–1945*, ed. Christian Bachelier (Paris: Gallimard, 1990), 105.

12 Jean-Paul Sartre, "La nationalisation de la littérature" (1945), in *Situations II* (Paris: Gallimard, 1948), 31–53, at 35.

13 István Déak, "Introduction," in *The Politics of Retribution in Europe: World War II and Its Aftermath*, eds. István Déak, Jan T. Gross, and Tony Judt (Princeton: Princeton University Press, 2000), 3–14, at 4.

14 Quoted in Margret Boveri, *Treason in the Twentieth Century*, trans. Jonathan Steinberg (London: Macdonald, 1961), 22. On treason's expansion to include propaganda, see Otto Kirchheimer, *Political Justice: The Use of Legal Procedure for Political Ends* (Princeton: Princeton University Press, 1961), 41.

15 "Gringoire ou le gredin devenue ermite," *Combat*, February 20, 1943.

16 Tom Harrison, "Who'll Win?" *Political Quarterly* 15.1 (January-March 1944): 21–32, at 25.

17 Brasillach's case is well-known because of Alice Kaplan's *The Collaborator: The Trial and Execution of Robert Brasillach* (Chicago: University of Chicago Press, 2001).

18 Jacques Isorni, *Le procès de Robert Brasillach* (Paris: Flammarion, 1946), 177.

19 The doctrine of "mere words" can be found in *Wimmer v. United States* (1920) 264 F. 11, 12.

20 Archibald MacLeish to T. S. Eliot, n.d. [summer 1945], Library of Congress (LOC), Archibald MacLeish Papers.

21 István Deák, *Europe on Trial: The Story of Collaboration, Resistance, and Retribution During World War II* (Boulder, CO: Westview Press, 2015), 8.

22 Tony Judt, *Postwar: A History of Europe since 1945* (New York: Penguin, 2005), 41; Keith Lowe, *Savage Continent: Europe in the Aftermath of World War II* (New York: Viking Press, 2012).

23 A. M. Meerloo, *Aftermath of Peace: Psychological Essays* (New York: International Universities Press, 1946), 41, 52.

24 Florimond Bonte, "La haine, devoir nationale," *L'Humanité*, January 10, 1945, 1; Jean Galtier-Broissière, *Mon journal depuis la libération* (Paris: La Jeune Parque, 1945), 109.

25 Henry Mason, *The Purge of Dutch Quislings: Emergency Justice in the Netherlands* (The Hague: Martinus Nijhoff, 1952), 70.

26 James D. Wilkinson, *The Intellectual Resistance in Europe* (Cambridge: Harvard University Press, 1981), 65.

27 Alexander V. Prusin, "Traitors or War Criminals: Collaboration on Trial in Soviet Courts in the 1940s," in *Stalin's Soviet Justice: "Show" Trials, War Crimes Trials, and Nuremberg*, ed. David M. Crowe (London: Bloomsbury Academic, 2019), 879–903, at 87.

28 Victor Gollancz, *Our Threatened Values* (London: Victor Gollancz, 1946), 45–6.

29 Marcel Aymé, *La tête des autres* (Paris: Bernard Grasset, 1952), 70.

30 See Minou Arjomand, *Staged: Show Trials, Political Theater, and the Aesthetics of Judgment* (New York: Columbia University Press, 2018).

31 *L'Humanité*, May 8, 1945, 1.

32 Letter to Foreign Office, January 2, 1946, KV 2/3581.

33 Henry De Montherlant, *Mémoire* (Paris: Gallimard, 1976), 289.

34 Quoted in Alan Riding, *And the Show Went On: Cultural Life in Nazi-Occupied Paris* (New York: Knopf, 2010), 317.

35 On severity of punishment and time from war, see Judith Keene, *Treason on the Airwaves: Three Allied Broadcasters on Axis Radio During World War II* (Lincoln: University of Nebraska Press, 2010 [2009]), 6–7.

36 Report, March 13, 1941, KV 2/898.

37 Theobald Mathew to Hartley Shawcross, October 10, 1945, KV 2/3581.
38 Ferdinand Earle to Dorothy Pound, Lilly, Pound II, Box 4.
39 Charles De Gaulle, *Mémoires de guerre* (Paris: Plon, 1999), 711.
40 DOJ argument in Hearing on Motions, April 2, 1947, in *USA v. Douglas Chandler*, April 2, 1947, National Archives, NAI 131089941 (Stenographic Record of *USA v. Chandler*).
41 William Shirer, *Berlin Diary: The Journal of a Foreign Correspondent, 1934–1941* (New York: Knopf, 1941), 228.
42 Graham Greene to Vivien Greene, August 30, 1939, in *A Life in Letters*, ed. Richard Greene (London: Abacus, 2007), 99; George Orwell, "Poetry and the Microphone" (1943), in *Collected Essays, Journalism and Letters of George Orwell*, eds. Sonia Orwell and Ian Angus (New York: Harcourt, Brace, Jovanovich, 1971), 2: 381.
43 On MoI and the publishing industry, see John Brophy, *Britain Needs Books* (London: National Book Council, 1941), 35–6.
44 See, more generally, Brett Gary, *The Nervous Liberals: Propaganda Anxieties from World War I to the Cold War* (New York: Columbia University Press, 1999) and Holly Cowan Shulman, *The Voice of America: Propaganda and Democracy, 1941–1945* (Madison: University of Wisconsin Press, 1990).
45 Antonio Papa, *Storia politica della radio in Italia, Dalla Guerra d'Etiopia al crollo del fascismo, 1935–1943* (Naples: Guida Editori, 1978), 105.
46 See John Carver Edwards, *Berlin Calling: American Broadcasters in Service to the Third Reich* (New York: Praeger, 1991).
47 Andrew MacLaren, Hansard, HC Debate, October 11, 1939, vol. 352, c. 415.
48 Quoted in Valerie Holman, "Carefully Concealed Connections: The Ministry of Information and British Publishing, 1939–1946," *Book History* 8 (2005): 197–226, at 212–13.
49 Hadley Cantril and Gordon W. Allport, *The Psychology of Radio* (New York: Harper & Brothers, 1935), 3.
50 T. W. Adorno, "The Radio Voice," in *Current of Music: Elements of a Radio Theory*, ed. Robert Hullot-Kentor (Cambridge: Polity Press, 2009), 379, 376.
51 Major Frederic Evans, "The Re-Education of Germany," *Political Quarterly* 16.1 (January-March 1945): 21–30, at 22.
52 Quoted in Horst J. P. Bergmeier and Rainer E. Lotz, *Hitler's Airwaves: The Inside Story of Radio Broadcasting and Propaganda Swing* (New Haven: Yale University Press, 1997), 3.
53 Kay Chadwick, "Our Enemy's Enemy: Selling Britain to Occupied France on the BBC French Service," *Media History* 21.4 (2015): 426–42, at 427.
54 Rebecca West, *The Meaning of Treason* (Harmondsworth: Penguin, 1965 [1949]), 13. See as well Melissa Dinsman, *Modernism at the Microphone: Radio, Propaganda, and Literary Aesthetics During World War II* (London: Bloomsbury Academic, 2015).
55 "Hamburg Broadcast Propaganda: Summary of the Results of an Enquiry Into the Extent and Effect of Its Impact on the British Public During Mid-Winter 1939/40," BBC R9/14; "Do You Listen to Hamburg? Lord Haw-Haw Has a Place in Hitler's Scheme for a Nazi Victory," 1941, BBC R43/198.
56 Directive Respondent 2374, Directive Questionnaire, January 1940, Mass Observation Archive, Sussex.
57 Mass-Observation, *War Begins at Home* (London: Chatto and Windus, 1940), v.
58 Hubert Cole, "I've Been a Silly Ass," *Illustrated* (London), December 7, 1946, 9; *Daily Mirror*, June 28, 1941, 1.
59 *Daily Mirror*, June 28, 1941, 1.
60 "British Civilians Working for the Enemy," September 13, 1945, KV 2/3581.
61 Statement of Edwin Hermann Frederick Lynn Schneider, May 21, 1945, KV 2/246.
62 *United States v. Douglas Chandler*, June 6, 1947, 69.

63 Maximilian Koessler, "Subject, Citizen, National, and Permanent Allegiance," *Yale Law Journal* 56 (1946): 58–76, at 68. The legal scholar who found only a void in the Constitutional Convention debates on treason was James Willard Hurst, *Law of Treason in the United States* (Westport: Greenwood, 1971), 144. For a contemporary assessment of allegiance and citizenship, see Youngjae Lee, "Punishing Disloyalty? Treason, Espionage, and the Transgression of Political Boundaries," *Law and Philosophy* 31 (2012): 299–342, and Ashwini Vasanthakumar, "Treason, Expatriation and "So-Called" Americans: Recovering the Role of Allegiance in Citizenship," *The Georgetown Journal of Law and Public Policy* 12 (2014): 187–224. On treason's illiberal nature, see George P. Fletcher, *Loyalty: An Essay on the Morality of Relationships* (New York: Oxford University Press, 1993), 41–2.

64 David Eversley to Rebecca West, January 12, 1947, Tulsa, RWC, 39.21.

65 Arthur Koestler, *Darkness at Noon*, trans. Daphne Hardy (London: Jonathan Cape, 1940), 101.

66 Kirchheimer, *Political Justice*, 76.

67 *Leviathan*, II.17.

68 Versions of this argument are found in Boveri, *Treason in the Twentieth Century*, 13, and Carl J. Friedrich, *The Pathology of Politics: Violence, Betrayal, Corruption, Secrecy, and Propaganda* (New York: Harper & Row, 1972), 86.

69 Sharika Thiranagama and Tobias Kelly, "Introduction: Specters of Treason," in *Traitors: Suspicion, Intimacy, and the Ethics of State-Building*, eds. Sharika Thiranagama and Tobias Kelly (Philadelphia: University of Pennsylvania Press, 2010), 1–23, at 3.

70 Carl Schmitt, *The Concept of the Political*, trans. George Schwab (Chicago: University of Chicago Press, 1996), 27.

71 E. H. Carr, *Nationalism and After* (New York: Macmillan, 1945), 40.

72 *Ex parte Bollman* 8 U.S. 125; John Barrell, *Imagining the King's Death: Figurative Treason, Fantasies of Regicide, 1793–1796* (Oxford: Oxford University Press, 2000).

73 Nachman Ben-Yehuda, *Betrayal and Treason: Violations of Trust and Loyalty* (Boulder, CO: Westview, 2001), 108.

74 A contemporaneous history of postwar justice can be found in D. N. Pritt, "The Trial of War Criminals," *Political Quarterly* 16.3 (July-September 1945): 195–204.

75 John Angus Macnab, Home Office, Advisory Committee to Consider Appeals Against Orders of Internment, Notes of a meeting held at 6 Burlington Gardens, January 18, 1943, KV 2/2474.

76 Quoted in J. H. Leek, "Treason and the Constitution," *The Journal of Politics* 13.4 (November 1951): 604–22, at 604.

77 Directive to the Commander in Chief of the U.S. Occupation Forces (JCS 1067) (April 1945), in Department of State, *Germany 1947–1949: The Story in Documents* (Washington, D.C.: GPO, 1950), 22–8.

78 See Howard S. Becker, *Art Worlds*, 25th anniversary ed. (Berkeley: University of California Press, 2008), 187. Prominent exceptions include Cristina Vatulescu's account of Eastern European internal security services in *Police Aesthetics: Literature, Film, and the Secret Police in Soviet Times* (Stanford: Stanford University Press, 2010) and Robert Darnton's *Censors at Work: How States Shaped Literature* (New York: Norton, 2014).

79 Roland Barthes, "The Death of the Author," in *Image - Music - Text*, trans. Stephen Heath (London: Fontana Press, 1977 [1968]), 142–8, at 147.

80 Howard Woolston, "Free Speech in War Time," *American Sociological Review* 7.2 (April 1942): 185–93, at 190. On authorship and the legal signature, see Peggy Kamuf, *Signature Pieces: On the Institution of Authorship* (Ithaca: Cornell University Press, 1988).

81 Quoted in Werner Sollors, *The Temptation of Despair: Tales of the 1940s* (Cambridge: Harvard University Press, 2014), 9.

82 Armand Petitjean, "Pour l'après-guerre," in *Combats préliminaires* (Paris: Gallimard, 1941), 124–37.

83 Tristan Tzara, "Le surréalisme et l'après-guerre," in *Œuvres complètes*, 6 volumes, ed. Henri Béhar (Paris: Flammarion, 1975–1991), 5: 59–80, at 77.

84 Aachen might have surrendered on October 21, 1944, and then all of Germany over six months later, on May 8, 1945 (VE Day), but the United States remained legally at war with Germany until July 1951 (a peace treaty was signed with Japan only in April of the next year). For some, the war ended before VE Day (Paris was liberated in August 1944; Tito and the partisans had liberated almost all of Yugoslavia even earlier), while for others, liberation and VE Day only ushered in more fighting, "war after the war" in places like Greece or Italy. On the general problem of dating postwars, see Larry May, *After War Ends: A Philosophical Perspective* (Cambridge: Cambridge University Press, 2012) and Mary L. Dudziak, *War Time: An Idea, Its History, Its Consequences* (New York: Oxford University Press, 2012).

CHAPTER 1
NO LAUGHING MATTER: THE PEOPLE'S WAR, FEATURING HAW-HAW AND WOOSTER

As a country that did not suffer occupation or invasion (save for the Channel Islands), the question of treason was fundamentally different in Great Britain than elsewhere in Europe. While often said to be a matter of dates, treason, in most cases, is a matter of space. Proximity to the enemy provides occasions to collaborate and rewards for doing so. Few British subjects, save for captured POWs (Prisoners of War), found themselves in a position to help Nazi Germany when Berlin was so distant and the supposedly ubiquitous "Fritz" eavesdropping in pubs was a fanciful Ministry of Information invention. Regardless, widespread hysteria that disloyal Britons were waiting for the signal to drape swastikas over Big Ben—Churchill believed the country harbored 20,000 Nazi sympathizers—made everyone on the lookout for traitors, and not just men in brogues washing out of the sea. The threat from within led to "careless talk costs lives" becoming a national motto. Any young man not in uniform was reckoned a fifth columnist while German-Jewish refugees were detained in the same camps as native Hitlerites ("a Hun," one exalted peer exclaimed, "will always be a Hun").[1]

While the geography of the Second World War "ran off the edges of maps," as Elizabeth Bowen indicated in *The Heat of the Day* (1948), the finest novel to emerge out of the blackout years, the radio war had a reassuring constancy: every night after the 9 o'clock News Bulletin, listeners—and millions of them, around 30 percent of the population, did just this—sought out Lord Haw-Haw's take on the day's events.[2] They did so out of boredom, for with cinemas and dance halls shut, all one had was the radio, and Haw-Haw was undeniably entertaining; they did so because, addicted to news, they were "ransacking the wavebands" and hearing the other side was an exemplary act of that most British of values, fair play; they did so because others were doing it, so having listened one could take part in office or shop talk the next morning.[3] In some locales in Kent, it was actually easier to pick up a strong German signal than the BBC. German radio targeted a wide range of native opinion, from trade unionists, pacifists, and the Christian faithful; it also stoked the national grievances of the Welsh, Scots, and Irish. Its theatrical presentation—"No propaganda without its *Dramaturgie*," Zeesen station's director noted—contrasted favorably to the drab home fare of redacted news and church organ recitals.[4] "Our news is so brief," a cook-housekeeper told Mass Observation in 1940, "what there is of it," she added disdainfully, referring to the strict MoI censorship.[5] In wartime, though, the Home Secretary explained, mass listenership was needed:

> At present we can pick up in England from eight to 10 German stations daily. If our own broadcasts are not attractive, if the news is dry, if the entertainment is mediocre, and if the music is of a low standard, which is what people complain of, the listener just turns the button and he gets a foreign broadcast. He may very well tune in to a German programme for its entertainment value, but he also gets a full measure of German propaganda, skilfully delivered and in excellent English. Do not let us undervalue the possible effects of this.[6]

From early on in the war, there was a sense that the radio out of Hamburg, Bremen, or Zeesen redirected people's beliefs and undermined confidence in the war effort. Tales of Nazi triumphs and British isolation were readily confirmed by military maps until the tide swung at El-Alamein in late 1942. The spectral voice haunting wartime Britain belonged to the Brooklyn-born, Galway-reared and London-formed William Joyce, who was dubbed "Lord Haw-Haw," but there were countless other British voices on the German air, among them the most popular comic writer of the century, P. G. Wodehouse.

The British government eventually applied incredibly repressive measures to meet threats from abroad and within, but at its darkest hour, traitors abroad did not figure high on the list of war priorities for the simple reason that these renegades would have to be captured—and it was fanciful to believe, in 1940 or 1941, that the British army would one fair day stroll down Unter den Linden. There was, at first, no systematic recording of German propaganda to collect evidence for eventual prosecution. The BBC Monitoring Services recorded foreign broadcasts on waxed discs that were reused. It was unclear whether a permanent physical record was worth the trouble or expense: "I have never heard of a gramophone record being used in criminal proceedings," an MI5 officer tartly noted in September 1941. While a few months later the office of the Director of Public Prosecutions (DPP) noted that mechanical recordings could be entered into evidence, it was only in September 1942 that Special Branch established a recording plan (and hoped that the BBC would do the job). And it was only in early 1943 that William Joyce's broadcasts were recorded for the purpose of postwar prosecution. Joyce, at least, used his name on the air and had an identifiable voice; most broadcasters were anonymous. From an intelligence point of view, then, it was felt to be "valueless as well as very costly" to record most talks. Radio renegades were slippery fish: few revealed their name on the air; few permanent records were made of their talks; documentary evidence was hard to come by when the archives from German stations were either deliberately destroyed or had been buried in the rubble; and witnesses were drawn from a murky pool of fellow renegades and Nazi officials.[7] As war fortunes changed, though, a newfound urgency was given to planning postwar prosecutions for traitors. Much of this urgency was fueled by the fact that Britain was standing alone and suffering greatly (see Figure 1.1). More than two million homes, by June 1941, were damaged by bombs. Until as late as mid-1944, civilian casualties outnumbered military ones. The ledgers in the account book of sacrifice contained entries of homes destroyed and families broken up, so when renegade broadcasters sounded "better fed and better clothed than we were," treason was no laughing matter.[8]

Figure 1.1 The effects of German bombing on Great Britain. Courtesy of Franklin D. Roosevelt Presidential Library & Museum. Public domain.

British States of Treason

In the third book of the *Institutes of the Laws of England,* Edward Coke, who as Attorney General led the prosecution against the Gunpowder Plot conspirators, framed the legal importance of the 1351 Treason Act: "For except it be Magna Charta, no other Act of Parliament hath had more honour given unto it by the King, Lords spirituall and temporall, and the Commons of the Realm … then [*sic*] this Act concerning Treason hath had."[9] The American colonists thought so highly of the British law of treason they flouted that whole parts of it were copied in the Constitution. For all its longevity and influence, the statutory definition of high treason was composed in Norman French, codified in a Parliament whose proceedings were taken down in Latin, and addressed a people who spoke English. The relevant part of the act, in a modern English translation that corrects the original's loose grammar and shifting voice, reads

> When a Man doth compass or imagine the Death of our Lord the King, or of our Lady his [Queen] or of their eldest Son and Heir; or if a Man do violate the King's Companion or the King's eldest Daughter unmarried, or the Wife [of] the

> King's eldest Son and Heir; or if a Man do levy War against our Lord the King in his Realm, or be adherent to the King's Enemies in his Realm, giving to them Aid and Comfort in the Realm, or elsewhere … the Cases above rehearsed ought to be judged Treason which extends to our Lord the King, and his Royal Majesty.

Many commentators have noted that high treason is defined not against "the Crown, not the commonweal, not the government, not an abstract state, but the person of the king."[10] Allegiance is owed to the King and that King's body, which is evident in how the act mimics the King's voice ("the King, at the request of the Lords and of the Commons, hath made a Declaration as hereafter followeth"). There was good reason in medieval times, where oaths of allegiance laid down mutual obligations for a dizzying array of relationships, to cast treason as a personal betrayal.

Blackstone held that the 1351 Treason Act was "declaratory": it did not create new legal categories but merely affirmed and clarified common law.[11] Over time, though, the use of the terms "compass and imagine" resulted in an expansion of treason's orbit. Indictments under "imagining" the king's death predominated after the act was passed.[12] As a synonym for "intend" or "design," to "imagine" the king's death did not mean dreaming about doing so, thinking in one's own head about it, but rather a purposive plan to carry out an act.[13] But the term was loose enough to serve as the basis for a number of prosecutions where the sole evidence was some verbal or written act:

> Words and writings which commented on the king and his behaviour in what was regarded as a malicious manner were often the basis of these indictments. If the words did not suggest a direct intent to bring about the king's demise then they were held to do so indirectly and the accused found guilty of treason just the same.[14]

Up to the fifteenth century, the harm of those words was judged through the lens of the king's health: if he were to read or hear those words, would his health, or humors, be upset, thus endangering his life? If it seems a stretch for a written text to cause such severe physical harm, at least a dozen individuals were executed for "commenting adversely on the behaviour of royal advisers, criticizing the sexual life or procreative ability of the monarch, misinterpreting government policies in a dangerous manner, showing open hostility to the ruling class or spreading rumours about general disaffection."[15] In a curious case of repression unconsciously exposing itself, the 1534 treasonable-words statute enumerated the terms of abuse that Henry VIII could not be called ("Heretick, Schismatic, Tyrant, Infidel or Usurper of the Crown").[16]

The problem with prosecuting speech for treason was that words spoken in a public assembly or a hushed tête-à-tête are misremembered or misunderstood; the meaning of oral communication depends on context, tone, even hand gestures or posture. As Coke put it, "bare words may make an heretick, but not a traitor without an overt act."[17] Writing, though, was an overt act—*scribere est agere*, to write is to act, the judge in Algernon Sydney's treason trial noted—and publishing even more so. As literacy expanded and new print technologies accelerated the circulation of texts, treasonous print matter became a vexing issue. For Thomas Hobbes, the ease with which "seducers" circulated treasonous ideas in print was one of the major reasons for the country's ills: since "the power of the mighty hath no foundation but in the opinion and belief of the people," words could never be innocuous.[18]

On top of an expansive definition of treason, the legal protections for the accused were nugatory. There was a requirement, sanctioned by Biblical law (Deut. 17:6), that two witnesses to a capital crime were needed, but the testimony of one witness to one treasonous act and a second witness to another was also accepted. Sydney was convicted by "scraps of paper" in a desk drawer that were "never shewed any Body."[19] Sydney's request for a copy of the indictment was denied, as was his request for an attorney. "We shall deny you nothing that is Law," the Lord Chief Justice ruled: "You shall have the right that becomes a Subject in your condition."[20] That condition was not an enviable one. Accused traitors were not given a copy of the indictment, could not be represented by counsel, and could not call or cross-examine witnesses.[21] That changed only with the 1695 Treason Act: "Whereas nothing is more just and reasonable" than the right to defend oneself when "Lives Honour Estates Bloud and Posterity … may bee lost and destroyed," those accused of treason "should not bee debarred of all just and equal Means for Defence of their Innocencies."[22] The accused would be issued the indictment and have the right to two attorneys. Advance notice of witnesses (and jurors) was to be given and only evidence related to the indictment was admissible. These protections were extended, a century later, to all major crimes—so it was out of the exceptional case of treason that fundamental protections in the right to a fair trial came into being.

While the pointed use of treason diminished due to the growing importance of political liberties, the incorporation of new territories like Scotland and Ireland, to say nothing of the far-flung empire, made questions of national belonging more acute, politically as well as legally (the protections to those accused of treason offered in the 1695 Act, for instance, were extended to Ireland only in 1821). The treason conviction of Arthur Lynch, an Australian-born Irishman who arrived in South Africa as a correspondent for the Parisian *Le Journal* but quickly set up an Irish Brigade allied with the Boers and later became an MP for Galway, shows the complexities involved: "I opposed the policy of the Government, but the principles that spurred me on were my love for Ireland and for Australia, and my passionate desires for what I considered national progress."[23] The Irish question continued to bedevil British courts, as the first conviction for treason in the Second World War (although for the minor crime of felony treason) was handed out to an IRA man who exclaimed in a Belfast court that "it is not treason to fight for one's country."[24]

While the core of British treason law in the run-up to the Second World War remained the 1351 Treason Act's emphasis on allegiance owed the sovereign, moments of national crisis had always expanded treason's orbit. The 1939 Defence of the Realm Act (DORA) gave "almost dictatorial powers" to the executive: any order or regulation felt necessary to winning the war could be issued, which meant that the property and legal rights of British subjects could be suspended and any existing Act of Parliament could be modified or nullified by decree.[25] The only quibble of resistance in the ninety-minute parliamentary debate was a meek reminder that serious abuses had been committed during the First World War: "Cut out this controversy, let's have national unity" is how one MP characterized the prevailing sentiment.[26] But even such expansive powers were not enough once war started. DORA's powers were extended in late May 1940: "Every private interest must give way to the urgent needs of the community," Clement Atlee noted, which meant giving the government "complete control over persons and property ... of all persons, rich and poor, employer and workman, man or woman, and all property."[27] DORA's expansion was prompted by the dire military situation (the German invasion of Norway, the Low Countries and France) and growing fears of fifth-column elements (two days earlier, a clerk in the American Embassy with links to the British far-right was discovered to have copied thousands of secret cables between Churchill and Roosevelt). "At a time like this, when Britain is fighting for her very existence," the *Belfast Telegraph* opined, "it is above all things necessary to deal sternly with enemies inside our gates."[28] The government could now direct, under penalty, anyone to work here rather than there, to produce this rather than that; it could also detain, with habeas corpus suspended, those thought likely to endanger the country. Coordinated raids across the country swept up thousands of British fascists.

Piggybacking on to that decree was the Treachery Act of 1940, which extended the death penalty to acts of treachery (espionage or sabotage) committed by foreign agents. It also directed that treachery trials should follow "the ordinary procedure of the courts, without the special forms and dignities of a treason trial."[29] Turning treachery into a capital crime showed the government's resolve: "you cannot deal with traitors," stated an Ulster Unionist MP and man of the cloth, "if you wear kid gloves."[30] The Act was a product of "the harsh necessities of the times," and those times—and here a contemporary legal journal spared no rhetoric, sidestepped no alliteration—were nothing other than "alarming emergency, the heyday of treachery, sabotage, stealthy stratagems and devilish designs to reduce free peoples into terror and subjection."[31] While twenty or so foreign agents were eventually executed under the Treachery Act, the simplified court procedure was also used in cases involving native Britons for such acts as writing to a German consul or supplying information about shipping routes. The high burden of proof required in treason cases made it preferable to charge offenders with "treachery" even though the acts fitting those crimes were roughly equivalent.

Having on the book two different crimes with varying judicial procedures for the same act was not ideal. The other problem, as Attorney General D. B. Somervell detailed in a May 1944 opinion, was that renegade broadcasters were not technically guilty of treachery:

> We are satisfied that reading out a broadcast is an act, but we are of opinion that the words here used, although of course they might affect morale, are not within the words "designed or likely to give assistance to the naval, military or air operations of the enemy, or to impede such operations of His Majesty's Forces."[32]

With war winds now blowing favorably, the prospect of capturing renegade broadcasters became real—but also the eventual headache of having cumbersome treason trials or, less ideally, resorting to charges under DORA, which did not carry a capital sentence. A memo to the Cabinet from late March 1945 flagged this as an issue of "immediate importance": the special procedures for treason trials would "prove a hindrance to the speedy and effective prosecution for treason of British subjects who may come into the hands of the authorities as the occupation of Germany proceeds."[33] The solution favored by the DPP, what eventually become the 1945 Treason Act, streamlined treason procedures to the ones already introduced in the Treachery Act. Treason no longer had to be proved through two eyewitnesses to the same overt act (or one eyewitness each to two separate overt acts). Some protections dubbed "archaic" or "out of date" were also waived, among them the presence of three sitting judges, the provision, ten days before trial, of a full list of witnesses and jurors, and the limitation of evidence at trial to matters dealing with an overt act specified in the indictment. The standard for treason trials did not bottom out entirely since what now applied was the procedure in murder trials. The Act nonetheless removed the symbolic elevation of treason as a crime apart.

There were good reasons in mid-May 1945 to make treason banal. The most important was the capture, earlier that month, of the war's most notorious renegade. William Joyce was detained abroad for over six weeks because the government did not want to risk repatriating him until after the Treason Act became law (he was sent home the morning after it received royal assent). The government was also gearing up for scores of treason prosecutions—by April 1946, 125 alleged wartime collaborators would be apprehended—and investing each trial with Regency-era pomp and ceremony would clog the courts. How the tide swings: whereas before the accused in treason trials had been hampered from conducting a robust defense, the remedies to that injustice had created too many protections. The best resting point was making treason a crime like any other, tried under the same conditions in a "general system of criminal procedure [that] is the fairest in the world."[34] Just how fair that system would be was soon put to the test.

The total number of Britons indicted for broadcasting on German radio reached twenty-one, although the number of active collaborators was far greater. The sentences varied enormously, from six months to life imprisonment or the death penalty. Dual nationals were generally exempted from postwar prosecution because their "dominant" nationality was felt to be German, a view grounded in notions of affect rather than law. At a certain point the appetite for continuing prosecutions simply flagged. The strict evidentiary requirements were difficult to meet and resulted in unsatisfactory sentences, such as Norman Baillie-Stewart being charged with Defence Regulation offenses but spared a treason trial because the exact date of his naturalization as a German citizen could not be determined. Establishing the identity of some renegades could be a tedious procedure, and corralling eyewitnesses to treason was difficult in the postwar disorder. Even when it would have been easy to establish egregious forms of collaboration, as occurred in the Channel Islands, there was little appetite to press the full force of the law (in this case because of the embarrassment of having so many cases to try).[35] The pendulum swung quickly from harsh vengeance to boundless mercy. The Lord Chief

Justice, "who certainly has not a reputation for tenderness," made it clear to the DPP in June 1947 that "renegade prosecutions should stop."[36] As the war receded in time, the luxury of perspective revealed that legal proceedings had failed to deliver justice. The discrepancy in sentencing galled: five years for writing letters presumably never read on how fine conditions were in Germany but only nine months for broadcasting defeatist comments and Nazi propaganda. One of the first traitors to be captured and tried, and who thus had the misfortune of being put on trial when emotions were at their fever pitch, was William Joyce, the most notorious radio voice of the war but someone who had never been a British subject.

Case One: William Joyce and the Scar of "Germany Calling"

The two most consequential postwar British war crimes trials both opened, fittingly enough, on 1945's Day of Atonement (September 17). The first, a British Military Court, convened under a Royal Warrant and operating under international law, was set up in a converted gymnasium in the old Hanseatic town of Lüneburg. Forty-five individuals, among them Josef Kramer, the "Beast of Belsen," were collectively tried for war crimes at Bergen-Belsen and Auschwitz. On top of oral testimony and written affidavits, motion pictures were introduced as evidence to document what prosecutors called mass murder on an unprecedented scale. Despite the undoubted importance of the first Allied tribunal on the Nazi plan for the "deliberate destruction of the Jewish race," it was the second trial opening that cloudy Monday morning that hit closer to home.[37] In the dock of the Old Bailey stood a former captive of the British garrison at Lüneberg, William Joyce, aka Lord Haw-Haw. It was still dark when a long queue for one of the twenty general-public seats in the Central Criminal Court began to form. If that weekend Londoners had celebrated the fifth anniversary of the Battle of Britain by marveling at 25 RAF squadrons flying low over the capital or inspecting captured German aircraft exhibited in Hyde Park and Trafalgar Square, those in line for the Joyce trial saw the Luftwaffe's handiwork up close, a 1941 bombing that had sliced open the building's ashen stone façade "as if it were a cake."[38] Bare electric bulbs illuminated the oak-paneled Court No. 1, whose shattered glass skylight was boarded up. Heavy blackout tarring on the windows further darkened the mood. That much needed repairing was obvious, but the repairs required were not just physical, the rebuilding of destroyed bricks and stones and glass, but also moral, seeking out justice against those who had inflicted all this damage. The line dividing justice and vengeance was very thin; during the course of Joyce's trial, it became increasingly difficult to see whether it had been crossed.

When Joyce was captured in May 1945 outside Flensburg, near the Danish border, many in Whitehall must have secretly wished that the aim of the arresting officer—who shot Joyce in the leg—had been truer. As it was, the DPP pressed for a "leading state trial" that could exorcise the iniquity of Joyce and expose the evils of Nazi propaganda.[39] The Crown was led by Attorney General Shawcross (see Figure 1.2). Forty-three years old, recently re-married, with dashing good looks, Shawcross was nervous about such

Figure 1.2 Portrait of Hartley Shawcross. Courtesy of National Portrait Gallery.

a high-profile case in his first Old Bailey appearance as Attorney General. The ballast of state was anchored by Treasury counsels Lawrence Byrne and Gerald Howard, both of whom would later be called up to judgeships. Joyce's legal team consisted of Gerald Slade, a future judge on the King's Bench Division who later defended John Amery; Derek Curtis-Bennett, who would go on to defend Klaus Fuchs and serial killer John Christie; and James Burge, who would defend Stephen Ward in the Profumo affair. Presiding over this assembly of legal talent was Justice Frederick Tucker, a South-African-born judge who later became a privy counsellor and Lord Justice of Appeal.

Shawcross opened the case by proclaiming treason "the gravest crime known to our law." This trial would be greater than the defendant:

> I daresay that in the years to come in the pages of history it will count for nothing what happens to William Joyce in the course of this trial. He will leave no mark upon those pages, but it may count a great deal that we who in our various activities are concerned in this trial to do and comport ourselves in accordance with the best traditions of English law, that we should try this man according to the law without fear or favour, affection or ill-will, on the evidence, unprejudiced by any preconceived notions, coldly, dispassionately, on the evidence, and on that alone. So best shall we sustain that great record of impartiality and equal justice which British courts and British juries hold in the eyes of the whole civilised world.

Though personally opposed to the death penalty, Shawcross enjoined the jurors to transform themselves into agents of the hallowed traditions of British justice, perhaps the last bulwark of Albion's power now that its empire was limp and broken. This symbolic merger of the jurors with British law and justice had its own logic when the issue was treason: as upholders of the nation, the jury had to defend itself. The Crown claimed that whether Joyce's broadcasts "did Germany more harm than good is a matter about which it will not be necessary for us to speculate."[40] As a purely legal point, the material impact of a treasonous act is irrelevant because the compelling fact is the intention to commit treason. Practically, though, it was the deep-seated fear of Haw-Haw's broadcasts and the broader history of the "war of words" that made a conviction so important.

Joyce's trial remains a dark blight in the annals of British justice. Fearing a furious "public outcry" if Joyce did not pay with his life, the government resorted to underhand tactics to secure a conviction.[41] The Security Services intercepted correspondence addressed to his family, friends, even his solicitor.[42] The judge who oversaw the proceedings had called Joyce a traitor in a 1940 case and walked into the courtroom carrying a black cap, the traditional accoutrement when sentencing a man to death. If Joyce were somehow acquitted on the three charges of treason, an unopened indictment, for treachery, was lying in wait; if he squirmed free of that, the American Department of Justice promised to "grab him quick" for a trial across the pond.[43] Radio Moscow, while irritated with British legal trappings ("the judges took an incredibly long time putting on their wigs"), predicted the right outcome would come to pass: "Naturally Courts cannot ignore the formalities or evade them, but there is a limit to everything."[44]

The intent of a treasonous act is usually established by a longer history of disloyalty, but at Joyce's trial the only evidence of intent came from a sworn statement he had given after being captured:

> I was actuated not by the desire for personal gain, material or otherwise, but solely by political conviction. I was brought up as an extreme Conservative with strong Imperialist ideas, but very early in my career, namely in 1923, became attracted to Fascism and subsequently to National Socialism. Between the years 1923 and 1939 I pursued vigorous political activities in England, at times as a Conservative but mainly as a Fascist or National Socialist.[45]

The chief Crown witness who presented the evidence that ultimately led to Joyce's conviction confirmed that he had heard a number of Joyce's public speeches in the 1930s but did not go into any great detail about them. Even though Joyce started in the fascist movement through the pen and became a leading figure in fascist periodical culture, the trial removed any signs of Joyce as an author, obviating any need to consider whether the court was prosecuting an opinion.

Most received views of Joyce today stem from Rebecca West's reportage in *The Meaning of Treason*. As a piece of contemporary journalism, West's description of the Joyce trial is rightly considered a classic; but it is not surprising to consider that West, writing on deadline for *The New Yorker*, failed to get the story right, and that her own prejudices, especially when it came to Joyce's Irish roots, colored her writing. Born in Brooklyn in 1906, Joyce was an American citizen by birth but grew up in Galway, in a family devoted to the ideals of Empire. When scarcely a teenager, he became a "scout" for the Black and Tans, a paramilitary organization brought in to stomp out the Irish independence movement. Wildly indiscreet about his pro-British loyalties, "W. E. Joyce" was dubbed a "Proved Spy" on an IRA kill list.[46] His family was given "a week's notice to clear out of the country or be shot."[47] Upon his arrival in London in 1922, Joyce signed up to join the Officer Training Corps at London University (he received a first-class honors degree in English literature from Birkbeck) and gravitated toward far-right political parties. The British Fascisti was Joyce's training ground in fascism. He acquired a badge of notoriety as the "quiet and highly respected member" who was razored during a political meeting in October 1924.[48] The attack was blamed on a "Jewish Communist," but, as Joyce confided to a former Galway acquaintance, it was likely payback, "Sinn Feiners" coming to settle scores.[49] In March 1933 Joyce joined the British Union of Fascists (BUF), quickly rising to become its Director of Research. If the popular imagination in 1945 and since has relegated Joyce to the role of minor fascist hack, the truth was that he was a key figure in the party, coordinating its activity nationwide and monitoring press coverage. Maxwell Knight, working undercover in the BUF, considered Joyce "a greater force than [Oswald] Mosley himself."[50] He crisscrossed the country on lecture tours, his appearances advertised by surname alone. If the BUF had twenty or so "first-class" speakers, only three were truly "outstanding," *Fascist Week* noted, and Joyce was one of them.[51]

Joyce was central to the network of fascist print culture that included *Blackshirt*, *Fascist Week*, *Action*, and a separate press for books and pamphlets. His start in the movement came in October 1933 with *Dictatorship*, a two-and-a-half-penny pamphlet. While a confused jumbling of conceptual ideas (equality was a complete fiction but present inequalities required fascism; fascism was "scientific" rule but also revolutionary; dictatorship did not require one man but could be led by "a new aristocracy"), the pamphlet marked Joyce out as a house intellectual with "extensive knowledge" and "white-hot prose."[52] While the British fascists vigorously attacked the existing intellectual caste (the "grotesque species" who were the "high-priests of Modernism" or, as Joyce put it, "the sickening miasma of Bloomsbury masochism"), they held a Romantic conception of intellectuals as the ones to set the course and guide the future.[53] On top of pamphlets, Joyce wrote essays for *The Fascist Quarterly* and became one of the most popular writers in *Action*, a popular weekly. His columns (forty-seven over a thirteen-month period) harped on the Jewish-Bolshevik threat, fascism's growing strength in Britain, and the sham democracy of Westminster (on the BUF as an alternative to the current order, see Figure 1.3). The most revealing personal obsession was a total anti-Semitism that picked up on even the most trivial signs (the genteel pastime of punting being spoiled by Jews who "dislocate the traffic of the river").[54] On modern culture Joyce was roundly against the "ultra-moderns" and "surrealists," calling himself a traditionalist who believed in the order and beauty that had once graced the art of "white civilization."[55]

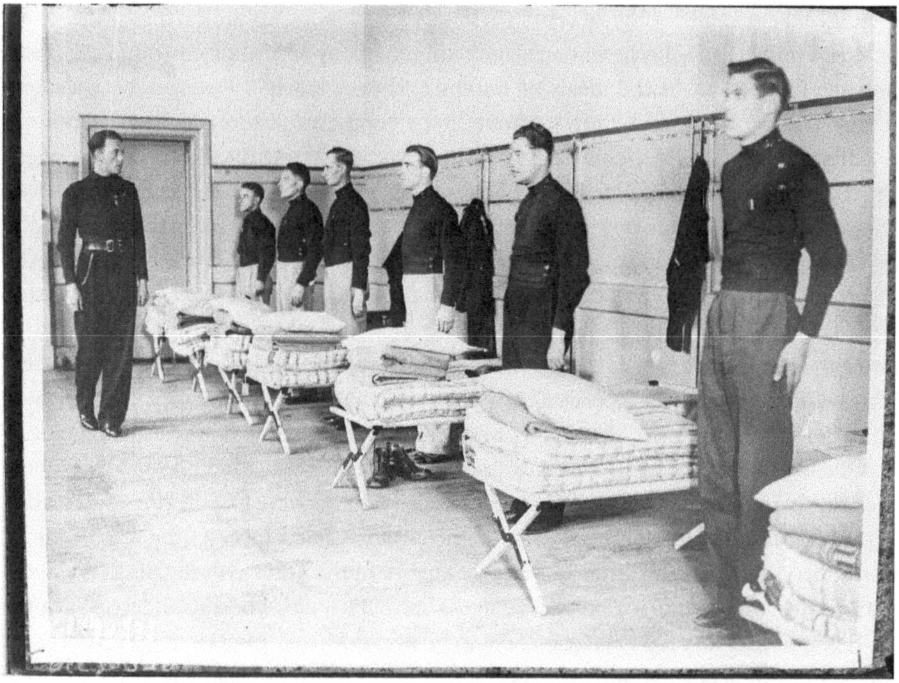

Figure 1.3 Inspection of British Union of Fascists dormitory, 1932. Courtesy of Gallica/BnF, all rights reserved.

In 1937, after a failed attempt to get a seat on the London City Council for Shoreditch, Joyce was expelled from the (now re-named) British Union. The official reason was that the BU's "precarious" finances required "a reduction and consolidation" of party staff; the more likely explanation is that Joyce had become a challenger to the throne.[56] Joyce did not go quietly, suing for back pay and setting up the National Socialist League (NSL) with John Beckett, a former Labour MP who considered Mosley soft on the Jewish question, and John Angus Macnab, a Rugby- and Oxford-educated classics master who idolized Joyce (the two ran a tutoring business together). The NSL was a hardline but ultimately fringe fascist group with a tiny, and then further dwindling, membership. Its program was laid out in *National Socialism Now* (1937), a pamphlet-cum-essay whose diagnosis of the current malaise held no surprises: massive income inequality and widespread "hunger, poverty, ruin" putting to bed any notion that Britain was a land of freedom; an emperor-has-no-clothes imperial policy, with India and Ireland drifting away; a bloated and corrupt party system failing to represent the interests of the people; the dark specter of Bolshevism brought into the land through alien sources; the puppeteering of the economic, political, and cultural spheres by a Jewish cabal.[57] The fascist medicine included a House of Commons represented by guilds, "an Empire united and indivisible," and the expulsion of Jews.[58] The national socialist, "the true rebel, the divinely inspired revolutionary, who lives to make destiny, not to be enslaved by it," would restore a mythical Britain, sketched out in purple prose:

> For all of us British people, there is a land in which we have played our part, great or humble, in the drama of life, a land where we have had our happy days, as well as the sad. We generally forget the spring morning, with the splendid sun sparkling on the dew in the green fields, the white lanes with their smiling hedges in summer, the rich tint of the leaves in the declining autumn afternoon, the first nip of winter, the English Christmas with our nearest and dearest, the mists on the fens, the gigantic bustle of our great cities, the fire-breathing giants of the night in the Black Country or by South Shields, the long, snaky monsters that bring happiness, sorrow, hope or anxiety into Euston or King's Cross, the ocean battering away at the rocks of Devon, the Cockney, with his Shoreditch barrow, making fun of every moment in his struggling little life, the broad Mersey restively bringing the challenge of the sea into the heart of Liverpool, the godly majesty of the Highlands, the serene power in the mountains of North Wales, even the rain blending so strangely with the romance of our early days, when, as children, we played in it—all these things are most often out of our minds; but if it ever happens to us to see the chalk cliffs receding for the last time as the water widens between us and our homeland, then the memories will come in a choking flood, and we shall know our land when it is too late.[59]

That prophetic image of the receding white cliffs would become a bitter reality two years later: "We kept our eyes fixed upon the Dover cliffs," Joyce later recalled about his 1939 departure to Berlin, "until the haze drew over them that impenetrable veil which, for us, was the end of an old life and the beginning of a new."[60]

Germany Calling

Arriving in Berlin in late August 1939, Joyce soon joined the English *Redaktion*, a small outfit that needed fresh blood since its heavy, unsubtle propaganda was "making itself ridiculous," as Eduard Dietze, who joined up at the same time, recalled.[61] Almost immediately after Joyce began broadcasting, a former BU member notified MI5 that Joyce's signature lines from the 1930s lecture circuit were airing on German radio. In mid-December, a *Sunday Mirror* headline screamed "Lord Haw-Haw's Ex-Wife Tells: He's an Englishman!"; then, in April 1940, *Life* magazine ran a picture of him in an article on radio traitors. In early April 1941 the open secret was fully acknowledged on air:

> I, William Joyce, will merely say that I left England because I would not fight for Jewry against the Fuehrer and National Socialism, and because I believe most ardently, as I do today, that victory with a perpetuation of the old system would be an incomparably greater evil for England than defeat coupled with a possibility of building something new, something really nationalist, something truly socialist.[62]

In July 1942, Joyce was promoted to "Chefkommentator der Ländergruppe England," with a monthly pay of 1,200 Reichsmarks (RM) (for Joyce as a man about town, see Figure 1.4). There was widespread appreciation in the Propaganda Ministry for his broadcasts, which were routinely described as *ausgezeichnet* (excellent), *fabelhaft* (fabulous), *vorbildlich* (exemplary), and *erstklassig* (first class). Naturalized as a German citizen in September 1941, Joyce was paraded to POW camps to drum up recruits for the British Free Corps.[63]

Only partial transcripts from four broadcasts were replayed at Joyce's trial (January 30, 1943, April 8, 1943, July 12, 1943, and August 30, 1944). The first broadcast was mainly a proclamation by Hitler, with little commentary by Joyce, as Judge Tucker pointed out after much confusion; the other three were anti-British screeds, heavy on Jewish conspiracies and *tu quoque* retorts on Allied injustice. A wide survey of Joyce's broadcasts throughout the war indicates that they tended to replay old hits from his fascist days, which followed the Nazi propaganda line anyway: the sham of democracy in Westminster, the selling out of England to Jewish interests, the crumbling of Empire. Postwar testimony from fellow radio employees stressed that Joyce "only read things of his own authorship."[64]

These broadcasts made Joyce "a daily perpetrator of High Treason," as he admitted in *Twilight Over England* (1940).[65] First published in German as *Dämmerung über England* (see Figure 1.5), *Twilight* was a conversion narrative of a boy raised "in a creed of fanatical patriotism" (7) who had awakened to do his "humble part" (8) for the "inevitable" German "victory" (11). Blame was laid squarely upon the country that had let down its people: "I lived for months," Joyce recalled, "with real friends who loved England

Figure 1.4 William Joyce, 1941 photo. Warsaw Press, 2-16636. Courtesy of National Digital Library, Poland.

Figure 1.5 Front cover of Joyce, *Dämmerung über England* (*Twilight over England*), published by Internationaler Verlag (Berlin). Public Domain.

and could not get enough to eat from her" (17). As a tale of decline, *Twilight* ranges from the "materialism of finance" to the failure of British politics after the First World War: "The system of government in Britain today deserves one description only: it is a plutocratic oligarchy, materialist in philosophy, Jewish in purpose, and tyrannous in effect" (53). When Berlin was captured, MI5 officers were instructed that anyone able to "identify JOYCE as the author of the book ... should be despatched to England by air immediately."[66] With no documents or witnesses to Joyce's authorship discovered, and, amazingly enough, no copy of the book on hand, *Twilight* was never introduced as evidence at trial.

Accumulating material evidence proved surprisingly difficult. The BBC was not keen to "take part in what might be described as the sordid work of prosecution."[67] It was only in late January 1943 that it began permanent recordings of Berlin radio, although the Special Branch officers complained that "not very good" reception muddled their transcription efforts (then, comically, they could not read back their shorthand).[68] There were other instances of human error, such as Joyce's security services file being mislaid, with an official dryly noting that "the matter may have escaped attention."[69]

Evidence-gathering efforts became more urgent as the prospect of Allied victory loomed. In an end-days diary he began keeping in early 1945, Joyce realized that he was considered a criminal fugitive: "I still love England and hate to think that I am to be regarded as a traitor to her, which, in my opinion I am not."[70] The change in fortunes was painful:

> It is 12.08. There seems to be a never-ending raid on Berlin. A whole procession is passive over us. ... I think that the proceedings may be very lengthy. It seems as if the whole bloody menagerie were being paraded. What worries me is lunch. I could almost eat the f-Bunker.[71]

With the *Rundfunkhaus* no longer suitable for broadcasting, operations were decamped to Apen, twenty kilometers from the Dutch border, and then Hamburg. Joyce gave one of his final broadcasts on April 27, 1945, slurring his words ("in homely language," one reviewer noted, "he was well and truly plastered").[72] A few days later Joyce and his wife fled to Flensburg, where a Nazi rump government led by Admiral Dönitz had assembled. Life on the run did not suit Joyce, who was captured after two British soldiers recognized his voice: "You wouldn't be William Joyce, by any chance, would you?" Shot in the right buttock, the person who had taunted Britain was conveyed on a stretcher to hospital, inert, his drowsy eyes gazing in the distance as soldiers with drawn rifles posed for the trophy shot (see Figure 1.6). Joyce could not resist a barb: "In civilized countries wounded men are not peepshows."[73]

The Trial of a False Passport

The central question in Joyce's trial was not whether he had committed treason but whether he could commit treason at all: "Did this prisoner owe a duty of allegiance to the British Crown?"[74] It is unimaginable that this question had not been cleared up before trial. The Crown, in fact, already had an answer, though not a palatable one. After his capture, Joyce stated that he had been born in America, that his father had been naturalized as an American, and that he had become a German citizen during the war. His family might have been considered British in the long years he lived in England, but

Figure 1.6 Capture of William Joyce, Flensburg, Germany, May 29, 1945. Bert Hardy, Army No. 5 Army Film & Photographic Unit. Imperial War Museums BU 6911.

"whether we were or not" he did not know.[75] Joyce's former fascist associates had been telling MI5 interrogators the same thing for years, and Joyce had said as much on air ("I was born in Brooklyn and have acquired German nationality").[76] The implications of Joyce's birth only began to be considered in March 1944, with frantic dispatches across the Atlantic asking the FBI to rifle through naturalization records and birth registries. While coming to accept that Joyce had been born in Brooklyn in 1906, the British government at first erroneously concluded that he was "a natural-born British subject."[77]

Determining whether Joyce was a British subject was no simple matter. In fairness, he was not alone: "There must be a multitude of persons," Francis Piggott observed in 1907, "who cannot say with certainty whether they are British subjects or not."[78] As the two-volume treatise by the Chief Justice of Hong Kong noted, British nationality law depended on a series of recent legislative acts—many of them poorly drafted—and common law; as an empire, nationality had a wide reach, subtle shades, and perplexing individual cases. It was also of recent vintage, with little case law before the eighteenth century. Britain's imperial expansion widened the orbit of possible subjects, but territory could be conceded, or lost, its administration contested. The grant of various degrees of autonomy to multiple dominions created further ripples. There was also a shift in Joyce's lifetime from nationality as a matter of organic belonging and affect to a purely administrative and bureaucratic matter—yet there was still quite a degree of latitude, even by official bodies, on how nationality was understood. In 1917, Joyce's mother was told by police in Lancashire that she could not apply for a wartime ration book because she was an American citizen, but in Galway a Royal Irish Constabulary officer refused to believe that the Joyces were aliens since Michael was "one of the most respectable, law-abiding and loyal men in this locality."[79] In the postwar trials, dual nationals and even individuals with "a long German or Italian residence and background" were generally spared prosecution, on the grounds that their "dominant" nationality or affective bonds were foreign.[80] Joyce's wife, Margaret, who worked in the propaganda services, too, was not prosecuted despite her case being very "similar" to her husband's; instead, she was returned "to Germany as a German subject."[81] Considering her an enemy alien who did not owe allegiance to the Crown (when she was indisputably a natural-born British subject) while executing her husband for treason (though he indisputably had never been a British subject) spoke loudly of how politics determined Joyce's fate.

Common law had long held that British nationality was indelible, *nemo potest exuere patriam*—in vulgar terms, the winning ticket of first prize in the lottery of life could not be thrown away. A natural-born subject's allegiance was "natural, absolute, pure, and indefinite" (*ligeantia naturalis, absoluta, pura, et indefinita*).[82] This changed with the 1870 Naturalization Act, which stipulated the loss of British nationality for subjects who became citizens of another state. The children of former British subjects, it logically followed, and case law confirmed, were not natural-born British subjects. When Joyce was born in 1906, both his parents had relinquished their British nationality. When the family moved back to Britain, his parents did not apply to have their British nationality reinstated.

The most one could say was that Joyce had engaged in a "life-long masquerade as a British subject," to quote Rebecca West.[83] Four times in his opening statement Shawcross used some variant of the metaphor that Joyce "clothed himself in the full status of a British subject": he had "not merely clothed himself with the status of a British subject; he had, so to speak, enveloped himself in the Union Jack."[84] This metaphor cut its own logic in a treason trial: nationality could not be taken on and off when it suited, as Joyce had done; conversely, nationality as a uniform drew an implicit association with the fraught symbolism of the Blackshirt. If this metaphor had its own pull, the Crown witnesses had nothing to offer but Joyce calling himself British. The rejoinder from the defense was irrefutable:

> by screaming from the housetops fifty thousand times that I am a British subject I do not become one … by making fifty thousand declarations that I am a British

> subject I do not become one … by swearing an oath that I am a British subject … I do not become one. (58)

By the end of the trial's first day, Shawcross conceded that he would not "press that point" of Joyce being a British subject, to Justice Tucker's approval: "I think everybody must agree that the evidence which has been tendered is really overwhelming" (97).

The treason case against Joyce did not collapse since the Crown had planned for this eventuality. The first two charges—broadcasting for the enemy from September 18, 1939, to May 29, 1945, and becoming naturalized as a German subject—were premised on Joyce owing allegiance as a British subject. The third charge—that Joyce had violated his allegiance to the King while holding a valid British passport (it expired on July 2, 1940)—was premised on the idea that a passport holder received protection from the Crown and thus owed allegiance in turn. Basing the trial on solely this charge would have been problematic. Would the public accept that a foreigner could be hung for treason for acts committed abroad because he had lied to get a passport? There was also a legal reason to start the trial with the knowingly false claim that Joyce was a British subject: the Crown could widen the timeline of treasonous acts and thus introduce its most compelling evidence (the later broadcasts were not only more hateful, but they were all the Crown had in terms of permanent recordings).

The overused metaphor of Joyce draping himself in British cloth turned out to be no metaphor at all; it was the famous dark-blue cloth covering of a British passport book that made him a traitor. The novel theory put forward by the Crown was that a passport, even one acquired fraudulently, offered its holder protection. This interpretation was suggested to Shawcross by Hersch Lauterpacht, a key figure in the development of international criminal tribunals and human rights law.[85] Through a passport, Shawcross asserted, Joyce could invoke the assistance of "the whole of the diplomatic and consular machinery of the State":

> The Crown really does assume—and I am not using language of any kind of exaggeration when I say so—grave responsibilities to protect a person to whom it issues a passport; and equally, of course, it may be under grave responsibilities to other Powers in respect of the acts of the passport-holder abroad.[86]

A British passport theoretically relieved Joyce of conscription in the German Army and entitled him to re-enter Britain. It also may have been used to secure employment, Shawcross speculated, since Joyce's value to German radio was in his being a British subject (although surely what mattered most was being perceived by listeners as British). Prodded by Justice Tucker to condense his theory, Shawcross promised to put "the whole thing in a sentence":

> I would submit on behalf of the Crown that it is unthinkable that a person who has apparently been domiciled in this country; who has the whole of his family living in this country and who leaves the whole of his family, his relatives, his father and

> mother and sisters and brothers with the exception of his wife in this country; who has secured from this country the substantial matter of protection that the issue of a passport involves; who has secured the right to return to this country at any time as a British subject; who has declared himself to be a British subject; who uses the passport and travels on it as a British subject, even perhaps as in this case secures employment on it—it is in my submission unthinkable that such a person should not at the corresponding date owe allegiance to the Crown. (111)

If there was some sophistry in making this out to be a single sentence, the arguments smacked of legal hair-splitting and desperation, the deplorable fact, as Shawcross noted a few years later, that "it is possible to find … an authority for almost any proposition that you like to put up."[87]

Before wider arguments began on the implication of Joyce holding a passport, Justice Tucker admitted to a wide ignorance on the legal status of passports. He was not alone. When a Middle Temple barrister gave a talk on passports in March 1946, "passport" was put in quotation marks, as if it were some newfangled, incomprehensible invention.[88] Put into mass circulation after the French Revolution, the passport system flourished in the first part of the nineteenth century as part of a wider movement by European states to issue identification documents to control their populations and stymy the movement of radicals. By the end of the nineteenth century, though, passports came to be seen as "despotic" and "an unnecessary barrier to the freedom of communications" and movement.[89] Passports came back in use after the First World War and soon became a necessity for travelers seeking to cross borders—to great annoyance within *The Times* letter page, which was full of complaints about extortionate fees and the indignity of foreigners questioning the *bona fides* of British subjects.

As passport use increased, so too did case law. One thing was clear: the link between a passport and citizenship was tenuous, if not nil. Because different states issued passports to a wide variety of peoples, "it is impossible to establish a connection in international law between the issuance of a passport and the acquisition or tenure of nationality."[90] In *Urtetiqui v D'Arcy* (1835), the US Supreme Court called a passport a "political document" addressed to foreign states and in no way evidence of citizenship.[91] A foreign state was under no obligation to accept that a passport established its bearer's nationality.[92] The 1939 ruling in *Rex v. Ketter*, which concerned the deportation of an alien who held a British passport signed by the High Commissioner in Palestine, noted that it was difficult to imagine that a passport "could lead the appellant to think that he was a British subject, and it is still more difficult to see how it could make him one."[93] By extension, it was even more difficult to conceive that a passport acquired fraudulently could impact nationality. Adding to the problem in the Crown case was that diplomatic protection was not a right. There was no legal duty for a state to protect its citizens, a Foreign Office official later noted: "The mere holder of a British passport is of course entitled to nothing. If he is not a British subject we deny protection and take the first opportunity to impound the passport."[94] In a February 1946 memo (misplaced from the official files for over a year), the Head of the Consular Department at the Foreign Office fumed at how Joyce's trial "went off the rails": "the holder of a British passport carries no rights whatever to protection."[95] Thinking otherwise would impose "an onerous burden" upon embassies.[96] A passport, in sum, was merely a shortcut to establish nationality, but "other and better evidence" could displace that *prima facie* view.[97] In Joyce's trial the Crown placed the passport as a material object above the state of affairs it was meant to speak to, Joyce's nationality, which was the legally significant matter.

Despite these limitations to the Crown's case, on which was added the practical matter that there was no trace of Joyce's British passport or any evidence to suggest that he had used it, Shawcross argued that Joyce had affirmed multiple times—despite notices "in heavily leaded type" warning of the grave consequences of false declarations on passport applications—that he was a natural-born British subject.[98] Those declarations, Joyce's lawyer argued, had absolutely no bearing on the matter at hand: "We are concerned here with a British passport which has in fact been issued to an American subject. The Crown has no jurisdiction to issue British passports to American subjects" (118). That was not entirely true; the Crown could do as it liked with passports, issuing them to pets and plants if it wished, although it would be diplomatically troublesome to identify foreign nationals as one's own. It was ultimately a question of law as to whether holding a passport obliged allegiance, and on this matter Justice Tucker sided with the Crown. In his summing-up to the jury, Tucker stated that while Joyce had never been a British subject, he had incontestably owed local allegiance when residing within the realm and that this allegiance persisted when he left the country armed with a British passport:

> You cannot become a British citizen by carrying a British passport … None the less I think it is the law that if man who owes allegiance by having made his home here, having come to live permanently, thereby acquiring allegiance as he undoubtedly does—if he then steps out of this Realm armed with the protection which is normally afforded to a British subject (improperly obtained maybe, but none the less obtained) if he leaves this Realm, as the Attorney-General called it, wrapped up in the Union Jack, that is to say, using and availing himself of the protection of the Crown in an executive capacity which covers him while he is abroad, then in my view he has not thereby divested himself of the allegiance which he already owed. (149–50)

That ruling in law sealed Joyce's fate. The evidence the Crown had assembled against Joyce had hardly been stunning. The only witness to his traitorous activities, a Detective Inspector at Special Branch, had never spoken to Joyce, had no memory of the precise date or time when he heard Joyce broadcast, could not recall the station he heard Joyce on, and confused everyone with a shorthand transcription of a broadcast that did not distinguish Joyce's personal commentary from direct quotes from a Hitler speech. The only admissible evidence that remained was a 1939 broadcast which falsely stated that Dover and Folkestone had been bombed by the Luftwaffe. That threadbare testimony from a single uncorroborated witness—"they wouldn't have a dog hanged on no more than that" rued a contemporary American legal scholar—was the only evidence of Joyce's adherence to the enemy.[99] But since it was admitted that Joyce had broadcast on German radio in 1939, the judge's instructions to the jury were for them to pass judgment on a series of largely rhetorical questions: "Do you think it is essential for propaganda that it should either be false or true? Propaganda may be true and some may be false, may it not? Does it matter whether it is false or true if it is broadcast over the enemy radio system? What is the purpose and object of a broadcast from Germany in English? What is the purpose of it? To assist the Germans or to assist the English?"[100] The jury had barely time for a cupper before shuffling back with a guilty verdict.

The Times praised the trial as being "conducted in accordance with the highest standards of British justice," noting that even if Joyce had never been British, the capital sentence was entirely merited due to "the detestation and contempt which his conduct provoked … If WILLIAM JOYCE had had his way the abomination of Nazism would have been fastened upon Britain and the world."[101] Six weeks later, the Law Courts in the Strand dismissed Joyce's appeal. The court of last resort was in the House of Lords. Hearings began on December 10, a few days after John Amery had pled guilty to treason at the Old Bailey. The same arguments were presented, and the Lords found—in a ruling that was only publicly disclosed in February, after Joyce was already six feet under—the appeal without merit, although Lord Porter voted to overturn the conviction on the grounds that it was up to the jury to determine what Joyce had done with his passport and whether such actions showcased allegiance. In most cases a dissenting vote would have stayed the death penalty, but Joyce was sent back to Wandsworth to await his execution—without even having the reasons for the dismissal. On top of the press throng and Rebecca West there to document his execution, the crowd that had assembled included fascist supporters but also ordinary members of the British public, like two working men from Glasgow down on holiday, a mother living nearby who wanted to show her ten-year-old daughter what disobedience wrought, and an ex-servicemen with a bulldog ready to be unleashed if the fascists caused trouble. What was noticeably missing was a sense that the law had been well served by the public hanging.

Case Two: Wodehouse in Wonderland

One of the few advantages of wartime internment by the enemy is the sweet relief of not having to file one's taxes. But since the tax authorities back home can always rule otherwise, especially if the business of authoring can still be profitably carried out, one may well regret not having kept track of professional expenses. With no bookshops, no occasion for travel, and not much in the way of incidentals like stamps and envelopes, these would be limited. Having so little to claim creates its own trouble, it being well-known that nothing so jolts a taxman's left eyebrow as wild, year-to-year fluctuations in the same box. Thankfully in those lean times there was the typewriter rental, 18 RM per month, paid out to Oberlieutenant Buchelt of Ilag VIII in Tost, in German-controlled Poland. About six months of that to deduct from the 250 RM that came in for the radio broadcasts in July 1941. If one only had the receipts.

It is easy to parody P. G. Wodehouse's wartime plight ("they find you, you know," he said disbelievingly when told that he was probably off the hook with the IRS).[102] If the war years were a black mark for Wodehouse, it was not because he was found guilty of any crime. The standard view, largely adopting George Orwell's celebrated essay on the case, is that the summer 1941 broadcasts from Berlin "do not convict Wodehouse of anything worse than stupidity," of being Bertie without Jeeves.[103] The five talks were light in tone and touch, "perfectly harmless," Wodehouse said at the end of his life, "just a comic description of my adventures in camp."[104] The furor that erupted in the press was an obvious instance of wartime deranging the senses, and thankfully everybody agreed afterwards that it was all a big misunderstanding. Sir Pelham Grenville, "Plum" to his friends, would always remain "an Englishman for all seasons," the unsurpassed comic writer of the twentieth century.[105]

A closer examination of the Wodehouse case reveals a complicated story of how professional authorship in wartime could lead to political irresponsibility. "As long as I had a typewriter and plenty of paper and a room to work in I'm fine" was how Wodehouse summed up his internment.[106] His stated intention in broadcasting, to let readers back in America know that all was fine, posited a narrow view of authorship as continuous production, "writing all the time."[107] But all that writing found no outlet after his name was disgraced and the British security services investigated him for treason. Even if he was never convicted of a crime, the desire to rehabilitate his reputation became an obsession, firstly in the unpublished (and then destroyed) manuscript "Wodehouse in Wonderland" and then in a series of postwar autobiographical works. When *Encounter* suggested publishing some of the broadcasts in the early 1950s, he agreed—but then altered the texts (to freshen up the jokes, he said). A critic who wrote a 20,000-word chapter on the broadcasts got the hint when Wodehouse refused to send it back.[108] To borrow a phrase from *Money in the Bank*, the novel he wrote while in a German internment camp, all this was unmistakably some "oompus-boompus" calling for re-appraisal.

From Low Wood to Nazi Air

When war broke out in September 1939, Wodehouse was living in Le Touquet, a "foreign pleasure resort" on France's northwestern coast.[109] Having spent most of the year convinced that peace would hold ("no war in our lifetime is my feeling," he confided in April; no chance of Germany risking war, he wagered in July), once war broke out it was unclear what a nearly sixty-year-old funnyman could do.[110] These were busy times for him: the BBC began airing Ukridge adaptations in January 1940 ("the Wodehouse brand of humour broadcasts well," a critic noted); the *Saturday Evening Post* serialized *Quick Service* that spring; a collection of Drones Club stories came out in late April under the soon-to-be-dream title *Eggs, Beans, and Crumpets*; and a new novel, *Joy in the Morning*, was in the works.[111] During the *Sitzkrieg* "no popular fiction was in greater demand" than Wodehouse's, with RAF pilots said to be especially enthralled with Blandings (on Wodehouse's celebrity, see Figure 1.7).[112]

Figure 1.7 P. G. Wodehouse, celebrity author. Courtesy of National Portrait Gallery.

After the German occupation of Le Touquet began on May 22, 1940, not much changed for Wodehouse save for the obligation to report daily to a German official in town. A group of American writers, editors and theater producers petitioned for his safe passage back to Manhattan on the grounds that "without exception, his writings are of a light, humorous order, completely free of propaganda."[113] The official German response was that Wodehouse was "quite comfortable" and no one should feel any "anxiety" about his fate.[114] Five days later he was given ten minutes to pack (in the trunk went "a copy of Shakespeare, a pair of pajamas, and a mutton chop," but no passport).[115] The town Wodehouse left behind would be ravaged by war: 800,00 German mines were laid and around 30 percent of the homes were destroyed, the others looted. Even though Wodehouse's villa was spared thanks to a protection order the German authorities issued "in view of the propaganda value of his work," there was no question of returning for good after the war, especially when bartenders at the clubhouse refused to serve him a drink.[116]

Wodehouse shuttled through a succession of internment camps in France and Belgium before reaching Tost, in Upper Silesia, where he stayed from September 1940 to June 1941. Ilag VIII housed over one thousand civil internees in a converted mental asylum. Wodehouse's internment diary was marked by a chirpy "prison brings out all that is best in us all" tone. "I must make a note of this day," he wrote after nearly six months of internment, "as one of the absolutely flawless ones of my life." The German officers and soldiers were kind fellows forced to play a disagreeable part: there was the "very decent" sergeant escorting them onto the bus, the "very pleasant German soldier" giving out cigarettes, the "nice old German general" instructing a soldier to carry Wodehouse's heavy suitcase, the "very tough looking German private" who did the "most touching thing" by offering soup, the "charming German corporal who spoke perfect English and had read all my books," and so on.. He felt that he was right in "what I have always said, that Germans are swell guys, and the only barrier between us is the one of language. I have never met an English-speaking German whom I didn't like instantly." The journal has little political commentary, although the casual anti-Semitism ("Distinct lowering of the tone" after the arrival of sixteen new Jewish prisoners, the "Jew in spectacles" on double rations who was "the most unpopular man in camp," etc.) is jarring.[117]

After Civilian Prisoner Number 796 rented a typewriter, he telegrammed his New York-based agent, "Am quite happy here and have thought out new novel. Am hoping be able write it."[118] For friends and supporters, it was a relief to read in the *New York Times* that Plum was "cheerfully" working "undisturbed each morning and afternoon" on what eventually became *Money in the Bank* (interment gave him "plenty of time to think of funny things").[119] After a personal essay on his internment was published in the *Saturday Evening Post* in July 1941, *Money in the Bank*—"the only novel I should imagine," he later noted, "that has ever been written in an internment camp"—was serialized in the same venue that autumn (before being released as a single volume in January 1942).[120] The moral dilemma other writers faced—what did it mean to publish when the Nazis controlled the literary field?—was different for Wodehouse, whose work was published in still-neutral America. Yet without explicit German approval his work would never have seen the light of day. The instincts of the professional author—"I just wanted to write, and was prepared to write anything that had a chance of getting into print"—were ill-suited to the ethics of the situation.[121]

In late June 1941, the Associated Press reported that Wodehouse was freed from Tost and staying at the Adlon Hotel in Berlin. The immediate reaction was one of relief, especially for Plum's daughter: "It's most wonderful news," she told the *Daily Mirror*,

"Father will now be able to write in peace."[122] A day later, though, it was reported that Wodehouse would broadcast a series of "weekly" radio talks on German radio. That news was followed by Wodehouse lauding the German sense of humor in Swedish daily *Aftonbladet* and seeming indifferent to the war when speaking to the *New York Times* ("Naturally, I hope the war is over soon," he confided, "but if I am able to continue my work I will be satisfied. All I ask is a table, a typewriter, and no interruptions"). The food at the five-star Adlon was "very good," he told American readers, but, with only three meals per day, insufficient; in camp, Red Cross parcels allowed him to "nibble chocolate in between."[123] If these were jokes, newsprint flattened them. The flippant tone continued in a radio broadcast beamed to New York a few days later.[124] The actual result of the war—then entering a critical phase, with Operation Barbarossa smashing through Russian lines—was filtered through the lens of his fictional world: "I'll tell you something about the war and my work that's been bothering me a good deal. I'm wondering whether the kind of people and the kind of England I write about will live after the war—whether England wins or not, I mean."[125]

The impact of that radio talk was momentous. The *Daily Mirror*'s front page the following day carried a mug shot of Wodehouse, captioned in bold as—"A MAN WHO LETS DOWN HIS OWN COUNTRY"—alongside the pointed question "The Price Is?": "He lived luxuriously because Britain laughed with him, but when the laughter was out of his country's heart, Wodehouse was not ready to share her suffering. He hadn't the guts (or was it that he hadn't the wish?) even to stick it out in the internment camp."[126] The *Sunday Times* opined that there was "deep resentment" toward the country's most beloved author.[127] Questions were asked in the Commons if appearing on Berlin radio was an offense under the Treachery Act; while no names blotted Hansard, there could be no doubt what prompted the enquiry. The inescapable conclusion was that Wodehouse "bought his freedom and comfort at the price of helping the enemy."[128] In the literary pages, A. A. Milne noted that the rights of genius to be "above the battle" no longer applied: "every man" must now "come down into the arena, pledge himself to the cause in which he believes, and suffer for it."[129]

That motif of suffering was the key trope for Wodehouse's case. Most renegades, the postwar prosecution service later noted, were actuated by "selfish motives," enjoying "the comforts of the liberty which their work as willing pawns in the hands of the enemy afforded them … As against this, we have the loyalty and courage of those British subjects who suffered all the hardships which internment meant."[130] By escaping the suffering other internees were going through, which itself was conjoined with the sacrifice of a native population strafed by Luftwaffe bombers and thinned out by rationing, Wodehouse had violated the moral pact of the "people's war."[131] The high cost of that was made clear in a violent BBC broadcast by Daily Mirror columnist "Cassandra" on the "story of a rich man trying to make his last and greatest sale—that of his own country."[132]

Against these slew of charges Wodehouse contemplated hiring a German lawyer to sue for libel. He was mystified by the uproar over broadcasts which he considered "simply comic accounts of my camp life in lightest possible vein."[133] Most critics have followed that view. "There is not a single sentence that is pro-Nazi" in the talks, Iain Sproat argues.[134]

Frances Donaldson says that it is "established beyond doubt" that the talks were "harmless in themselves and harmless in intention."[135] Robert Hall, Jr., says that the broadcasts presented "a straightforward narrative, wholly unpolitical," and goes so far as to repeat the claim—eagerly touted by Wodehouse after the war but entirely unfounded—that they were taught in American military colleges as examples of "subtle anti-German propaganda."[136] The sweet rhythms of the Wodehouse style are in full display in the broadcasts; after the war he considered them "one of the best things I ever wrote."[137] But that, perhaps, is the issue. What does it mean to go on Berlin radio with "a slight goofiness," as the opening line of the first broadcast puts it, to lay on the jokes thick and fast?[138]

The first broadcast treats the afternoon in which Wodehouse's internment was ordered; broadcasts two, three and four cover about eight weeks in total (one week each for Loos and Liège, the subjects of broadcasts two and three, respectively, and about five weeks to the camp at Huy, the subject of broadcast four); and then the final broadcast covers forty-two weeks at Tost. The broadcasts flatten time: the shock and trauma of the internment order merit its own treatment while nearly a year's worth of captivity is reduced to a single broadcast because time within camp is unstructured and devoid of meaning. The only thing of note that happens within camp is feeding time, but once one meal is described, every other meal follows as a tasteless succession of leftovers. The weight of the narrative also occludes the full German involvement in his captivity. The first three camps were outside German territory and staffed by French and Belgian officials, but these ostensible allies turn out to be more sadistic than the Germans. The German guards at Tost are playfully nicknamed "Pluto, Rosebud, Ginger and Donald Duck," reducing Nazi brutality to a Disney comic strip; the über-organization of the German camp leads to a satire of bloated bureaucracy ("Room Wardens ward the rooms, the Floor Wardens ward the floor, the Adjutants bustle about, trying to look busy"). Tost was "a great improvement on our previous resting places" since it was "a real camp, and not a makeshift"; that final broadcast ends with a paean to the camaraderie of the internees who had been transformed into a "student body" horsing around and playing jokes: "I never met a more cheerful crowd, and I loved them like brothers."[139] That sentiment was not always reciprocated.

Investigations

With Wodehouse in German-controlled territory throughout the war, his MI5 file was patchy: "little reliable information … was available in 1941," when his broadcasts aired, "and little additional information became available during the course of the war."[140] The file contained the broadcasts, which were "innocuous" but still incriminating because they had been relayed on the air, and hundreds of press clippings.[141] Then, in November 1942, Wodehouse sent a letter to the Foreign Office whose tortuous syntax was a far cry from the crystal clarity of his house style:

> In the hope that by doing so I shall be able to re-establish myself in the eyes of the British Government and people and to remove the bad impression created by my

> unfortunate broadcasts over the German short wave system ... may I be allowed to put before you the circumstances connected with these, I am not attempting to minimize my blunder, which I realise was inexcusable, but I feel that I can place certain facts before His Majesty's Government which will show that I was guilty of nothing more than a blunder.[142]

The first "fact"—"I was released, as were all the internees who had reached that age, because I was sixty years old"—was false (Wodehouse was a few months shy of sixty when he was released; moreover, there were scores of internees at Tost above that age). Claiming that he went on the air because unanswered fan letters were "preying" on his mind, Wodehouse noted that he quickly realized his mistake and had acted irreproachably afterwards (although it was widely reported that he had signed a contract for a Berlin film studio and that he was the beneficiary of "courtesy marks"). Unsurprisingly, the letter cut no ice: when a few months later the Germans offered to allow the Wodehouses to move to Sweden in exchange for the release of two German subjects, Whitehall refused.

To show that the Nazi regime valued culture, details about Wodehouse's doings were regularly released. Made available for interviews with foreign media outlets, Wodehouse told *Aftonbladet* that he was "no traitor" and had no desire to do propaganda for either side; he would focus only on his writing.[143] In 1943, as the bombing campaign of Berlin intensified, Wodehouse was allowed—and even paid 100,000 francs in moving expenses—to settle in Paris. The Wodehouses had rooms at the Bristol and took their meals in the hotel's diplomatic dining room, which was reserved for German officers.[144]

Even if Wodehouse spent most of the war years writing, the radio broadcasts and other questionable events (like selling film adaptation rights to a German production company) landed him on the British Renegades Warning List. After the liberation of Paris in August 1944, Wodehouse, to "clear up" the "highly embarrassing" suspicion of treason, made his whereabouts known.[145] The Security Services, fearing that Wodehouse might become a victim of the *épuration sauvage*, pressed for his repatriation, but a senior Home Office official noted that it would be "politically embarrassing" to have him on British soil and not immediately put on trial for treason.[146] As an MI5 agent later admitted, "WODEHOUSE would have been a bad case to be the first prosecution of its kind [radio treason]."[147] The evidence against him was incomplete and unproven; there were no legal precedents guiding radio treason trials; and while he was reviled, no one thought him malicious like Haw-Haw.

A seasoned MI5 officer, Major E. J. P. Cussen, who later became a judge, was sent to Paris to interrogate Wodehouse under caution. Wodehouse's statement covered his early literary career and then went into great depth on the war years. One issue Wodehouse stressed was that he "always had plenty of money" ("I never received financial assistance in any form from the German authorities either directly or indirectly"). Wodehouse claimed he had no reason to bargain his way out of Tost since he was "definitely happy," with "congenial work to occupy me and a great variety of pleasant company." He conceded that his broadcasting had been foolish but insisted that nothing more sinister than wishing to acknowledge his loyal readers drove it. There was also possibly some vanity in hoping that people would "admire me for having kept cheerful under difficult conditions," but that was no capital crime.[148] (As he later put it, "if you are going to condemn authors for being smug, you will hardly know where to start."[149]) He also claimed that since his war had been such a busy one from a writing point of view, he had had no time to work for the Germans:

> Since I was released from Tost I have written about 80 pages which were needed to complete the novel "Joy in the Morning" which I had been writing while I was interned, almost the whole of the novel called "Full Moon" which I had begun in camp, a book of camp reminiscences, a novel entitled "Spring Fever," ten short stories and about 100 pages of a novel tentatively called "Uncle Dynamite." This amounts to between 350,000 and 400,000 words and in addition to this there was the time involved in thinking out the plots. This is designed to shew that I could not have been engaged in doing secret propaganda for the enemy.[150]

More concretely, Wodehouse provided his camp diary and an accounting of his wartime finances. The latter document was short on details and raised more questions than it answered. On top of personal loans, most of his money came from selling jewelry for incredible sums (a bracelet for 40,000 RM, a wristwatch for 5,000 RM—that timepiece alone had the same value as a top-of-the-line Mercedes). If there was a minor oversight in not including the 250 RM received for the radio broadcasts, Wodehouse failed to mention the 36,000 RM sale of film rights in 1942. Two days later Wodehouse amended the financial statement to include that sale, stressing that *Heavy Weather* "could not possibly be twisted for propaganda purposes" (he had "insisted" on inserting a clause stipulating that the eventual film remain free of propaganda, as if such a clause had any legal force in the Third Reich) and that he had been promised the film would not be released "until after the War" (presumably only if Germany won).[151] He did not mention that the initial negotiations allowed much greater latitude to the Berliner Film Company: he was paid "a sum of money which binds me to sell my novels for pictures to them alone for a year," the film company was allowed to choose which work to adapt, and Wodehouse would be paid extra to write the screenplay.[152] He also did not mention that *Der Meisterdetektiv*, the adaptation of what was, in fact, *Summer Lightning*, had actually been released two months earlier. If this sale fell afoul of the Trading with the Enemy Act, Wodehouse dramatically announced, "I must of course accept the penalty," although he hoped for clemency since he had "acted in perfect innocence" in thinking that the law did not apply "to a transaction of a purely artistic nature."[153] Equally troubling was a recent transfer that September of 560,000 francs from Germany without much in the way of accounting or explanation. A day later Wodehouse, clearly panicking, gave a further statement on his wartime finances that was "correct to the best of my belief."[154]

Cussen's report, which ran to fifteen single-spaced pages and included, in its appendix, Wodehouse's statement and nearly forty pages of documents, was completed at the end of the month. It began by foregrounding Wodehouse as "the wellknown [*sic*] author" and "a wellknown [*sic*] public figure." Framing Wodehouse as "a rich man" who "lived a very comfortable life," the report implicitly raised doubts that he could have supported the misery of internment. Being shorn of "the advice of his wife, his literary agents, his accountants and the like" had thrust Wodehouse in the entirely unfamiliar territory of having "to make decisions for himself." From Cussen's perspective, Wodehouse was both "lacking in worldly wisdom" and "very susceptible to any form of flattery," so it would not have taken much for his behavior to become ill-judged. Cussen would "not be surprised" if further interviews showed other errors in judgement.[155]

This call for more interviews (of residents of Le Touquet, internees at Tost, and German officers) and documentary evidence (from German records in Berlin and Paris) was the report's unbroken chorus: each section detailing a particular episode or action invariably concludes with a statement to the effect that "factual evidence ... later obtained" would probably recast Wodehouse's account, which in many respects was "vague in the extreme." When it came to the crux of the case, how and why he went on the air, Wodehouse was unable "to recollect with any clarity the events." Relying "on WODEHOUSE alone" was entirely unsatisfactory, Cussen stressed.[156] One particular issue, Wodehouse's behavior in camp, was of special interest. Behavior in German captivity was a sensitive topic, with "stool pigeons" (POWs who collaborated with the Germans or undermined camp morale) receiving, on average, longer sentences than even volunteers for the British Free Corps.[157] In Wodehouse's case, Cussen had seven sworn statements from former internees that did not paint a rosy picture. While these statements were pulled from Wodehouse's MI5 file when it was declassified, making it impossible to evaluate the evidence now, Cussen's use of those statements indicates that there were grounds to investigate further. Two days after Cussen's report was filed, an ex-internee from Tost claimed that Wodehouse "could hardly be called an internee, for he never spoke to the others"; a week later, another former internee added that Wodehouse "spoke in monosyllables, and discussed nothing."[158] These retrospective statements, which appeared in the British press, did not confirm Wodehouse's claim of camp bonhomie. George Gregson, an ex-RAF Captain during the First World War who roomed with Wodehouse at Tost, wrote in his camp journal in February 1941,

> We hear that P. G. Wodehouse has—through interviews—told the world what a splendid place it is and how well we are treated, etc....! Well, two days ago he told Dut that he did not mind which side won as long as the war finished soon—and that shows his mentality as a so-called Englishman ... such men can do a lot of harm and, although successful in fiction in peacetime, they should stick to the truth in wartime.[159]

Cussen's report concluded with a call that could not be interpreted as an absolution: "In my opinion it will not be possible to arrive at a final conclusion on this case until the various enquiries which I have indicated are made in Germany."[160] The Security Services agreed that further "enquiries in Berlin" were needed and recommended the prosecution of Wodehouse under either treason or assisting the enemy (under Regulation 2A, which carried the maximum penalty of lifetime imprisonment).[161]

Despite MI5's desire to continue the investigation, it was pre-emptively stopped in late November 1944, months before Allied troops entered Germany, on the grounds that "there is not sufficient evidence to justify a prosecution of this man."[162] There were any number of reasons the DPP decided to stop investigating. The key witnesses and documents would have to be found in the ashes of a soon-to-be defeated Germany, without any assurance that incriminating material would be found, and, in the meantime, Wodehouse would have to be detained abroad or returned to British soil, both courses of action presenting their own headaches. These problems could be overcome, as the successful prosecutions of other British renegade broadcasters later showed, but the other renegade broadcasters (with the exception of Norman Baillie-Stewart) came from marginal, lower-class backgrounds, while Wodehouse was a favored author of the mandarin class. The hot-blooded venality of those who sought out punishment—the *John Bull* types who said to Wodehouse "you will remain outside the pale"—could be dismissed by more sanguine steerers of state.[163] None of that has ever been explicitly spelled out but it did not have to be; the force of culture and institutional norms lie very much in what remains unsaid. Considering the later pusillanimity toward Kim Philby and Anthony Blunt, it is reasonable to speculate that a certain stratum of the establishment protected Wodehouse, who was "extremely foolish" but no war criminal, as "Bobbety" (a Dominions Office official) told "My dear Linky" (Lord Quickswood, Hugh Cecil, best man at Churchill's wedding).[164]

There was also a more immediate reason to stop further investigations: at this point in late November, Wodehouse was detained under suspicion of collaboration by the French. It was unclear how the French could prosecute a British subject for acts committed in Germany, but legal sophistry in the postwar period permitted all sorts of previously inconceivable actions (as the Joyce case showed). Since the severity of French justice toward collaborators was a frightening sight across the Channel, the new Foreign Office line—that Wodehouse was "a wronged British subject whom we should champion in every possible way"—reflected changing views back home.[165]

Wodehouse's case caused considerable headaches for diplomats and intelligence officers. The Foreign Office wished to tell the French that "we should not be sorry to see Wodehouse deported," but categorically refused to have him returned to the only country with a legal duty to accept him.[166] British diplomats in Paris kept telling Whitehall that the French wanted to "meet our wishes if they can be informed of what our wishes are."[167] The lack of clear policy eventually reached Churchill's desk:

> Would it be too much to ask the French to let him live under mild surveillance out of the way so long as he can find the money to do so? Maybe he has quite enough to pay his expenses without being a burden on the country. We would prefer not ever to hear about him again and this would be best in the general interest. His name stinks here, but he would not be sent to prison. However if there is no other resort, he should be sent over here and if there is no charge against him, he can live secluded in some place or go to hell as soon as there is a vacant passage.[168]

One memo officialized this by saying that the government position was to "not wish to hear of Mr Wodehouse again," as if covering eyes and ears amounted to a policy.[169] Foreign Secretary Eden, practically, asked for Treasury restrictions to be lifted so that Wodehouse could access "a sufficient amount of his own fortune."[170] This would have to be done quietly to avoid the "unanswerable outcry if it became known that a man who had rendered nothing but ill-service to his country was receiving specially favourable treatment."[171] (Some flexibility was shown when Ethel was back in London in 1948, with Treasury allowing for her bills at the Ritz to be paid out of still-frozen accounts.)[172] At some point Wodehouse's friends back in Britain wondered if the government could lend a helping hand in "the project of facilitating Mr. Wodehouse's departure from France for neutral territory," as if the State were a haulage broker.[173] The French, who released Wodehouse from detention after nearly four months, required him to live sixty kilometers outside of Paris, much to the chagrin of Ethel (who enquired, tone-deaf to the ongoing austerity, "I do not know what we can do or where we can go. What about Chartres? Is that a nice town? Can you get food and drink there and are there hotels?").[174] The British government prodded Wodehouse to find safety by making it very clear that he should never set foot on British soil; as the Foreign Office noted to the consular staff in Paris, "We should still like you to take all possible steps to keep Mr. Wodehouse away from this country."[175]

Wodehouse remained unconvinced of the risks he courted in returning back to Britain until a family friend, Thelma Cazalet-Keir, visited him in Paris. Having worked tirelessly on his behalf as a Conservative MP for Islington East (like many Tories, she lost her seat in the 1945 General Election), Cazalet-Keir advised him to avoid Britain until the major treason trials getting underway that autumn were completed. In 1946 Wodehouse paid over 400 pounds to Christopher Shawcross (the younger brother of Hartley Shawcross, the Attorney General) and Raymond Needham for a comprehensive overview of his case and the question of his return to Britain. The Attorney General had recently stated in Parliament that no assurances could be given to Wodehouse if he ever returned due to the principle laid out in the Joyce trial that broadcasting on the enemy airwaves was itself a treasonous act. Wodehouse was distraught about this development, writing to Cussen,

> The pronouncement of the Judge in the Joyce case bars me from coming to England. Right. But for how long? Indefinitely? For ever?
>
> If for ever, how do I live? The present regulations of the Bank of England seem to make it impossible for me to touch my money over there.[176]

In Christopher Shawcross's read of the situation, a British jury would consider broadcasting on enemy radio to be an act tending to aid the King's enemies. It mattered little what was said on the air; if anything, the less political the talk was the more problematic it could turn out:

> a series of talks by such a well-known and respected person as he would tend to induce English and American listeners to tune-in to the German broadcasts. This

> in itself would help the enemy, and the less tendentious his talks were the more the enemy would be helped in this respect, as listeners would be both encouraged to listen and induced to believe.[177]

The two attorneys asked Wodehouse to submit a full account "of all his dealings and contacts with the Germans" for the past ten to fifteen years, omitting "nothing which might be regarded as unfavourable to him, however irrelevant he may consider it to be." Wodehouse complied and also sent a complete manuscript of the now-destroyed "Wodehouse in Wonderland," in the hope that his justification for going on the air would be acceptable. The two, in a joint opinion, disabused him of that notion:

> Any broadcasting over the German radio by an Englishman as prominent and well-known to the United States as Mr. Wodehouse would be likely to help the enemy. The German radio system was completely under the control of the enemy government, and, indeed, of its Propaganda Department. Had the Germans not thought it would be to their benefit they would not have invited Mr. Wodehouse to broadcast.
>
> It is no answer to say that because they were not in the least pro-German the actual character and contents of the talks transmitted were of no assistance to the enemy. Indeed, the contrary could be argued. Thus if Mr. Wodehouse had broadcast lavish and fulsome praise of the Nazis and extolled their qualities and stated that Britain ought not to go on fighting them, American listeners would probably have discounted what he said, as having been said perversely or under pressure.[178]

While all of this was damning, Wodehouse was told that a prosecution for treason was unlikely, probably because the evidentiary requirements were so high and the stipulated punishment so extreme. The government would have a good case under Regulation 2A of the Defence Regulations, carrying a punishment from two months' imprisonment to a life sentence. It would ultimately be up to a jury to decide his guilt, and the joint opinion noted that a jury could find good reasons to be severe. Wodehouse had sought this legal opinion because he desperately wanted to return to Britain ("Mr. Wodehouse is indignant that there should now be any question of his being prosecuted"), but the barristers noted that "his feelings are beside the point." They were convinced that any return to Britain posed grave dangers: "To sum up, our opinion is that if Mr. Wodehouse returned to England at the present time he would be in grave danger of being apprehended soon after his arrival and put upon trial."[179] It finally became clear to Wodehouse that he had no legal defense. A year later, when he was safely back in America, another enquiry was raised by a solicitor who queried the solicitor general about what would happen if Plummie ever returned to native soil: would there be, "to borrow his own terminology, phonus-bolonus, oompus-boompus, or ranny gazoo?"[180] The author who had embodied Britain and transported a certain sense of Britishness to the world, the most popular living writer of his time, finally understood that the only home left to him was whatever could be fashioned out of his pen.

The barristers had no way of knowing that the Wodehouse case would be re-opened later that year thanks to a French discovery of files from the German Embassy in Paris, one of which put Wodehouse on the same list of beneficiaries of Reich funding as the Librairie Rive Gauche and John Amery. Ethel, it seems, received four payments in 1944 amounting to 400,000 francs.[181] These "so-called 'special payments'" seemed to suggest that Wodehouse was being paid a monthly wage of 60,000 francs (for comparison, an accountant in Paris made about 5,000 francs per month at the time).[182] This new discovery led the DPP to reverse its position on prosecuting Wodehouse: "The Director said that he now takes the view that, if WODEHOUSE ever comes to this country, he should be prosecuted."[183] As the investigating officer noted in a March 1947 report, a number of documents "strongly suggest that WODEHOUSE was working for, and being paid a monthly salary by, the German Embassy."[184] These documents, though, were "not conclusive," as they only showed payments made, not services rendered. To find out why Wodehouse was paid from May to August 1944 would require interviewing German Embassy staff from the time. Some of the circumstantial nuggets in the documents include a query about whether the Wodehouses could receive the same rations of soap and cigarettes as German Embassy employees, to which an official noted that he had "no objection to their being treated in this respect 'like the other employees of the Language Service.'"[185] Another document noted that Wodehouse was employed with the Berliner Film Company and "in addition is working for the German authorities."[186] Trying to track down former employees of the German Embassy in Paris was difficult when one only had surnames to go on, and in July 1947 the inquiry was called off:

> It is now clear that to identify, locate and eventually interrogate these men would involve an immense amount of trouble for a number of people, since WODEHOUSE has departed to the U.S.A. and there is really no longer any reasonable likelihood of his being prosecuted here, whatever the four Germans might say. I do not think there is any useful purpose in pursuing this enquiry.[187]

The intelligence officer, G. E. Wakefield, a Gray's Inn barrister who worked for MI5, added that the existing documents "do indicate, although perhaps they do not prove conclusively," that Wodehouse was receiving regular German payments.[188] He was unsure what Wodehouse was doing to deserve that but speculated that it was probably "not of a very treasonable character."[189] That may have been true, but the two witnesses whose identities were then known (although without current addresses) would have been better placed to speak on the matter. The investigation was stopped not because it lacked merit—if anything, there were more unanswered questions about Wodehouse's conduct in 1947 than there ever had been, and more leads to follow—but because he was now safely in America and the "season" of postwar trials of British renegades had ended.

It was very much the case of good riddance, a sentiment that even bureaucratic language could transmit: "It looks as if the file might now be closed, never, let us hope, to be re-opened."[190] Wodehouse pressed for this closure to be made public—"what is needed is an official statement" declaring that he would not be prosecuted so as to counter "the prevalent opinion ... that I did German propaganda on the radio and am pro-Nazi"—but that audacious request was refused.[191] Even Wodehouse's private approaches to ensure that he would not be prosecuted if he returned to Britain, which continued throughout the 1950s and even as late as 1965, yielded no assurances. It was probably true that the zeal for any treason prosecution, never very high among the establishment figures who tended to excuse Wodehouse's conduct, was close to nil, but such a statement would be read as exculpatory (which is why Wodehouse wanted it). If he really wanted absolution, let him return to Britain and risk arrest: "It is for Mr. Wodehouse to decide whether he wishes to place himself upon his country" and allow "a jury of his fellow countrymen" to settle the matter of his guilt or innocence.[192] That was not a ticket Wodehouse wished to purchase.

Revisions

Wodehouse's main concern after he arrived back in America in late April 1947 (see Figure 1.8) was to get his writing career back on track. During the war he had written four

Figure 1.8 P. G. Wodehouse and his wife traveling to America. Courtesy of National Portrait Gallery.

novels, only one of which had gotten into print. American magazines were not rushing to commission work, with the *Saturday Evening Post* fearing "a storm of protest" if the Wodehouse name appeared in print.[193] The only reason *Money in the Bank* came out in Britain (in May 1946) was that Wodehouse threatened to change publishers (Jenkins profited nicely off the book, which sold over 25,000 copies in a month).[194] *Joy in the Morning*, which was released in the United States in August 1946 as *Jeeves in the Morning*, pointed to the heavy cloud over the author's fate and the desire to put it all behind him:

> After the thing was all over, when peril had ceased to loom and happy endings had been distributed in heaping handfuls and we were driving home with our hats on the side of our heads, having shaken the dust of Steeple Bumpleigh from our tires, I confessed to Jeeves that there had been moments during the recent proceedings when Bertram Wooster, though no weakling, had come very near to despair.[195]

In the world of fiction all it took was Jeeves and his richly deserved reputation ("You can't go on as you have gone on so long, dishing out aid and comfort to all and sundry, without acquiring a certain reputation, if only in the family circle") to save Bertie from a "monstrous persecution."[196] Wodehouse had to engineer his own rehabilitation, which he feared would be a hard slog: "It will be said," he wrote his publishers, "that here is a man who is well known to be a Nazi collaborator, and now that the war is over he thinks he can quietly slip back into his former position in America."[197]

Prompted by the desire to clear his name, Wodehouse began a book of camp reminiscences as early as November 1941. The problem was finding not only a suitable form but also an appropriate tone. All those years writing in a light, breezy comic style, with a ready turn of phrase to leaven the joke, were poor preparation for what the book demanded. Wodehouse was of two minds about what that might be; a comic book would be "resented" by some readers, while a "serious treatment" would "make heavy weather over the really trivial things that happened to me."[198] In one of his more belligerent moods Wodehouse felt that "no harm could be done by publishing a defense" and asked MI5 to supply him with full transcripts of his radio broadcasts so that they could be inserted into the book as documentary evidence of his innocence.[199]

For Wodehouse's agents and publishers, the problem was also one of timing, with an exasperated Wodehouse admitting that "overwhelming pressure" from his London agents led him to postpone publication "till this Belsen business has become a thing of the past."[200] In May 1946, Wodehouse explained the fate of his book in a letter to *Variety*:

> When I came out of camp I wrote a book about my experiences as an internee, the second chapter of which dealt with the broadcasts. I had hoped to publish this as my first postwar production, but Doubleday, my publishers, advised putting it off for a while and are bringing out a "Jeeves" novel in the early fall.[201]

Banking on Wodehouse's fiction was a surer bet. Just as Ezra Pound's publishers sought to erect a wall between his aesthetic works and his political and economic writings,

Wodehouse's publishers had no reason to shift attention to a form that would only alienate readers.

Although the full draft of the book was destroyed, three chapters from it remain, one entitled "Apologia," in which he countered the main charges against him, and two detailing the last days in Le Touquet before his internment. One quickly understands why Wodehouse's entourage discouraged publication. Framing his tale as "the story of how I was misjudged and misunderstood," Wodehouse stuck to his guns. It mattered little if people believed his defense: "I have never valued popularity, and I shall not be crushed by unpopularity." As he was an author apart ("not one of those authors who pine and droop if excluded from literary luncheons, literary teas, prize-givings, symposia and other rewards of successful authorship"), the stance he would take was not to "protest and splutter and call upon saints to bear witness to my innocence," adopting "the cringing attitude of a beaten dog that hopes to be taken back into favour," but "merely [to] place the facts before the reader and leave them to be judged." But rather than present those facts, Wodehouse could not fathom why the case was worth answering at all. Belittling the "global howl" against his broadcasts, "which exceeded in volume and intensity anything I had experienced since the time in my boyhood when I broke the curate's umbrella and my aunts started writing letters to one another about it," the apologia manages to strike a tone that is strident and flippant—hardly a winning combination.[202]

While the camp book was eventually destroyed, questions about Wodehouse's wartime broadcasting remained. Penguin, set to re-issue five backlist Wodehouse volumes in spring 1953, asked the BBC to see transcripts of the radio broadcasts so that its sales staff could "give a true answer to the book sellers on whom they are calling when questions relating to these broadcasts are asked them."[203] Around the same time Wodehouse had a chance to clear the air in the three autobiographical memoirs that appeared around this time: *Performing Flea* (1953), *Bring on the Girls* (1953), co-authored with Broadway collaborator Guy Bolton, and *Over Seventy* (1957). This turn to memoir proved difficult for a writer who largely avoided significant emotions or personal revelations in his books. Entertainment was Wodehouse's calling card, and he did not see why scruples about facts should get in the way of that in the memoirs: "We shall have to let truth go to the wall," he told Bolton, "if it interferes with entertainment."[204]

Perfoming Flea takes its title from the wartime controversy, Sean O'Casey's complaint that Wodehouse was English literature's "performing flea." Because it collects over 130 letters from Wodehouse (from 1920 to 1952), with minimal editorial intrusion, the reader may be forgiven in trusting the authenticity of the text. As plans for the book were afoot, Wodehouse told Townend that they were free to manipulate the letters as they saw fit: "The great thing, as I see it, is not to feel ourselves confined to the actual letters. I mean, nobody knows what was actually in the letters, so we can fake as much as we like."[205] When it came to the broadcasts, which were slated to be included in the volume, Wodehouse shuddered upon re-reading them and decided it best to excise them from the volume.

The question of the broadcasts resurfaced when *Encounter*, one of the premier journals in the early Cold War, asked if they could be reprinted. The aim, as Wodehouse proclaimed in the letter which prefaced their publication, was "to print the broadcasts just for the record" so as to show that he had said nothing harmful on the German radio. An unsuspecting reader could once again be forgiven in thinking that what was printed was a documentary record—but it turns out that Wodehouse revised the broadcasts so as to make the writing fresher and also less politically suspect. If the first broadcast spoke of how "you inevitably begin to fraternize" with the occupying Germans, the *Encounter* version speaks of how "familiarity so breeds indifference," seeming to suggest that Wodehouse had adopted the stony attitude of silent resistance celebrated in *Le Silence de la Mer* (1942). There was no "beaming" toward German officers, as the original broadcasts had it; in its place, *Encounter*'s readers see Wodehouse putting up with "men in steel helmets riding round your lawn."[206]

The publication of *Performing Flea*, with its sections from "Wodehouse in Wonderland," and the (altered) broadcasts in *Encounter* were the final step in Wodehouse's engagement with the wartime controversy. Naturalized an American citizen in 1955 but still dissuaded from stepping foot back in Britain, Wodehouse no longer wanted the war brought up in any form. When Richard Usborne began assembling the first major book of Wodehouse criticism, with a great deal of help from Wodehouse personally, the draft chapter entitled "Internee" made Wodehouse "absolutely furious." He not only excised the chapter but also cut all references to the broadcasts from the manuscript.[207] To his London publisher's solicitor suggestion that a "factual chapter" on the broadcasts be added as an appendix, Wodehouse's response was firm: "I am against this. Ignore the whole thing, I say. I feel very strongly about this."[208] Not only did he refuse to let Usborne publish on the affair, but he also personally "destroyed all that broadcasts material. I felt strongly that after you had cut it out of the book there was nothing to prevent Usborne selling the stuff as an article to some magazine, and destroying the stuff would at least compel him to do all his scavenging all over again."[209] This went well beyond freshening up a phrase or two or tossing out a dead line, but the silence Wodehouse adopted continued until he died at the ripe old age of ninety-three as Sir Pelham Granville.

Conclusion

For a country with a significant prewar native fascist movement, Britain had, in the end, very few cases of wartime treason. That was mainly due to the May 1940 mass internment of native fascists: thousands of British Union members and sympathizers were rounded up and interned under DORA, which granted the state extraordinary powers. (German nationals were also interned, although the vast majority in the country were now refugees fleeing Hitler who ended up committing the right kind of treason during the war.) In the literary field, the sprawling media ecosystem of fascist print culture—venues like *Action* and *Blackshirt*—were shut down. It helped as well that the prevailing ideology of the literary sphere in the 1930s was roundly anti-fascist, and with the Soviet Union a fellow ally during the war, communists and fellow travelers were brought into the fold as well. Whatever anarchist or anti-establishment sympathies writers might have harbored were checked by the rush to fill government ministries and the security services with writers. The MoI employed hundreds of writers, as did the BBC; even the Security Services found writers useful, receiving intelligence reports from established figures like Elizabeth Bowen. The State had never had such unrivaled powers in literary production and culture, Cyril Connolly famously noted in *Horizon*. All this meant that writers and intellectuals who, before the war, had pro-fascist sympathies had few venues open to them, and a post-publication censorship system ensured that dissent was quickly shut down.

Although Britain had not been occupied, it had suffered immensely during the war, with civilians targeted and their homes destroyed. Dutch psychologist A. M. Meerloo, who was in the Dutch resistance before escaping to England predicted that England's postwar attitudes toward renegades would oscillate between unbridled vengeance and boundless mercy. Hatred was a "contagious collective phenomenon" that would spread through the population and target a "defenseless scapegoat"—but once the ugly reality of retribution became evident to the population, there would be a recoil away from continuing the harsh line of punishment.[210] Meerloo's assessment proved prescient. As a scapegoat, one could hardly find a more fitting figure than William Joyce, with his tiny body, scarred face, affected voice, Irish roots, and lower-middle-class origins. That Haw-Haw was the main figure of hate during the war, a ubiquitous presence on the airwaves, also drove the postwar reaction toward him: there was no question of letting him escape punishment on a technicality, even if the technicality in question was at the core of the legal case. But the ugly reality of hanging a man who owed no allegiance to the Crown left a bitter taste; and when it came time to take seriously the very serious questions posed by Wodehouse's wartime conduct, the appetite was gone. The legal precedent in the Joyce case, that any appearance on Berlin radio was *de facto* treasonous, brooked no argument in Wodehouse's case. But with protectors in high places who had grown up on his tales, Wodehouse benefited from an immense amount of sympathy for the view that he was so deep in his fantasy world that he could not possibly make cogent moral decisions in the real world. His machinist view of authorship—he was nothing but a writing machine, attached to his typewriter, committed to producing for his readers, and no war could ever change that—contributed to that sense of authorship as a profession apart, oblivious to reality. The deeply-engrained British disregard for intellectuals (although it was unclear if Wodehouse fell under that category) also made it easy to dismiss the "innocuous" talks on Berlin radio. Wodehouse could be considered part of the upper stratum of literary culture because his origins—those public school years at Dulwich—matched the self-reproduction at the heart of the intellectual field. Joyce, though, despite his first-class honors degree, doctoral studies, lecture tours, and taste for classical culture, could never be accepted as an intellectual. He tried too hard to enter a sphere that was closed off to him, just as he had tried too hard to be a British patriot when he would always be nothing but a man from the bog. While it could hardly have been surprising for politics to drive the postwar trials of renegades, the British postwar showed, more than anything, the national and class inflections of authorship.

Notes

1 Lord Marchwood, Hansard, HL Deb, May 23, 1940, vol. 116, *c.* 422.
2 Elizabeth Bowen, *The Heat of the Day* (London: Vintage, 1998 [1948]), 308.
3 "Hamburg Broadcast Propaganda," March 8, 1940, BBC Archives, R9/14. See as well M. A. Doherty, *Nazi Wireless Propaganda: Lord Haw-Haw and British Public Opinion in the Second World War* (Edinburgh: Edinburgh University Press, 2000).
4 Quoted in E. Tangye Lean, *Voices in the Darkness: The Story of the European Radio War* (London: Secker and Warburg, 1943), 29.
5 Directive Respondent 2396, January 1940, Mass-Observation Archive (Sussex).
6 Sir Samuel Hoare, Hansard, HC Deb, October 11, 1939, vol. 352, *c.* 398–9.
7 Quotes from various notes in KV 4/117; general information about British renegades drawn from KV 2/3581 and KV 2/430.
8 West, *Meaning of Treason*, 13.
9 Edward Coke, *Institutes of the Laws of England*, part III: *Concerning High Treason and Other Pleases of the Crown, and Criminal Causes* (London: Brooke, 1797), I.2.
10 Lisa Steffen, *Defining a British State: Treason and National Identity, 1608–1820* (Basingstoke: Palgrave Macmillan, 2001), 9.
11 William Blackstone, *Commentaries on the Laws of England in Four Books*, 2 vols. (Philadelphia: J. B. Lippincott, 1893 [1753]), 1: 86.
12 John Bellamy, *The Tudor Law of Treason: An Introduction* (London: Routledge and Kegan Paul, 1979), 11.
13 John Barrell, *Imagining the King's Death: Figurative Treason, Fantasies of Regicide, 1793–1796* (Oxford: Oxford University Press, 2000), 31.
14 Bellamy, *Tudor Law*, 11.
15 Ibid., 45; Roger B. Manning, "The Origins of the Doctrine of Sedition," *Albion* 12.2 (Summer 1980): 99–121, at 103–4.
16 26 Hen. 8 c. 13.
17 Coke, *Institutes*, I.14.
18 Thomas Hobbes, *Behemoth, or the Long Parliament*, ed. Ferdinand Tönnies (Chicago: University of Chicago Press, 1990), 16.
19 *The Arraignment, Tryal & Condemnation of Algernon Sydney, Esq. for High-Treason* (London, 1683), 34, 46.
20 Ibid., 10.
21 Gerald P. Bodet, "Sir Edward Coke's Third Institutes: A Primer for Treason Defendants," *The University of Toronto Law Journal* 20.4 (Autumn 1970): 469–77, at 471.
22 *Statutes of the Realm: Volume 7, 1695–1701*, ed. John Raithby (London, 1820): 6–7.
23 Quoted in John Bulloch, *Akin to Treason* (London: Arthur Barker, 1966), 6. Lynch was pardoned and was subsequently made a colonel in the British Army during the First World War, tasked with recruiting soldiers in Ireland!
24 "I. R. A. Man Gets Seven Years," *Daily Mirror*, November 25, 1939, 18.
25 Frederick Bellenger, Hansard, HC Deb, August 24, 1939, vol. 351, *c.* 82.
26 Sir Richard Acland, Hansard, HC Deb, August 24, 1939, vol. 351, *c.* 80.
27 Clement Attlee, Hansard, HC Deb, May 22, 1940, vol. 361, *c.* 151–2.
28 "Enemies Within," *Belfast Telegraph*, November 8, 1940, 4.
29 Sir John Anderson, Hansard, HC Deb, May 22, 1940, vol. 361, *c.* 187.
30 James Little, Hansard HC Deb, May 22, 1940, vol. 361, *c.* 234.
31 "Criminal Law: Legislation," *Annual Survey of English Law* 1940, 238–49, at 238.
32 KV 4/117.
33 CAB 66/64/4.

34 Sir Donald Somervell, Hansard, HC Deb, June 11, 1945, vol. 411, *c*. 1393–4.
35 Madeleine Bunting, *The Model Occupation: The Channel Islands Under German Rule, 1940–1945* (New York: Harper Collins, 1995), 260–5.
36 Theobald Mathew to Rebecca West, June 25, 1947, Tulsa, RWC, 33.8.
37 *Law Reports of Trials of War Criminals, Selected and Prepared by the United Nations War Crimes Commission*, vol. 2: The Belsen Trial (London: HMSO, 1947), 106.
38 Rebecca West, "The Crown Versus William Joyce," *New Yorker*, September 29, 1945, 30–42, at 30.
39 W. E. Hinchley Cooke, note, November 11, 1944, KV 2/245.
40 Quotes from C. E. Bechhofer Roberts, ed., *The Trial of William Joyce* (London: Jarrolds, 1946), 30–1.
41 G. E. Wakefield, note, July 10, 1945, KV 2/246.
42 G. E. Wakefield and E. P. Cussen, Report, November 1, 1945, KV 2/248.
43 *New York Times*, September 19, 1945, 10.
44 Radio Moscow, "Joyce Must Not Evade Punishment," September 19, 1945, in KV 2/247.
45 *Trial of William Joyce*, 36–7.
46 "Enemy Address, Dublin, Dunleary," n.d., IEMA, CP/5/1/6.
47 Evidence of Frank Joyce to the Advisory Committee, 1940, KV 2/249.
48 *Leeds Mercury*, October 25, 1924, 2.
49 *Stirling Observer*, February 4, 1941, 2.
50 Report, January 28, 1935, KV 2/245.
51 *Fascist Week*, December 1–7, 1933, 4.
52 William Joyce, *Dicatorship* (London: BUF, 1933), *passim*; *Blackshirt*, January 9, 1937, 5.
53 E. C. Cornforth, "The Twilight of British Culture," *Blackshirt*, November 2, 1934, 8; and William Joyce, *Action*, June 18, 1936, 2.
54 William Joyce, *Action*, May 21, 1936, 2.
55 William Joyce, *Action*, November 21, 1936, 12.
56 Oswald Mosley, "The Future of the British Union," *Blackshirt*, March 20, 1937, 1.
57 Joyce, *National Socialism Now* (London:National Socialist League, 1937), 32.
58 Ibid., 60.
59 Ibid., 70–1.
60 William Joyce, "My Decision to Join the Nazis," August 28, 1944, KV 2/245.
61 Statement by Eduard Dietze, May 29, 1945, KV 2/248.
62 Quoted in Peter Martland, *Lord Haw Haw: The English Voice of Nazi Germany* (Richmond: National Archives, 2003), 51.
63 Colin Holmes, *Searching for Lord Haw-Haw: The Political Lives of William Joyce* (London: Routledge, 2016), 207.
64 Statement by E. R. A. Dietze, May 29, 1945, KV 2/246.
65 William Joyce, *Twilight Over England* (London: Imperial War Museum, 1992 [1940]), 7.
66 E. J. P. Cussen, September 7, 1945, KV 2/246.
67 E. B. Stamp, note, September 23, 1942, KV 4/117.
68 T. M. Shelford, note, February 2, 1943, KV 4/117.
69 E. B. Stamp, note, August 1, 1942, KV 4/117.
70 Joyce, diary, March 29, 1945, KV 2/250.
71 Ibid., February 27, 1945.
72 *Evening News*, May 1, 1945, in KV 2/246.
73 *The Times*, May 30, 1945, 4.
74 *Trial of William Joyce*, 31.
75 D. H. Sinclair, report, June 14, 1945, KV 2/246.
76 *Shields Daily News*, July 14, 1941, 4.

77 Note, October 16, 1944, KV 2/245
78 Francis Piggott, *Nationality, Including Naturalization and English Law on the High Seas and Beyond the Realm*, 2 vols. (London: William Clowes and Sons, 1907), 1: i. See also J. Mervyn Jones, *British Nationality Law*, rev. ed. (Oxford: Clarendon Press, 1956).
79 G. B. Rutledge, County Inspector, Royal Irish Constabulary, June 28, 1917, CRIM 1/483.
80 Theobald Mathew to Hartley Shawcross, October 10, 1945, KV 2/3581.
81 HO 45/25779; FO 945/783.
82 *Calvin's Case* (1707), in *English Reports Full Reprint* 77, 377–411, at 383.
83 West, *Meaning of Treason*, 25.
84 *Trial of William Joyce*, 32, 34–5.
85 See H. Lauterpacht, "Allegiance, Diplomatic Protection and Criminal Jurisdiction Over Aliens," *The Cambridge Law Journal* 9.3 (1947): 330–48, at 335.
86 *Trial of William Joyce*, 107, 108.
87 Hartley Shawcross, "The State and the Law," *The Modern Law Review* 11.1 (January 1948): 1–8, at 1.
88 Kenneth Diplock, "Passports and Protection in International Law," *Transactions for the Year* 32 (1946): 42–59.
89 Egidio Reale, "The Passport Question," *Foreign Affairs* 9.3 (April 1931): 506–9, at 506.
90 Richard Plender, *International Migration Law*, 2nd rev. ed. (Dordrecht: Martinus Nijhoff, 1988), 150.
91 *Urtetiqui v. D'Arcy*, 34 U.S. 692 (1835), 699.
92 See also Edwin Borchard, *The Diplomatic Protection of Citizens Abroad, or the Law of International Claims* (New York: Banks Law, 1916), 29, and John Vincent Barry, "Treason, Passports and the Ideal of Fair Trial," *Res Judicatae* 7.3 (1955): 276–303, at 303.
93 "*Rex v. Ketter*," *The Law Times* 160 (1939): 306–9, at 307. See also Green Haywood Hackaworth, *Digest of International Law*, vol. 3 (Washington, D.C.: Government Printing Office, 1942), 470.
94 Note, November 26, 1947, FO 372/6877.
95 Geoffrey Allchin, note, February 1946, FO 372/6877.
96 Ibid.
97 Diplock, "Passports and Protection," 56.
98 *Trial of William Joyce*, 33.
99 W. H. Lawrence, "Rex v. Lord Haw-Haw," *Hastings Law Journal* 2 (1951): 73–9, at 79.
100 *Trial of William Joyce*, 156.
101 *The Times*, September 20, 1945, 5.
102 Wodehouse quoted in Harry W. Flannery, *Assignment to Berlin* (London: Michael Joseph, 1942), 118.
103 George Orwell, "In Defence of P. G. Wodehouse," in *The Complete Works of George Orwell*, vol. 17: *I Belong to the Left, 1945*, ed. Peter Davison (London: Secker & Warburg, 1998), 51–63, at 53.
104 P. G. Wodehouse (PGW), "The Art of Fiction LX," *The Paris Review* 64 (1975): 149–171, at 167.
105 Robert McCrum, *Wodehouse: A Life* (London: Penguin, 2005 [2004]), 5.
106 Radio interview with Harry Flannery, June 26, 1941, in Cussen Report, September 28, 1944, KV 2/75.
107 PGW, "The Art of Fiction LX," 170.
108 Richard Usborne, who worked at the BBC Monitoring Service during the war, leaves much unsaid about the destroyed chapter: "But he [Wodehouse] didn't like the result and the chapter never came to print"; in *Wodehouse at Work to the End* (London: Barrie and Jenkins, 1976), 12.

109 PGW, "Uncle Fred in Springtime," in *Uncle Fred: An Omnibus* (London: Penguin, 1992), 1–213, at 8.
110 PGW to William Townend, April 23, 1939, in P. G. Wodehouse, *A Life in Letters*, ed. Sophie Ratcliffe (London: Hutchinson, 2011), 278; PGW to Mrs. William Cazalet, July 10, 1939, BL MS 129/2/4.
111 *Birmingham Mail*, January 27, 1940, 7.
112 *Birmingham Mail*, August 12, 1944, 3. On RAF pilots, see *Liverpool Echo*, 30 January 1940, 2.
113 Petition to Herr Hans Thomsen, Chargé d'Affaires, German Embassy, Washington, D.C., BL MS 129/2/5.
114 *Belfast Telegraph*, July 16, 1940, 8.
115 Ethel Wodehouse to Diana and Denis Mackail, June 26, 1945, BL MS 129/2/4.
116 Letter, February 3, 1944, in G. E. Wakefield report, March 7, 1947, in KV 2/75. On Wodehouse's frosty postwar reception in Le Touquet, see Charles Graves, "French Resorts Three Years After 'D'-Day: How Le Touquet Paris-Plage and Other Seaside Places Are Faring," *Sphere*, June 14, 1947, 346.
117 Quotes from the "Camp Note Book" reproduced in Frances Donaldson, *P. G. Wodehouse: A Biography* (London: Weidenfeld and Nicolson, 1982), 170–205. The original is now in the Wodehouse collection at the British Library.
118 PGW to Paul Reynolds, in *A Life in Letters*, 293 (telegram reprinted in *Time*, December 30, 1940, 43).
119 Angus Thuermer, "Wodehouse Works on New Book in 'Padded Cell' at German Camp," *NYT*, December 27, 1940, 3; Gunnar Müllern, "Wodehouse Frigiven, Far Till Slott I Bayern," *Aftonbladet*, June 25, 1941, 1, 15, at 15.
120 PGW, *Performing Flea: A Self-Portrait in Letters* (London: Wyman and Sons, 1954), 112. See as well my article "Writing Internment: Wodehouse's *Money in the Bank*," *Literature and History* 34.1 (June 2025): 25–40.
121 PGW, "Over Seventy," in *Wodehouse on Wodehouse* (Harmondsworth: Penguin, 1981), 465–645, at 486.
122 *Daily Mirror*, June 26, 1941, 2.
123 *NYT*, June 26, 1941, 3.
124 The broadcast is transcribed in Flannery, *Assignment to Berlin*, 245–7.
125 BL MS 129/2/5.
126 *Daily Mirror*, June 28, 1941, 1.
127 *Sunday Times*, June 29, 1941.
128 *Birmingham Daily Post*, July 9, 1941, 2.
129 A. A. Milne, Letter-to-the-editor, *Daily Telegraph*, July 3, 1941.
130 Letter to Theobald Mathew, September 13, 1945, KV 2/3581.
131 On "self-sacrificing citizens" as the key element of British patriotic discourse during the war, see Sonya O. Rose, *Which People's War? National Identity and Citizenship in Wartime Britain, 1939–1945* (Oxford: Oxford University Press, 2004), 14.
132 William Connor, "Postscript," in Donaldson, *P. G. Wodehouse: A Biography*, 243.
133 PGW to Wesley Stout, 1941, quoted in Donaldson, *P. G. Wodehouse: A Biography*, 254.
134 Iain Sproat, *Wodehouse at War* (London: Ticknor and Fields, 1981), 51.
135 Donaldson, *P. G. Wodehouse: A Biography*, 228.
136 Robert A. Hall, Jr., "The Persecution of P. G. Wodehouse," *Institute for Historical Review* 7.3 (Fall 1986): 345–51. See also Anthony Lane, "Beyond a Joke," *The New Yorker*, April 19, 2004, 138–149.
137 Quoted in Donaldson, *P. G. Wodehouse: A Biography*, 221
138 Quoted in Sproat, *Wodehouse at War*, 107.
139 Quotes from Sproat, *Wodehouse at War*, 126, 127, 128.

140 Cussen Report, September 28, 1944, KV 2/75.
141 Note, June 28, 1941, KV 2/74.
142 PGW to Foreign Office, November 21, 1942, KV 2/75.
143 Curt Knöppel, "Mr Wodehouse lättar sitt hjärta," *Aftonbladet*, November 27, 1942, 1, 19.
144 Note, November 25, 1946, FO 369/3509.
145 PGW to Home Secretary Herbert Morrison, September 4, 1944, KV 2/75.
146 T. M. Shelford, note, August 31, 1944, KV 2/75.
147 B. A. Hill to G. E. Wakefield, December 18, 1946, KV 2/75.
148 PGW Statement, September 12, 1944, KV 2/75.
149 PGW, "Apologia," NYPL.
150 PGW Statement, September 12, 1944, KV 2/75.
151 PGW to Major Cussen, September 14, 1944, KV 2/75.
152 PGW to Anga von Bodenhausen, March 30, 1942, in *A Life in Letters*, 322.
153 Board of Trade to Sir Donald Somervell, July 1942, LO 2/1166; PGW to Major Cussen, September 14, 1944, KV 2/75.
154 Further Statement by Pelham Grenville Wodehouse, September 15, 1944, KV 2/75.
155 Cussen Report, September 28, 1944, KV 2/75.
156 Quotes from Cussen Report, September 28, 1944, KV 2/75.
157 On stool pigeons, see S. L. B. 3 Progress Report, KV 2/3581.
158 *Middlesex Chronicle*, September 30, 1944, 5; *Surrey Advertiser*, October 7, 1944, 5.
159 George Gregson, Wartime Diary, February 26, 1941, at http://www.holywellhousepublishing.co.uk/PDF/GG3-George_Gregson%27s_Diary.pdf. Last accessed: January 19, 2026.
160 Cussen Report, September 28, 1944, KV 2/75.
161 Letter to L. M. Vincent Evans, October 3, 1944, KV 2/75.
162 DPP, note, November 23, 1944, BL MS 129/2/8.
163 "Mr. P. G. Wodehouse, Somewhere in Paris," *John Bull*, September 16, 1944, 6.
164 Letter to Lord Quickswood, December 8, 1944, FO 369/2963.
165 D. P. Reilly, Minute, January 5, 1945, FO 660/229. On a possible trial, see E. Pizané to Adrian Holman, December 25, 1944, FO 369/3121.
166 Minute, November 27, 1944, FO 369/2963.
167 Paris to Foreign Office, December 5, 1944, FO 369/2963.
168 Churchill to Foreign Secretary Eden, December 7, 1944, FO 369/2963.
169 Foreign Office memo, December 20, 1944, FO 369/2963.
170 Foreign Secretary Eden to Lord Halifax, telegram, February 6, 1945, FO 115/4179.
171 Draft letter, G. C. Harvey to Duff Cooper, February 28, 1945, FO 369/3121.
172 Malcolm Muggeridge, *Like It Was: The Diaries of Malcolm Muggeridge*, ed. John Bright-Holmes (London: Collins, 1981), 302.
173 Foreign Office to Berne, February 17, 1945, FO 369/3121.
174 *Manchester Evening News*, November 23, 1944, 1. See also Noel Barber, "Tea With Mr. Wodehouse," *Continental Daily Mail*, September 2, 1945.
175 Foreign Office to Consular Section, British Embassy, Paris, September 13, 1945, FO 369/3121.
176 PGW to Major Edward Cussen, February 1, 1946, in *A Life in Letters*, 379.
177 Advice by Christopher Shawcross, May 29, 1946, BL MS 129/2/9.
178 C.N. Shawcross and Raymond Needham, joint opinion, June 13, 1946, BL MS 129/2/9.
179 Ibid.
180 Hesketh Pearson to Frank Soskice, July 10, 1947, LO 2/1166.
181 The first mention of the 400,000-franc payment is in Foreign Office note, November 25, 1946, FO 369/3509.

182 G. E. Wakefield, report, March 7, 1947, KV 2/75. On French salaries in the period, see Jacques Lehoulier, "Chronique des salaires: Le mouvement des salaires en France depuis 1938," *Journal de la société statistique de Paris* 86 (1945): 172–6, at 173.
183 B. A. Hill to G. E. Wakefield, December 18, 1946, KV 2/75.
184 G. E. Wakefield, report, March 7, 1947, KV 2/75.
185 Ibid.
186 Ibid.
187 G. E. Wakefield to G. C. Allchin, July 25, 1947, FO 369/3786C.
188 Ibid.
189 Ibid.
190 G. C. Allchin to G. E. Wakefield, July 28, 1947, FO 369/3786C.
191 PGW to E. J. P. Cussen, November 2, 1945, KV 2/75.
192 Attorney General Hartley Shawcross, note, August 8, 1947, LO 2/1166.
193 PGW to William Townend, September 13, 1945, *A Life in Letters*, 370.
194 David A. Jasen, *P. G. Wodehouse: A Portrait of a Master* (London: Garnstone Press, 1975), 203.
195 PGW, *Joy in the Morning* (Stockholm: Continental Book Company, 1947 [1946]), 9.
196 Ibid., 14, 249.
197 PGW to Nelson Doubleday, March 11, 1946, *A Life in Letters*, 401.
198 PGW to William Townend, February 24, 1945, *A Life in Letters*, 357.
199 PGW to Malcolm Muggeridge, April 16, 1945, *A Life in Letters*, 362.
200 PGW to William Townend, November 8, 1945, *A Life in Letters*, 374
201 Quoted in Jasen, *P. G. Wodehouse: A Portrait of a Master*, 200.
202 Quotes from PGW, "Apologia," NYPL.
203 R. G. W. Lane to Marie Slocombe, January 9, 1953, in BBC RCONTI (910).
204 PGW to Guy Bolton, November 4, 1952, *A Life in Letters*, 12.
205 PGW to William Townend, October 16, 1951, *A Life in Letters*, 444.
206 PGW, "Berlin Broadcasts (I)," *Encounter*, October 1954, 17–24.
207 PGW to J. D. Grimsdick, November 28, 1960, *A Life in Letters*, 499.
208 Ibid., 501.
209 PGW to J. D. Grimsdick, January 31, 1961, *A Life in Letters*, 502.
210 Meerloo, *Aftermath of Peace*, 41, 52.

CHAPTER 2
AMERICAN BUGHOUSE: EZRA POUND AND THE STRANGE FRUITS OF TREASON

On October 1, 1942, Franklin Delano Roosevelt was in a "fighting mood" after completing a two-week, 8,754-mile trip inspecting war munitions plants in twenty-four states. FDR had seen the American people doing their darn best—unlike, he sarcastically noted to the press throng eager for news (his trip had been subject to a complete media blackout, a first in American history), some folks in Washington.[1] Although he did not name names, that afternoon FDR penned a note to Attorney General Francis Biddle, whose soft attitude to sedition and treason had been a source of annoyance for months:

> There are a number of Americans in Europe who are aiding Hitler et al. on the radio. Why should we not proceed to indict them for treason even though we might not be able to try them until after the war? I understand Ezra Pound, Best, Anderson and a few others are broadcasting for Axis microphones.[2]

American literary history, and the history of literary modernism, would be very different had the might of the American state not been pressed into indicting, capturing, and institutionalizing Pound for his wartime broadcasts from Rome. Pound's legal troubles catalyzed a major effort to rehabilitate his poetic standing, transforming him from minor unreadable poet (the 1945 view) to a writer whose name defined an entire era.

America's postwar treatment and understanding of authorial treason will be examined through the protracted Pound affair. Focusing on Pound perhaps does not need any justification, although it should be noted that his wartime behavior was not exceptional (as FDR's memo indicates, he was merely one of a group of renegade broadcasters) and he did not undergo a criminal trial (much less suffer a miscarriage of justice like Iva D'Aquino, "Tokyo Rose"). Yet Pound's case was the most high-profile and symbolically rich in addressing questions related to authorship, free expression, and the status of the intellectual in postwar America. He was the first renegade broadcaster captured and flown back for trial. His legal proceedings were meant to set the tone for subsequent prosecutions, which had to grapple with the new legal understanding of treason in *Cramer* (1945), a Supreme Court decision issued just days before fighting in Europe ended and with an eye to postwar trials. Pound's "case" extended out for nearly a dozen years, resulting in a number of substitute proceedings against him in the literary and popular press.

American States of Treason

The US Constitution famously defines only one crime:

> Treason against the United States, shall consist only in levying war against them, or in adhering to their Enemies, giving them Aid and Comfort. No person shall be convicted of Treason unless on the Testimony of two Witnesses to the same overt Act, or on Confession in open Court. (Article III, section 3)

Although adopting almost verbatim the British definition of treason from the 1351 Treason Act and the evidentiary requirement from the 1696 Trial of Treasons Act, the situation of the American colonists was radically different. How the new state would understand loyalty and betrayal was a topic of deep personal interest for those who escaped the hangman's noose only because their treason had been victorious. "The basic law of treason in this country," the Supreme Court noted, "was framed by men who ... were taught by experience and by history to fear abuse of the treason charge almost as much as they feared treason itself."[3] Yet allegiance to the new nation was not a given with Shays' Rebellion, continued Loyalist sympathies, and the presence of foreign powers on all sides (the British in Canada, Spain in the south, the French in the Midwest and Canada), as well as Native Americans who were considered natural enemies. For Thomas Jefferson, "Treason ... when real, merits the highest punishment. But most codes ... do not distinguish between acts against the *government*, and acts against the *oppressions of the government*."[4]

The American government's "remarkably liberal" view of treason resulted in relatively few treason prosecutions.[5] Considering the divided allegiance of the early Republic (between states and the federal government), the existence of armed challenges to sovereign authority that punctuated the country's history, the major social challenge posed by slavery, the massive stretches of unchartered land, the treasonous acts of secession that led to the Civil War, and a significant history of colonial expansion, that is remarkable. The opposing side of the coin would note that the restrictive nature of the Treason Clause made the government turn to sedition charges. The Alien and Sedition Acts were used to punish anti-government speech, and the 1940 Smith Act made it illegal to "advocate, abet, advise, or teach the duty, necessity, desirability, or propriety of overthrowing or destroying any government in the United States by force or violence." There were practical reasons as well to not press the loaded charge of treason. Anything but mass amnesty after the Civil War would have made national healing impossible. The existence of a large land mass, plentiful resources, and geographic separation from any significant external threats also lessened the potential danger of any individual treason.

It was more recent history, though, that was on Francis Biddle's mind when he began his tenure as Attorney General in autumn 1941 (see Figure 2.1). Vowing to avoid the "extravagant abuse of prosecutions for sedition" that occurred during the First World War, when over 2,000 federal prosecutions amounted to a "blanket suppression of all

Figure 2.1 Francis Biddle, US Attorney General and later judge at the International Military Tribunal of War Criminals at Nuremberg. Photo 1945, United States. Holocaust Memorial Museum, photo #81945. Courtesy of National Archives and Records Administration, College Park. Public Domain.

'disloyal utterances.'" Biddle subscribed to the Jeffersonian belief that treason prosecutions were used by abusive governments to stifle legitimate dissent (an idea informing "If This Be Treason," a two-act play he wrote years later).[6] In December 1941, he ordered that no prosecutor could initiate sedition or treason prosecutions without his sign-off; as he later rationalized, "I announced that freedom of speech should be curtailed only when public safety was directly imperiled."[7] Perhaps "the verdict of history will bear you out," Biddle's most trusted confidant, James Rowe, Jr., told him in March 1942, but the immediate problem was the perception that "you and the Department in general are 'civil liberties boys' and 'softies.'"[8] A Louisiana Congressman seethed against the DOJ's "benign policy ... towards treasonable publications"; in Cabinet meetings FDR hounded his former Groton, Harvard College, and Harvard Law classmate to stop anti-war writings.[9] Seditious speech should be made DOJ's top priority, Biddle was advised: "our actions are far from satisfactory ... I can think of nothing more important at present for the Department of Justice than to get on top of, and perhaps a little ahead of, this situation in relation to the President."[10]

That was hard to do given FDR's contempt toward "bogus traitors who use the sacred freedom of press to echo the sentiments of the propagandists of Tokyo and Berlin."[11] Even liberal venues like *The Nation* saw protecting the fascist press "in the name of democracy" as wrongheaded: "They should be exterminated exactly as if they were enemy machine-gun nests in the Bataan jungle ... Opinion is one of their most effective weapons, and to allow them to use it against us is reckless to the point of insanity."[12] The ACLU refused to aid "defendants ... co-operating with or acting on behalf of the enemy."[13] And the enemy, in the American imagination, was lurking within, ready to strike. The mass internment of Japanese-Americans was the most striking manifestation of that fear, but the panic was more generalized. John Roy Carlson's explosive account of American fascist organizations, *Under Cover* (1943), claimed that defeatist propaganda had "permeated deep into the American mind."[14] The *Washington Star* estimated that there were nearly eight million fascist sympathizers in the land; Alan Hynd's *Passport to Treason* (1943) warned that "more than one hundred thousand loyal Germans now living in the United States" were ready to do Hitler's bidding.[15] *Life*'s eleven-page article "Voices of Defeat," in April 1942, attacked those who "abuse free speech" and "sow lies and hate inside our lines."[16]

Was it treason, though, to express political beliefs on foreign radio when it was "well-settled," as the 1920 *Wimmer* decision noted, that "one cannot, by mere words, be guilty of treason"?[17] It was only in February 1943 that the DOJ began to consider broadcasting on foreign stations as a crime. Boris Bittker, who went on to become the Sterling Professor of Law at Yale, was uncompromising in his analysis of radio treason:

> These American citizens have adhered to the enemies of the United States in a very real sense. Not only do their broadcasts evince a complete acceptance of the enemy's philosophy, but in making them, they are cooperating with the enemy as fully as though they were volunteers in his armies. They could hardly take steps to establish their adherence more firmly, except by an open renunciation of American citizenship and an acceptance of Axis citizenship.[18]

A few days after Bittker's nine-page memo moved up the bureaucratic chain, the DOJ announced that six individuals would soon be indicted for treason, among them Ezra Pound. It took a few months for the DOJ to prepare comprehensive reports on a number of radio broadcasters, and then grand jury indictments were handed down in late July. The only snag: no one had any experience prosecuting treason, and the courts, with so few cases, had issued very little guidance on what constituted the crime.[19]

The Supreme Court finally laid out, in April 1945, its interpretation of the treason clause in *Cramer*, a case concerning a German-American who met with a Reich intelligence agent. Although the conviction could have been overturned on procedural grounds, Chief Justice Harlan Stone wanted to use the case to issue a controlling interpretation of the Treason Clause.[20] The brief was given to Justice Robert Jackson, who would soon shine as Chief United States Prosecutor at Nuremberg. In a July 1944 memo, Jackson indicated that the meaning of the Treason Clause could not be divorced from how the founders "accomplished the great work of their lives ... under the shadow of treason prosecution"; moreover, he observed,

> in 150 years of our history not one prosecution for treason or sedition has occurred that after a few years was considered to have in any degree contributed to the nation's security or stability. The Civil War shows that possibility of treason prosecution does not deter resistance when there is a sense of grievance widely held, whether justified or not. If treason and sedition prosecutions must be resorted to against masses, they are futile and if needed only against a few are rarely needed at all.[21]

Fellow justices Frank Murphy and Felix Frankfurter went even further in believing that the Constitutional construction made it "almost impossible to commit treason."[22]

Jackson's majority opinion adopted a middle-of-the-road approach, restricting the freedom of the government in prosecuting treason but mindful that the crime posed real threats. He noted that treason had two elements: "adherence to the enemy and rendering him aid and comfort." Supporting the enemy "intellectually or emotionally" was not treason if no act providing aid or comfort was given; likewise, aiding or comforting the enemy was not treason "if there is no intent to betray."[23] The problem, though, was conjoining the overt act with the intention of adhering to the enemy. Establishing intent required entering into "the state of mind and heart of the defendant," which two witnesses could not do.[24] The only solution was to "draw usual reasonable inferences" by placing the overt act in an "environment" or "setting": "Environment illuminates the meaning of acts, as context does that of words."[25] The overt act and its intention could not be divorced: "An overt act, in criminal law, is an outward act done in pursuance and in manifestation of an intent or design."[26] Curiously, while intent was becoming enshrined as the determinative factor in the jurisprudential understanding of treason, literary critics began to consign it as unknowable and irrelevant. Wimsatt and Beardsley's influential article on the "intentional fallacy" argued that intent could never be established with absolute certainty; and even if established, intent should not displace the text, which was what a critical reading had to focus on.[27] For the literary scholar, the "overt act" of the literary text was complete in itself, but, for Jackson, the overt act was only treason if intended as such. That was entirely in line with basic understandings of criminal law, in which intent was a critical factor for evaluating punishment (the harm of homicide and involuntary manslaughter are the same, but, because of intent, the two are not punished equivalently).

The requirement Jackson set in place resulted in very high evidentiary standards for treason. The overt act not only had to provide "actual" aid and comfort but also manifestly indicate adherence to the enemy's cause. In *Total War and the Constitution* (1947), Edward Corwin predicted that the *Cramer* decision would result in "the near elimination of treason from the calendar of provable crimes under the Constitution."[28] One can even speculate that this was the Court's intention, as Jackson's decision noted that while the bar for treason was high, nothing prevented Congress from legislating against the danger, citing the Espionage Act, the Smith Act, and the Trading with the

Enemy Act.[29] Postwar history confirmed the utility of this approach: the Rosenbergs were charged under the Espionage Act, and Congress passed the Internal Security Act of 1950 and the Communist Control Act of 1954 to criminalize behavior that might otherwise have been considered treasonous.

The critics who thought that *Cramer* spelled the end of treason as a viable criminal charge were proven wrong. Pound's prosecution for treason pressed forward, and after he was ruled mentally unfit to stand trial, the DOJ dispatched more agents abroad to collect evidence on renegades. No one could accuse the DOJ of being soft on John Provoo, who faced two federal treason trials that lasted over a decade between them (as a homosexual and Buddhist, Provoo may have felt that different prejudices animated the zealotry to convict).[30] As it was, a number of treason prosecutions were successful in the immediate post-*Cramer* era. The Supreme Court upheld *Haupt*, in which the father of an executed German saboteur was convicted of providing aid and comfort to his son, while the other post-war treason prosecutions mainly concerned "radio traitors."[31] In most cases, the defense strategy centered on jurisdiction, improper venue, or the treason statute not applying extraterritorially—but not the question of intent. In all of these cases bar one, the conviction for treason was upheld after appeal, showing that the stringent requirements set forth in *Cramer* were no obstacle to prosecution.

Cramer's understanding of the link between intent and the overt act was actually straightforward for radio propagandists. A footnote in *Cramer* stated that "subscribing an oath of allegiance or accepting pay from an enemy" signified *prima facie* adherence to the enemy.[32] That gave confidence to prosecutors, as did a further elaboration from the dissenting opinion: "one cannot do an act which he knows will give aid and comfort to a person he knows to be an enemy of the United States and then seek to disclaim criminal intent and knowledge by saying that one's motive was not to aid the enemy."[33] In later years, Pound would repeat the refrain "no treason without intent," alleging that the statement given before his Radio Roma broadcasts (that he was speaking as an American citizen without breaching any of the duties or obligations thereof) proved that his intent was not treasonous. But Pound was falsely equating motive with intent; even the noblest motives do not trump the willful step taken to commit an act that results in a crime. The words spoken on enemy microphones did not even need to be heard for them to be treasonous, as simply making the recording signified an active intent to collaborate with an enemy power. A radio traitor, a higher court affirmed in Douglas Chandler's case, "trafficked with the enemy and as their paid agent collaborated in the execution of a program of psychological warfare designed by the enemy to weaken the power of the United States to wage war successfully."[34] Mere words could be treason since "the communication of an idea, whether by speech or writing, is as much an act as is throwing a brick."[35]

Throwing Bricks: Ezra on the Air

Treason was on Ezra Pound's mind in 1933 (Figure 2.2). A few days after composing the preface to *Jefferson and/or Mussolini* on "18th September, Anno XI," he argued for "a new

Figure 2.2 Ezra Pound, Passport Photo, 1919. Public Domain.

definition" of treason in his *New English Weekly* column and then, a week later, followed that up with a column entitled "Treachery."[36] Anno XII started with Pound lambasting the "enormity of this treason" of American intellectuals, and then, in the January 1934 essay "Judas Had It," belittling the idea that free speech existed in America.[37] All this followed his first and only meeting, in January 1933, with someone he was "perfectly willing to take orders" from, Mussolini.[38] Which was *Patria Mia*? Could Pound still write "as an Idahoan," as he did to Senator William Borah in late November 1933; was he really a "Jeffersonian republican," as he put it in *ABC of Economics*; or were these claims fatuous and misleading when he had not stepped foot in his native country for over two decades and was beginning to feel "PRO-MUSSOLINI 100%"?[39]

"What we need," Pound wrote,

> is a new definition of treason. A country can be betrayed in more than one fashion, and the more we learn of the past forty years' history, the more clear it becomes that the worst enemies of any and every nation in our time have been those within and not without the gates.
> As I believe in the rot and corruption of these men, as I believe their rottenness is more rotten, their foulness more foul than any printable language, so I believe them to be one and all craven cowards ...
> I honestly think some of these people might be less enthusiastic about the blood game if more private citizens knew where they lived, what they looked like, and if there were more men who would feel no qualms of conscience about shooting them on, or preferably before, the next outbreak of hostilities.

If calling for "private citizens" to shoot that "gang of lice" undermined the progressive thrust of Pound's redefinition of treason, that kind of direct action appealed to him:

> At any rate, I think a few of us should vow ourselves to personal action in the next conflict. It will be different from Mr. Rolland puffing out words from Geneva ... I think action will be necessary, but it will have to be action outside what is now recognized as the field of politeness.[40]

While acting outside "the field of politeness" understates Pound's subsequent action ("We must start hating sometime," is how he put it in an unpublished 1934 article), it was a way of coming to grips with his frustrations as a writer and how he sought to transcend the narrow confines of modernist authorship ("My contemporaries in licherchoor mostly sheer sapheads with NO civic sense, iggurunt as ham ... poor in sperriit, but just NOBUDDY done TOLD 'em anything about ANYthing").[41] The days of "In a Station of the Metro," with its sculptural chiseling of word, image and form, were over. By the late 1930s Pound was converted to a series of dogmatic propositions about usury, the international Jewish conspiracy, the sellout of Western democracy, the mendacity of FDR, the greatness of Benito. These subjects, repeated *ad nauseum*, did not lend themselves to the best of Pound, movement, development, thought, subtlety; they existed as fixed ideas, tropes of the Judeo-Bolshevik menace and the Italian renascence fighting it.

Those ideas gravitated from the printed page to the ether. "Took me 2 years to get hold of their microphone," Pound later reflected on his travails to broadcast on the Ente Italiano per le Audizioni Radiofoniche (EIAR).[42] Having lived in Italy since 1924, Pound was aware of the repressive speech laws in place and the importance of propaganda to a regime whose guiding ideology was *Mussolini ha sempre ragione*.[43] EIAR signals began reaching America's shores in 1934, and after war broke out its propaganda was ramped up to mobilize votes in favor of neutrality. Having first signaled his desire to work for the fascist regime in November 1939, Pound was offered a trial broadcast in January 1941. He was then given a contract for two political broadcasts per week and five general broadcasts per month.[44] If the work was taxing, "nothing left over in the head after the day's output," it paid well: the FBI estimated that Pound took in 30,000 lire in the first eight months of 1942.[45]

When Pound began broadcasting, he pointedly wondered if his scripts should be composed "with calm and detail / or let the anger boil?"[46] Pound chose the latter—"I don't so much write as I roar," he told his American publisher at New Directions, James Laughlin—but this choice also accorded with what he believed successful propaganda required.[47] He told William Joyce that he would "be glad to profit by experienced criticism" from propaganda's contemporary master, whose broadcasts he listened to "daily."[48] In May 1941 Pound outlined for his EIAR bosses what propaganda to America required: short, simplistic, humorous broadcasts ("they are children") with constantly repeated "key phrases."[49] He later crafted a series of quasi-Imagist rules for propaganda: "Do not use two words to say what ONE will convey"; "Think of the hearer"; "Think of the sound of your sentences."[50]

All this had to be learned from scratch: "New technique for Uncle Ez. A poem has to be good in 200 years/ or it is bad. Quite different technique for talk that has to take effect NOW or never."[51] Yet Pound was convinced that immediate effects could be delivered through literary techniques: "For radio broadcasts, a dynamic idea is presented under various forms so as not to arouse suspicions, for the purpose of irony, fantasy, metaphor, etc."[52] The best way to "hold the attention of the listener" was through "variety" and "the unexpected," which required a balance between "diversity in the methods and tones of various broadcasts" and "repetition."[53] Direct argument was of "NO use! The jew can argue the hind leg off a mule … If a radio speaker relies on logic, he is dished."[54] This, he wrote, is how "we" should respond to British propaganda:

> We must be the ones to impose the argument, picking out the field of those arguments on which they want to remain silent, where they do not dare express themselves. … we can destroy and disrupt their entire system of propaganda or an entire division by demonstrating their game.[55]

Radio Rome was there to "win the ideological war" and "create revolutions in England," or "at least place obstacles in enemy's way."[56] "Coordinate" slogans, he advised; then "*ripetere, ripetere, ripetere*."[57]

Before the war, Pound had made loud noises about how authors needed to sign their works: "The man who dares not sign his opinions is beneath all legally expressible contempt."[58] Yet wartime realities had changed his view of authorship:

> The anonymous stuff is in some ways better than the personal/ When anonymous I can be omniscient/ when I speak in my own voice I have to be modest and stick to what I have seen first hand.[59]

America's entry into the war did not sideline Pound from the "fight" between "two systems of IDEAS."[60] Although pulled from signed broadcasts, at least 17 "original manuscripts prepared by Pound" were aired anonymously from December 9, 1941, to January 21, 1942.[61] These anonymous notes argued that America provoked Japan's aggression and called FDR a "psychopathic lunatic" engaging in a wag-the-dog war to benefit the "plutocracy" that would "reduce the american farmers to the level of russian serfs" (whereas "the AXIS stands for the homestead").[62] In February 1942 Pound wrote over thirty anonymous notes. Nazism, one claimed, would enjoy "sheer and TOATL [*sic*] gratitude from a large number of american citizens" if brought to its shores.[63] The "omniscience" anonymity offered turned out to be prejudice: "Now the BIG jews KNOW that this war is the result of a jew plot to ruin ALL the aryan nations of Europe. And plenty of aryans know this … the yidds look as if they would win that part of their program. The program BEFORE the POGRAM."[64] Sometimes Pound left the decision of attribution to his superiors: "anon/ or not, as you like," he noted for one submission; "by me, or by 'an American' as you like, possibly stronger with my name on it," he wrote of another.[65] This as-you-like-it transfer of authorship—a metaphorical waiver of copyright—would have been strong evidence in terms of establishing treasonous intent.

Pound's first signed broadcast after Pearl Harbor, entitled "On Resuming," showed how the personal could become propaganda. The broadcast is marked by the serenity of someone seeking "wisdom from the ancients" as he is "trying to figure things out" and worrying about the proper pronunciation of *Li Ki* (or *Lǐjì*), the Book of Rites. These flights of fancy gave the illusion that Pound was in full control of his broadcasts, as the introduction to his post-Pearl Harbor broadcasts (which Pound drafted) seemed to imply:

> Rome Radio, acting in accordance with the fascist policy of intellectual freedom and free expression of opinion by those who are qualified to hold it, has offered Dr. Ezra Pound the use of the microphone twice a week. It is understood that he will not be asked to say anything whatsoever that goes against his conscience, or anything incompatible with his duties as a citizen of the United States of America.[66]

Pound kept coming back to this disclaimer after the war to claim that his broadcasts were free expressions of his beliefs, but confining free speech to "those who are qualified to hold it" implies a certain level of trust that Pound would not deviate from the fascist message. And, indeed, in "On Resuming," Pound goes from Chinese ideograms to declaring that America "had been for months ILLEGALLY at war" for the benefit of the "few bloodthirsty kikes who OWN gold." Telling listeners that war with Japan could have been avoided had he been sent there "with any sort of official powers" (a claim he kept repeating after the war), Pound ended the broadcast with the eerily prescient words, "Whom God would destroy, he first sends to the bug house."[67]

If Pound's broadcasts were idiosyncratic, they nonetheless toed the basic line of Axis propaganda, especially when it came to anti-Semitism:

> The Kike is out for all power. The Kike and the unmitigated evil that has been centered in LONDON … against all that is decent in America. Against the total American heritage. This is my war all right, I have been in it for 20 years.[68]

A broadcast targeting the "white remnants of England" spoke of British society being controlled by "the Kahal, the Jew's central committee of bleeders": "YOU HAVE NO RACE left in your government."[69] "No nation has ever survived a plague of the jews at the top," his pseudonymous persona "American Imperialist" explained: "RACES have been undermined by infiltration ... The United States shows NO apparent consciousness of the symptoms of her own weakness."[70] Pound's anti-Semitism was entirely in line with, if not in advance of, Italian policy: as one EIAR official advised in 1940, Rome had to "to intensify anti-Jewish propaganda in all sectors, especially when it comes to English-language transmissions."[71]

"My job, as I see it," Pound noted, "is to save what's left of America."[72] The treason being committed was not his:

> any man who submits to Roosevelt's treason to the Republic commits breech of citizens' duty ... There is NO patriotism in submitting to the prolonged and multiple frauds of the Roosevelt administration. And to try to make the present support of these frauds figure as LOYALTY to the American union, to the American Constitution, to the American heritage is just so much dirt, or buncomb.[73]

"You are," Pound stated in a broadcast that he insisted be anonymous, "your OWN fifth column."[74] While the governments of Britain and America were committing "treason, low treason, high treason, red, green, pink, purple treason," he had been saying the same thing "during the past 20 years."[75] Pointing out the continuity of his thought—a tactic used by a number of other writers accused of treason—shielded one from accusations of selling out. The prior legality of those sentiments also showed that treason was merely a matter of dates.

One of those critical dates was late July 1943, when Mussolini was deposed from power and Pound was formally indicted for treason. If one goes by the published edition of Pound's wartime broadcasts, it seems as if Pound stopped broadcasting at that point. In fact, Pound stayed on the air until the war's dying days. Telling William Joyce that he yearned for "more German contacts," Pound offered to join him in Berlin (but only "by official invite with paid expenses"), signing off with "Heil Hitler" and "nach Vladivostock."[76] This desire for closer ties with German propaganda was achieved after Mussolini was installed as the figurehead of the Repubblica Sociale Italiana (RSI), commonly called the Salò Republic, in autumn 1943. An RSI official noted the importance of propaganda to the new regime: "Comrades, pay attention to words: they can hurt, poison or even kill. It is now up to us to find the word, sound it loudly, make it triumph together with the voice of Italy finally freed from treason."[77] Pound was eager to do his bit: "give me a bed, a bowl of soup, and a microphone."[78] If the "light will rise again," he wrote, it would be through the proper framing of Salò's actions: "The Fascist regime is only as good as its propaganda."[79] In mid-November 1943 he addressed Mussolini:

> Duce,
>
> I don't think that it is either useful or necessary that the radio remains London's monopoly in English language. I could fight their infamous propaganda. I don't need a ministry, but without a microphone ich Kann nicht senden.[80]

A week later, Pound was up in Salò and then Milan, where he recorded three broadcasts (one produced by a German radio engineer). "Tell everyone," he told his wife, Dorothy, "that the new government is alive."[81] Pound enthusiastically backed the new regime's repressive purge—one letter to a senior RSI official calls for the heads of "the dogs who were systematically treacherous during the twenty-one years"—and he found the 1943 Manifesto di Verona, which designated all Jews as foreign nationals, leading to their deportation to death camps, "magnificent."[82]

Pound was restless for action: he had grand plans for a major educational reform; he was convinced that soldiers needed Confucius translations; he wanted to edit a weekly out of Rapallo; he proposed a "BIBLIOTECA FASCISTA" "to combat the poison of mercantilist works of the usurers and their followers."[83] Pound was convinced that Salò needed to take the lead on propaganda: "*Noi dobbiamo andare sempre un po avanti, fare la scopera per prima*" (We have to go a bit further ahead, make the discovery first).[84] One acquaintance marveled at how Pound "believed in us more than we believed in ourselves."[85] This belief was tested, though, by the regime's limited resources. It was "always kid gloves," Pound complained; he railed against "the ignorance of the Republican Fascist propagandists," "the lack of publishing facilities," the fact that the RSI "has not published my new slogans."[86] As it was, six Pound pamphlets were printed at government expense, *Jefferson and/or Mussolini* was reprinted, and two Confucius translations were issued, to "be taken into the trenches."[87] His two Italian Cantos (LXXII and LXXIII) appeared in *Marina Repubblicana*; large propaganda posters in Rapallo had slogans authored by Pound; and "Ez. P." was a thin disguise for over sixty items in *Il Popolo di Alessandria.*

When it came to direct collaboration with the Germans, the possibility of broadcasting from Berlin appeared again in January 1944.[88] In the end, Pound stayed in Rapallo, although in May 1944 that meant vacating his flat. With Rapallo subject to bombings (its main plaza was hit badly), Pound found some relief in sending "short items" to the Germans and pressing for "more INTERCOURSE between the two parts of the axis."[89] Those German broadcasts were prefaced with the phrase *Nein, ich ~~kampfe~~ sphrcye nicht gengen mein Vaterland* [No, I do not ~~fight~~ speak against my fatherland].[90] With that, and the claim that he had been paid by the Republican Fascist Accounting Office on orders of the Ministry of Popular Culture of the Republican Fascist Government, Pound later claimed that he had not supplied German propaganda.[91] Invoicing aside, those items were read on *Jerry's Front Callin'*, a German show targeting Allied troops. "Every human being who is not a hopeless idiotic worm," Pound told GIs, "should realize that fascism is superior in every way to Russian Jewocracy and that capitalism stinks."[92] One undated 1945 script showed how Pound's message conformed to German propaganda:

> Frankie said that the United States would fight to the last goy in defence of jewisch interests … Roosie will lay down the lives of all the non-jew americans in the interest of Leghman & Cohen and company. Expense is no object. What is war to kike, if not a grand sales campaign. Roosie will go on/ unless somebody has the sense to stop him/ … HIS war is aimed at enriching the jew/ and to that end

> he will continue so long as there is an acre of land or an unmortgadge dollar bill in the possession of any american NON-jew. Well now you know wot you are fightin' for.[93]

Pound continued offering unsolicited views on how to improve the message to the "children" that made up the American radio audience, and his devotion to the cause remained true until the very end (his last propaganda script was dated mid-April 1945).[94] Within two weeks he would be in captivity—but the story of Pound's investigation, indictment and eventual capture was complicated by competing pressures within the American government machinery that showcased the different ways in which wartime treason was understood.

Investigations

Pound was no stranger to state security services. His far-flung correspondence during the First World War caught the eyes of the British Censor, and in the 1930s his letters to prominent leftists (like Nancy Cunard and Claud Cockburn) and fascists (like the editor of *Action*) brought renewed scrutiny. Even with France falling in June 1940, MI5 agents found time to report on two foreign nationals ("Both Ezra and Dorothy POUND are of strongly Fascist and anti-Semitic sympathies").[95] For the American government, interest in Pound resurfaced after FDR's October 1942 memo on renegade broadcasters. Two weeks later, the FBI formally opened its investigation: "All possible background of subject should be developed, reflecting subject's activities, and sympathies in the U.S. prior to travel abroad and those activities engaged in by subject since residing in Europe."[96]

The Baltimore field office, presumably because of its proximity to the Federal Communications Commission's listening station in Maryland, took the lead. G-men were dispatched to Idaho to verify Pound's birth (confoundingly, the territory did not keep city, country, or state records before 1907). More promisingly, one source from New York, who had returned from Italy in early 1941, "personally saw POUND reading a propaganda script."[97] One major challenge was identifying Pound's voice on air, which sources characterized as "similar to a Southern negro's," "preacher-like," "high squeaky," downright "peculiar."[98] William Carlos Williams (despite being redacted, an interviewee's identity can sometimes be surmised) threw a spanner in the works by claiming that "in recent broadcasts … the voice did not closely resemble POUND as he had known him, and, in his opinion, believed that possibly DR. EZRA POUND had been interned and some other individual was impersonating his voice."[99] While a few sources identified Pound's voice in an audio lineup, one pointedly told the FBI "that he, as well as any acquaintances of POUND, should they be called [as witnesses], probably all would state that they believed he has become mentally unbalanced."[100] More than a few sources called Pound "unsound," "irrational," "mentally unbalanced," suffering from a "mental condition," quite simply a "crackpot."[101] Williams repeated what he had already said in print, that Pound "had gone completely insane as far as any sense of reason and judgement was concerned."[102] This mental imbalance did not sound like a medical condition, though, when three separate sources stated that Pound's mental state was due to him being "very bitter about America because publishers had refused his books"—that sounded like motive.[103]

The FBI's investigation led to a federal grand jury handing down a treason indictment in late July 1943. Having "devoted his efforts and personal attention to the composition of texts, speeches, and announcements," the indictment noted

> that Ezra Pound, the defendant herein, at Rome, Italy, and other places within the territory of the Kingdom of Italy … being a citizen of the United States, and a person owing allegiance to the United States, in violation of his said duty of allegiance, knowingly, intentionally, willfully, unlawfully, feloniously, traitorously, and treasonably did adhere to the enemies of the United States.

The unexpected bad poetry of adverbial accumulation came to a head in thirteen specific occasions where Pound had "broadcast and caused to be transmitted by radio apparatus, owned and operated by the Kingdom of Italy, to citizens and other residents of the United States within the United States" messages which said, "in substance, that citizens of the United States should not support the United States in the conduct of said war."[104]

The DOJ's "background" to the indictment fused Pound the broadcaster with Pound the writer:

> [Pound] enjoyed a limited popularity both in England and the United States as a poet. Like many of the "modern poets" of that period, he employed a distinctive and unorthodox style which, to most of the reading public, proved incomprehensible …
>
> The lack of popular appreciation is known to have embittered him, first, against the United States, which he considered a cultural backwoods, and later England …
>
> Pound's style as a broadcaster has much in common with his style as a writer: much of what he says is meaningless and incoherent, further complicated, at times, by the use of words of his own coinage. The general trend of his comments, however, follows the familiar Axis propaganda line: that international Jewry is the root of the world's difficulties, that the United States is being used as a pawn by the British, and that the fascist way of life is the hope of the world. Through most of his remarks runs a deep undercurrent of contempt for America and democracy.[105]

Once the obfuscation of Pound's style was cleared away, essentially, what remained was anti-Semitism and Axis propaganda. Pound's style was, in other words, literary coating. The motivation to broadcast—Pound's frustration at being out in the cold in literary America—added to this sense of personal grievance as fueling his broadcasting.

Starting in October 1943, the FBI began receiving reports from its boot on the ground, Special Agent Frank Amprim. A Michigan lawyer of "Italian genealogy" with a "mustache that doesn't enhance his appearance any," Amprim's wider remit in Italy was to investigate "renegade Americans from the prosecution angle."[106] He had three main objectives in the Pound case: securing documentary evidence; locating witnesses; and obtaining information on Pound's whereabouts. The big break was discovering Pound's EIAR file in June 1944. Amprim assembled six disks with recordings, collected thirteen record books "containing entries of the times Pound came to Rome," found a record of payments in the Bank of Italy archives, and located a number of witnesses who either saw Pound broadcast or receive payment for doing so.[107] Back home, though, Pound's capture was not a high priority. When Biddle wrote to the Secretary of War in January 1944, he spoke passively of what should be done "in the event that Dr. Pound is taken into custody."[108] It was hardly a secret that he had been living in Rapallo, and Amprim had also noted down this address.[109]

In the end, Pound was not captured by the American army but by two partisans, who, luckily for him, were motivated by money rather than vengeance. In the heady days after the fall of Salò and the defeat of the German army, a wave of violence was unleashed throughout northern Italy. Death warrants had been issued for collaborators as early as February 1945: "All criminals must be eliminated! The Fascist plague must be extirpated! With Jacobin resolution the knife must cut deeply into the wound until all the gangrene has been cut out."[110] With contemporary reports estimating nearly 20,000 former fascists hunted down and killed in two months, one Allied administrator noted that "any person tainted with Fascist has been extremely fortunate if he has remained alive ... The methods have been cruel and summary—perhaps sometimes unjust—but thorough."[111] Pound was relieved to be handed over to the American military, who took him to the Counter Intelligence Center in Genoa. A day later Amprim arrived to interrogate Pound, who was disoriented but reverted to type by insisting that a cablegram be sent to Truman stating he was the ideal person to negotiate a separate peace with Japan.

These eccentric requests aside, Pound was happy to talk. His six-page statement laid out the chronology of his engagement with fascism, admitted that he initiated the request to broadcast and was always fighting for air time, acknowledged that he was paid by the regime, and expressed his willingness to stand trial in the United States.[112] Incomprehensibly giving the fascist salute on "numerous occasions," Pound also typed out a five-page supplementary statement that plumbed the philosophical and historical roots of his thought (which included famine in 1766 B.C. in China, medieval just price doctrine, the founding of the state bank of England, and Lenin's theory of imperialism).[113] He also granted the FBI permission to search his home, with Dorothy given detailed instructions on where to find documents (a bag in a wardrobe, a suitcase in the hall, etc.).

The American high command in Rome issued a press release about Pound's capture, which was picked up by British papers and *The Stars and Stripes* (with the headline "Traitor Pound Reported Captured Near Genoa"). An enterprising *Chicago Sun* reporter came away with good copy after Pound railed against FDR and Churchill while calling Hitler "a Jeanne d'Arc, a saint ... a martyr." These were not, the reporter emphasized, the ravings of "a senile old sinner who has gone off his rocker"; Pound was "probably the only man ever to be interviewed while awaiting trial for treason who talked more

Figure 2.3 Ezra Pound Mug Shot, US Army photo, 1945. Public domain.

of various interpretations of Oriental ideographs than ... of his own impending trial."[114] But there was no clear sense as to when that would be. The FBI agents had requested that Pound be moved, to which military command issued the typically military order of moving him somewhere else so that the same state of affairs would continue until a further order: "Transfer without delay under guard to MTOUSA Disciplinary Training Center for confinement pending disposition instructions. Exercise utmost security measures to prevent escape or suicide. No press interviews authorized. Accord no preferential treatment."[115]

The Disciplinary Training Center (DTC), a stockade three miles north of Pisa, held "the slime and filth of the Mediterranean Theatre of Operations: convicted rapists, murderers, and traitors who had been members of our Armed Forces."[116] Arriving there on May 24, Pound would stay for nearly six months (Figure 2.3). While exempt from the fourteen-hour workdays imposed on the "trainees," his lot was hardly enviable. He was held in a "gorilla cage" (the term is used in Canto LXXXIII) that had been specially outfitted for him (see Figure 2.4). The exposed cage sucked in dust from the nearby road, roasted in the sun, and had no cover for rain. At night a bright reflector light disturbed his sleep on the concrete floor. By order no one could speak to him. The only authorized reading material was the Holy Book, though Pound had with him the Mencius he had been translating when captured. The sole relief consisted of nightly visits to the infirmary for eye drops to treat an inflammation. Eventually some mercy was granted, and he was allowed to use the dispensary's typewriter at night.

That permission was granted because of raised fears for Pound's mental state. The expert psychiatrists who later testified to his mental incapacity honed in on the early Pisa experience as the catalyst for his mental breakdown. Army doctors, in fact, had acted quickly after Pound suffered from a "spell" in early June. Although finding "no evidence of psychosis, neurosis or psychopathy," an Army psychiatrist warned that "prolonged exposure in present environment may precipitate a mental breakdown, of which premonitory symptoms are discernible. Early transfer to the United States or to an institution in this theatre with more adequate facilities for care is recommended."[117] The camp commander concurred, telling the War Department that "premonitory symtoms [*sic*] are discernible of mental breakdown. Return to UNITED STATES recommended without delay."[118] But with Washington unwilling to repatriate Pound until the treason case was shored up—the War Crimes Office noted in early July that the "long delay in holding Dr. Ezra Pound has been due to the necessity of securing two witnesses of the overt act of treason upon which to predicate the trial of the case"—the best solution was to make Pound comfortable.[119] He was moved into the medical compound and given access to reading and writing materials. His condition was carefully monitored:

> The prisoner was kept in rather close confinement during his first weeks in the D.T.C. He developed symptoms of anxiety, fatiguability, had difficulty in concentrating, and some momentary lapses of memory. When removed from strict confinement, and given more freedom of movement, and improved physical facilities, the above noted symptoms rapidly cleared up.[120]

Figure 2.4 Gorilla cage, United States Army Disciplinary Training Center, Pisa, 1945. Photo by US Army. Public domain.

By the time he was permitted to correspond with Dorothy in late September, Pound stated that he was well fed and hungry for news.[121] A week later he wondered whether his translations from the Chinese would be published and sent her some 70 to 80 pages of cantos, of which, in his opinion, some were quite good, while the others were at least understandable.[122] In early October he penned a release request, referring to himself in the third person throughout:

> While no man can assume responsibility for the actions of another, anyone who has observed the prisoner during the past four or five months is aware that he is serious and reliable. If sent to Rapallo he would presumably stay there if he agreed to do so.
>
> Given his age and literary position he is not the man to spend the rest of his life as a fugitive from justice; in which condition he could not publish his work, and his studies would be very considerably hampered.[123]

A particular notion of authorship underpinned the request: because an author had to live openly, needed access to publishers and readers, and banked on his reputation, Pound would not be a fugitive from justice (unlike other suspected war criminals or traitors). While happy to let Pound author away on a typewriter, the last thing the military contemplated was releasing him on the grounds that authors abided by a code of honor, a notion the war years had proven patently false.

Back in Washington, the DOJ staff attorneys were not convinced that a criminal case could succeed. In late June Amprim was instructed to bring in actionable evidence:

> Examination information and documentary material furnished by you reflects only general data. Nowhere have two witnesses to same overt act of treason been developed. Discontinue all general investigation in case and concentrate on development of two witnesses to same overt act.[124]

FBI Director J. Edgar Hoover also wanted forensic evidence, such as typewriting and handwriting samples. Four extra agents were assigned. On top of the chaotic conditions and the destruction of material evidence, the irresolvable problem was that the Italian radio employees could only testify to seeing Pound speak—but, not knowing English, the content of his speech was unintelligible to them. FCC recordings could not prove who was speaking (and in many cases were of very poor quality). A DOJ suggestion that Pound be asked to cooperate actually bore fruit, as he gave some leads on how to find witnesses of him broadcasting and being paid.

By late summer, Amprim was confident that he had secured enough evidence for a new indictment. A three-page memo dated September 7, 1945, outlined the witnesses who could testify that "Subject Wrote Original Manuscripts," "that Ezra Pound Made Recordings," "that Pound's Recordings Were Broadcast Over Radio EIAR," "that Pound Made the Broadcasts in His Own Voice," and "that Pound Received Money from the Italian Ministry of Popular Culture for Making Broadcasts." While "no one actually saw Pound prepare the manuscripts" and EIAR practice was to have only one technician on site at recordings, Amprim was confident that the witnesses and documents "tell the story of Pound's activities from the time he wrote the manuscripts until the time he received his money."[125] While the DOJ remained anxious about the two-witness requirement, by late October the sheer bulk of evidence warranted Pound's removal for trial. The FBI agents were repatriated, and "round trip transportation, food and lodging and reasonable additional cash compensation" were offered to twelve witnesses.[126] For individuals with questionable wartime pasts in an occupied, cash-poor country, that generous offer was irresistible.

The normal journey for army transports involved landing in New York City, but the military acceded to DOJ's request that Pound's plane land, for jurisdictional reasons, in D.C. (the Chandler and Best trials took place in Boston because bad weather had forced their plane to land in Massachusetts).[127] For the DOJ, it was symbolically important to hold the treason trial in the capital. There were also practical advantages: DOJ attorneys would not have to travel, the political implications of the trial could be more sensitively judged, and the D.C. jury pool included a sizeable number of civil servants who would not be sympathetic to Pound's anti-government screeds. There had been little let up on that front, as one of the guards on the nearly thirty-hour flight noted that Pound spoke eagerly and at length on the gold standard, Roosevelt's moral failings, and how his knowledge of Asia was more important than any possible treason.[128] When the plane finally landed in D.C. at 22:30 on November 18, Pound hectored the pack of waiting journalists and photographers, "Does anyone have the faintest idea of what I actually said in Rome?"[129]

Defending Pound

On the same day that the Nuremberg War Crimes Trials were officially convened, a tired-looking, red-bearded poet propagandist in GI-issued grey sweatshirt, baggy trousers, and shoes three sizes too big was shepherded into Washington, D.C.'s District Court House for a preliminary arraignment. Pound made clear what he had been saying for months, that he would defend himself, but Judge Bolitha Laws ruled that the matter was too serious for that, which Pound conceded before turning out his empty pockets. Dorothy, who had disagreed bitterly with Ezra's plan to defend himself, had been trying to find a suitable lawyer. Laughlin steered interest toward Julien Cornell, a skiing buddy and future lawyer for New Directions. Born into a Quaker family, Cornell had entered Swarthmore at the age of sixteen before going on to Yale Law School.[130] As the chief counsel for the ACLU's committee on conscious objectors, Cornell knew what it meant to have a defendant pilloried by the public and understood how hard it was for courts to go against "the compelling temper of the times."[131] He had also written two well-regarded books on the need for tolerance from those "who place moral duties above duty to the State."[132] While siding with the underdog, Cornell preferred to "establish a friendly and co-operative relationship" with prosecutors to settle cases amicably.[133] Cornell was also a convinced internationalist whose *New World Primer* (1947), later published by New Directions, lamented the "folly of nationalism" and "fetish of sovereignty" that were producing "anarchy and chaos."[134]

Cornell first met Pound the day after the preliminary arraignment (which he could not attend):

> I found the poor devil in a rather desperate condition. He is very wobbly in his mind and while his talk is entirely rational, he flits from one idea to another and is unable to concentrate even to the extent of answering a single question without immediately wandering off the subject.

One moment Pound was saying that he could make peace with Stalin or Tokyo, the next that "the greatest benefit which can come to a poet is to be hung." After piecing together what had happened in Pisa, Cornell came to the conclusion that Pound "went out of his mind" and raised the possibility of an insanity defense. Pound admitted "that the idea had already occurred to him."[135]

At the formal arraignment one week later, the defendant stood mute while Cornell made clear that he did not wish to be appointed lead counsel. But the die was cast for Pound's future defense with Cornell's bail application: "I believe that he is still insane and that if he remains in prison he may never recover, and not only will he be unable to stand trial on this indictment, but one of the greatest literary geniuses of these times will be permanently eclipsed."[136] While Pound's longtime solicitor in London, Arthur Moore, warned that an insanity plea "may not meet with the approval of Pound when he feels better," Cornell's defense had its advantages.[137] The first was practical: the longer the trial was postponed, the more removed the war would be. Daily reports of servicemen coming home (27,500 lucky boys on the day before Thanksgiving that year) would recede into memory, passions for vengeance would be dulled. The government would also have to continue supporting the Italian nationals flown in to testify.[138] Cornell had not yet stumbled on the main advantage of his course of action: since Pound's "state of mild paranoia which is most common among great artists" was chronic but not dangerous, a prolonged hospitalization with no medical benefits would amount to a form of incarceration, a denial of *habeas corpus* for someone technically innocent.[139]

In court Cornell relied on a recently-published *PM* symposium for an account of Pound's career, quoting laurels received, dropping names, trumpeting adjectives (a "roving mind," the "monumental" *Cantos*, the "amazingly clear exposition" of *ABC of Economics*).[140] While bemoaning the "ridiculous broadcasts" full of "anti-Semitic and vulgar utterances," Cornell also painted Pound as a victim with nothing to hide (he "accosted the first American he saw," he was taken into custody "at his own request").[141] A long account dramatized the brutal treatment in Pisa that led to his client's mental collapse ("After enduring the tropical sun all day, neither sleep nor rest came with the night—electric lights glared into the poet's cage and burned into his bloodshot eyes").[142] Events over the weekend at the district jail—a jailbreak that flared up Pound's anxieties—were thrown in for good measure. The lead prosecutor, Isaiah Matlack, who had headed the War Frauds Unit in New York City, found Cornell's gambit a "complete surprise": he had expected a request for an early trial, with Pound to fight the charges on the basis of treasonable intent or a free-speech defense.[143] Just a week earlier, the accused had stood up in the same courtroom and demanded to act as his own lawyer. Reports that summer and autumn indicated that Pound was in fine physical and mental health, so it was difficult to understand how his condition could have deteriorated. Placed in a difficult position, the prosecution agreed to have Pound removed to Gallinger Hospital for a psychiatric evaluation.

Three psychiatrists were appointed: Dr. Marion R. King, medical director of the Bureau of Prisons; Dr. Joseph L. Gilbert, the head of the psychiatric ward at Gallinger; and Dr. Winfred Overholser, the superintendent of Saint Elizabeths, a 6,000-patient federal mental hospital. The defense, after having first approached Overholser, hired its own expert in Wendell Muncie, an associate professor at Johns Hopkins.[144] Cornell sent Muncie a long letter with an account of Pound's career and his detention in Pisa. He also asked the expert to read Pound's writings attentively, among them excerpts from the then-unpublished *Pisan Cantos*, for evidence of mental illness (these writings demonstrated, Cornell believed, the "descent … from genius to filth").[145] Normal practice dictated that each expert evaluate the patient separately. Overholser, though, felt that the psychiatrists needed "to reach an agreement" so that competing diagnoses would not slug it out in court, a process that he felt "unworthy of the profession."[146] Overholser, the secretary-treasurer of the American Psychiatric Association and a recognized authority with numerous scientific publications, was a powerful figure in American psychiatry.[147] The others were not so distinguished. King had little training in psychiatry while Gilbert worked in a two-person psychiatric ward that had recently been investigated for poor services (Overholser had been on the investigating commission). That Overholser put pressure on the other psychiatrists to side with his assessment that Pound was mentally ill can be seen in how King changed course from stating that Pound "cannot be considered mentally ill" to signing the unanimous report delivered four days later:

> The defendant, now 60 years of age and in generally good physical condition, was a precocious student, specializing in literature. He has been a voluntary expatriate for nearly 40 years, living in England and France, and for the past 21 years in Italy, making an uncertain living by writing poetry and criticism. His poetry and literary criticism have achieved considerable recognition, but of recent years his preoccupation with monetary theories and economics has apparently obstructed his literary productivity. He has long been recognized as eccentric, querulous, and egocentric.
>
> At the present time he exhibits extremely poor judgment as to his situation, its seriousness and the manner in which the charges are to be met. He insists that his broadcasts were not treasonable, but that all of his radio activities have stemmed from his self-appointed mission to "save the Constitution." He is abnormally grandiose, is expansive and exuberant in manner, exhibiting pressure of speech, discursiveness, and distractibility.
>
> In our opinion, with advancing years his personality, for many years abnormal, has undergone further distortion to the extent that he is now suffering from a paranoid state which renders him mentally unfit to advise properly with counsel or to participate intelligently and reasonably in his own defense. He is, in other words, insane and mentally unfit for trial, and is in need of care in a mental hospital.[148]

The report raised any number of questions (and a number of conspiracy theories).[149] Suffering from a "paranoid state" was not a medical condition, and Pound's fixed beliefs (the machinations of Jewish high finance, the duplicity and rottenness of Western liberalism, the need for major economic reforms) were social opinions, not psychiatric delusions. One can leave aside the biographical sketch's coded language ("precocious student" bringing to mind Leopold and Loeb, the implication being that mental prowess correlates to character flaws; speaking of Pound's "uncertain living" tied authorship to precarity, which by its very nature contributes to mental instability) and questionable speculation (straying from poetry and literary criticism as a dereliction of authorly duty and professional expertise). The starting point seems to be that Pound could not comprehend how the government could charge him with treason. But this was not a failure of comprehension in the sense of Pound not knowing that he was being charged with treason or not understanding the crime's legal definition; the incomprehension was his insistence upon innocence. By this circuitous logic, Pound could only assist counsel in his defense by admitting his guilt.

While stating that Pound's mental state was "for many years abnormal," the report did not establish whether that amounted to insanity during the war years. The report also conflated insanity and mental competence to stand trial. Insanity had a clear legal basis through the M'Naghten test:

> It must be clearly proved that, at the time of the committing of the act, the party accused was laboring under such a defect of reason, from disease of the mind, as not to know the nature and quality of the act he was doing; or, if he did know it, that he did not know he was doing what was wrong.[150]

This test asked if the defendant was cognizant of his or her actions while committing them. If anything, the foreword Pound drafted to his talks on Radio Roma manifested an active effort to deflect possible criticism of his actions as treasonous, implying awareness of how those acts could be perceived. Fitness to stand trial was a different matter. In English common law the unfit plea was intended to relieve the severely mentally disabled from criminal proceedings. The bar for mental competence was extremely low: knowing one's location, the date and year, who was President, and so on. The DOJ, once-bitten, twice-shy after the Pound case, eventually adopted a three-part test to administer to all renegade broadcasters before any return for trial:

> [1] Is the subject able to comprehend her present condition and peril with reference to the prospective treason charge that is facing her.
> [2] Would she if indicted be mentally and rationally capable of understanding the nature of the treason indictment which would be returned against her.
> [3] Is she presently sufficiently rational to consult with counsel, prepare and assist in the preparation of her defense, and take the witness stand in her own behalf if indicted.[151]

This test applied the more stringent view of mental competence then being used in some jurisdictions (the Supreme Court formalized it as the prevailing standard in 1960).[152] The psychiatric report employed similar language when stating that Pound "is now suffering from a paranoid state which renders him mentally unfit to advise properly with counsel or to participate intelligently and reasonably in his own defense." This was the main issue in the case, not him being "insane," a term that was employed casually in the report, without any medical or legal basis, but which made the best newspaper copy.

The report was not made public until it was read out by Judge Laws one week later. The prosecuting attorneys publicly vowed to contest the findings. Internally, though, the DOJ was resigned: "This would seem to settle the matter. I assume Overholser's word is final in the matter."[153] It was difficult to contest a unanimous psychiatric finding, especially when three of the experts were government officials. Some DOJ lawyers were also relieved since there was an undercurrent of misgiving about the case. The witnesses flown in from Italy (busy amusing themselves on the government dime at a resort in Hot Springs, Virginia) did not inspire much confidence. The public show of opposition and determination was a classic bureaucratic exercise in covering one's ass: no one could fault the DOJ if a "technicality" spared Pound.

Mental Competence on Trial

From 10:00 a.m. until 12:30 p.m. and then from 2:00 p.m. until 3:55 p.m. on February 13, 1945, a jury heard expert testimony on Pound's mental state: four hours of testimony summing up a life that was then arbitrated in three minutes. The only witnesses called were the psychiatrists who had signed the common report in December. Yet in the intervening period, the staff psychiatrists at Saint Elizabeths had come to a radically different conclusion. When Pound was admitted on December 21, 1945, he launched into a lengthy defense of his broadcasts "in a chronologically systematic fashion," telling the admitting physician that he had been "performing a patriotic duty."[154] At the formal admission conference a week later, the six assembled psychiatrists "couldn't elicit any symptoms of psychosis at all … no delusions, no thought disorder, and no disturbance of orientation. He definitely did not seem to be insane."[155] Continuous contact with Pound showed him to be a troublesome patient, prone to exaggeration, oscillating wildly from nervous excitability to overwhelming fatigue, but not insane or mentally unfit to stand trial. After communicating these concerns to the court, Judge Laws ordered the four experts to re-examine Pound.

At the follow-up hearing in February, the DOJ did not contest the composition of the expert panel or call to the stand any staff psychiatrist who disagreed with the initial finding. That day in court was a kind of puppet theater. After sending FBI agents to a war-ridden country to search for bits of paper in the rubble of archives and track down individuals who had no reason to be found, constructing a special cage for the accused, providing round-the-clock medical care, flying him back with three guards, two of them colonels, and transporting eyewitnesses to American hotels and resorts—after all that, the government wilted. It would have been easy to press King on why his evaluation had changed or ask Overholser why his staff disputed the diagnosis. Overholser practically invited questioning on this matter when stating that he was carrying "the report made by the other physicians at the hospital," but the prosecutors did not ask him to read it out and even failed to bring up the conflicting diagnosis, a fantastic situation considering that the hearing had been postponed for that very reason.[156] For some, the government laying down its gloves was a convenient out for a trial that, due to its unprecedented nature, might have been a roll of the dice; the more cynical saw brandishing Pound as "insane" as an effective way to silence him.[157] The more mundane explanation for the

DOJ's baby-toothed prosecution was that contesting three government experts would have undermined their professional and institutional standing. King was the medical director of the Federal Bureau of Prisons, a DOJ unit, and Overholser supervised Saint Elizabeths, a federal hospital instrumental in providing care for returning veterans. That the DOJ did not fold because it was Pound in the dock or because it did not wish to prosecute radio treason can be seen by the direct fallout of the case. Attorney General Tom C. Clark announced immediately after the hearing that a special emissary would be sent to Europe "to bring every single American who played the Axis game swiftly to trial. No effort will be spared because we must show the world that we are not sloppy sentimentalists where the crime of high treason is concerned."[158] In the coming months, a number of broadcasters were captured, rearrested, interned, or brought back for trial.

The DOJ actually came to regret its initial acquiescence. In 1948, a local doctor told the DOJ that someone "interested in poetry" had told him that "Pound is quite sane ... and is continually in communication with many leading poets and literary figures."[159] Although this was just hearsay, the DOJ dispatched a letter asking if Pound "is now sufficiently sane to stand trial on the charges against him."[160] Overholser replied that "Pound was not mentally competent to stand trial ... and it is unlikely that there would be any substantial improvement in his condition."[161] DOJ officials began to suspect that Overholser was actively working to ensure "that Pound not be brought to trial."[162] (Pound's room, at which Overholser was a frequent visitor, was just across the hallway from the Superintendent's 8,000-square-foot apartment.)[163] DOJ agents were sent to St. Liz two to three times per year to pressure Overholser into clearing him as fit to stand trial.[164] Insisting that Pound "does no writing and very little reading," Overholser told the medical director of the DOJ's Bureau of Prisons that Pound was "mentally incompetent yet ... does not fit well into any of the psychiatric categories."[165] The DOJ pressed again in 1954: "You will appreciate that this Department would be derelict in the discharge of its duties if it failed to bring to trial on such a serious charge a man who seemingly is mentally capable of translating and publishing poetry but allegedly is not mentally capable of being brought to justice."[166] Overholser stuck to the original diagnosis, blithely (and falsely) claiming that all of Pound's postwar literary productions and translations were "substantially completed" before he was admitted to hospital.[167]

Back to 1946. The first witness, Wendell Muncie, the defense's expert psychiatrist, indicated that Pound held "a number of rather fixed ideas which are either clearly delusional or verging on the delusional"—these included saving the Constitution, assuring peace if only Confucius were more widely read, and that he "has no peer in the intellectual field." Muncie noted that after having gone through "a great deal" of Pound's writings he had found evidence to support the contention "that there has been for a number of years a deterioration of the mental processes." What most bothered Muncie was Pound's inability to stay on topic: "that is the astonishing thing, if you touch on his case and hospitalization, Confucius and these other things [the economic situation, Japan] seemed to get roped in, and you end up with a confusion of thought." Under cross-examination, Muncie kept referring to how Pound did not understand "the reality of the situation," citing exaggerated beliefs in the power of writing and the conviction that his broadcasting was the act of a patriot. These beliefs showed that Pound "was out of touch with a very large segment of the world ... You and I are living in what one is pleased to call the realities of the situation." The delusions that Muncie pointed to were none other than the core beliefs of a certain strain of modernist authorship: the idea that the world can be remade through language, the indubitable supremacy of individual consciousness, the artist's role as savior and reformer, and the rejection of the common reality that had been so facilely trapped into heavy Victorian exteriors. Yet when asked about the connection between Pound's authorship and treason, Muncie denied that it had any bearing—if Pound were a man "off the street," the same conclusion would be drawn.[168]

Authorship and writing were unacknowledged specters at the hearing. The prosecution asked every expert witness if there was a connection between Pound's profession and his mental state. Even if King believed that all poets were a species apart (grandiose, with an inflated self-regard), Pound had erred by straying from the literary field. Based on a "careful consideration" of Pound's "achievements and progress," the exemplary evidence of his paranoid state was how he "deviated from his chosen profession" and became "preoccupied with economic and governmental problems." The "intense feeling" these subjects aroused in him—the sublimation of the artist's personality into the object, as it were—was "quite characteristic of paranoid conditions." In other words, it was Pound's unorthodox authorship that led to his mental breakdown. These "hobbies, or these special interests" engulfed Pound and "interfered largely with his own profession, without any profit or gain incidentally." The impact of all this came out in his poetry as well. Although admitting to not being an expert (he had read "some" poetry by Pound and "some" poetry by other poets), King felt that Pound's recent work was "incoherent and impossible for me to understand, as compared with the earlier" poetry, which this occasional reader found "coherent."[169]

The other specter of authorship at the hearing, and one which appeared in the testimony of every psychiatrist, was Pound's disjointed discourse (had they read the *Cantos*?). Although the term was not used, this essentially amounted to equating Pound's speech with stream of consciousness. No one, Overholser claimed, could follow "bunches of ideas" that were "rambling and illogical." Asking Pound a direct question, Gilbert said, led to "rambling discourses on matters that had no relation to the question." Pound might be, Muncie speculated, "making a statement about a number of topics which may be clear in his mind but cannot be clear in the examiner's mind." Pound was always getting "sidetracked," King noted, which signified an inability to engage in a "logical, reasonable, and persistent manner."[170] Pound's speech was the living embodiment of the much-decried modernist literary innovation of stream of consciousness (which Pound was in some sense responsible for by shepherding *Ulysses* into print). While that technique had been validated as artistic in the law—"Joyce has attempted it seems to me, with astonishing success to show how the screen of consciousness with its ever-shifting kaleidoscopic impressions carries, as it were on a plastic palimpsest, not only what is in the focus of each man's observation of the actual things about him, but also in a penumbral zone residua of past impressions, some recent and some drawn up by association from the domain of the subconscious," affirmed Justice Woolsey in 1933—stream of consciousness continued to excite anxious commentaries for its willful obscurity and disregard for the common reader.[171] If Pound's manner of talking failed to conform to empiricist rationality, the psychiatrists went one further by classifying it as a sign of mental illness.

These spurious associations between authorship and mental incapacity went uncontested. There was a resigned air to the prosecution's questioning despite every psychiatrist admitting that Pound understood that he was indicted for treason, understood the legal meaning of that charge, was able to furnish details of his past and wartime actions, and could conceivably convey that information to counsel. After the jury delivered its verdict, Pound "seemed very cheered" and told Laughlin to "thank Julien for saving his life." The next day in hospital, Laughlin found Pound "in excellent spirits and not a bit downcast. He realizes that he is not insane but is willing to have the world think so if it will enable him to live to go on with his work."[172]

Legal Afterlives

After the ruling of mental incompetence was issued in February 1946, Cornell began gearing up for an eventual release. The first step was to get Pound transferred to a private hospital, even though "public opinion may make it difficult to persuade the court to permit such removal at the present time."[173] A private sanatorium smacked of privilege while state mental hospitals (especially after "Bedlam 1946," a *Life* magazine exposé replete with graphic pictures of naked, emaciated inmates) conjured up high walls and straitjackets.[174] A private sanatorium would also be a financial burden. The Treasury Department had frozen Pound's American bank accounts on the grounds that he was an Italian national ("are yYOU stark raving?? When the hell and WHO proclaimed me a italian national ... IF I were Italian, how the heel do they xcharge me as an American?").[175] For Dorothy, accustomed to financial security but now fretting about the expense of renting a shabby flat to be near her husband, the prospect of paying for a private hospital (anywhere from 80 to 100 dollars per week, she was told) was unimaginable. At the same time, she realized that Ezra needed to "rest and be carefully treated ... I cannot let him just rot at St Elizabeth's until he dies."[176]

Determined "to get Ezra out of hock," Cornell was convinced that postwar politics was keeping Pound locked up: "Sooner or later the folks in Washington will decide that the war is over."[177] The intensified East-West conflict and rising fears about communist spies made it harder for the country to get off a war footing, but Cornell was also unlucky in Pound refusing to move on. As Moore had predicted, Pound wanted not just to be released but to be applauded for his broadcasts. Pound grew increasingly annoyed that he was not defended on those terms: "J.C. has never bothered to find out what EP's position was," he complained; "E.P. accepted ONLY such <u>parts</u> of fascism as accord with U.S. Constitution," he affirmed; and, as Dorothy put it, "EP did NOT transmit Axis propaganda."[178] Olga Rudge wanted a freedom-of-speech defense, but Cornell

Figure 2.5 Hitchcock Hall, St. Elizabeths Hospital. Photo by Jack E. Boucher, National Park Service. Courtesy of Library of Congress Prints and Photographs Division.

was convinced that Pound's "treasonable statements" fell afoul of the otherwise wide protections afforded to speech.[179]

In January 1947 Cornell petitioned the court to release Pound into private care since "the defendant is not violent, does not require close confinement and the public safety would not be impaired if he were allowed the degree of liberty which a private sanatorium permits for patients who are mildly insane."[180] The DOJ was not pleased with Overholser's suggestion that such a transfer would be medically appropriate, as it had heard quite a different tale from him.[181] Although finding the prosecution lawyers "stodgy and stupid" and the judge "completely impassive," Cornell was pleased with the outcome of the hearing: Pound would be moved out of Howard Hall, where patients under criminal indictment were held, and continue his treatment among the general population at St. Liz (see Figure 2.5).[182] He would benefit from longer visiting hours and greater access to the hospital's extensive grounds; in his single room, he could have a typewriter and papers.

Whatever privileges Pound had inside, outside St. Liz's walls he was a ward of the court. Without the right to sign legal documents, he was stripped of the primary marker of authorship, a signature. A dispute with Liveright, which continued to publish *Personae* despite the copyright having expired, clarified the need to regain some control over his authorship. On October 30, 1946, the "Committee for the Estate of Ezra Pound" was formally instated, its day-to-day running entirely under Dorothy's purview (it was a committee of one). The Committee conducted all the unseen work required of a professional author with an extensive backlist who continued to produce new works, but it also took active steps in what would now be called reputation management. It made, for instance, decisions on the suitability of certain foreign translators and guarded the "Pound" brand by authorizing the use of the name to certain acolytes (Peter Russell, for instance, setting up "The Pound Press"). At times the Committee was a mere figurehead for legal purposes; one contract for the publication of *Women of Trachis*, for instance, stipulated that no alterations could be made "without Mr Ezra Pound's consent," begging the question of who was in charge.[183]

The more humdrum affair of the Committee concerned finances. The yearly audits ordered by the courts bothered Ezra to no end: "the god damn pikers cop everything, and inspect committee accounts to prevent my giving my grandson a $5 Xmas present, cause gooks aint allowed to give away money."[184] Among the physical assets of the Committee were folding chairs used on the St. Liz lawn, Pound's books and writing materials, even his watch. Dorothy had legal control over these items as well as over various bank accounts, which allowed her to authorize $20 per month for "miscellaneous personal expenditures" for Ezra.[185] The estate's financial health improved over time. The first audit, covering the period from November 1946 to October 1947, indicated a total balance of $2,154.17—but most of the holdings were in a blocked account. The 1949 audit revealed that the estate's total assets had grown to over $5,000.[186] The Committee continued to manage Pound's estate after his release; removing guardianship required Pound to no longer be deemed "incompetent," thus opening up the possibility of a fresh treason indictment.[187] To the end of his life, then, Pound's authorship was not under his control.

While Dorothy was happy to steward Pound's literary career, she was the ultimate stumbling block to his release. Having received assurances from Overholser that Pound was incurable, Cornell filed a writ of habeas corpus in February 1948:

> In the case of my husband, EZRA POUND, there is no reasonable possibility that he will recover his sanity, and, therefore, he can never be brought to trial under the indictment. It is also clear that his insanity is of a mild sort which does not require his continued hospitalization. Under these circumstances, if my husband is held indefinitely in confinement, he will in effect be confined for the rest of his life, solely because an indictment is pending against him which can never be resolved by trial.[188]

After the initial application was denied, Cornell filed an appeal and promised to fight all the way to the Supreme Court. But Dorothy abruptly changed her mind:

> Please withdraw the appeal at once. ~~You should have consulted me before filing one~~. My husband is not fit to appear in court, & must still be kept as quiet as possible; the least thing shakes his nerves up terribly. I want nothing attempted now until the Nov. elections are over. There are also April elections in Italy to be considered. I do not wish to [go] outside Judge Laws' jurisdiction – & certainly

> not up to the Supreme Court while Frankfurter is there. I feel no confidence in the case being decided "without intolerance" … Also please note that I will not be responsible for any further expenses.[189]

Only a few weeks earlier she had told Cornell that it was "high time" for Ezra to be released, discussing possible destinations (if not Italy, then perhaps Spain—but, as Cornell pointed out, fascist Spain would not look good).[190] But sanctioning the first step in that direction proved too much for Dorothy, who claimed that Ezra "says he'd better stay where he is, as he can at least get a little Chinese work done—+ the life is very regular."[191] Arthur Moore speculated that Dorothy "may find the cost of his future maintenance too much for her to bear alone"; Laughlin felt that she was "a little bit batty too."[192] Things got nowhere after Cornell left the country, in early 1949, to take up a position with the American Friends Service Committee in Geneva. Upon his return, he continued to act as Pound's counsel but found himself sidelined. Working contacts at the ACLU in 1957, he told Dorothy that it was interested in helping to release Pound, but she rebuffed the offer. In December of that year he confessed, "So far as I know, there is no move under foot looking toward Pound's release."[193] It was no small vindication that the chosen line of argumentation which freed Pound a few months later was the exact same one he had put forward a decade earlier. The issue in releasing Pound, in other words, was not so much the law but politics, literary politics included.

Literary Battles: Blacklists and Prizes

If Pound's writings are a starting point for literary modernism today, things looked very different in 1945. The vast majority of academics and critics considered him a second-rate poet, much inferior to Eliot; to the "ordinary literate American," one such specimen noted, he was an "utter stranger."[194] As Hugh Kenner openly wondered in 1949, "why is he [Pound] so little discussed and, one suspects, less read?"[195] The transformation from unreadable minor poet to lionized classic was more than literary *Fortuna* changing course. The treason indictment was the catalyst for a "campaign to re-establish his [literary] standing" that removed any consideration of politics or morals: "Ezra Pound's poetry is good—very good—notwithstanding his political folly … A poem is a thing in itself. You judge it by itself and of itself—not by the politics of the man who wrote it."[196] But literary politics could not always be kept at bay. In early 1946, Random House blacklisted Pound because of his fascist politics; three years later, the tables were turned when he was awarded the Bollingen Prize. If these literary affairs functioned as substitutes for the missing criminal trial, Pound was "less important than the symbol" he had become about a host of postwar controversies related to freedom of expression, the autonomy of art, and modernism.[197]

The first *Kulturkampf*, set off a few days before the decisive hearing on Pound's mental state, was an instance of what now would be called cancel culture. Legendary editor Bennett Cerf announced that Pound's poetry would be removed from a forthcoming anthology so as to not sully Random House's name with the work of a "traitor":

> Damn it … this war is not over … The same ideology that caused it—the ideology that Pound has preached—is still all too prevalent … [e]very time you parade the work of a man who represents such ideas, especially while he still lives, you are in a sense glorying him, and giving tacit approval to his point of view.[198]

It was not just the anthology's editor, Conrad Aiken, who "raised hell" over a "ridiculous and hypocritical" decision: within two weeks, Cerf received letters "from every corner of the country": "142 opposed … 140 approved the exclusion … Seven people simply could not make up their minds, and took the trouble to tell me so!"[199] But the issue was more complex than a yes-or-no vote, as the letters to Cerf revealed a range of views on postwar authorship and showcased the depth of feeling the Pound case aroused.

Some readers wanted to keep alive "the burning flames of righteous wrath and moral indignation": "Stand by the gun, man," Cerf was implored, "there are plenty of us to pass the ammo."[200] Others supported excluding Pound on the grounds that his poetry was "empty artifice" (so said E. O. James, a Shakespeare scholar at Mills College) or "distinctly sixth grade work" (even in comparison to other poetry by the insane, wrote Elizabeth Millet Chase, who ironically would go on to write scores of poems as a mental patient herself).[201] The biggest fault line was over the various professional responsibilities of "Cerf-man, Cerf-publisher; Pound-man, Pound-poet."[202] If publishers held "as important and as strategic a position" in the cultural field as writers, then they had pedagogical and moral responsibilities toward readers who "often do not trust their own judgement as to what constitutes good literature."[203] Picking up on the New-Critical language of the "intentional fallacy," a number of readers stressed that "[a]n artist's work … is something entirely divorced from the artist" and could only be judged "on the basis of literary merit."[204]

The most spirited replies concerned censorship. Cerf's exclusion was firmly in line with the wartime liberal *doxa* that freedom of speech could not be granted to fascists: "How many Belsama and Buchenwalds do we have to have to learn how the fascist uses his freedom of speech?" asked the editor of *The Christian Register*, whose January 1946 number was on that very topic.[205] But opinion was beginning to shift as censorship moved from a necessary wartime evil to a domestic risk with state censorship boards, loyalty oaths and McCarthyite suspicion. No one individual could be entrusted to act as censor, Cerf was told; let the great wisdom of the people decide what was pernicious; do not think, the scolding went, that one could have anything less than absolute freedom of speech, for even the narrowest opening would result in abuses: the Nazis had started with "persecution" of unpopular ideas before undertaking "suppression and extermination of all literature not in political agreement with the dominant party."[206] As the delightfully-named Betty Bold put it, "Freedom of speech becomes a farcical term if less than complete freedom is meant."[207] The instrumental argument was simpler: censorship resulted in "unintentional advertising" and turned the banned object into forbidden fruit.[208]

After wading through the avalanche of letters, of which nearly forty were printed in the *Saturday Review of Literature*, Cerf reversed course one month later by admitting that it was impossible to get off the slippery slope. With less good grace, he added, "I still maintain that the war of ideas is not over; indeed, it seems scarcely to have begun. I still think that Ezra Pound and men like him are the scum of the earth, and must be fought without quarter and without cease."[209] If Cornell felt that this *mea culpa* rose to a "technical libel," the more important thing for Laughlin was that Cerf "ate crow," stumped up $300 to reprint the twelve excised Pound poems and inserted an apology in all new editions of the anthology which stated that "it may be wrong to confuse Pound the poet with Pound the man."[210] The separation in the literary field between art and politics was becoming complete.

That separation became a critical part in the story of *The Pisan Cantos* receiving the inaugural Bollingen Prize. Set up to reward the most significant book of poetry by an American citizen, the cash prize of $1,000 was administered by the Library of Congress, whose Fellows in American Letters constituted the jury (chaired by Léonie Adams and including Aiken, W. H. Auden, T. S. Eliot, Katherine Garrison Chapin, the wife of Francis Biddle, Robert Lowell, Karl Shapiro, and Robert Penn Warren). At its first meeting, in November 1948, Allen Tate warned of "embarrassing" "political implications" if Pound were picked.[211] When announcing the prize in February 1949, the jury sought to shield its decision from criticism:

> The fellows are aware that objections may be made to awarding a prize to a man situated as is Mr. Pound. In their view, however, the possibility of such objection did not alter the responsibility assumed by the Jury of Selection. This was to make a choice for the award among the eligible books, provided any one merited such recognition, according to the stated terms of the Bollingen Prize. To permit other considerations than that of poetic achievement to sway the decision would destroy the significance of the award and would in principle deny the validity of that objective perception of value on which civilized society must rest.[212]

If there was a certain passivity in speaking of "a man situated as is Mr. Pound," the statement foregrounded the jury's mission to select the volume that "represents the highest achievement of American poetry in the year for which the award is made." While "highest achievement" could be interpreted in various ways (the biggest seller, the most publicized, the most improbable), the jury took "poetic achievement" to mean "objective perception of value," the well-wrought urn of New Critical fame. But there was also a Cold War political undertone in claiming that a "civilized society" required an apolitical theory of art (unlike the other side, afraid as it was to allow an art of free expression). It was unclear, though, how a book infused with politics, as *The Pisan Cantos* was, could be read absent its core.

Even if some headline-writers were titillated to employ arresting epithets like "mad poet" or "fascist traitor," the public controversy was muted at first.[213] The higher values expressed by the Fellows—"an objective criterion of beauty and excellence, akin to a belief in an objective truth," the *New York Herald Tribunal* opined, "is fundamental to a free and rational society"—were deemed more important.[214] There was some self-satisfaction in thinking that the arts were not shackled by the State: no way could this happen in Soviet Russia! This was the thrust of Dwight Macdonald's view that the award was "the brightest political act in a dark period."[215] *Partisan Review* editor William Barrett was uncertain: could "technical embellishments" really "transform vicious and ugly matter into beautiful poetry"?[216] Sensing that the main problem was Pound's anti-Semitism, Auden retorted that "all gentiles" had at one point held anti-Semitic thoughts or feelings.[217] Clement Greenberg and Karl Shapiro were livid; "As a Jew," Greenberg wrote, "I myself cannot help being offended by the matter of Pound's latest poetry; and since 1943 things like that make me feel *physically* afraid too."[218] Tate also took the charge personally, but the other way round, challenging Barrett to a duel.

This tiresome debate would soon pass, Jas Laughlin opined. Having been off skiing in Europe when the prize was announced, he launched a marketing campaign around the award, convinced that the public would be "impressed by the weight of the Committee which made the award, and the fact that it came from the Library of Congress."[219] That looked to be true until two articles by Robert Hillyer appeared several months later in the *Saturday Review of Literature*. Although largely forgotten today, Hillyer was the serving President of the Poetry Society of America and a Pulitzer Prize winner. A traditionalist who believed that poetry could elevate humdrum experience "into something more lasting and beautiful," Hillyer had been on the faculty at Harvard but was then based at Kenyon College (his anti-modernist screeds against "the new critic, happy jargoneer, | Who makes obscure what once was fairly clear" came from inside the belly of the *Kenyon-Review* whale).[220] The ensuing controversy—*SRL* printed over 100 letters, *Poetry* issued a pamphlet defending Pound—even came to a head in the halls of Congress, which cancelled all official prizes by the Library of Congress as a result. For the first time in a long time, poetry was news in America.

In "Treason's Strange Fruit," the first of two essays, Hillyer not only condemned Pound's writings as "vehicles of contempt for America" but also took to task the broader institutional forces behind the prize.[221] The first visual in the essay was not of Pound but a top-hat-wearing T. S. Eliot—who was the subject of Hillyer's follow-up article a week later, "T. S. Eliot and the 'New Criticism.'" Hillyer focused more on the institutional dynamics in rewarding Pound than *The Pisan Cantos*, a book he dismissed as "rubbish."[222] An *SRL* editor privately told Archibald MacLeish that the prize had become "a focal point" for "increasing dissatisfaction" with modern poetry; it was also, he told Malcolm Cowley, just a way to "start a controversy" to fill up "three exciting issues" ("it went on for six").[223] As Hillyer put it, there was a cancerous growth within American literary culture: the institutional prestige of critics who championed modernism and New Criticism eviscerated morality, politics, significant emotion, and community standards.[224] "As a citizen," Hillyer was shocked that the government could honor an indicted traitor. The stage was set for "the literary battle of the year."[225] *The Pisan Cantos* was a mere prop in this dispute, as *Poetry* complained: "They have used the admittedly troublesome case of Ezra Pound as a pretext for their general condemnation of the poetic achievement of the whole period … They have examined us all in the works of Ezra Pound, and they have condemned us."[226]

The ensuing controversy raised Pound's public profile, which translated into more readers. The first print run of *Selected Poems*—which at 3,400 copies was a sizeable figure for a volume of verse—sold out within one year, and in late 1950 a second printing of 4,500 copies was ordered.[227] Observing "the yells of editorial outrage … the columns of rant," Hugh Kenner became convinced "nobody in 1949 knew how to talk about Pound's poetry"—and so he began *The Poetry of Ezra Pound*, his 1951 book that catapulted Pound's reputation (and Kenner's academic standing).[228] Pound felt vindicated by the award but showed little gratitude when Bollingen chairperson Léonie Adams began to visit him at St. Elizabeths. He tried to get Adams to send out a press release on Library of Congress letterhead with "a list of important people about 100 who praised him"—the catch was that she had to sign the communiqué he had drafted as her own.[229] This tactic of using other individuals as a front for Pound's authorship was not a one-off but very much part of his postwar history.

Rise from the Smoke Hole: Anonymous Propaganda from the Bughouse

Rise through the smoke hole: that could well be the story of Pound's twelve years at Saint Elizabeths.[230] In early 1948, after Dorothy pulled the plug on any further legal action, it seemed as if Pound would spend the rest of his days in an 8x10 cell. He may not have gone in for Bingo, group singing, or watching variety shows on a 12-inch Philco television set, but he was given wide latitude to make his stay pleasant. Those liberties included free use of the lawn under Dorothy's escort, a tennis court for daily sessions when the weather was fine, extended visiting hours, a room of his own with a typewriter, and twice-daily mail deliveries bringing in news from hundreds of correspondents across the globe.[231] No group therapy, no menial work details, no invasive medical interventions: Pound was allowed to arrange his time as he pleased, with only occasional, disengaged chats for the case file ("the minute yu are confronted with a psychiatrist turn yr/ back and LEAVE. Quite useless to waste yr/ time talking to vermin").[232] To the doctors he complained of "great fatigue and weakness" but, as one physician noted, "this fatiguability is much less evidenced when he is working on his manuscripts in his room alone."[233]

A number of illustrious poets—Eliot, Elizabeth Bishop, Robert Lowell, and Marianne Moore—visited regularly. Pound also took great comfort in overseeing a number of young disciples and admirers. At the "EZUversity" on St. Elizabeths' lawns, the assembled were led in readings of the classics and assigned various missions, from writing the great American novel to investigating the (abyssmal) state of American culture. "If you come out here," he warned, "you're in danger of getting put to work."[234] Spurred by his belief that "resistence [*sic*] has got to be ONE by ONE, the word from ONE person to one person," daily missives were postmarked to far-flung locales.[235] The earliest biographies of Pound—by Eustace Mullins, Noel Stock, and Michael Reck—all came from visitors or correspondents from the St. Liz period. Pound was especially keen to cultivate academics, even if he disparaged the ignorance propagated by American universities, because "it is in them circles … that the keys to jails are kept."[236] One of the disciple reviews from St. Liz, *Academia Bulletin*, was explicit in this interest (its original title was *Academia Poundiana*). While Fredric Jameson and Malcolm Bradbury did not have their visitor requests granted, Kenner, then finishing a doctorate at Yale, became a regular, as did his friend from back home in Canada, Marshall McLuhan. Some academics were put to "work," such as Wellesley professor D. D. Paige, who edited a volume of Pound's letters that did much to rehabilitate his standing as a major figure for literary modernism. Giovanni Giovannini, a professor at nearby Catholic University, later became one of Pound's literary executors.[237] But it was not always smooth sailing in the ivory tower. John Edwards, whose *Ezra Pound Newsletter* came out of Berkeley, became a *persona non grata* in Poundian circles, as did University of Alabama's Douglas Hammond.

While the daily sessions on the lawns and the endless letter-writing gave Pound a sense of purpose, over time he grew frustrated with the walls. His publishers were bent on "remaking" his postwar image by drawing a strict line between "aesthetic" writings and polemical pieces on politics or economics.[238] Presenting Pound "as a poet & a literary thinker" while "leaving out all cursed economics + politics" was seen by Laughlin and Eliot as the road to rehabilitation, much to Pound's dismay at only "NON-Critical E.Prose" being published.[239] Already in May 1946 Dorothy confided that Pound felt "the necessity for some kind of small-review + publishing-house" to put out works that New Directions and Faber & Faber refused.[240] "The STRATEGIC aim" of such work, he told a British correspondent, "is the kind of publicity that will accelerate EZ' liberation."[241]

To a friend who enquired about poetry, Pound brusquely replied, "Birds don't sing in cages."[242] The following message-poem from 1947 seemed to say it all:

Lunatix
 do
 not
 work
 E.P.
 S.Liz
Tanks[243]

If that was the public message, privately Pound hankered to fight "this bath of mendacity and obscurantism in the WHOLE daily and periodical press."[244] But that fight required "LITERARY camouflage."[245] Openly taking credit for writing could lead the DOJ to conclude that he was fit to stand trial. Then there was the fact that some anonymous missives—"surely if the Jews have an Israel, the allergic might also desire a country where they, as one cultivated chinaman once put it, might pass their lives without ever meeting a semite"—were politically toxic.[246] In the paranoid political climate of the early Cold War, Pound concluded, "the ONLY way to get calm perusal/" was to write anonymously.[247] When one of his disciples republished his money pamphlets in 1950, Pound was furious, as it was "a danger rather than a help" to be openly credited with authorship.[248] "Nothing since 1939 to be shown to anyone," Pound instructed Laughlin; private letters were "strictly 'anonymous.'"[249] A number of disciples gave Pound free rein in articles that were signed by another ("So let me have anything you want shoved into this article and you may regard it as your own," Ronald Duncan told Pound) or sent scripts for his approval.[250] "Nothing to be done without imprimatur of senior professor of St Lizzie's," wrote Norman Holmes Pearson, himself a distinguished professor of literature at Yale and former OSS agent, who offered to serve as "letter-drop, cut-out, or whatever undercover terms seem best."[251]

While never contributing to *The Elizabeth: A Paper By and For the Patients*, Pound wrote scores of anonymous notes for a series of little reviews put out by disciples, among them *Four Pages* (Galveston and South Wales), *NINE* (London), *Voice* (Belfast), *Mood* (St. Louis), *Academia Bulletin* (D.C), *Strike* (D.C), *Edge* and *The New Times* (Melbourne). These ephemeral reviews, supplemented by single-issue publishing houses, constituted a distinct print culture ecosystem for postwar Poundian thought. As Dallam Simpson, editor of *Four Pages* and publisher of The Cleaners' Press, told Peter Russell, editor of *NINE* and publisher of The Pound Press, there needed to be "a systematic attempt to get, not only the part of EP's work that Eliot and Laughlin like, but the whole of it into print."[252] The guiding motivations for these journals varied as much as Pound's work cut a wide cloth; some were mainly interested in social credit (*Edge, New Times*); others mainly marshalled his racial and political ideas (*Academia Bulletin, Strike*); and still others focused on his cultural views (*Four Pages, NINE*). These coterie venues constituted a lifeblood for Pound, who swore by them: "NO ONE is educated till they have digested the Sq $ series/"; the Melbourne-based *Edge* was "best since Little Review in 1918."[253]

Pound's anonymous propaganda offensive also went beyond "small sectarian muggyzeens."[254] High-culture venues, like *Quarterly Review*, ran special issues on him. He served as an informal advisor to the newly-founded *Hudson Review* (which published Pound translations and a number of Cantos) and the *Yale Poetry Review*, whose managing editor was given reading lists and inserted into Pound's epistolary network.[255] Tom Carter, who ran *Shenandoah*, later admitted that three issues were essentially edited by Pound. After stepping down from the review, Carter refused to start up a sixteen-page quarterly that Pound promised to subsidize, resulting in "several bitter letters" from Pound "about my not joining His Holy Wars."[256] Tom Cole had a similar experience at *Imagi*, with Pound trying to get the review to go "off the other end with notices etc of economics."[257]

Pound's anonymous propaganda offensives required the collaboration of disciples who were, at best, incompetent and, at worst, harmful. Incompetence rankled, forcing an increasingly exasperated Pound to wonder how simple instructions had to be for them to be carried out: "DEEElayz, DEElayz. any time I count on any sort of punctuality among my friends the byby gets colic or a tupewriter busts or a printer goes on strike at sight of IDEOGRAMS/ etc. AND in 9 years/ impossible to get Los Poundistas to speak to each other."[258] As he heckled another interlocutor: "yr/ generation is sodam slow to wrath/ I dunno WHEN a few you will git ORGANIZATION and get grampaw's woiks into print and availability."[259] When the poet Robert Creeley was trying to set up a little review, Pound dispatched some disciples to help out, prompting Creeley to lash out, "No damn use positing any one of the many idiots surrounding you are of USE only because they happen to have TWO legs."[260]

The flipside of incompetence was zealotry exceeding good sense. Simpson wanted to expose Pound's participation in *Four Pages*; other disciples shared private correspondence or tried to sell it (as Peter Russell did on two occasions). The politics of some of his disciples—Eustace Mullins, who wrote a hagiography of Pound, was the director of the Aryan League of America; John Kasper, who ran the Square Dollar Series and the "Make It New" bookstore in Greenwich Village, was a diehard segregationist and white supremacist—also brought disrepute and unwanted publicity.[261] In both cases, Pound stoutly defended the "mere indiscretion[s]" that such positions entailed, noting, in Kasper's case, for example, that one could not "expect the wisdom of Solon from a y.m. whose parents thanked me for straightening him out AFTER he had been extremely muddled by four years in a jewisch beanery in jew York / Columbia JEWniversity."[262] Given that Pound never fundamentally changed his anti-Semitic views ("Obviously it is kikes keeping me in here"), it was little wonder that political extremists continued to gravitate toward him.[263] It was "a pity," though, as the British writer Denis Goacher, who came to St. Liz for an extended stay in the early 1950s, put it, "to have to waste time saving E.P. from his more hysterical disciples."[264]

Final Release

If the non-trial of Ezra Pound meant that his case came to be litigated "in the newspapers and magazines and, still less officially, the classrooms and living rooms of the postwar United States," the lack of a public tribunal denied Pound the official absolution he craved.[265] This sense of being wronged was encouraged by supporters who considered Pound's case as "again Socrates in his prison cell."[266] Pound studied the history of treason, especially the writings of British jurists Sir Edward Coke and Blackstone, and closely followed the trials of other renegades (he assembled clippings on the Chandler case and closely followed what was happening to Louis-Ferdinand Céline). Coming to believe that there could be "no treason without intention," Pound became the greatest stumbling block to any eventual release, objecting to any course of action that did not have as its aim "vindication from on high," "a gilt-edged certificate proclaiming him a patriot who was Right All the Time."[267] Pound's lack of cooperation and the questionable company he kept complicated everything, Eliot bemoaned, with crackpot schemes encouraged and practical ones dismissed.[268]

The story of Pound's eventual release was less a question of law than of several factors working together to create a favorable climate for the law being bent. And, more than anything, there was the question of time. In 1951, when Olga Rudge made the trip from Italy to visit Pound, she hired a young Washington attorney with connections on Capitol Hill, Rufus King, to look into Pound's case. King laid out three possibilities, all of them bad: a trial that might go in Pound's favor but whose strain "would kill him"; asking for a pardon, which "implied an admission of guilt" and thus was a non-starter; or continuing with the status quo until dying in hospital.[269] With such unpalatable options, no wonder that little effort was made on the legal front. Two years later, Cornell pressed to resubmit a *habeas corpus* petition, but Dorothy blocked it. She also rebuffed the ACLU's offer of legal aid (it saw a perfect test case not for freedom of speech, as Pound might have wished, but for the indefinite confinement of the mentally ill charged with a crime).[270]

In the absence of any legal action, some supporters, especially outside America, believed in the need for coordinated action. The Italian gang—Olivia Rossetti Agresti, Olga Rudge, John Drummond—were especially active. Pound's case became a *cause célèbre* for writers and intellectuals abroad. Eva Hesse, Pound's German translator, signaled that his detention "makes name of U.S. democ'y stink throughout the world of letters."[271] Laughlin, then publishing *Perspectives USA*, a Cold War cultural diplomacy review, argued that Pound's confinement confirmed the prevailing view that the United States had "no regard for cultural values."[272] Archibald MacLeish yanked the same chain when writing to Milton Eisenhower: "nations are judged in the perspective of history by the way they treat their poets, philosophers, artists and teachers."[273] UN Secretary General Dag Hammarskjöld named Pound among the "seers ... and explorers" and wrote personally to the State Department to call for "a solution to this humanitarian problem."[274] Internationalizing Pound's case had its own risks, though. As Eliot warned, it smacked of meddling in the country's internal affairs (something America routinely did toward others but disliked intensely when the volley was returned). Raising the profile of Pound's case also ensured that there would be loud objections if he were ever released on the grounds that he was (or had been) a good poet, as that implied a law for genius and then another for everyone else.

Those who worked most closely on Pound's behalf tried to calibrate their interventions to the political winds. The refrain "wait until after the election" peppered the letters of Cornell, Eliot, Laughlin, Moore, and MacLeish. The latter, with his extensive experience in the State Department during the war, close friendships with many establishment figures, and current position of professor of poetry at Harvard, was ideally positioned to link the literary field with Washington hardball. Robert Frost received a visit from MacLeish and the two strategized about how to proceed; Hemingway and Eliot were kept in touch by letter. Not every writer wished to help Pound's case (Auden, 1955: "Sorry I have nothing, absolutely nothing to say about him"), but those who did—Cummings, Eliot, Faulkner, Frost, Hemingway, Williams—were recognized lions.[275]

These efforts by writers and intellectuals, both in the United States and abroad, needed to be translated into effective political action. Replacing Cornell, who was far removed from the corridors of power, was an important step. While Pound was taken by a small-town Virginia lawyer who regularly visited St. Liz, the services of Washington power-broker Thurman Arnold were retained in January 1955. Arnold had run the anti-trust division at the DOJ during the war (raising Dorothy's suspicions: "he must know all the wrong people ... I wouldn't trust him an inch") and was a named partner at one of the capital's most powerful law firms, Arnold, Fortas & Porter.[276] As a former elected official (he had been mayor of Laramie, Wyoming, and that state's sole representative to the House of Representatives in the 1920s), he also commanded respect among

Figure 2.6 Ezra Pound with Representative Usher Burdick, 1958. Public domain.

politicians.[277] Another important step was an official Congressional report commissioned by Usher Burdick, an iconoclastic Republican from North Dakota who was one of the fiercest critics of the UN system ("an ungodly menace") but also a fluent Sioux speaker, supporter of civil rights and the sole Republican to vote against the Communist Control Act (see Figure 2.6).[278] Burdick had heard from John Kasper (in the oddest of circumstances: congressional hearings on a proposed federally-funded psychiatric hospital in Alaska which smacked of "Siberia, U.S.A." to the far-right; coincidentally enough, Overholser was on the fact-finding trip to inspect the proposed site in 1949) that the United States had a political prisoner in the form of Ezra Pound.[279] The ensuing report that Burdick ordered from the Library of Congress's Legislative Reference Section came to be known, after its lead author, as the Sieber report. A progressive civil rights activist and poet from North Carolina, Hal Sieber was not the most natural ally of Pound ideologically, but he admired Pound's poetry and received a great deal of material on Pound's situation from fellow North Carolina poet Charleen Swansea and other visitors to St. Elizabeths.[280] Giovanni Giovannini, perhaps Pound's closest ally in the academy, did "work in the dark" to influence the report, which came out in March 1958.[281] The Sieber Report detailed the positive press coverage for Pound in recent years—Samuel Hynes in *Commonweal*, editorials in *Life* and *New Republic* calling for his release, a long piece in *Esquire*—and sidestepped the legal controversy of whether his broadcasts constituted treason, or whether Pound was sane or not, and even parroted Pound's claim that it was "unaristotelian" to call him an anti-Semite.[282]

With establishment figures and mainstream press organs backing his release, and now a Congressional report that smoothed the way for such a course of action, the political fallout of releasing Pound was minimized. The medical evidence, that Pound's condition was "permanent and incurable," spoke to the impossibility of a trial, as did the fact that so much time had passed since the eyewitnesses to Pound's broadcasting had idly accumulated *per diems*. Those eyewitnesses were shaky enough in 1945, but the idea of them in an American courtroom in the late 1950s stretched the credible. If there was no statute of limitations on treason in America (in the UK, it was three years), thirteen years had passed since the war had ended, so keeping a war criminal locked up was out of step with the times (France had passed a general amnesty in 1951; in West Germany there were amnesty laws in 1951 and 1954). West Germany was America's closest ally in Europe, as was Japan in Asia; if bitter enemies could now be embraced, what sense was it to seek vengeance upon an old man?[283] By some symbolic reckoning, the many years Pound spent at St. Liz were recast as a prison sentence.

The release of the Sieber Report led to the DOJ being asked about Pound's case, and rather than repeating standard lines an opening was breeched: the case was being re-evaluated. That was all Arnold needed to file a *habeas corpus* writ arguing that because Pound's condition was "permanent and incurable," there was no compelling reason for the government to bear the charge of interning him and that refusing his release would be tantamount to a life sentence.[284] Attached to the motion was a statement by Robert Frost which squarely dismissed Pound's supposed patriotism as "nonsense" but nonetheless called for "magnanimity" toward a "great poet" whose current plight was a "disgrace."[285] The hearing on April 18, 1958, before the same judge, Bolitha Laws, who presided over the case in 1945 and 1946, took only twenty minutes. The government did not contest the motion even though there was no legal reason to waive the power to prosecute a federal crime and the Supreme Court had, two years earlier, ruled that the incurably insane could remain committed in federal custody since there was no "finality of judgment" in the field of psychiatry.[286] As it was, Pound's internment in St. Elizabeths was annulled. For Pound's supporters it finally seemed "that the last war is over, <u>now</u> … The war is <u>over</u>, my stars."[287]

In formal legal terms, a *nolle prosequi* was granted—this meant that the prosecutors agreed to not pursue the case, but this was no acquittal, as a new indictment for the same charge could be issued if new evidence appeared. While there were some predictable complaints about Pound getting off "scot free," most of the press coverage underscored the magnanimity of the government's decision and the prestigious writers who had lobbied for Pound's release.[288] It helped, too, that Congress was on Easter recess. The ACLU objected to what it saw as preferential treatment being given to a celebrity, but Thurman Arnold responded that it was celebrity that had kept Pound in the jug so long. He also denied reports that a "deal" was struck, whereby the court action would not be contested if Pound agreed to leave the country.[289] But that was exactly what he did—within weeks, he was on a liner sailing back to Italy. When he arrived in Naples, he (in)famously gave a fascist salute. Until the end of his days, he remained unrepentant toward his actions—"The treason was carried out in the White House, in the head organizations of American finance, not in Rapallo"—but also a ward of the court, his signature void of any legal impact.[290]

Conclusion

If Pound's case has become the most emblematic instance of literary treason from the Second World War, the drawn-out "trials" in courtrooms, newspapers, literary reviews, faculty offices and among the wider public were instrumental in elevating Pound's literary standing from an expatriate poet of little-review fame to one of the defining figures of modernism. The Pound affair also exposed nascent Cold War tensions in the American literary sphere over the limits of free expression (in the Random House affair) and supposed apoliticism of art (in the Bollingen controversy). As a wider point, questions of authorship and authorial responsibility lay at the heart of the case. Firstly, Pound's decision to broadcast and his wider engagement with politics could not be separated from his understanding of authors as "antennae of the race," with a unique mission to lay out the public good in advance of prevailing beliefs. If that work usually led to contempt, it could not, in his thinking, give rise to prosecution or be framed as criminal. This framing of authorship as a public mission was at odds with the increasingly professionalized understandings of literary authorship that separated the literary sphere from a wider society which had become dominant ever since the mid-nineteenth century. While the inability to hew closely to a purely professional engagement with literature led Pound to take to the air, it also, paradoxically, saved him from the awful consequences of his broadcasting. The psychological assessment that Pound was mentally incompetent was informed by an overly restrictive view of authorship: by straying from the literary into such domains as politics and economics, Pound was considered to have betrayed his literary genius and undermined his professional responsibilities. For a poet to do more than produce rhymes was to subvert what was expected of a versemaker. In some ways, the fantasies of modernist autonomy—the literary text as an end and complete in itself, the author as a figure exterior to the text and the social world—had become operative in the Pound affair, resulting in the diagnosis that straying from the purely literary was, for authors, a sign of degeneration. The constant movement on Pound's part also impacted his discourse, resulting in an external manifestation of that most modernist of narrative techniques, stream of consciousness—and for the psychologists, that meant a mind out of order, legally equivalent to a child or a deranged individual.

The case also hinged on questions of intent. Pound's view that there could be "no treason without intent" accorded with the Supreme Court's understanding of treason in *Cramer*, but the "intentional fallacy" was increasingly seen in the literary field as a critical *faux pas*. There was, in truth, a series of category errors at work here. Pound may well have been motivated by the desire to return America to its prior greatness, but the acts he took to accomplish that end—going on foreign radio—had a more immediate impact in furthering the war aims of a foreign state. And for those who denied the existence or knowability of intent, the war seemed to show that the meaning of an act or a text could not be understood in isolation but depended on a variety of factors, such as immediate context, timing and material form.

Finally, the case spotlighted the contestation over the most visible sign of authorship, the equivalence between author, text, and signature. Pound had long held, because of his strong beliefs in authorship, that authors were obliged to sign their texts. But during the war, Pound decided that Radio Roma could use his texts anonymously or broadcast them under a series of pseudonyms because doing so would increase their propaganda value, complicating Pound's claim that he was speaking as a free citizen of America (signing off on his authorship effectively gave his literary property to an enemy state). After Pound was deemed mentally incompetent, though, his signature was no longer his to give away; it was, in fact, voided of any legal standing or value. To the end of his life, Pound was not a legal entity but a legal fiction, a committee of one. It was a convenient fiction in some ways, though, as many of those closest to Pound freely signed his work in their name, taking part in "literary camouflage" to disguise his authorship.

Notes

1 *NYT*, October 2, 1942, 1.
2 FDR to Francis Biddle, October 1, 1942, DOJ Pound.
3 *Cramer v. United States*, 325 U.S. 1 (1945), 21. See also Bradley Chapin, *The American Law of Treason: Revolutionary and Early National Origins* (Seattle: University of Washington Press, 1964).
4 J. H. Leek, "Treason and the Constitution," *The Journal of Politics* 13.4 (November 1951): 604–22, at 622.
5 Quoted in Leek, "Treason and the Constitution," 604.
6 Francis Biddle, *In Brief Authority* (Garden City, NY: Doubleday, 1962), 234; Geoffrey R. Stone, *Perilous Times: Free Speech in Wartime* (New York: W.W. Norton, 2004), 173. On Biddle's play, see Georgetown, Francis Biddle Papers, box 10, file 31.
7 Biddle, *In Brief Authority*, 235.
8 James Rowe, Jr., to Francis Biddle, March 23, 1942, in FDR Presidential Library, Biddle Papers, Box 1, File "Propaganda, Domestic."
9 Quoted in Patrick S. Washburn, *A Question of Sedition: The Federal Government's Investigation of the Black Press During World War II* (Oxford: Oxford University Press, 1986), 68.
10 James Rowe, Jr., to Francis Biddle, April 29, 1942, in FDR Biddle, Box 1, File "James Rowe, Jr."
11 Fireside Chat, April 28, 1942, at https://www.presidency.ucsb.edu/documents/fireside-chat-5.
12 Freda Kirchwey, "Curb the Fascist Press!", *The Nation*, March 28, 1942, 357–8.
13 ACLU to Attorney General Francis Biddle, January 4, 1943, Princeton, ACLU Archive, MC#001, 859.10.
14 John Roy Carlson, *Under Cover: My Four Years in the Nazi Underworld of America* (New York: E. P. Dutton, 1943), 9.
15 *Washington Star*, May 10, 1942, in FDR Biddle, Scrapbook; Alan Hynd, *Passport to Treason: The Inside Story of Spies in America* (New York: Robert M. McBridge & Company, 1943), 26.

16 "Voices of Defeat," *Life*, April 13, 1942, 86, 88, 90–4, 97–100, at 86, 88.
17 *Wimmer v. United States*, 264 F. 11, 12–13 (6th Cir. 1920).
18 Boris Bittker to Oscar Cox, February 9, 1943, DOJ Pound.
19 Willard Hurst, "Treason in the United States. III. Under the Constitution," *Harvard Law Review* 58.6 (July 1945): 806–57, at 806–7.
20 Chief Justice Harlan F. Stone, memo, March 22, 1944, in LOC, Robert H. Jackson Papers, box 131.
21 Robert Jackson, Memo, July 12, 1944, in LOC Jackson, box 131.
22 Frank Murphy to Robert Jackson, n.d., in LOC Jackson, box 131.
23 *Cramer*, 29. The Lex Julia Majestatis considered the two elements of treason separately, stipulating that "the law will punish the intention, and the perpetration of the crime with equal severity" (Cod. 9,8,5). Similarly, "compassing or imagining" the King's death in English treason law dealt largely with intention.
24 Robert Jackson, memo, April 18, 1944, LOC Jackson, box 131.
25 *Cramer*, 31, 33.
26 *Cramer*, footnote 7. Footnote 7 cites *United States v Haupt*, 47 F. Supp. 836, 839, *rev'd on other grounds*, 136 F.2d 661.
27 W. K. Wimsatt, Jr., and M. C. Beardsley, "The Intentional Fallacy," *The Sewanee Review* 54.3 (July–September 1946): 468–88.
28 Edward S. Corwin, *Total War and the Constitution* (New York: Alfred A. Knopf, 1947), 125–6.
29 Paul T. Crane, "Did the Court Kill the Treason Charge: Reassessing *Cramer v. United States* and Its Significance," *Florida State University Law Review* 36 (2009): 635–96, at 661, 665–6.
30 See Barak Kushner, "Treacherous Allies: The Cold War in East Asia and American Postwar Anxiety," *Journal of Contemporary History* 45.4 (2010): 812–43.
31 Two treason convictions did not concern radio propaganda: Tomoya Kawakita, who while employed for a Japanese company tortured American POWs, and Martin Monti, a serviceman who stole a plane and flew it behind enemy lines, attempting to enroll in the Luftwaffe.
32 *Cramer*, note 42.
33 *Cramer*, 54. This language was repeated in similar terms in the charge to the jury in the Chandler case.
34 *Chandler v. United States*, 171 F.2d 921, 939 (1st Cir. 1948).
35 *Chandler*, 938.
36 Ezra Pound [EP], *Jefferson and/or Mussolini: L'Idea Statale, Fascism as I Have Seen It* (London: Stanley Nott, 1935), ix; EP, "Is It War?", *Time and Tide*, September 30, 1933: 1148–9, in *Ezra Pound's Poetry and Prose: Contributions to Periodicals*, ed. Lea Baecherl, A. Walton Litz, and James Longenbach, 11 vols. (New York: Garland, 1991), 6: 79–80, at 79. Hereafter cited as *P&P*. All previously published Pound material reprinted by permission of New Directions Publishing Corp.
37 EP, "Abject and Utter Farce," *Harkness Hoot* 4.2 (November 1933): 6–14, in *P&P*, 6: 87–94, at 88; "Judas Had It," *Outrider* 1.2 (January 1934): 1,3, in *P&P*, 6: 119.
38 EP to Ubaldo delgi Ulberti, April 5, 1934; quoted in Catherine E. Paul, *Fascist Directive: Ezra Pound and Italian Cultural Nationalism* (Clemson, SC: Clemson University Press, 2016), 146.
39 EP to William Borah, November 27, 1933, in *The Correspondence of Ezra Pound and Senator William Borah*, ed. Sarah C. Holmes (Urbana: University of Illinois Press, 2001), 1; EP, *ABC of Economics* (London: Faber and Faber, 1933), 53; EP to Gaetano Polverelli, quoted in Matthew Feldman, *Ezra Pound's Fascist Propaganda, 1933–1945* (London: Palgrave Macmillan, 2013), 21.
40 EP, "Is It War?", *P&P* 6: 79–80.
41 EP, "Clean It," HRC, EP Collection, 2.7; EP to Ingrid Davies, July 30, 1955, HRC, EP Collection, 6.1.

42 Quoted in Mary de Rachewiltz, "Fragments of an Atmosphere," *Agenda* (1979/80): 157–70, at 162. On the EIAR, see Alberto Monticone, *Il Fascismo al Microfono: Radio e politica in Italia (1924–1945)* (Roma: Edizioni Studium, 1978), Francesca Cavarocchi, *Avanguardie dello spirit: Il fascismo e la propaganda culturale all'estero* (Rome: Carocci, 2010); Luigi Petrella, *Staging the Fascist War: The Ministry of Popular Culture and Italian Propaganda on the Home Front, 1938–1943* (Oxford: Peter Lang, 2016), and Antonio Papa, *Storia politica della radio in Italia, Dalla Guerra d'Etiopia al crollo del fascismo, 1935–1943* (Naples: Guida Editori, 1978).

43 Robert O. Paxton, *The Anatomy of Fascism* (London: Allen Lane, 2004), 17; on Italy as a "propaganda state," see R. J. B. Bosworth, *Mussolini's Italy: Life Under the Dictatorship, 1915–1945* (New York: Penguin, 2006), 414.

44 Ministero della Cultura Popolare to EP, January 18, 1941, YBL MSS 43, 34.1439.

45 EP to Viola Baxter Jordan, August 4, 1941, YBL MSS 175, 2.76; Frank Amprim to J. Edgar Hoover, May 26, 1945, FBI Pound, I.11, 1089–1092. See pay slips in YBL MSS 53, 39.896–7.

46 EP to Adriano Ungaro, February 6, 1941, quoted in Tim Redman, *Ezra Pound and Italian Fascism* (Cambridge: Cambridge University Press, 1991), 209.

47 EP to James Laughlin, June 28, 1941, in *Ezra Pound and James Laughlin: Selected Letters*, ed. David M. Gordon (New York: Norton, 1994), 132.

48 EP to William Joyce, n.d. [1941], YBL MSS 43, 26.1117.

49 EP to the Ministero della Cultura Popolare, May 4, 1941, YBL MSS 43, 34.1439.

50 Untitled and undated document, YBL MSS 43, 128.5299.

51 EP to William Joyce, July 19, 1941, YBL MSS 43, 26.1117.

52 FBI Pound, I.8, 867.

53 FBI Pound, I.8, 871.

54 "Verso Impostazione," n.d., YBL, MSS 43, 128.5299.

55 "Bisogna," n.d. [January 1943?], YBL MSS 43, 128.5290.

56 FBI Pound, I.8, 867.

57 FBI Pound, I.8, 871.

58 EP, "The Ignorant Ignorami," letter to the editor (October 22, 1934), *The New York Herald*, in *P&P* 6: 206.

59 EP to Adriano Ungaro, June 27, 1941, quoted in Redman, *Pound and Italian Fascism*, 211.

60 EP to di Marzio, December 28, 1941, quoted in Tim Redman, "The Repatriation of Pound, 1939–1942: A View from the Archives," *Paideuma* 8.3 (Winter 1979): 447–57, at 456.

61 Office Memorandum from the Chief of Internal Security to the Chief of Communications and Records, May 30, 1945, DOJ Pound. The relevant archival files for anonymous broadcasts by Pound from December 1941 to January 1942 contain over 30 original texts, with Pound sometimes writing up to three broadcasts per day.

62 Various broadcasts in YBL MSS 43, 127.5264–5.

63 No title, February 27, 1942 (anonymous), YBL MSS 43, 127.5267.

64 "Naiveté," February 13, 1942 (anonymous), YBL MSS 43, 127.5267.

65 "Jackalls and Vermin," February 11, 1942, YBL MSS 43, 127.5267; "American Carelessness," n.d., YBL MSS 43, 128.5323.

66 Quoted in Leonard W. Doob, "Introduction," in *"Ezra Pound Speaking": Radio Speeches of World War II*, ed. Leonard W. Doob (Westport, CT: Greenwood Press, 1978), xi–xv, at xiii.

67 "On Resuming" (January 29, 1942), *Radio Speeches*, 23–7.

68 "Universality" (May 4, 1942), *Radio Speeches*, 120.

69 "England" (March 15, 1942), *Radio Speeches*, 59–62.

70 American Imperialist, no title, April 13, 1942, YBL MSS 43, 126.5223.

71 "Relazione tecnica di Giovanni Telesio, funzionario dell'Ispettorato per la Radiodiffusione e la Televisione, sull'organizzazione radiofonica tedesca," October 1, 1940, in Franco Monteleone,

La Radio italiana nel periodo fascista: Studio e documenti: 1922–1945 (Venice: Marsilio, 1976), 278–86, at 280.
72 "Napoleon, etc." (March 2, 1942), *Radio Speeches*, 49.
73 "MacLEISH" (April 23, 1942), *Radio Speeches*, 104.
74 American Imperialist, no title, n.d. [June 1943], YBL MSS 43, 126.5233.
75 "Violence" (June 15, 1942), *Radio Speeches*, 172.
76 EP to William Joyce, July 19, 1941, YBL MSS 43, 26.1117.
77 Giorgio Almirante, "To Unite" (1944), quoted in Luisa Quartermaine, *Mussolini's Last Republic: Propaganda and Politics in the Italian Social Republic (R.S.I.), 1943–45* (Exeter: Elm Bank, 2000), 180–1.
78 Quoted in Rachewiltz, "Fragments of an Atmosphere," 169.
79 EP, "D'accordo," *Il Popolo di Alessandria*, June 8, 1944, in *P&P* 7: 234; EP to Fernando Mezzasoma, February 27, 1944, quoted in C. David Heymann, *Ezra Pound, The Last Rower: A Political Profile* (New York: Seaver Books, 1976), 333.
80 Quoted in James Strachey Barnes, *A British Fascist in the Second World War: The Italian War Diary of James Strachey Barnes, 1943–45*, ed. Claudia Baldoli and Brendan Fleming (London: Bloomsbury, 2014), 116, 217.
81 EP to DP, November 26, 1943, quoted in A. David Moody, *Ezra Pound: Poet: A Portrait of the Man and His Work*, vol. 3: *The Tragic Years, 1939–1972* (Oxford: Oxford University Press, 2015), 3: 71.
82 EP to Alessandro Pavolini, January 18, 1944, FBI Pound, I.10. See H. James Burgwyn, *Mussolini and the Salò Republic, 1943–1945: The Failure of a Puppet Regime* (London: Palgrave Macmillan, 2018), 42–5, 52–5.
83 EP, note to the Servizio Ufficio Razza, n.d., YBL MSS 43, 127.5282.
84 EP, note, n.d., YBL MSS 43, 127.5282.
85 Francesco Monotti, quoted in Moody, *Ezra Pound: Poet*, 3: 70.
86 EP to Alessandro Pavolini, January 18, 1944, FBI Pound, I.10, 1004; memo, Pound correspondence, FBI Pound, I.11, 1175 (which summarizes from correspondence in Pound's personal folder at the Ministry of Popular Culture of the RSI; those complaints come from letters dated January 16, 1944, and January 26, 1944).
87 EP to Ubaldi degli Uberti, November 2, 1944, FBI Pound, I.7, 767.
88 Georg von Lilienfeld to EP, January 2, 1944, YBL MSS 53, 2.43.
89 EP to Adolf Mahr, 1945, quoted in Feldman, *Ezra Pound's Fascist Propaganda*, 159.
90 No title, November 23, 1944, YBL MSS 43, 128.5291.
91 Sworn Statement by EP, May 7, 1945, in Ezra and Dorothy Pound, *Letters in Captivity, 1945–1946*, ed. Omar Pound and Robert Spoo (Oxford: Oxford University Press, 1999), 65.
92 Quoted in Heymann, *Last Rower*, 142.
93 EP to Carl Goedel, n.d., YBL MSS 43, 18.846.
94 EP, no title, December 1944, YBL MSS 43, 127.5282; EP, note, March 28 [1944], YBL MSS 43, 127.5282.
95 MI5 Report on Pound, June 19, 1940, KV 2/875.
96 Memo on Ezra Pound, November 30, 1942, FBI Pound, I.1, 73.
97 New York City OFR, January 1, 1943, I.2, 131. All field reports from FBI Pound cited as OFR.
98 Washington, D.C., OFR, January 13, 1943, I.2, 141; Boston OFR, February 6, 1943, I.2, 167; Washington, D.C., OFR, February 13, 1943 (I.2, 172), March 16, 1943 (I.2, 201).
99 Newark OFR, March 17, 1943, I.2, 206.
100 New York City OFR, April 27, 1943, I.2, 234.
101 Washington, D.C., OFR, January 13, 1943, I.2, 143; Boston OFR, February 6, 1943, I.2, 165, 166; OFRs (collated), February 16, 1943, I.2, 180, 177.

102 Newark OFR, March 17, 1943, I.2, 206. In a 1941 essay, Williams had noted: "Pound is another case for the psychiatrists and it doesn't call for a great expert at that. His position today is the result of deficiencies, long apparent to his friends, which have finally overthrown him." See his "Ezra Pound: Lord Ga-Ga!", *Decision* 1.3 (September 1941): 16–24, at 16.
103 Los Angeles OFR, March 2, 1943, I.2, 193; see also Salt Lake City OFR, April 2, 1943, I.2, 213–4, and OFRs (collated), February 16, 1943, I.2, 177.
104 Grand Jury indictment, July 26, 1943, FBI Pound, I.3, 292.
105 DOJ Press Release, July 26, 1943, Georgetown FBP, 7.68.
106 Frank L. Amprim File, FOIA Request 1415563-000; Amprim to Colonel Earle B. Nichols, March 25, 1945, in National Archives (College Park, MD), RG 65, 61-109877-Sec. 1; FBI Memo, August 23, 1944, FBI Pound, I.3, 375.
107 Memo, August 23, 1944, FBI Pound, I.3, 376.
108 Francis Biddle to Henry L. Stimson, January 24, 1944, National Archives, NAI 3376702, box 4.
109 Amprim to Lt. Colonel Stephen J. Spingarn, April 27, 1945, National Archives, NAI 7362005, Ezra Pound XE004765, container 616.
110 Giorgio Amendola, *Unità*, April 29, 1945, quoted in Burgwyn, *Mussolini and Salò*, 307.
111 Quoted in Roy Palmer Domenico, *Italian Fascists on Trial, 1943–1948* (Chapel Hill: University of North Carolina Press, 1991), 148.
112 Sworn Statement by EP, May 7, 1945, in *Letters Captivity*, 61–7.
113 Amprim to J. Edgar Hoover, July 12, 1945, FBI Pound, I.7, 838; EP, Supplement to Sworn Statement, May 8, 1945, in *Letters Captivity*, 69–77.
114 Edd Johnson, "Pound, Accused of Treason, Calls Hitler Saint, Martyr," *Chicago Sun*, May 8, 1945; reprinted in Humphrey Carpenter, *A Serious Character: The Life of Ezra Pound* (London: Faber and Faber, 1988), 650–2.
115 AFHQ Message Center, FX 79856, May 22, 1945, WO 204/12602.
116 Robert L. Allen, "The Cage," *Esquire*, February 1958; reprinted in *A Casebook on Ezra Pound*, ed. William Van O'Connor and Edward Stone (New York: Thomas Y. Crowell Company, 1959), 33–8, at 33.
117 Psychiatric report by Captain R. W. Fenner, June 14, 1945; psychiatric report by Captain Walter H. Baer, June 15, 1945, quoted in Ben D. Kimpel and T. C. Duncan Eaves, "More on Pound's Prison Experience," *American Literature* 53.3 (November 1981): 469–76, at 471–2.
118 Major General M. G. White to AGWAR Washington, June 21, 1945, WO 204/12602.
119 Brig. Gen. John M. Weir to Judge Advocate, Mediterranean Theatre, July 3, 1945, quoted in Kimpel and Eaves, "More on Pound's Prison Experience," 470.
120 Psychiatric evaluation by William Weisdorf, July 17, 1945, quoted in Kimpel and Eaves, "More on Pound's Prison Experience," 472–3.
121 EP to DP, September 20, 1945, in *Letters Captivity*, 89.
122 EP to DP, September 28, 1945, in *Letters Captivity*, 97.
123 Ezra Pound [signed], n.d., WO 204/12602.
124 Military Command to Amprim, June 25, 1945, FBI Pound, I.6, 619.
125 Amprim to J. Edgar Hoover, September 7, 1945, FBI Pound, I.10, 1071.
126 DOJ cablegram, October 22, 1945, FBI Pound, I.11, 1253.
127 AGWAR to COMGENMED, November 16, 1945, WO 204/12602.
128 Affidavit of P. V. Holder, November 20, 1945, in *Letters Captivity*, 199.
129 *Washington Post*, November 19, 1945, 1.
130 On Cornell, see his self-published memoir, *Lexcetera* (Central Valley, NY: n.p., 1971), as well as Swarthmore College Archives, RG 6, Series 10, No. 1000116 (Alumni: Cornell, Julien Class of 1930).
131 Cornell, *Lexcetera*, 86; Julien Cornell to ACLU, February 17, 1944, Swarthmore College Peace Collection, Julien Cornell Collection (JCC), DG 010, Box 2.

132 Cornell to Winslow Ames, October 15, 1945, Swarthmore, JCC, Box 3; Julien Cornell, *The Conscientious Objector and the Law* (New York: John Day 1943), 1. See also *Conscience and the State: Legal and Administrative Problems of Conscientious Objectors, 1943–1944* (New York: John Day, 1944).

133 Cornell to A. J. Muste, October 22, 1942, Swarthmore, JCC, Box 1.

134 Julien Cornell, *New World Primer* (New York: New Directions, 1947), 11, 12.

135 Cornell to Laughlin, November 21, 1945, in Julien Cornell, *The Trial of Ezra Pound* (New York: John Day, 1966), 13–4. Hereafter cited as *Trial EP*.

136 *Trial EP*, 16.

137 Moore to Cornell, December 4, 1945, YBL MSS 176, 1.25.

138 Cornell referred to "the gang of Italian ~~dago~~ witnesses who are living in a swank hotel at government expense" as the reason for the government pushing for a swift trial; see Cornell to Laughlin, November 28, 1945, YBL MSS 176, 1.14.

139 Cornell to Moore, December 24, 1945, HRC Pound, 11.7.

140 "Affidavit," *Trial EP*, 18–9.

141 Moody, *Ezra Pound: Poet*, 3: 182; *Trial EP*, 19.

142 *Trial EP*, 20, 21.

143 *New York Herald Tribune*, November 28, 1945, in *Trial EP*, 24.

144 On November 30, 1945, Cornell wrote to Overholser asking if he would conduct the examination of Pound, but Overholser demurred, noting that as a government official he could not do that (see Cornell to Overholser, November 30, 1945, YBL MSS 176, 1.31). On the four psychiatrists, see E. Fuller Torrey, *The Roots of Treason: Ezra Pound and the Secrets of St. Elizabeths* (London: Sidgwick & Jackson, 1984), 187–91. On Muncie, see Interview with Dr. Wendell Muncie (1975), Victor Almon McKusick Collection, item no. 200548, uploaded at https://soundcloud.com/hopkins-medical-archives/wendell-muncie-interviewed-by-robert-goodman-and-john-bertolatus-1975. Accessed: January 21, 2026.

145 Cornell to Muncie, December 6, 1945, YBL MSS 176, 2.45.

146 *Trial EP*, 36.

147 See LOC, Winfred Overholser Papers, Scrapbooks.

148 King, quoted in Moody, *Ezra Pound: Poet*, 3: 189; psychiatric report in Cornell to Arthur Moore, December 13, 1945, HRC, 11.7.

149 The psychiatric finding showed how "American authorities and officials" were rushing to "acquit all those Nazi sympathizers, Nazis and reactionaries" so that it could curry favor with anti-communist forces ("Cazul Tradatorului Ezra Pond [*sic*] Departe a fi Solvat" [The Case of Ezra Pound Far from Being Resolved], *Românul American*, January 5, 1946, 2). An opposing conspiracy theory saw a liberal metropolitan elite bent on protecting Pound. A contemporary medical critique of the finding can be found in Fredric Wertham, "The Road to Rapallo," *American Journal of Psychotherapy* 3.4 (October 1949): 585–600.

150 9 Eng. Rep. 718, 722 (1843).

151 Theron L. Caudle to Kenneth C. Royall, May 7, 1947, DOJ Gillars.

152 *Dusky v. United States*, 362 U.S. 402 (1960).

153 William Foley, memo, November 29, 1945, DOJ Pound.

154 Examination of Dr. Parker, December 21, 1945, quoted in Moody, *Ezra Pound: Poet*, 3: 193.

155 Quoted in Torrey, *Roots of Treason*, 203.

156 *Trial EP*, 187.

157 Montgomery Belgion, *Victors' Justice: A Letter Intended to Have Been Sent to a Friend Recently in Germany* (Chicago: Regnery, 1949), 86. For Henry Swabey, "He has doubtless given offence by showing who the real enemies of his country are, and the fear that he would continue to do so has led its rulers to apply the muzzle." In "The Crime of Ezra Pound," *The Social Crediter*, March 31, 1951, 2. Eustace Mullins actually believed that Pound deliberately sought

out an indictment for treason so that he would have "an opportunity to discuss openly his economic ideas" (224)—but the state did not wish to provide that stage; see Eustace Mullins, *This Difficult Individual, Ezra Pound* (New York: Fleet Publishing, 1961).

158 *Washington Star*, February 19, 1946.
159 William Foley, memo, October 28, 1948, DOJ Pound.
160 DOJ to Overholser, November 1, 1948, DOJ Pound.
161 Quoted in William Foley to James McInerney, June 5, 1950, DOJ Pound.
162 William Foley, memo, April 23, 1952, DOJ Pound.
163 "Memo regarding Winfred Overholser, M.D., Superintendent, Saint Elizabeths Hospital, Washington, DC," in National Archives, RG 418, Box 30; Thomas Otto, *St. Elizabeths Hospital: A History* (Washington, D.C.: U.S. General Services Administration, 2013), 293.
164 Rufus King to T. S. Eliot, October 27, 1953, Lilly, Pound II, Box 4.
165 Overholser to Stanley E. Krumbiegel, August 18, 1953, National Archives, Ezra Pound Case File, Box 2.
166 William F. Tompkins to Overholser, September 30, 1954, DOJ Pound.
167 Overholser to William F. Tompkins, October 13, 1954, National Archives, Ezra Pound Case File, box 2.
168 *Trial EP*, 160–71.
169 Ibid., 175–85.
170 Ibid., 188, 205, 158, 177.
171 *United States v. One Book Called "Ulysses,"* 5 F. Supp. 182, 183 (1933).
172 Laughlin to Eliot, February 15, 1946, Lilly, Pound II, Box 9.
173 Cornell to Arthur V. Moore, April 16, 1946, YBL MSS 176, 1.27.
174 Albert Q. Maisel, "Bedlam 1946: Most U.S. Mental Hospitals Are a Shame and a Disgrace," *Life*, May 6, 1946, 102–10, 112, 115–16, 118.
175 EP to Cornell, n.d., YBL MSS 176, 2.49.
176 DP to Cornell, November 6, 1946, YBL MSS 176, I.36.
177 Cornell to Laughlin, January 27, 1947, YBL MSS 176, 1.18.
178 EP to Cornell, n.d., YBL MSS 176, 2.50; DP to Cornell, September 25, 1947, YBL MSS 176, 1.38.
179 Cornell to Olga Rudge, March 8, 1948, YBL MSS 176, 2.56.
180 Motion for bail, January 1947, YBL MSS 176, 3.95.
181 T. Vincent Quinn, Assistant Attorney General, to Overholser, March 3, 1948, National Archives, Ezra Pound Case File, Box 1.
182 Cornell to Laughlin, January 30, 1947, YBL MSS 176, 1.18.
183 Houghton, AMS 2077, Box 720.
184 EP to Ingrid Davies, March 2, 1955, HRC Pound, 5.13.
185 Order to Pay Maintenance Allowance to Patient's Son, and For an Allowance for Patient's Taxes and Miscellaneous Personal Expenditures, January 26, 1950, Lilly, Pound VI, Box 2, Folder 68.
186 See Lilly, Pound VI, Box 1, Folders 24, 25.
187 Moore to EP, June 7, 1959, Lilly, Pound VI, Box 3.
188 Writ of habeas corpus on behalf of Ezra Pound, February 17, 1948, YBL MSS 176, 3.96.
189 DP to Cornell, March 13, 1948, YBL MSS 176, 1.42.
190 DP to Cornell, January 26, 1948, YBL MSS 176, 1.42.
191 DP to Moore, March 15, 1948, Lilly, Pound VI, Box 3.
192 Moore to Cornell, March 19, 1948, YBL MSS 176, 1.28; Laughlin to Cornell, December 14, 1948, Houghton, AMS 2077, item 399.
193 Cornell to John Edwards, December 2, 1957, YBL MSS 176, 1.5.
194 Bernice Carey to Bennett Cerf, February 24, 1946, Princeton, AM13111, folder 3.

195 Hugh Kenner, "In the Caged Panther's Eyes," *Hudson Review* 1.4 (Winter 1949): 580–6, at 580.

196 Laughlin to Eliot, December 23, 1945, Lilly, Pound II, Box 9; Laughlin, "Editor's Notes," *New Directions* 9 (1946); quoted in Greg Barnhisel, *James Laughlin, New Directions, and the Remaking of Ezra Pound* (Amherst: University of Massachusetts Press, 2005), 92.

197 Ann Smith to Bennett Cerf, n.d., Princeton, AM13111, folder 21.

198 Bennett Cerf, "Trade Winds: The Case of Ezra Pound," *SRL*, February 9, 1946, 26–7, at 27.

199 Bennett Cerf, *At Random: The Reminiscences of Bennett Cerf* (New York: Random House, 1977), 172; Conrad Aiken to Charles Norman, October 30, 1946, University of Pennsylvania, Kislak, Ms. Coll. 183, folder 18; Conrad Aiken to James Laughlin, July 18, 1945, Houghton, AMS 2077, item 21; Bennett Cerf, "Trade Winds," *Saturday Review of Literature*, March 16, 1946, 32.

200 Rabbi Jacob Philip Rudin to Cerf, February 13, 1946, Princeton, AM 131111, folder 19; Neville to Cerf, February 21, 1946, folder 17.

201 James to Cerf, February 15, 1946, Princeton, AM 131111, folder 11; Chase to Cerf, February 13, 1946, folder 4.

202 Margaret Ballard to Cerf, February 19, 1946, Princeton, AM 131111, folder 2.

203 Patrick LePaitre to Cerf, February 8, 1946, Princeton, AM 131111, folder 13; Bernice Carey to Cerf, February 24, 1946, folder 3.

204 Edgell to Cerf, February 11, 1946, Princeton, AM 131111, folder 6; Behrens to Cerf, February 15, 1946, folder 2.

205 Stephen H. Fritchman to Cerf, February 19, 1946, Princeton, AM 131111, folder 8.

206 Esther Alger to Cerf, February 10, 1946, Princeton, AM 131111, folder 1.

207 Betty Bold to Cerf, February 16, 1946, Princeton, AM 131111, folder 2.

208 Helen Ramsey to Cerf, February 15, 1946, Princeton, AM 131111, folder 18.

209 Cerf, "Trade Winds," *SRL*, March 16, 1946, 32.

210 Cornell to EP, May 2, 1946, YBL MSS 176, 2.48; Laughlin to TSE, May 22, 1946, Houghton, AMS 2077, item 513; Cerf to Cornell, May 21, 1946, YBL MSS 176, 1.2.

211 "Report to the Librarian of Congress on a Meeting of the Fellows of the Library of Congress in American Letters, November 18–19, 1948," Georgetown, Katherine Biddle Papers (KBP), 37.29.

212 "*The Pisan Cantos* Wins for Ezra Pound First Award of Bollingen in Poetry," Library of Congress Press Release No. 542, February 20, 1949, in O'Connor and Stone, *Casebook*, 44–5, at 45.

213 Ray West, "Extracts from a Journal: 1949," in O'Connor and Stone, *Casebook*, 67–73, at 67.

214 Quoted in Michael Coyle and Roxana Preda, *Ezra Pound and the Career of Modern Criticism: Professional Attention* (Rochester, NY: Camden House, 2018), 25.

215 Dwight Macdonald, "Homage to Twelve Judges," *Politics* 6.1 (Winter 1949): 1–2.

216 William Barrett, "A Prize for Ezra Pound," *Partisan Review* 16.4 (April 1949): 344–7, at 344, 347.

217 W. H. Auden, "The Question of the Pound Award," *Partisan Review* 16.5 (May 1949): 513.

218 Clement Greenberg, "The Question of the Pound Award," *Partisan Review* 16.5 (May 1949): 515.

219 Laughlin to EP, March 28, 1949, IU Lilly, Pound II, box 9; details of marketing blitz in Laughlin to TSE, March 24, 1949, Houghton, AMS 2027, item 513.

220 Robert Hillyer, *In Pursuit of Poetry* (New York: McGraw-Hill, 1960), 7; Hillyer, "In My Library, Late Afternoon," in *Collected Poems* (New York: Knopf, 1961), 21.

221 Robert Hillyer, "Treason's Strange Fruit: The Case of Ezra Pound and the Bollingen Award," *Saturday Review of Literature*, June 11, 1949: 9–11, 28, at 9.

222 Hillyer, "Treason's Strange Fruit," 11.

223 Harrison Smith to Archibald MacLeish, May 20, 1949, Houghton, AMS2029; Smith to Malcolm Cowley, quoted in Karen Leick, "Ezra Pound v. *The Saturday Review of Literature*," *Journal of Modern Literature* 25.2 (Winter 2001–2): 19–37, at 19. See, more broadly, Alan Filreis, *Counter-Revolution of the Word: The Conservative Attack on Modern Poetry, 1945–1960* (Chapel Hill: Univeristy of North Carolina Press, 2008).
224 Robert Hillyer, "Poetry's New Priesthood," *SRL*, June 18, 1949, 7–8, 38, at 38.
225 Malcolm Cowley, "The Battle Over Ezra Pound," *New Republic*, October 3, 1949, 17–20, at 17.
226 "The Anti-Poet All Told," *Poetry* 74.5 (August 1949): 274–85, at 278.
227 Barnhisel, *Remaking*, 135.
228 Hugh Kenner, "Retrospect 1985," HRC, Hugh Kenner Collection.
229 Katherine Biddle, Journal, April 21, 1949, Georgetown, KBP.
230 Marcella [Spann] Booth, "Through the Smoke Hole: Ezra Pound's Last Year at St. Elizabeths," *Paideuma* 3 (Winter 1974): 329–34, at 329.
231 This account is drawn from "Monthly Report for month of January 1946," in National Archives, Records of Saint Elizabeths Hospital (RG 418), Administrative Files, Ca. 1921–1964, Box 75; and LOC, Winfred Overholser Papers, Scrapbooks. See more generally Daniel Swift, *The Bughouse: The Poetry, Politics and Madness of Ezra Pound* (New York: Farrar, Straus and Giroux, 2017).
232 EP to Ingrid Davies, December 8, 1954, HRC Pound, 5.13.
233 Samuel A. Silk to Olga Rudge, May 4, 1948, National Archives, Ezra Pound Case File, Box 1.
234 Bill MacNaughton, "Pound, A Brief Memoir: 'Chi Lavora, Ora,'" *Paideuma* 3 (Winter 1974): 319–24, at 319.
235 EP to Ingrid Davies, May 7, 1955, HRC Pound, 6.1.
236 EP to Ingrid Davies, March 28, 1955, HRC Pound, 5.15.
237 See Georgetown, Giovanni Giovannini Papers.
238 Robert Corrigan, "Literature and Politics: The Case of Ezra Pound Reconsidered," *Prospects* 2 (1976): 463–82, at 474.
239 Agnes Bedford to Dorothy Pound, December 1, 1947, Lilly, Pound II; EP to Noel Stock, June 5, 1955, HRC Pound, 9.6.
240 DP to Moore, May 8, 1946, Lilly, Pound VI, Box 3.
241 EP to Denis Goacher, May 18, 1954, HRC Pound, 7.4.
242 Ronald Duncan, "A Memoir of Ezra Pound," HRC, Ronald Duncan Collection, 18.10.
243 *P&P*, 8: 348.
244 EP to Ingrid Davies, May 7, 1955, HRC Pound, 6.1.
245 EP to Dallam Simpson, n.d. [early 1948], HRC Pound, 9.2.
246 EP to Noel Stock, August 1, 1955, quoted in Michael J. Alleman, "A Pound of Flesh: Ezra Pound at St. Elizabeths," unpublished PhD dissertation, University of Dallas, 2007, 59.
247 EP to Denis Goacher, February 19, 1953, HRC Pound, 7.4.
248 DP to Moore, January 15, 1950, Lilly, Pound VI, Box 3.
249 EP marginalia in James Laughlin to EP, September 26, 1950, Lilly, Pound II, Box 9; EP to Ingrid Davies, March 18, 1955, HRC Pound, 5.14.
250 Ronald Duncan to EP, September 2, 1949, Lilly, Pound II, Box 4.
251 Norman Holmes Pearson to EP, February 14, 1956, YBL MSS 43, 40.1677.
252 Simpson to Russell, n.d., HRC Pound, 14.5. For an extended reading of *Four Pages*, see my article "Pound's *Four Pages*: 'Literary Camouflage' and Postwar Anonymous Propaganda," *PMLA* 137.3 (May 2022): 424–41.
253 EP to Ronald Duncan, November 13, [1950], HRC Pound, 6.5; EP to Virginia Cazort Risse, January 17, [1957], HRC Pound, 8.6.
254 EP to Ronald Duncan, April 19, 1953, HRC Pound, 6.5.

255 The massive archive on Pound's relationship with Frederick Morgan is at Princeton, C1091, Hudson Review Archives, Series III.
256 Tom Carter to New Directions, May 20, 1960, Lilly, Pound II, Box 2.
257 Thomas Cole to EP, October 3, 1952, Lilly, Pound II, Box 2.
258 EP to Brigit Patmore, November 20, 1954, HRC Pound, 8.2.
259 EP to Virginia Cazort Risse, May 24, 1955, HRC Pound, 8.5.
260 Robert Creeley to EP, September 1950, Lilly, Pound II, Box 3.
261 On the "lunatic fringe," as Harry M. Meacham called it (*The Caged Panther: Ezra Pound at Saint Elizabeths* [New York: Twayne, 1967], 55), see Alec Marsh, *John Kasper and Ezra Pound: Saving the Republic* (London: Bloomsbury Academic, 2015).
262 EP to Norman Holmes Pearson, n.d. [1957], YBL MSS 43, 40.1680.
263 EP to Archibald MacLeish, June 13, 1957, LOC, Archibald MacLeish Papers.
264 Denis Goacher to EP, May 9, 1953, YBL MSS 43, 19.842.
265 Kamran Javadizadeh, "The Institutionalization of the Postwar Poet," *Modernism/Modernity* 23.1 (January 2016): 113–39, at 116.
266 Olivia Rossetti Agresti to Noel Stock, December 21, 1957, HRC Pound, 11.3.
267 Laughlin to Eliot, November 10, 1950, Houghton, AMS 2077, item 513; Hugh Kenner to Moore, June 7, 1955, Lilly, Pound II.
268 Eliot to MacLeish, July 13, 1956, LOC, MacLeish Papers, Box 5.
269 Rufus King to T. S. Eliot, October 27, 1953, Lilly, Pound II.
270 "Intra-Office Buck Sheet," August 28, 1957, Princeton, ACLU MC#001, 1060.17.
271 Eva Hesse to EP, December 14, 1950, Lilly, Pound II.
272 Laughlin to Eliot, November 13, 1956, Houghton, AMS 2077, item 513.
273 Archibald MacLeish to Milton Eisenhower, January 11, 1957, LOC, MacLeish Papers.
274 Dag Hammarskjöld to Francis O. Wilcox, March 15, 1956, quoted in Marie-Noëlle Little, *The Knight and the Troubadour: Dag Hammarskjöld and Ezra Pound* (Uppsala: Dag Hammarskjöld Foundation, 2011), 97.
275 As quoted in Robert MacGregor to Laughlin, December 8, 1955, Houghton, AMS 2077, item 95.
276 DP to Moore, January 30, 1955, Lilly, Pound VI, Box 3.
277 See Arnold's memoir, *Fair Fights and Foul: A Dissenting Lawyer's Life* (New York: Harcourt, Brace & World, 1965), and the massive digitization of selections of his archive at the University of Wyoming.
278 See Bernard Lemelin, "Congressman Usher Burdick of North Dakota and the 'Ungodly Menace': Anti-United Nations Rhetoric, 1950–1958," *Great Plains Quarterly* 22 (2002): 163–81, at 169.
279 Kasper also added, for good measure, that "almost 100 percent of all psychiatric therapy is Jewish." Quoted in Claus-M. Naske, "Bob Bartlett and the Alaska Mental Health Act," *The Pacific Northwest Quarterly* 71.1 (January 1980): 31–9, at 39. The mystery of how Kasper was invited to testify before Congress as a "bookseller" from Merchantville, New Jersey, is cleared up by fellow St. Liz disciple Bill McNaughton, who claims that Kasper was romantically involved with one of Burdick's aides; see his "The Secret History of St. Elizabeths," *Paideuma* 30.1/2 (Spring/Fall 2001): 69–96, at 92.
280 See Charleen Swansea Papers #4027, Southern Historical Collection, The Wilson Library at the University of North Carolina at Chapel Hill. Swansea's letters to Sieber are contained in the Hal Sieber Collection, Saint Andrews University, Box 3.
281 Giovanni Giovannini to EP, October 22, 1957, YBL MSS 43, 19.833.
282 "The Medical, Legal, Literary, and Political Status of Ezra Weston (Loomis) Pound," Congressional Record Appendix A3894, April 29, 1958, at A3899.

283 This was the gist of James J. Kilpatrick's editorial "Ezra Pound: Set Him Free!", *Richmond News-Leader*, February 7, 1958. Kilpatrick was a prominent conservative and segregationist.

284 Motion to Dismiss Indictment, YBL MSS 176, 3.98.

285 Statement of Robert Frost, YBL MSS 176, 3.98. Frost was ushered into print during the First World War by Pound, but he did not care for the man: "neither you nor I," he told MacLeish, "would want to take him into our family or even into our neighborhood" (Frost to MacLeish, June 25, 1957, LOC, Archibald MacLeish Papers).

286 *Greenwood v. United States*, 350 U.S. 366 (1956), 375.

287 Denis Goacher to EP, April 20, 1958, YBL MSS43, 19.845.

288 Quoted in a press release by the Defenders of the American Constitution, April 1958, enclosed in EP to Ingrid Davies, April 10, 1958, HRC 6.3.

289 Thurman Arnold to ACLU, May 1, 1958, Princeton, ACLU, MC#001, 1060.17.

290 Pound interview in *Dagens Nyheter*, November 5, 1958, quoted in Meacham, *Caged Panther*, 37.

CHAPTER 3
A "HANDFUL" OF *MISÉRABLES*: INSTITUTIONS AND TRIALS OF THE FRENCH POSTWAR PURGE

Having cartwheeled through a series of avant-garde *isms* in an effort to "destroy literature," Paul Éluard emerged as the great poet of the French literary resistance. The "honor of poets," as his 1943 edited collection of clandestine poetry was titled, consisted of continuing the fight for "Liberté," the title of an incantatory lyric airdropped into the French countryside during the war. Upon liberation, though, honor was steered on a different course in Éluard's poetry, to a startling emotional point: hatred. In the 1945 collection *Au rendez-vous allemand*, hatred emerges as the rallying cry for all who desire justice. In "Avis" a man condemned to death by the Germans takes comfort in the knowledge that "he did not have one comrade | But millions and millions | To avenge him." The messianic imagery of the resistance martyr continues in "Courage": "The best among us died for the rest of us | And here their blood finds our heart." "Hatred," as "The Beautiful Balances of the Enemy" puts it, "delivers justice to our suffering." This was not a poetry of doubt or uncertainty, one which could be read in between the lines for seven types of ambiguity: "I see what I see / What I know / What is true." To speak of pity or mercy for collaborators was not an exercise in charity but a denial of justice:

> There is no stone more precious
> Than the desire to avenge the innocent
> There is no sky brighter
> Than the morning where the traitors perish
> There is no greeting on the earth
> So long as one can pardon the executioners.[1]

Éluard's desire to unleash hatred was a widely shared sentiment, with *L'Humanité* coming to speak of "hatred" as a "national duty."[2] During the war clandestine papers, produced and distributed under great risk, routinely reminded readers of their duty in language that, befitting the times, was *sanguinaire*: "Kill the Germans in order to purify our land, kill him because he kills ours, kill him in order to be free. Kill the traitors, kill those who denounce, those who have aided the enemy … Strike them down as mad dogs … Destroy them as you would vermin."[3] As early as 1941 local resistance groups began drawing up blacklists with the names, occupations, even addresses, of sellouts who had to pay the price.[4] One of those writers targeted, Marcel Jouhandeau, figured that "there won't be enough rope to hang" all those named in *Franc-Tireur*, *Libération*, *Résistance*, *Défense de la France*, and *Le Populaire*.[5] Secret tribunals issued calls for patriots to track down guilty collaborators. "Wherever they may be, whatever they might do," a pamphlet parachuted into France in 1943 intoned, "the traitors will be punished."[6] *La voix des traîtres* chronicled the names, deeds, and sayings of the collaborators who deserved the harshest of punishments, preferably without trial.[7] The "same furor that rises in all of us" now, one resistant noted, "unites us all."[8] The hymn sheet of hate infected even the moderate Christian venue *Esprit*: "Enough of this blind poison flowing through all our veins," it noted in December 1944, "and for this, whatever measures are needed, however brutal they have to be."[9] "Since June 1940," Simone de Beauvoir summarizes, "we have learned rage and hate."[10]

In this feverish atmosphere, Herbert Lottman estimates that from autumn 1943 to D-Day around 2,500 summary executions took place (admittedly, an even greater number of resistance fighters suffered at the hands of the Germans).[11] Around 30 percent of those polled by resistance militants in May 1944 felt that the "people's desire for revenge" should be allowed to "explode."[12] "Aux armes, citoyens!" screamed one headline.[13] Within a few hours of Paris's liberation (see Figure 3.1), the Conseil National de la Résistance called for collaborators to be shot at once. In Nice, there were

Figure 3.1 Surrender of German soldiers and officers at the Liberation of Paris, August 25, 1944. Photo 65639(20), Franklin D. Roosevelt Presidential Library & Museum. Public domain.

perhaps one hundred summary executions in two days; in the Dordogne, the reign of terror reportedly lasted three months.[14] Since the *sine qua non* of the resistance was clandestinity, anyone could claim to have been on the right side. Many of the so-called *résistants de septembre* (individuals who joined the resistance after the Liberation) were notoriously cruel, either driven by the “shame … at their inaction” or simply profiting from the lawless times to settle personal scores.[15]

While curtailing the *épuration sauvage* was necessary, a wholesale legal purge had its own problems. With the prospect of France’s liberation looming in April 1944, Charles De Gaulle agreed that “some traitors … some cowards … some fools” deserved the severest punishment, but, in an outline of what would eventually become the resistance myth, he noted that “the immense mass of the French people” had acted honorably during the war.[16] That message was repeated in mid-October (only “a handful of *misérables*” were guilty of treason while “the immense majority of us were and are French in good faith”) and then again in his New Year’s Eve message.[17] In the heat of the moment, not everyone agreed. A June 1945 *Esprit* editorial estimated that one-quarter of population had actively collaborated. The difference between De Gaulle’s “une poignée” (a handful) and *Esprit*’s tens of millions was not simply mathematical. A head of state could not let the wheels of justice become embroiled in a never-ending expiation, pursuing a course no matter the consequences. *Esprit*’s figure was inexact, but, given the opportunities for close contact that four years of occupation presented, it could not have been far off.

In the literary field, the German occupation ensured that no venue was outside the sphere of propaganda. Every published book required a Propaganda-Abteilung Frankreich authorization number, effectively giving it a Reich imprimatur.[18] The daily press could hardly stray from the official propaganda line. For their part, French publishers rushed to enforce a strict censorship, which led to some absurd situations, like Vichy banning a certain work but the Germans allowing it on the grounds of artistic expression (this was the case for one of Cocteau’s wartime plays). The smaller size of the literary field—in 1938 publishing houses used 38,000 tons of paper, but in the first six months of 1944, only around 1,500 tons were available—meant that the message of the few printed works was amplified.[19] The working definition of collaboration in a September 1944 decree that suspended all pro-German print outlets was simply appearing after the June 1940 armistice. As the resistance slogan had it, *littérature legal veut dire: littérature de trahison* (legal literature simply means the literature of treason).[20] By that formula, the number of collaborators in the press and literary field was in the thousands. That September decree, for instance, resulted in 900 periodicals “under the control of the enemy” being suspended; one could multiply that figure by however many writers, editors, and staff were needed to put out and distribute each venue.[21] Those untold thousands, the argument went, knew what they were doing, what they had accepted, as no writer or publisher could be unaware of how the literary field had been completely reordered and reorganized along ideological lines.[22] The problem with this formal definition of collaboration was that Louis Aragon, Simone de Beauvoir, Albert Camus, Éluard, Irene Némirovsky, and Jean-Paul Sartre had work appear in mainstream venues during the war—and by no reasonable definition of collaboration could they be accused of siding with the Germans.

Writing and authorship were central concerns for the postwar legal purge. In a mirror image of how the German occupier and Vichy had instituted strict controls over what could be published, the newly installed provisional government issued its own index of banned works and notorious writers.[23] The symbolic value of bringing to justice writers who had sided with the Germans was incontestable, especially so in France, where writers were prized for their contributions to the *rayonnement* of its culture. The Ministry of Interior's guidelines on arresting collaborators listed "writers and journalists" as priority targets: "Because of their high standing which gave them the role of guides and role models in the nation, they are particularly responsible and should be among the first, and among the harshest, punished."[24] The first treason charge in the Paris Cour de Justice was lodged not at a high official or a *milice* figure but Georges Suarez, an editorialist for *Aujourd'hui* largely known for his hagiographies of Clemenceau and Briand (different times, different heroes!). Other writers quickly followed in the dock: Stéphane Lauzanne, the long-time editor of *Le Matin*; Paul Chack, a writer of high sea tales; and then, in December 1944, Henri Béraud, the Goncourt winner from modernism's *annus mirabilis*, 1922, was sentenced to death (his sentence was commuted). The rush to prosecute writers could be explained by the ease with which their convictions could be secured. Unlike financial or political collaboration, writers openly signed their texts, resulting in a trove of damning evidence: "No need for witnesses, no need even to hear the accused: the only thing needed would be to reread them."[25] The schema for judging writers was well-known: the *dossier d'instruction* contained clippings from a selection of writings, grouped along thematic lines (support for collaboration or the German New Order; anti-British, anti-American, or anti-Soviet sentiments; anti-De Gaulle sentiments; and, finally, although accorded much less importance at the time, anti-Semitic or racialist utterances); the arraignment spun a narrative of ideological waywardness and venality; and then, during the trial, the child's game of pinning the authorship of excerpts upon the accused. One author complained to De Gaulle that the *métier* of the pen was being unfairly targeted: "Writers and journalists who by their signatures accepted responsibility for their acts are subjected to the full force of the law. On the other hand, a remarkable clemency, and sometimes total immunity, applies to other forms of collaboration, even the most serious, the basest, or the most efficacious."[26] For his part, De Gaulle reportedly believed that "two categories of traitors … deserved no pity: talented writers and army officers."[27] As if taking a cue from Plato's *Republic*, he bemoaned how the "eloquent excitations" of collaborationist writers had pushed "poor gullible" members of the public to crimes and atrocities.[28]

The French purge has been the subject of much debate in the intervening years, from popular history books to encyclopedic, 700-page tomes. Alice Kaplan's meticulous examination of the case of Robert Brasillach depicted the vagaries of justice in the period, Philip Watts showed how the climate of treason trials influenced the development of postwar French literature and critical theory, and Jeanyves Guérin documented the proliferation and metaphorical significance of blacklists in the country's literary landscape.[29] The purge seems to never go away; recent debates about re-issuing Louis-Ferdinand Céline's anti-Semitic works in a Pléiade edition or the publication of newly discovered wartime writings serve as a trial *manqué* of the justice never delivered to Destouches. The judgment *Esprit* handed down in January 1945—that the purge was "too benign for some, too severe for others" but "incoherent to all"—has never gone away.[30] What is often missing from these discussions, though, is a clear understanding of the legal processes and institutional forms involved. Especially missing in the discussion is an appreciation of how professional writers' associations and bodies played critical roles in the purge. These professional bodies were a continuation of the wartime clandestine networks and continued in that same spirit at first, attempting to instill a harsh justice on writers who had collaborated, but the institutionalization of those bodies did not translate into a smooth justice.

French States of Treason

For a country that pioneered notions of sovereignty, state centralization, and national belonging, France has a curiously muddled legal history when it comes to treason. In the *ancien régime*, treason (and its linked crime, *lèse-majesté*) was understood as disobedience to the *roi*, a personal attachment that forbade attacks on the king's body or property but also included such matters as corresponding with the king's enemies. It was with the French Revolution that treason acquired its own legislative and judicial apparatus. (Coincidentally, the term *épuration*, or purge, also came to the fore during the Revolution's Jacobin period.[31]) The 1791 Penal Code that targeted the émigrés cast treason as a military crime of bearing arms against the French state. A political view of treason appeared in the Constitution of the Year III (1795): blocking the legislative functioning of the Primary Assembly was called an instance of high treason, thus linking treason to the exercise of democratic sovereignty. But that political understanding of treason was not pursued in the penal codes of 1810 and 1832, or the 1857 Code of military justice, which all defined treason as a crime against the external security (*sureté*) of the nation. The 1848 Constitution, moreover, removed treason from the list of capital crimes. The ill-defined nature of the crime helps explain why, during its most famous test, the Dreyfus affair, passions ran so high.[32]

The danger of treason to the nation was recognized in the run-up to the Second World War when treason was made, once again, a capital crime. But that late July 1939 law (and accompanying decree-law of April 1940) did not go as far as many had wanted when it came to *trahison morale* (supporting a foreign power ideologically). There remained a strong material bent to the understanding of aid and assistance to a foreign enemy, as treason was defined to involve bearing arms for the enemy or delivering to a foreign power "either French troops or territories, cities, fortresses, works, posts, magazines, arsenals, materials, munitions, ships, buildings or aerial navigation centers."[33] Even acts resulting in French soldiers defecting to an enemy power, which could conceivably be seen as the intended effect of propaganda, were primarily considered in the material sense of assisting the passage or transport of a French soldier to a foreign army. The legislation was up-to-date enough to ban sorties in French airspace on a foreign airship, but there was almost nothing about propaganda as such.

While treason remained legally anchored to questions of military security, the popular imaginary was engaged in a semantic redefinition of the term. The abrupt collapse of the Third Republic led to intense scrutiny on what had caused its defeat. For Vichy, the ministers who had weakened France and the "sinister Jew" contributing to "the diffusion of communist poison" were the traitors who had weakened France. This was the argument in Colonel E. Massol's *Pourquoi collaborer?*: "Treason, yes, there had been treason, but committed by our rulers who threw us into an absurd war."[34] Maurice Betz's captured prisoners came to understand that "we had been betrayed" by ministers playing parliamentary games while letting the army languish.[35] What the "Révolution nationale" needed was a purge of non-nationals, members of secret societies, and Jews. Removing the latter from public life was the precondition, in this logic, of a regenerated France: "épurer pur unir," as *Aujourd'hui* put it, to make France for the French.[36] On the flip side, those who resisted or contested the armistice saw Vichy's acceptance of a foreign military power on national soil as a flagrant act of treason. The object of a citizen's allegiance—should it side with Vichy's legal primacy or should it fall to some abstract notions of *la France eternelle* that lay defeated—was the unresolved question. The ambiguous term was not so much treason but, rather, France: was France a state of ideals (spin the wheel for the possible dates: 1789, 1815, 1848, 1871, 1914), or was it the government in power, no matter how odious (which meant Vichy)? Liberal political thought, from Hobbes on, preferred the latter: disagreements over the rightful sovereign were likely deadlier than whatever acts an uncontested but tyrannical ruler could commit. But that calculation of harm ignored the frightful power that modern states could harness, the awesome machinery of destruction an organized bureaucracy could deploy. In short, treason's ambiguous legal position between the sovereign in fact (the ability to make law) and the sovereign as an ideal (the ability to make just laws) was brutally exposed.

Like other exile governments, the French resistance began planning its postwar early. In July 1940 De Gaulle announced that a liberated France would "punish those responsible for its disasters"; the future architect of European unity, Maurice Schumann, spoke of the Free French compiling a "list" of "squealers, miserable judges, dishonored soldiers … who have sentenced themselves to death" by collaborating.[37] The starting point for the resistance was declaring the Vichy regime *nul et non avenu*.[38] The argument was that the armistice of June 16, 1940, had only temporarily suspended hostilities, so all post-armistice laws, decrees or regulations lacked legal force. When republican "legality" was re-instituted on August 9, 1944, over four years of French political life were wiped out in what was effectively a legal scorched-earth policy. It was an elegant theoretical fix, but one that did not accord with how individuals experienced the occupation. The vast majority of individuals who resisted Vichy understood that they were acting against the law and risked punishment; similarly, those who obeyed Vichy's laws could not imagine themselves to be committing a crime.[39] But without the legal fiction that Vichy did not exist, the only way to punish the collaboration would have been through a retroactive law.

The resistance lawyers at first believed that Article 75 of the Penal Code was supple enough, due to terms like "intelligence with the enemy," to punish collaboration. The Ordinance of June 27, 1944, defined collaboration as any act, writing or personal attitude which aided the enemy, harmed the French or Allied war effort, or jeopardized fundamental rights.[40] Then, in late August 1944, the law of national indignity was passed, with a new punishment—national degradation—for this retroactive crime.[41] Decrees and orders passed in the summer and autumn of 1944 set up the courts of justice (composed of one judge and four jury members), civic chambers (to pronounce upon cases of national indignity), and High Court (composed of three judges and twenty-four jury members) that would try these cases. These new institutional forms constituted a justice of exception: investigations were undertaken by a government minister rather than a judge of instruction; hearsay and circumstantial evidence were readily accepted ("it is notoriously known that"); the right to legal counsel was not complete; appeals were not heard; and, most worryingly, juries were drawn from the ranks of the resistance and parliamentarians with political axes to grind.[42] As Jean Paulhan later complained, the juries "knew that they were there to condemn. The [Communist] Party had told them so. The Republic seemed to have repeated that message. And they condemned."[43] At times juries would heckle the accused, ask for the proceedings to be shortened ("Bastard," "Twelve shots to the head"), so that the inevitable would take place more quickly.[44]

There were serious obstacles to history following the moral arc of justice. The military situation in the summer of 1944 remained uncertain, with German armies all over the national territory, and even reconquering territory did not automatically translate into favorable conditions for judicial proceedings. In Grenoble, for instance, the *Journal officiel*, which enumerated the composition and working of the new courts, did not arrive until late September 1944. Communications between the provinces and Paris remained spotty due to cut telegram and telephone lines and electricity shortages (Paris had around forty-five minutes of electricity per day).[45] The material obstacles were legion: transport had to be arranged for the accused, which required soldiers but also a vehicle with gasoline; typists had to be found and could not work without typewriters or paper and ink; offices needed desks and chairs; courtrooms that had been bombed had to be repaired and, crucially in that first winter, one of the coldest in living memory, heated. Ensuring the safety of the accused before trial, when prisons and internment centers were overcrowded, unsanitary, and subject to attacks from mobs, was trying enough given the shortage of security personnel, vehicles, and munitions, if not also, at times, the will to do so (as the minister of interior told De Gaulle in June 1945, there were multiple cases of the police or army joining the vigilantes). The *épuration sauvage* did not magically end because the semblance of a legal machinery was set up across the country. The first two weeks of January 1945 saw eleven summary executions and over eighty armed or bombing attacks against interned collaborators; six months later, a mob of nearly four hundred individuals stormed Cusset prison, near Vichy, where they took prisoners out of their cells to string them up by their feet or beat them senseless.

The institutions called up to deliver justice—including the civil service, the judiciary, the police, and the bar—could not fully do so, or at least not in good faith, until they, too, were purged (to some degree). Filling posts with honorable members of the resistance was no guarantee of competence or impartiality. Moreover, all this had to happen in a country still at war, with genuine fears that a *cinquième colonne* (fifth column) would imperil the liberation.[46] Lyon was only able to hold its first trial for collaboration two months after its liberation, and only thirteen individuals were tried that first month. By February 1945, a paltry forty-two cases had been tried in five months.[47] A huge number of *dossiers*—over 300,000, by one count—were opened in the country, but getting to trial was another matter.[48] Had normal legal procedure been followed, purge cases would have clogged the courts for an unthinkable fifteen to twenty years.[49] The legal purge, meant to be harsh and swift, proved to be neither. If De Gaulle had hoped to limit the purge to a "handful of *misérables*," by which logic it could be concluded within a few months, the High Court of Justice in Paris held its last trial in June 1949 and was only dissolved in 1958, years after the general amnesty laws were passed.[50]

Punishing the Pen: Institutions of Repression

One of the most exceptional aspects of the exceptional postwar French purge was its marked corporatist spirit: almost every single professional and occupational category, from actors, authors, bankers, civil servants, dentists, doctors, engineers, farmers, lawyers, professors, secretaries, teachers, to veterans, sought to cleanse its ranks of notorious collaborators.[51] It was not surprising that writers figured prominently in the occupational purge. Already during the war years resistance authors had banded together in the Comité national des écrivains (CNE). Founded in 1941 as an offshoot of the French Communist Party's (PCF) National Front of Writers, the CNE came to publish the clandestine monthly *Les Lettres Françaises* (see Figure 3.2). Even though that house organ called for writers of all stripes to work together, it never lost the tag of being a mouthpiece of the PCF. Given the PCF's hegemonic position in the domestic political sphere due to so much of the resistance stemming from its ranks, the CNE enjoyed unrivaled political and moral legitimacy in defining the postwar literary purge.[52] But navigating the move from clandestinity to sunlight created all sorts of problems: new members, new political stakes, and new institutional forms eventually splintered it.

Barely ten days after Paris's liberation, the CNE hosted a major meeting of writers from both zones in the capital. Top of the agenda was deciding how to punish collaborationist writers. The formula the CNE hit on was a blacklist: any venue publishing a collaborator would be boycotted by resistance writers. The first blacklist contained twelve names, all of them "big fish": Robert Brasillach, Céline, Alphonse de Chateaubriant, Jacques Chardonne, Drieu la Rochelle, Jean Giono, Charles Maurras, Henry de Montherlant, Armand Petitjean, and André Thérive. A week later the CNE expanded the blacklist to forty-four names, and by late October its blacklist had 165 names. The drafting of these blacklists was an aleatory process, with writers lobbying for friends to be saved and enemies put to the rack.[53] Many writers were startled by how easily the CNE adopted "the soul of cops [*flics*]" in its operations.[54] For Jean Paulhan, a CNE founder who turned

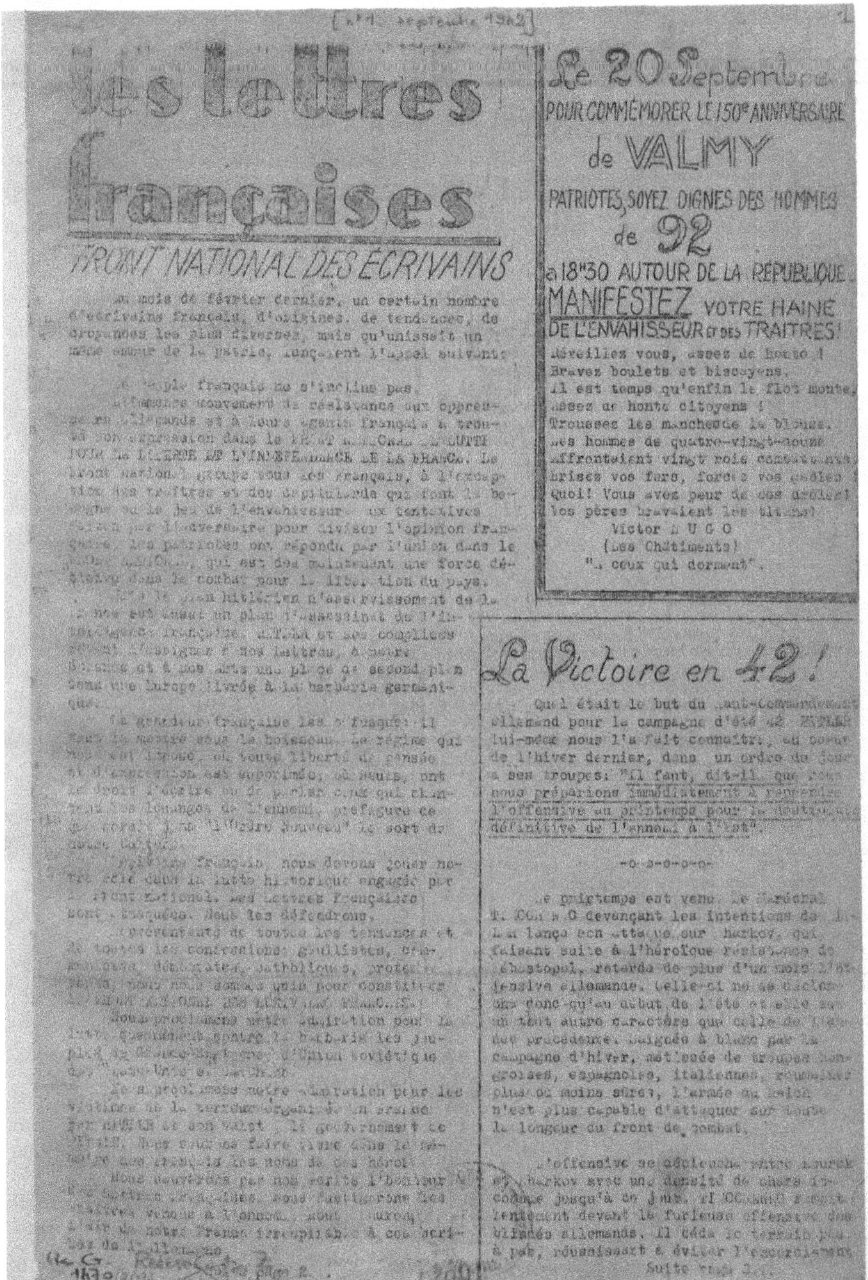

Les Lettres Françaises

FRONT NATIONAL DES ÉCRIVAINS

Le 20 Septembre
POUR COMMÉMORER LE 150e ANNIVERSAIRE
de VALMY
PATRIOTES, SOYEZ DIGNES DES HOMMES
de 92
à 18"30 AUTOUR DE LA RÉPUBLIQUE
MANIFESTEZ VOTRE HAINE
DE L'ENVAHISSEUR et des TRAITRES!

La Victoire en 42!

Figure 3.2 The clandestine paper *Les Lettres Françaises*, by the Comité National des Écrivains. Courtesy of Gallica/BnF, all rights reserved.

into its most vigorous opponent, the entire process was misguided when "error" was "the first right of the writer"; for others, punishing wayward writers was acceptable, but the manner in which it was done, without debate or discussion, largely driven by personal and political prejudices, was not.[55] That these blacklists were PR communiqués, not legal documents, became apparent when writers who had been in the resistance found themselves listed as collaborators or, more damningly, writers in the grave were summoned for punishment *outre-tombe*. While such errors were understandable given the informational chaos of the time, they nonetheless undermined the legitimacy of the lists.

The CNE's informal purge of the literary field was largely symbolic. In late May 1945 a government decree instituted, along similar lines to the occupational purge committees for doctors and actors, a Comité national d'épuration des gens de lettres, auteurs et compositeurs (National Purge Committee of Writers, Authors, and Composers).[56] It was composed of delegates from six professional associations: the Société des Gens de Lettres, the country's oldest professional body for writers, four other professional bodies (the Société des auteurs et compositeurs dramatiques, the Société des auteurs, compositeurs et editeurs de musique, the Société des aurateurs et conferenciers [orators and speakers], and the Association des écrivains combattants), and the CNE, which represented the literary resistance. The Comité National drafted a questionnaire that its constitutive associations sent to members. That questionnaire asked what individuals had published during the war but also probed into social advantages (the right to drive a car, personal dealings with Germans, etc.). Suspected collaborators were examined by a three-member committee, which prepared a preliminary dossier and then interrogated the accused (along with witnesses). Lawyers could be present, but dossiers were released only twenty-four hours before the interrogation. The punishments that the Comité National handed down mainly consisted of publication bans (although a work deemed to have "public, scientific or historical interest" could still be published, even if written by a banned writer). Writers could also have their royalties seized and transmitted to charities or the public purse.

The occupational purge committees were set up so that every profession could clean up its own house, thus restoring public confidence in that professional body. The expectation was that less serious cases of collaboration could be handled by confrères who understood the professional stakes and could act quickly. The difficulty for writers was that they did not make naturally competent jurists, interrogators or administrators (even with the *avocat general* of the Paris Court of Appeal, Gérard Frèche, being made president of the Comité National). The government did not help matters by taking three months to name the composition of the committee (as if the purge needed a long summer holiday), which pushed back the first formal interrogation of accused collaborators to January 1946. Then, once work began, there were all sorts of delays. It was not always easy to determine which body had priority over a certain dossier—a criminal tribunal, a civic court, another professional association?—and confusion naturally reigned if one body determined guilt and another innocence. (The principle of double jeopardy did not apply.) One obvious starting point was the CNE blacklist of over 160 names, but only a small number of blacklisted writers ended up being examined by the Comité National. The Comité's six different societies and associations were supposed to transmit files on their members to the national body, but those associations sometimes refused to send along dossiers if an internal purge procedure had been started.[57] (There were also palpable fears of dossiers being misplaced.) Not every professional body had the means or, more damning, the inclination to determine the guilt of its members: the Société des aurateurs et conferenciers, despite its field being that of lecturers and speakers, many of whom made a living through the radio or at public meetings, admitted that it had "no means to control" or inspect its members. It would only exclude members found guilty in a court of law.[58] The Société des auteurs et compositeurs dramatiques, whose members had not put on clandestine plays during the war years, washed its hands of the purge by excluding from its ranks only those members who had fled to Germany or were found guilty in criminal courts. At times the Comité National would ask for dossiers of individuals who were not members of any professional body, or the transmitted names were so John-Smithy generic—which Marcel Berger or Georges Robert?—that it was impossible to identify who was under suspicion. It surely did not help that the Comité National did not have a working telephone or that to hire an extra typist, or to get the one on its staff paid, a ministerial decree was required.[59]

Because the most notorious cases of collaboration were taken up by the special criminal courts set up after the war, the Comité National was left with ambiguous cases, ones where the evidence against the accused tended to be rumors or whispers, the gossip of concierges and neighbors. Its remit was wide, covering not only writings but also personal relations with the Germans and wartime privileges. Private mores, especially for celebrities—the "notorious pederast" Jean Cocteau consuming "mountains of drugs"; Sacha Guitry's extravagant lifestyle—were also signaled.[60] The key issue in many cases was a writer's "attitude" at a time when "the duty of all was to say nothing and to do nothing which could be interpreted by whomsoever as … antinational."[61] Terms like "defeatist" and "patriotic" functioned as code for guilt and innocence. Anonymous denunciations were added to individual dossiers. In some complicated cases a committee member would compile a report for the hearing with the investigated author. The committee's final judgment, which ranged from a few paragraphs to a few pages, was then issued.

After it began to meet regularly in January 1946, the Comité National was supposed to convene weekly, hearing anywhere from one to four cases per session. From January 7, 1946, to May 13, 1946, a total of thirteen meetings took place, with twenty-six cases heard. That was hardly quick justice. And it was not particularly severe justice either, as the penalties ranged from no sanction (six cases), six months (four cases), twelve months (six cases), eighteen months (three cases), and two years (the maximum punishment, handed down in seven cases), resulting in an average punishment of nearly sixteen months for those found guilty of collaboration. Given that many of the accused had been given informal publication bans in the autumn of 1944, the sentence had already been served. At one point in 1947 the Comité National did not even meet at all. Starting in 1949, it met only once per month, with fifteen minutes given for the examination of each case (the meeting of June 2, 1949, for instance, began at 3:00 p.m. and closed three hours later, with a total of thirteen dossiers heard).

It also rankled that the commissions set up for occupational purges were riddled with individuals with questionable wartime pasts. Urbain Falazie, who wrote over a dozen articles against De Gaulle, the communists, and the British government for *Mémorial de la Loire* from 1940 to 1942, served on the commission of the purge of the press. The wartime record of the secretary of the Syndicat des artistes, which was tasked with purging the cinema and the stage, included bylines in the infamously collaborationist paper *La Gerbe* and plays performed in German-requisitioned theatres. Not that Jean Darcante was alone, one detractor noted—the Syndicat was "exclusively composed of confrères" who, "under the cover of an opportune and opportunist resistance," were using their newly conferred powers "to eliminate as many artists as possible from the profession."[62] The Comité National had its own problems when in 1946, Charles Vildrac, officially a representative of the Society of Dramatic Authors but also a prominent CNE member, announced his resignation from the committee. He was not alone in determining that the Comité National had too many cases and not enough resources. When the Comité National's president, the attorney Frèche, also stepped away to take up his former position at the Court of Justice, the Comité entered a long hiatus, with over a year passing before it met again.[63] Rushing to finish off the literary purge in 1949 only added to the *opera buffa* of this ill-starred committee—at this point, most of France was keen to move on, not rifle through what was now a long-distant past for the sins of scribblers.

Treason's Footnote: Georges Suarez on Trial

As the first collaborator to be tried for treason before the Paris Court of Justice, Georges Suarez is often reduced to a footnote. Befitting his status as a forgotten minor writer, his trial is rarely discussed despite the contemporary interest in it (more than eighty journalists attended, many of them foreign correspondents, and almost every major French paper extensively commented on the trial) and its legacy in setting the course for the postwar literary purge. The questions raised in stark relief at this first major trial of literary treason—to what France did one owe allegiance; was writing an act or an expression of opinion; what else could writers do when the Germans controlled the entire literary field?—cast a long shadow over the literary purge.

Born in 1890 in Paris, Suarez was largely known for his biographies of Georges Clemenceau and Aristide Briand. He had co-founded, along with Joseph Kessel (a Jewish novelist and reporter who took part in the resistance) and Horace de Carbuccia (whose trial for collaboration languished for over a decade), the weekly *Gringoire* in the late 1920s. A decorated First World War veteran, Suarez had pushed for the harsh punishment of Germany before changing course in the 1930s, when he joined Jacques Doriot's Parti Populaire Français and advocated a Franco-German *rapprochement*. In the late 1930s he was the editor-in-chief of *Notre Temps*, Jean Luchaire's nationalist-imperialist Sunday review (slogan: "Remake France, Make Empire, Unite Europe").[64] In late November 1940 Suarez was offered the post of editorial director of *Aujourd'hui* after its founder, Henri Jeanson, a pacifist, anti-imperialist who was jailed by both the Third Republic and the Germans, refused to toe an anti-Semitic, collaborationist line. Suarez's first signed column appeared on December 3, 1940, under a masthead that identified him as the paper's "political director." Setting the tone for his control of the four-page daily, Suarez polemically argued that France's degenerate parliamentary democracy had ushered in war and disaster but now "our choice is made: our unlimited and unconditional trust lies with Pétain and the policies that his authority supports, those of Pierre Laval."[65] His column the following week (he began daily editorials in the new year) laid the blame for France's weakness on the "foreign anarchy" fomented by White Russians, Italian communists, Eastern European Jews, and Spanish refugees.[66] Under Suarez's leadership and editorial pen *Aujourd'hui* sent Hitler birthday greetings, condemned De Gaulle, blamed the resistance for German excesses, and, even as late as June 1944, called the Wehrmacht "liberators" who would "defend our soil"—in short, a prime example of a propaganda rag.[67] Despite that political coloring, *Aujourd'hui* also regularly published avant-garde modernists like Pierre Mac Orlan and Robert Desnos (who ended up dying at Theresienstadt in 1945).

Arrested in early October 1944, Suarez's trial began twenty days later in the Paris Court of Justice (Figure 3.3). His case had an undoubted symbolic importance, as his defense attorney underlined on the eve of the trial: "My client is unlucky. He is inaugurating the new Court of Justice, and this honor has resulted in publicity which makes his crime appear much worse than it was in reality."[68] The government had plenty of high-value collaborators overcrowding Fresnes prison—ministers, admirals, members of the French Academy, ambassadors, prefects, titans of industry—but it chose to begin treason proceedings in Paris with a writer.[69] But why choose Suarez? His literary standing could not compare to Pierre Drieu la Rochelle, who ran the *NRF*, or Louis-Ferdinand Céline, the major novelist whose anti-Semitic pamphlets were notorious, or the younger generation's bright star, Robert Brasillach, to say nothing of venerable names like Henry de Montherlant or Marcel Jouhandeau. What Suarez had was a relatively simple case, as his literary production during the war was largely confined to a single newspaper, and, perhaps most importantly, he had no true protectors in the literary field (Drieu la Rochelle was shielded from prosecution by André Malraux; figures like Montherlant or Brasillach were despised for their collaboration but admired for their other work; and while Céline was incomparably the most singularly talented of them all, and the most alone in terms of literary friends, he was in Germany). It was perhaps over-the-top to call Suarez "a man of letters of an incontestable value," as the police report called him, but he had been a fixture of French political writing for two decades.[70] His role in setting up *Gringoire*, which was one of the highest-selling literary periodicals in the 1930s, his lead position in Luchaire's *Notre Temps*, and the popularity of his political biographies testify to that. An exposé on the "fifth column" of the "Nazi press" in *L'Aurore*, which appeared even before Suarez was arrested, featured a caricature of him on the front page.[71] The fact that Suarez accepted the editorship of *Aujourd'hui* after its founder had refused to publish anti-Semitic, pro-German articles also made a

Figure 3.3 Trial of Georges Suarez, *France-Soir*, October 24, 1944. Courtesy of Gallica/BnF, all rights reserved.

compelling narrative for postwar prosecution. As a writer, Suarez was prominent enough that his punishment would be newsworthy, but enough of a hack that his elevation during the war years triggered resentment.

That Suarez was highly paid—his salary and expense account of around 70,000 francs made his monthly take several hundred times the salary of an average factory worker—also fueled charges that he was profiting handsomely from the occupation.[72]

Figuring out the "traitor's purse"—the financial rewards of collaboration—had become an important judicial question, with police investigators scrupulously examining bank and property records; to such dry figures was added salacious gossip from building concierges and waiters at fashionable restaurants. Publisher Bernard Grasset and his Italian wife, a police report determined, spent upwards of 20,000 francs per month on cigarettes alone.[73] To those who had "sacrificed the love of his country for the love of money," there was only one possible response: "he must pay his debt to France" with his life.[74] Suarez's outlandish pay fit the bill for his selling out.

The speed with which Suarez's case was prepared—not even three weeks between arrest and trial—was a direct result of the fact that the "black and white" evidence against a writer could be assembled with relative ease, requiring no more than scissors to cut out articles and a pencil to underline passages. Just over a dozen clippings were enough to seal Suarez's fate. In his initial police interrogation, Suarez insisted that "well before the war" he had supported close Franco-German ties and that everything he wrote during the war years was "sincere and in good faith"—he was not, in other words, a *vendu*, an opportunist trying to profit from the occupation. That Suarez was sensitive to that charge surfaced in his fanciful claim that he had soured on Pétain and collaboration but did not want to make that known lest he be criticized for "opportunism."[75] (Being an opportunist is code, in the literary field, for being a hack, without aesthetic or literary value; that charge had been leveled against Suarez years earlier and he particularly resented it, the judicial investigation noted.) Whether Suarez was a dyed-in-the-wool collaborator or an opportunist dissembling his real beliefs was six or one-half-dozen for prosecutors: while the animus toward sell-outs was real, an unshakeable faith in *rapprochement* was hardly a winning defense strategy. Curiously, the post-war investigators made use of Vichy intelligence reports dismissing Suarez as an "opportunist" who had "always been on the side of the strongest" and "had a finger in every pie."[76] If it had once been a hallmark of a writer to disown any attachment to a particular belief (Henry James and the ideal of artistry as being above the fray of mundane politics, impregnable to ideas), in Suarez's case this flexibility was likened to prostitution and selling out.

Escorted into the courtroom handcuffed by a guard a full foot taller than him, donning a beige overcoat more Côte d'Azur than penal colony, Suarez cut a lonely figure in the courtroom with a packed audience "there for the kill."[77] The defense began by questioning the validity of the tribunal to judge acts that were fully legal at the time they were committed. The court recessed to consider the motion and, unsurprisingly, declared itself competent. The opening statement by the government stressed Suarez's unique responsibility for what he wrote: *Aujourd'hui* was "under his control and under his responsibility and he himself wrote, almost every day, the lead article."[78] Suarez's room for maneuver, given the censorship in place and the expectation that newspapers reprint German and Vichy communiqués, was not a given, so it was important to establish that Suarez had a free hand to write as he saw fit. If every word was his own free choice, expressing his own beliefs, and if every word he signed was his, not dictated by another, then the 103 signed articles introduced into evidence showed that Suarez had been "a propagandist of total collaboration" (4). Suarez denied that supporting collaboration was treason (which, anyways, was "a word that people freely use in France to tar someone who does not think like you" [30]) as it had served the country's interests at the time. This was, in fact, the trial's loaded question: who had the right to define France's interests? And what was France during the war? For Suarez, it was the ruling power, which, under the armistice terms, meant Vichy and the German occupiers. For the provisional republic, which swept away Vichy's legal standing, fidelity to the law no longer implied legality: a higher spirit should have animated individual action during those times when no legitimate sovereign was in place.

The trial lasted six hours. The mood was somber. If trials did not need "a theatrical allure," one court reporter observed, they nonetheless needed "a certain grandeur," not the marked "mediocrity" on display: "Everyone, from the seat of the public minister to the defense bench, appeared to be discharging a duty as quickly as possible."[79] Even the prosecution could barely summon "much ardor" when the die was cast.[80] The case against Suarez consisted of laying out his career as a writer whose beliefs had swayed with the wind and siding with whoever employed him. *Aujourd'hui*'s finances were examined, with Suarez claiming, to generalized incredulity, that the paper never received a zinc Reichspfenning. His high salary was questioned, to which Suarez responded that he lived austerely—but also that he had managed to double *Aujourd'hui*'s circulation (a fact that could not have helped his case). Extracts from his written output were produced, with Suarez seemingly surprised by what he had written: "I haven't reread my articles" (38), he complained at one point, "Could you show me the texts?" (39). He also claimed that the prosecution was being selective with its choice of texts, picking only the most damning ones. Suarez was defending himself as a writer, seeking a rounded, coherent picture of his ideas through the entirety of his literary output, but for a criminal court that critical unity was irrelevant (that Suarez expressed pro-German propaganda in only 103 articles out of the 675 total he wrote during the war still made him guilty; one does not need to steal from every shop one enters). The "responsibility" of a writer, "one of the most noble professions in existence," the prosecutor noted, was to be aware of what words could do and to serve justice and humanity, not to sell out and support a regime of organized terror: "When one has the honor of holding a pen, when one has the honor to form the public opinion of one's co-citizens, one must think about one's responsibility" (53). The claim that Suarez was playing "a very subtle game, trying to protect the French against the occupier" (94), was rejected, as whatever *double jeu* he had undertaken to help a few friends was nothing compared to the harm for the wider public. The key argument was that Suarez's collaboration was vital for German war aims; the raft of writers, intellectuals and journalists who sided with the Germans created a "favorable climate" (87) for collaboration and undermined the resistance. A "simple reading" of Suarez's articles showed how far he had gone to justify German actions.[81] The intention of this propaganda was to reduce France to "the most vile, the most abject, the most profound servitude, the harshest and most abject slavery," resulting in nothing less than "the end of French culture and civilization."[82] This was not a case of putting an opinion on trial; Suarez would have been well within his rights to admire Hitler in 1938, but in times of war, writers had to be aware of the public impact of their writings.

(Was the public a monolith easily swayed by German propaganda or was it composed of resisters who dismissed anything official and only trusted the BBC? That inconvenient inconsistency was not raised at trial.)

Suarez's muddled answers made life difficult for his defense attorney, who during the closing arguments veered the discussion away from "the writings" to "the man," with much stress placed on Suarez's military record during the Great War and how the trauma from that war ("he was wounded, he was gassed") continued to the present day.[83] Suarez had taken a hard line against Germany in the 1920s, so much so that the German press covered him with "insults"; when the war started, he was a nationalist whose anti-German writings raised the Gestapo's suspicions; and some of his writings, like the biography of Clemenceau, were even banned by Vichy and the Germans![84] More than anything, the defense tried to paint a picture of Suarez as a lonely, isolated figure who was remarkably ill-informed. This scatter-gun defense tried to turn Suarez into a "pitiable victim" (103) who had committed not a crime but "an error, a profound error" (105) in judgment; he, too, had been swayed by German promises and propaganda. Finally, the great question at the end of the attorney's closing argument concerned what judgment might mean. Having Suarez's head would not change the ignominy of occupation; and with "all of France, but also the entire world" (106) watching, the great responsibility of history now shifted to the jury, who could not restore France's place in the world by turning Suarez into a scapegoat. The jury of two workers, one doctor, and a hospital orderly took only fifteen minutes to decide otherwise, sentencing Suarez to death. That sentence was carried out by a twelve-man firing squad a few weeks later after De Gaulle refused to commute the sentence. It was the case that examples were needed, and Suarez was a good one.

What undercut the clarity of the symbolism of punishing Suarez was a verdict in another trial that took place in the same courtroom the following week. Stéphane Lauzanne, who had directed *Le Matin* for over four decades, was given a twenty-year sentence, to be served in exile. The disparity in sentencing—Suarez ran a new paper, with a relatively limited circulation, while Lauzanne had, in one of the country's chief dailies, an incontestably larger mouthpiece at his disposal—was impossible to ignore. One seasoned court reporter thought that the "farce" of French justice that had marked the interwar years (the Stavisky Affair, etc.) was in fine fettle. A "minimum of coherence" was needed for the country to re-establish the rule of law, but that was nowhere to be found when the same crime resulted in vastly different outcomes. This was grist for the mill for "Montmartre *chansonniers*," but hardly ideal for the promises of quick, severe justice.[85] And it certainly undercut the idea that justice would be blind. If the evidence against writers consisted of what they wrote, their guilt depended much more on who they were (and who their friends might be).

Symbols of Young and Old: Brasillach and Maurras

The two most important postwar authors' trials in France opened within one week of one another in January 1945. The first, in Paris, concerned the leading voice of youth, the thirty-five-year-old Robert Brasillach; the second, in Lyon, involved the embodiment of the older generation, the seventy-six-year-old Charles Maurras. A member of the French Academy, Maurras had cast a long shadow over French political and literary life, with over five decades of public notoriety as the leader of Action Française (AF) and its eponymous newspaper. For his supporters, Maurras was an exponent of classical French rationalism, a staunch patriot whose writings were famous across the world; for detractors, he had "empoisoned generations" of French youth.[86] Brasillach was one of those young followers. After making his debut in regional papers as a *lycéen*, Brasillach quickly garnered academic and literary accolades—entry into the École Normale Supérieure, literary reviews for *Action Française*, books published by Plon and Denoël—to become one of the leading voices of the younger generation across multiple forms (novels, literary criticism, poetry, film). Both Maurras and Brasillach were disillusioned with the state of French society, which they saw as broken, corrupt, and decadent. But they sought different ways to get out of the mess they both so brilliantly polemicized against. Maurras stressed political battle ("politique d'abord," or politics first, was *Action française*'s slogan) while Brasillach tended toward aesthetic retreat. The two also differed with regards to the sources of their political thinking. Maurras, a child of the Dreyfus Affair, was deeply anchored in a French political and literary tradition that took France for the world. Brasillach was an internationalist, entranced by Léon Degrelle's Rexist movement in Belgium and moved by the stupendous crowds acclaiming Hitler at the 1937 Parteitag in Nuremburg. Maurras had a visceral anti-German hatred, a legacy of 1870 and 1914, while Brasillach, moved by the heights of German philosophy and music (Nietzsche, Wagner, all that *Kultur*), saw in emotionally sublime German a perfect partner for France's cool Cartesian spirit. During the war, Maurras's *Action Française* had decamped to Lyon, where it was published from October 1940 to August 1944. For his part, Brasillach had been an infantry officer on the Maginot Line when war broke out. He was captured in June 1940 and remained in a German POW camp until March 1941. Upon his return to Paris, Brasillach took up his post as editor at *Je suis partout*, where he wrote violent attacks upon Jews and communists in the most notorious Parisian collaborationist venue. The trials against Brasillach and Maurras were key events in expediting the purge, attracting major interest from the media and in the literary world. In both trials the central questions were the right of writers to express opinions and the responsibility they bore for their ideas, especially in "a country like ours which, laden with so many literary glories, had always conferred to the highest level the value of the pen."[87] Both trials probed the nature of authorship: was it a commutative property, whereby individual texts could be read separately to create a larger whole, or was it a transformative quality that could not be reduced to the sum of its parts?

The two trials took place in a feverish atmosphere, with loaded expectations as to the final verdict—although in Maurras's case, that also meant AF supporters vowing to strike back if their venerable leader was condemned. One week before Brasillach's trial opened, De Gaulle had commuted Henri Béraud's death sentence. While Béraud had been a celebrated writer in the 1920s, his virulent anti-Semitism and support for Vichy made him a prime suspect for the harshest penalty. Debates over the course of the purge—most famously, the exchange between François Mauriac, who pleaded for "charity" toward writers, and Albert Camus, who still held tight to a harsh policy of punishment—were in full tilt. Between the opening of Brasillach's trial on January 19 and Maurras's five days later, the provisional government, reacting to widespread dissatisfaction with the slowness of justice, announced that the purge would have to be wrapped up in a few months, contributing urgency to the proceedings. The difference in setting between Paris and Lyon was also critical. There was a widespread feeling in autumn 1944 that the purge was more vicious in the provinces, probably due to the scale of the *épuration sauvage* and also the delay in setting up the Paris Court of Justice. Lyon's military executioners worked at a Stakhanovite rhythm that autumn, trying traitors one day, executing them the next: five executions on October 3, five more the next day, two the day after, seven on October 6.[88] Once the Paris Court of Justice began trying cases in mid-October, though, issuing a series of capital punishments, the first of which struck Suarez, the balance seemed to shift. Having been occupied the entirety of the war, the consequences of collaboration—and the profits that could be made from it—were more striking in Paris. With "writers ... dropping like flies in our capital," Maurras's lawyer was not displeased that his client was being tried in Lyon.[89] By the time the trial began, months after the first arrests and trials in the region, the thirst for justice in Lyon seemed to be overshadowed by "the lack of provisions and the cold," with a noticeable public sentiment that "during the occupation we were better fed" and a "distrust" of the new "administrative elites" whose purge seemed to be "pathetic," as one ministerial report from January 1945 noted.[90]

The investigation into Brasillach amounted to no more than a two-hour police interrogation.[91] The dossier, a single file containing some clippings, was marked "*urgent*"—as his defense attorney later noted, "Urgent to judge him. Urgent to kill him."[92] One of the driving themes of the charges against "Midas" was that he was a sell-out. Firstly, he had been freed from a POW camp because the Germans considered him—rightly—as a pliable propagandist (see Figure 3.4). Throughout Europe the actions of POWs were harshly judged, with an expectation that a military code of valor would prevail—any POW who sought or received favors was universally reviled as the worst kind of traitor. Secondly, even if Brasillach's pay was not "excessive," his "constant collaboration" had resulted in a "material situation" that could not be compared to writers who braved the rigors and risks of clandestinity.[93] The "treason of the intellectual" that Brasillach committed resulted in him having "an audience, a public place, a political influence" (146).

Brasillach had a stellar counsel in his corner, Jacques Isorni, who later shot to fame as Pétain's lead attorney. The son of an immigrant, Isorni had been radiated from the Paris bar in 1941 but was later reinstated. He received the Brasillach dossier in October 1944. The government wanted to rush proceedings but could not find a suitable prosecutor (it eventually settled on Isorni's neighbor and friend, Marcel Reboul), so Isorni had time to prepare the defense, although access to his client at Fresnes prison was limited to a few minutes per week.[94] Preparations were not helped by the weather and deprivation: that winter was one of the coldest in memory, the Seine entirely frozen over, and there was

Figure 3.4 Robert Brasillach, left, next to Jacques Doriot, on the Eastern front. Public domain, via Wikimedia Commons.

no coal, no heating wood, no flour, no paper, no food. Isorni caught a severe case of laryngitis from his visits to unheated jails.

The defense Isorni settled on was to dissociate the polemicist of *Je suis partout* from the sensitive poet and cultivated writer: while the political writer had made errors, the poet was worth saving. The charge sheet against Brasillach already employed this division, separating the "political writer of an extreme violence" from the "essayist and literary critic of a great authority" whose novels were "of an incontestable literary value" (30). The politics Brasillach promoted were, moreover, the official ones of the time, which left no doubt that the charges against him were of a political nature: "We are here," Isorni told the court, "in a case of political justice" (48). The first line of defense was that the supposedly guilty texts were merely reflections of Vichy policy. The second was a bet that aesthetics should trump politics: Brasillach's aesthetic promise, given his youth, demanded cultivation, not the guillotine.

Legally, Isorni was aghast that the provisional republic presumed the right to judge collaboration when "almost the quasi-totality of the magistrates presiding over its courts of justice had taken an oath" to serve Vichy.[95] (Only a single serving magistrate in 1940 refused to take the oath to Pétain.) The presiding judge at Brasillach's trial, in fact, had a novel published in 1942, resulting in an interview in *Je suis partout*, which should have caused some blushes. The other major legal problem was that judging Brasillach before having judged Vichy was like "condemning the legs which walk before having judged the head."[96] In a situation where "you have a leader who commands and citizens who followed him," the provisional republic had a burden to prove that the head of state was guilty of crimes and not focus its efforts on targeting his followers.[97] Those legal arguments, though, were unlikely to sway the court, which had for months rejected all attempts to undermine its legitimacy or authority.

Politically, Brasillach stressed that his support for "Franco-German collaboration" had always been driven by his belief that this served the interests of France, which "had to continue to live" (81). Only a French-run government could discuss with the German occupiers "on an equal footing" (81). When it came to his visit to Weimar (in 1941) or his frequenting the Institut Allemand or the Rive Gauche bookshop, Brasillach spoke of an intellectual collaboration above politics, casting himself as a kind of "ambassador to a foreign country" who was trying to "understand Germany so as to discuss with her" (87). Perhaps in fairy tales like *Le silence de la mer*, Vercors's wartime novel about a cultivated German soldier billeted with a French family whose teenage daughter refuses to acknowledge his existence, it was possible to completely ignore the occupier, but in war no one could keep "his hands entirely pure" (92). In short, his intentions were honorable:

> My intention for France to be treated as a sovereign power and that in the case of a German victory it would be considered as a sovereign state in Europe at the same level as Germany was not an evil one, and certainly not treason towards my country. Perhaps I was mistaken in the means … but in the bottom of my heart what I desired … was in the name of France, of French grandeur and its glorious history. (105)

My writings, he insisted, "served, before anything else, my country" (108). He was willing to take responsibility for them, so long as the court considered his intentions, and not simply judged him for his errors.

Brasillach's responsibility for his writings, the prosecution countered, stemmed from his immense talent. He knew how to employ "all the seductions of persuasive eloquence" in "rich and colorful language"; with his "vast erudition," he possessed, "to the highest degree," the ability to unlock the meaning of other texts; he not only commented from the outside but had a "particular talent … of placing the reader in the spiritual intimacy" of ideas (126). Blessed with so many gifts, loaded with "success [and] authority" (127), Brasillach made a mockery of those talents by steering the country's youth to the enemy. The greater the talent, the more loaded the responsibility: that was very much the guiding principle in the trials of both Brasillach and Maurras.

Brasillach's "quasi-carnal love for brutal force" (142) led him into the arms of Germany. Treason's homosexual undertones—"he sleeps with Germany, and the day after this fornication, one slides into the palm of his hand a return ticket" (145)—made Brasillach's case even more damning.[98] The guilt lay in succumbing to those evil temptations and covering them with language that, in turn, led unsuspecting youth to collaboration. Brasillach was whore and pimp, profiting from his association with the Germans and doing their dirty work for them. Judging Brasillach by his own principles, the prosecution suggested, would mean nothing less than a summary execution. The provisional republic was showing undue generosity in even granting him a trial. Those were undoubtedly widespread sentiments at the time, but they were not dignified arguments and did not bolster the legitimacy of the proceedings. Isorni's defense took a different tack by speaking about literature. Brasillach was one of France's most promising writers: "He was the one who marvellously depicted ... our waking to life, our ecstasy before the riches of existence. He is the one who expressed our tastes, anxieties, combats, our first disillusions" (172–3). Someone who had "profoundly penetrated into the very soul of France" could not possibly have betrayed the country (173). To speak of his treason was to cut down "the literary glory of France" (173). The "greatest writers of our generation"—Paul Valéry, Paul Claudel, François Mauriac—had nothing but praise for Brasillach and pleaded for mercy. Reading out one of Brasillach's prison poems, Isorni pointedly asked, "Do civilized peoples shoot their poets?" (177). The trial against Brasillach was nothing other than a process of opinion, Isorni stressed several times (183, 187). A political belief could be wrong but that did not make it a crime. Should a "provisional" government pass a sentence that was "eternal" (208)? Isorni's rhetoric was overwhelming, but the jury saw no reason to spare Brasillach from execution on the premise that he had unfulfilled literary promise. Given the low regard toward collaborationist writers, no one was surprised by the severity of the punishment.

A few days later, on January 24, with Brasillach's death sentence fresh in everyone's minds, the trial against Maurras and his close collaborator Maurice Pujo began (Figure 3.5). It was always going to be difficult to try the country's most famous writer, both at home and abroad, but the task was considerably complicated by Maurras's almost total deafness, which obliged two stenographers to transcribe the proceedings for his benefit. (Although, as the joke had it, the old fellow was deaf but definitely not mute; the length of the proceedings dragged on due to his notorious long-windedness.) The evidence against *Action Française*, which had long been an anti-German venue, consisted of its unconditional support for Pétain and "daily invectives" against "Gaullists, Israelites, communists."[99] Its influence was considerable because the paper was "widely circulated" via Vichy's official channels.[100] Because his guilt lay in written texts, the government proposed to examine every single article in turn. Maurras objected to a method that did not allow for an understanding of "the ensemble of things" (17). The first question for the court, then, was to determine whether Maurras's authorship consisted of a sum of articles, each of which could be examined in isolation, or whether there was a more significant whole, a guiding philosophy or spirit, that had to be understood. Maurras was visibly agitated by the court's insistence on looking at individual articles: "Mr. President, there is Charles Maurras who is accused of having betrayed France," he interjected, speaking of himself in the third person, "Charles Maurras will have the freedom of his defense" (17). When presented with an article from October 1943 that advocated hard measures and denunciations of resisters, Maurras insisted that before discussing "details" one needed "a general exposition of the situation imposed upon me" (17). Even more, he complained,

Figure 3.5 The Trial of Charles Maurras in Lyon, *Globe*, February 8, 1945. Courtesy of Gallica/BnF, all rights reserved.

his articles were not presented in their entirety but rather as extracts typed up on "small papers very kindly cut up" (20), so not even the context or argumentative unity of any individual article could be understood. "Look again, Mr. President," he noted that first day, "the immense problem of cutting up bits of articles without seeing the relationship between them; we don't get anywhere, or, rather, we get to all the fantasies one wants" (29). Maurras's identification of the open-ended nature of literary language sounds strikingly postmodern, but as a shrewd literary critic and brilliant polemicist he long knew how language could be slippery. The problem for Maurras was that the judicial procedure of looking at isolated passages to determine criminal guilt (for crimes like obscenity or defamation) was a long-standing practice and not unique to France. After a war dominated by propaganda slogans, moreover, it was not surprising that prosecutors would treat texts that way.

More than anything, Maurras insisted, texts could only be deciphered after considering the context driving their enunciation. Understanding the author's intention was also, in his eyes, capital. His long-standing French patriotism (and visceral hatred of the Germans) colored everything he wrote: "I am accused of an abominable crime that is refuted by all my life, by all my life, by all that I have ever done" (30). There was nothing—"not a word, not an act, nothing, nothing, nothing" (47)—to document any possible contact with the Germans. "Day by day, for four years," he claimed, "I was the patriot writer, and the writer opposed to the German occupation" (48), the definite article very much in evidence in that claim. "No one who knows anything about contemporary literature," he summarized, "would contradict me when I say that there is not a single French writer who has shown throughout his entire career a similar horror to the German spirit and German domination as your humble servant" (144). Yet to believe that as an open supporter of Pétain he was "as much of a resistant as anyone else" (27), as Maurras claimed (although, in his eyes, Pétain was somehow "the very incarnation of resistance" [139]) was believable only if one accepted the premise that a strong Vichy was the best bulwark against Germany. For Maurras, Vichy was a French government that furthered French interests, not a stooge regime beholden to Germany and complicit in its terrors and crimes. His view depended on an uncomplicated view of the nation and one's allegiance to the *pays légal*, a curious position for someone who had always stressed the primacy of the *pays réel* (the mass of people and their mores that constituted the nation).

With his debilitating deafness, Maurras cut an isolated figure at the bench. His bearing throughout the trial—"aggressive, gesticulating, inexhaustible"—cut against the presiding judge and jurors.[101] "I am well aware that you do not want to believe any reasoning that comes from me" (49), he told the court, likening the trial to a "headless woman" full of "incoherence and madness" (50). The vain pettiness of this "immortal," as members of the French Academy were called, was readily apparent. At one point a witness statement by playwright Paul Claudel was read, which infuriated Maurras, who threatened to launch a counter-suit of calumny and defamation against a writer whose pompous, overblown style, full of "Hebrew vocalizations" (38), was nothing but "Dada" (46).[102] Although the presiding judge had wanted to examine the textual record article by article, Maurras pre-empted that investigation with a lengthy statement that went on for two days, an astounding one hundred thirty-five printed pages in the trial transcript which outlined his political, literary and philosophical beliefs *ab ovo*. His statement concluded with a rhetorical flourish against a political trial that covered up the real criminals and traitors (those who led France to the *débâcle*):

> Come, then, false informers, false transcribers or bad readers of the clearest texts: come, bad inventors of intentions which may well serve your interests but are not worthy of me. Come, messengers, servitors, instruments of factions and the factious. Come, false witnesses! ... Each of you will receive the direct jet of truth, the irresistible sparks of justice as the final act of service that I, though old and infirm, can still summon to deliver to my mother country. (154)

That Maurras still had rhetorical fireworks was apparent in this hijacking of the proceedings, which can only be explained by the presiding judge indulging the elderly writer as the international press looked on, a show of legality to deflect charges that the verdict was predetermined.

When the interrogation proper began, with the presiding judge addressing not so much Maurras but the stenographers ("demand Maurras," "ask him the following questions"), the answers were equally dogmatic. The occupation of France was likened to a game of musical chairs, with the German seat now taken by "the Jewish occupier"

(159). (His anti-Semitism, he noted in a rhetorical sleight-of-hand, was a classical, humanist, Christian one, with deep roots in French history, and had nothing to do with Nazi racialism.) The witnesses called to the stand were supremely inept, even with allowances made for the countless dodgy characters that the chaotic times sprouted. What sense could one make of an "occasional reader of *Action Française*" (180) who had an unnamable beef with Maurras? Testimony which tried to show that a denunciation in *Action Française* led to an arrest—nothing was a worse crime in postwar France—was pure speculation ("The article appeared and then," the defense attorney asked incredulously, "the Gestapo intervened?" [183]). When the accuser was told that in his first police statement he was unaware of the article's existence, and thus could not make a causal connection between article and arrest, the witness blithely answered, "I was wrong in my first deposition, but my second one is the right one" (187). The brother of the Foreign Minister, whose relationship to the case was unclear, simply expressed regret at "excesses of the pen and language" (180). The report on Maurras's wartime writings commissioned by the regional intelligence services contained egregious misreadings and invented quotes. How that task could be conferred to a thirty-one-year-old local teacher of no name or distinction who was under arrest for fraud and forgery was never cleared up. Then, continuing the snafu, the prosecution introduced into evidence a dossier of Maurras's printed articles that was hastily assembled, full of typographical errors, with phrases that did not appear in the print record, which undercut the supposed transparency of a text as undeniable (or even stable) evidence.

On the other side, the defense witnesses were a cascade of loyal Maurrasian followers. Central casting seemed to be behind the stereotypes assembled on the stand: the French prisoner who testified that a German officer called Maurras, in impeccable, unaccented French, "our most implacable enemy" (217); the concierge who noted that the communists who had ransacked *Action Française*'s offices made off with irons and radiators; the local tradesman, whose son was in the resistance, who had learned the meaning of honor from his signed copy of *L'Allemagne eternelle* (1921); the improbably named Mme la Comtesse Marie-Renée-Henriette de Dreuz-Brezé, a local writer and war nurse, who blissfully recalled the pleasures and enlightenment of an Action Française study circle at Verdun in 1914. The presiding judge grew weary of testimony that had nothing to do with the case at hand, which was not, he insisted, about Maurras's general beliefs but rather specific wartime writings, an admonition that did little to stop the parade of AF followers who vaunted the undiminished patriotism of their leader.

That was very much the issue in the case: was this about Maurras's beliefs or about his texts? The *requisitoire*, or closing argument, of the government stressed that the case would remain "entirely based on facts. I will not discuss any of Maurras's ideas" (244). The facts were as follows: before the war, when "the freedom of opinion was complete" (243), Maurras had every right to be a monarchist, against democracy, to attack communists and Jews. But once war started, taking a public stand in support of Vichy effectively meant supporting laws and acts that favored the occupier and thus acted against the interests of France. The term *les faits*—the facts—was repeated throughout the closing argument ("the facts are undeniable, cannot be discussed"; "the facts are established, clear, precise" [264]), as if a text, by reason of its solidity and materiality, gave rise to "facts" and not "opinions." This was very much in line with the view of authorship as a legal signature affixed to an individual instance, whereas Maurras's defense was based on a holistic view of authorship as an ensemble of acts with a deeper intentionality. As the defense's closing statement put it, the prosecutors never even tried to show any "guilty intention" (309), whereas anyone who went through Maurras's writings, including his poetry (which the defense's closing argument declaimed), could have a more complete picture of his worldview. "All of the case lies in the numerous articles" he wrote (249), and these articles were so clear in imputing guilt that there was "no need for commentaries" (250). "What else can one say, is there any need to discuss these lines?" the prosecutor noted (256). The meaning of these "facts" was "undeniable" (264): Maurras had done "an immense harm to France through his talent" and genius (265). But those were abstractions. In an effort to make more tangible the harm of these writings, the prosecutor stressed how *Action Française* denounced resisters, with individuals finding themselves arrested after their names appeared in the paper. The main charge against Maurras boiled down to him having denounced resisters and enjoined Vichy and the Gestapo to round up malefactors. One defense lawyer was aghast to see the trial of the most famous French intellectual reduced to a sordid case of gossip and innuendo, "the affair of a village lady accused of having denounced her neighbors" (274). How would history judge the French state in several centuries—and how would the world react to putting to the rack the country's most famous intellectual? The global implications of the trial (foreigners appreciated Maurras's "great value" [305]), and its historical legacy, were put forward by the defense as a way to remind jurors that their passions for retribution were momentary and localized—people in other countries and in different times would see that justice was disfigured out of a desire to "seek revenge" (306). If anything, the defense concluded, the only country that would benefit from Maurras being punished would, ironically, be Germany, the chief target of his vitriol.

Maurras was no stranger to courtrooms, but he could not have been under any illusions as to how serious this was. At the same time, the game was done before the trial started. Four days of testimony, with over a full day given over to Maurras reading out his prepared statement, would never convince anyone, even though the defense made a strong case by showing that no guilty intent was established and proved that Maurras never benefited financially from his ideas (he was no sell-out). The jurors came back with a guilty verdict, with a life sentence to be served in reclusion abroad, an act of mercy for a deaf eighty-year-old who no one wanted to see in front of a firing squad, save intransigent communists who were disgusted at how Maurras had managed to "save his head."[103]

In both trials, the evidence against Brasillach and Maurras consisted solely of their writings. There was little doubt that both had signed their names to wartime texts that had appeared in collaborationist venues. But did a signature result in complete and total responsibility for the text that was written, as the prosecution argued? The nature of wartime censorship undermined the traditional freedom of the writer, who had no choice but to color within the lines drawn by Vichy and the Germans. The second problem was determining what the isolated phrases of those wartime writings could mean. In Brasillach's trial, the prosecutor noted that with "many too articles" to consider, "we would never finish" if every single one were dissected (150)—so a select few were chosen as exemplary. In Maurras's trial, too, individual articles were examined in turn. Looking at isolated articles—or, what happened more often, isolated quotations—made sense when it came to highlighting their propaganda function, but it resulted in a transparent, simplified reading of text that could be wildly misleading. At times phrases were cut beyond recognition or transcribed incorrectly, so the material evidence was mistaken. In other instances, the texts were read naively, without any sophistication or nuance. The phrase that condemned Brasillach—the line about sleeping with Germany—was actually, his defense attorney noted, an allusion to Ernest Renan. The meaning of Brasillach's texts required a more sophisticated reading strategy than the one practiced by the police or the unassuming simple reader: "You have before you a man of letters with wide literary knowledge, and it so happens that not everyone is as knowledgeable as he is" (193).

Seeing authorship as simply the sum of individual writings denied the very complexity of a writer's thought and career. Both Brasillach and Maurras grounded their defense on what they saw as a coherent "ensemble" of authorship. Brasillach even went so far as to refuse to have any witnesses so that the court could judge him "only on his ideas" (13). Given how much he had written during the war—Brasillach estimated around 1,000 to 1,200 total pages—it was dishonest to pick out some select passages and cite them as representative of his thinking without any further explication as to what drove them. Every single piece of writing, he insisted, had to be judged as to what drove it (his intention) and what it could have meant "*à ce moment-là*" (71), at that moment in time (its context). Maurras pointed to a lifetime of agitating for France and French interests that was almost *prima facie* refutation of the charge of treason. For Brasillach, his support for collaboration was based on his view that this furthered French interests. Perhaps that was mistaken, but "the intention was not an error" (72).

Trying to show how writing led to consequences was an issue in both trials, although the State had no real theory or proof of incitement. For Brasillach, incitement was mainly a rhetorical question: "How many scatterbrained youths had you, by your articles, incited to the fight against the *maquis*? For how many crimes were you intellectually responsible?" (159). Maurras had been saying the same thing for so long that the crime no longer had a starting date—his crime was having laid the foundations of anti-democratic, anti-republican thought for decades (in Brasillach's trial: "It must not be forgotten that if you became a fascist, it is because Maurras, under the [Third] Republic, could write against the Republic" [166]). But in so doing the prosecution was dealing with milieus and environments, nothing tangible. At times there was an effort to link a particular article with a particular act, mainly when it came to a public denunciation and then a Gestapo or Vichy police arrest. Even if these attempted links strained credibility, they became central to the convictions of both writers. In both cases, there was a scrupulous effort to deny the central point of the trials, which was ruling on the political beliefs of the two authors, by stressing the direct harm of the denunciations: the speech in question was no longer political but rather an instance of direct harm by targeting a particular individual.

The problem was that the evidence in both cases was less than persuasive—but in the heat of the day, what mattered most was dressing the crime as that of a speech act rather than an opinion.

Céline, or the Vagaries of International Justice

Fittingly for a process that began in North Africa, the French postwar purge was eminently international. This was not so much due to France's extensive colonial possessions—most colonies threw in their lot with De Gaulle early on—but the heightened population flows in the chaos of the times. As the war began to turn, collaborators sought safety in places like Switzerland (Paul Morand), Spain (Abel Bonnard), and, of course, Germany, where a colony of Vichy administrators, politicians, and lackeys was relocated. The most conspicuous member of this enclave at Sigmaringen was Louis-Ferdinand Céline, who stayed nearly a year there before making off to Denmark. The Céline affair is instructive in showing the international dimensions of the French purge, its diplomatic maneuverings exposing the tensions of political justice.

Perhaps no French writer had such an explosive impact on French letters in the 1930s as Céline (Figure 3.6). His debut novel, *Voyage au bout de la nuit*, deployed a shrill,

Figure 3.6 Louis-Ferdinand Céline, 1932. Courtesy of Gallica/BnF.

punctuated staccato rhythm and inventive *argot* (slang) to denounce the horrors of the First World War and modernity. While Céline's prose sounded the death knell of classic French literary language, his politics were reactionary, with an anti-Semitism that was not "just a little bit for laughs, but ferociously, down to the bowels," as he announced in *Bagatelles pour un massacre*, his late 1930s polemic against "Jewish dictatorship."[104] A trained doctor, Céline also spoke of the "biological superiority" of Aryans in that book, which sold over 75,000 copies before it was withdrawn from circulation in May 1939 (for violating the April 1939 Marchandeau decree on defamation and incitement of hatred toward a specific race or religion).[105] Despite the natural affinities of Céline's anti-Semitism with Nazi racial thinking, during the war years Céline was not friendly with either Vichy or the Germans. His 1941 pamphlet *Les beaux draps*, which sold 15,000 copies in fifteen days, criticized Vichy for being too timid ("More Jews than ever on the streets, more Jews than ever in the press, more Jews than ever at the bar, more Jews than ever at the Sorbonne … France more than ever given over to Freemasons and Jews") and was soon removed from circulation.[106] His other major wartime text was the novel *Guignol's Band*, a nostalgic portrait of London during the First World War; otherwise, his wartime writings consisted of letters reprinted in newspapers, a few interviews, and some responses to surveys. He was not paid for these forays into print, which made the case against him challenging: here was a writer whose natural affinities were with Germany but who resisted any contact with the German authorities and openly despised Vichy. Two days after the D-Day landings, Céline received a German visa, in the hope of ending up in Copenhagen (in 1938, convinced that a war was coming, he had emptied his Lloyds Bank account in London and moved it to Copenhagen, and then, in 1942, through an intermediary in Berlin, he had had some gold deposited in a Danish bank). After a long stay in Germany, he, his partner, Lucette Destouches, and their cat, Bébert, made it to the Danish capital in late March 1945, around the same time that a French court issued an arrest warrant for treason against him. At first Céline lived under an assumed name (taken from a character in *Mort à credit*), but after Copenhagen was liberated in early May, he applied for a residence permit. The application noted that Céline was a "global celebrity" whose most recent writings, "of an anti-Semitic and pacifist inspiration," were banned in both France and Germany.[107] In December of that year, after news of his whereabouts began to appear in the French press and the Copenhagen daily *Politiken*, the French authorities formally requested Céline's arrest. He ended up languishing in an unheated room in Vestre Faengsel prison for fourteen months.

The French authorities put pressure on Copenhagen to extradite Céline, not only through formal letters to the Danish Foreign Ministry but also through a strategic use of the press in both countries.[108] Had that request succeeded, Céline feared that "they will kill me for sure, but only after having tortured me."[109] Any extradition, though, would have to abide by the joint Franco-Danish treaty of 1877. The list of extraditable crimes in that treaty included parricide, infanticide, murder, bigamy, rape, abortion, sexual assault, kidnapping, and counterfeiting, but not treason. Political crimes, in fact, were expressly forbidden as a motive for an extradition. There was a humanitarian rationale behind this (a political criminal was likely to suffer torture and be denied due process) but also an obvious element of *Realpolitik* (providing shelter to revolutionaries whose political goals matched one's own). For his part, Céline began to call himself a "political refugee" and pressed his attorney to apply for asylum.[110] To justify its extradition request, the French foreign ministry transmitted a series of briefs on Céline's crimes, but the charges were so vague (Céline had been a member of a pro-German doctor's group, he had "facilitated" German propaganda) that the Copenhagen chief of police quickly dismissed the request. A team assembled at the Ministry of Justice agreed, but it also noted that since Céline had no legal right to stay in the country, he could be extradited (or, at the very least, expelled—the only question being to where). The chief of the French legation could not conceal his displeasure at the flimsy evidence, telling his superiors at the Quai d'Orsay that he could no longer, with a straight face, press the case for extradition (privately, he was more cutting: "I am made ridiculous every week asking for Céline's extradition ... his dossier is empty! He doesn't risk a thing!").[111] He asked for "clearly specified" charges and not the "incredibly vague" accusations that made it seem as if Céline's crime was a "délit d'opinion," a crime of opinion, which would not get anywhere in a country firmly attached to the principle of free speech.[112] For such a "notorious collaborator," he noted after receiving yet another charge sheet from Paris full of innuendo, hearsay, and random quotes, it was inconceivable that a competent prosecutor could not assemble more persuasive evidence.[113]

Denmark had also been occupied during the war, and while that occupation was initially clement—Denmark was able to maintain its own political order and held multi-party elections—an organized resistance soon appeared. In the final two years of the war, Denmark was "administered" by the Wehrmacht, with all the repression that entailed. Copenhagen was thus sympathetic to the need for states to conduct postwar purges (40,000 Danes were interned that first summer, and over 13,000 would be found guilty of collaboration and sentenced to prison terms), but it also wanted to privilege the reinstatement of legalism and the rule of law.[114] Three Danish ministries ended up examining the Céline dossier: Foreign Affairs, which privileged maintaining close ties with France and playing its part in rendering "war criminals" to justice; Justice, which sought an absolute legality; and then "Special Affairs," the ministry set up to oversee the purge, which was led by Per Federspiel, a hallowed resistance figure who was a lawyer.[115] Different interests had to be balanced; for one thing, refusing to extradite Céline could result in Denmark being branded an unlawful international actor, undermining the creation of a stable international order by refusing to engage in the tracking down of war criminals. While some countries were beginning to refuse extradition requests for war criminals, and many countries were hesitant to repatriate Soviet POWs, Céline's was a high-profile case that would put Denmark on the map for all the wrong reasons. A refusal to extradite would also create a precedent that other war criminals could use to stay within Denmark's borders (and given the shared border with Germany and long occupation, there were more than a few in the country) or that other countries would refuse to extradite Danish war criminals, on the pretext that the prosecution was politically motivated. Yet a swift extradition without any legal basis of a political opponent could also undermine the international legal order by exposing the victor's justice behind postwar law. The Foreign Ministry was mindful of all these possible repercussions, and like many a bureaucracy, decided that the safest course in an unprecedented situation was to dither and stall until circumstances changed.[116] Even had it wanted to act, though, Special Affairs was firmly against extraditing Céline, with Federspiel judging the evidence against the writer unsubstantiated.

At first, this suited Céline, who had instructed his attorney Thorvald Mikkelsen, a well-connected, Francophile Dane, to stall for time: "It's a case of waiting two or three years," he noted in January 1946, until the terror in France subsided.[117] But stalling endlessly was not the plan, either. After a few months of prison, Céline had had enough: "The life that we are leading is no better than death; on the contrary, I would rather risk it once and for all" than deal with the continual delay and uncertainty of his fate: "At least there [France] I would be given the chance to defend myself—even if in vain. And then it would be done. The play would be over."[118] Prison and the "*harrowing incertitude*" of his case had led to a "major nervous depression, I am at the end of the rope."[119] If Denmark had been right to not extradite Céline, Mikkelsen noted almost a year after his client's arrest, it was not doing itself any honor to the rule of law by letting him rot in the kingdom: justice delayed was justice denied. Céline's letters to officialdom were increasingly shrill in denouncing the inhumane conditions of his internment and warning of an imminent breakdown. Céline's international celebrity ultimately moved the Danes to mitigate the harshness of internment by transferring him to recuperate at Rigshospitalet. Not that his time in hospital was any smoother: over twenty doctors signed an open letter saying that the patient under their charge was an incorrigible anti-Semite and collaborator who deserved to be behind bars, not taking up a bed that a former concentration-camp survivor could otherwise fill.

Back in France, with little prospect of Céline being extradited, the government decided to try him in absentia. The arrest warrant, on charges of treason (violating Article 75), had been issued in mid-April 1945, despite no copies of his political pamphlets in police custody (his publisher, Denoël, had been instructed to destroy all works by Céline). The *instruction du dossier*, the criminal investigative file, eventually spanned four-and-a-half years of police searches and interrogations "concerning the lifestyle, origins and morality of the indicted."[120] There were efforts, as late as 1948, to tie Céline down to wartime trips to Germany or Katyn. A "study of Céline's œuvre" went no further than the conventional division between "novelistic" and "pamphleteer." At first no movement was taken to try Céline because there were still hopes that he would be extradited, but by mid-1947 it was clear that the Danish authorities would not honor the request. The investigating magistrate assigned to Céline's case, Jean Seltensperger, was not convinced by the assembled evidence, but the principle of judicial independence eventually cracked after a press leak blamed him for delaying the case. The new magistrate knew how to read the tea leaves and promptly got the ball rolling. The case against Céline boiled down to the publication of *Les beaux draps*, the re-publication of *Bagatelles*, personal letters that appeared in *Au Pilori*, and Céline's membership in the "Cercle Européen," a collaborationist association. A work like *Bagatelles*, the charge sheet read, could be opened "at random" to find incriminating passages; it would be "too long and bothersome" to single out any page.[121] But instead of charging the writer with treason, Céline was charged under article 83-4 for committing "acts whose nature was to undermine national defense." The Paris Court of Appeal held a preliminary hearing on Céline's case in mid-December 1949, two weeks after the new magistrate, who had been in function for less than a month, issued his findings. A telegram demanded Céline to present himself to the court by the end of the year. His refusal to do so resulted in him being considered a fugitive from justice and thus opened the door for a trial in absentia.

Before the trial opened in late February, though, a number of intellectuals and writers came to Céline's side in a January 1950 *Libertaire* survey. He had often wondered if some eminent authors would defend him, but he was persuaded that with his foremost backer, his publisher, dead, he had no one to turn to: "I am lost here in total darkness."[122] The literary community in France had never truly welcomed him: "almost all French writers, young and old, a devilishly jealous race if there were ever one" had an unquenchable hatred of him, they having never "pardoned my sudden, spectacular debut in French letters. Those folks will not stop until I am executed."[123] Despite being convinced that "there are ten, there are a hundred, there a thousand … wanting me silent, killed, suppressed," Céline found some ready supporters for his cause.[124] American academics like Milton Hindus (see Figure 3.7) and French writers like Marcel Aymé stressed Céline's absolute independence from all political movements. Marcel Jouhandeau placed him in the tradition of Aristophanes, Juvenal, and Rabelais to state that his satire was a purely literary undertaking (that was how Céline saw it, too, claiming that the "outlandish character" and "enormous comedy" of his anti-Semitism made it "strictly literary").[125] The most even-handed defense came from Jean Galtier-Boissière, whose diaries were required reading to make sense of the times; he noted that Céline had never personally profited from his celebrity or literary standing during the war. Letters from abroad also came in, such as Henry Miller proffering the view that while "real rogues usually get off lightly," "someone who has contributed so much to world culture can be given some wiggle room."[126] The Swedish consul to France, Raoul Nordling, who had been instrumental in ensuring that the City of Light had not been razed by the Germans in 1944, sent in a letter calling for France to live up to its liberal, generous, humane past. These petitions, from both French and international figures, appealed to a certain image of France as a *pays de culture*. On the opposite side, though, a venomous pamphlet, *L'affaire Céline*, showed what Céline was up against. Penned by Maurice Vanino, a resistance figure, specialist in anti-Semitism, and war-crimes hunter, the pamphlet undercut Céline's literary originality and standing and reduced his writings to pure anti-Semitism advancing German war aims. Vanino's pamphlet parodied Céline's rapid-fire prose style to great effect, offering a line-by-line refutation by using Céline's own words to show bad faith, evil intentions, and treason. "The disciples of Céline have been punished—will the master escape all punishment?"[127] The tone of the pamphlet was not far off the scurrilous treatment Céline was receiving from the French press at the time, which ramped up interest in his case as the trial approached: *L'Humanité* claimed that he had been a Gestapo agent, *Regards* stated that he was living it up in a five-star hotel, *La Tribune des Nations* expressed regret that he had not been summarily shot in

Jeudi LETTRES · Vendredi TOURISME-AUTO · Samedi-Dimanche ARTS-LOISIRS-ÉCHECS · Lundi AVIATION · Mardi ÉCONOMIE · Mercredi LANGUE-JEUNESSE-UNIVERSITÉ

Un Juif témoigne pour Louis-Ferdinand Céline

Préface du Professeur Milton Hindus de l'Université de Chicago, à la traduction américaine de "Mort à Crédit"

Le Livre et l'Auteur

L.-F. CÉLINE (dessin de Jacques ZEITOUN)

« Je ne vois pas pourquoi on continue à lire les autres auteurs »

Un producteur de cauchemars

L'antisémitisme de Céline

Un succès universel

Je suis moi-même Juif

Milton HINDUS

Voyages dans la littérature vivante

LES LIVRES par Maurice NADEAU

La semaine littéraire

Makronissos laboratoire politique

Leçons par correspondance

Informations

Vous pourrez lire

SIGRID UNDSET

OLAV AUDUNSSØN

STOCK

l'un des plus beaux GIONO

Les Ames fortes

roman

Figure 3.7 "A Jew testifies for Louis-Ferdinand Céline," *Combat*, January 19, 1950. Courtesy of Gallica/BNF, all rights reserved.

1944, and so on.[128] *Combat*'s preview of his trial spelled out its likely end: "Alright then, five years in prison!"[129]

All those letters and petitions were in lieu of any formal defense of Céline, which was not admitted in a trial in absentia. For his part, Céline also wrote copiously in his own defense, with around twenty-five personal letters addressed to the various judges and magistrates overseeing the case. Those letters were ways for him to "refute the big picture and the tiny detail, the inept claims, almost everything, everything, lies, inventions, stupidities, bad faith, pretentions, wrong dates, everything."[130] Rather than allowing his lawyers in Denmark and France to press his case ("It's not easy to defend me," he candidly admitted), Céline preferred to try to persuade the French judges of his innocence, even though his literary style, with its excesses and personal victimhood, was far removed from the dry legal writing they were accustomed to reading.[131] This to a sitting judge ready to oversee the case in a few days: "But yes! I was Hitler's mistress! But yes! I delivered Pas-de-Calais to Keitel! The port of Toulon! I organized Oradour [an infamous massacre] with Abetz etc. … etc. … I must tell you—I am not guilty of anything—and even worse monstrosities, not at all."[132] Even the material form of these letters—mostly handwritten, on poor-quality paper—hardly fit the norm.[133] Yet their effect was not entirely nugatory; as one French lawyer put it, the prosecuting magistrate found Céline's letters "spontaneous and sincere": "Write him a packet of letters, funny ones; that will get you two close. He really admires you, so you might as well take advantage of that."[134]

Céline's defense—first set down in 1946, in a fifteen-page prison letter, and then again in 1950, before his trial in absentia—centered on the idea that he stood apart from politics or the public sphere, had never joined any groups, had never penned any articles, and had abstained from voting: "I have always remained strictly and only A WRITER"; "I am a writer and nothing but a writer"; "at no moment either before or during the war was I anything but a *writer*, in the pure sense of the term, if I may say so, *never* a journalist, *never* a propagandist, *never* a politician, never a soldier, *French, a doctor* and *a writer*—that is what I am and nothing else. *No compromises.*"[135] Even his refusal to install a telephone at home was a sign of his "horror" of the wider world.[136] If he had any political beliefs, they were complete pacifism and hatred of war in any form. He saw himself as a victim of sinister *complots* by his literary enemies, of which there were scores: "The crime is not mine but lies with those persecuting me. *And they know it*—that explains their rage, their babble, their bad faith."[137] He was not surprised given that the "persecution of writers" was a "national sport."[138] This view was so deeply engrained in Céline that it even figured in the international petition, instigated by Edgar Varèse and signed by Henry Miller, which spoke of personal revenge by literary rivals as the true motivation of the case against him. Other times he blamed his imprisonment entirely on "absolute Jewish vengeance."[139] There was no low he would not stoop to when painting his victimhood: "There is one persecuted individual in all this sordid affair and it's ME. It is *me* that I complain about, and I'm not done complaining. They talk to you about the suffering and martyrs of Buchenwald! We too had to endure suffering … the difference being that the Jews themselves had *pushed* for war while I wanted to stop it."[140] "The

Jews," a sentence that always began treacherously in Céline's prose, "should erect a statute for me for all the harm that I did not do to them. If I had been in charge of them, I could easily have deported an extra 300,000 to 400,000 to Poland."[141]

There was never much doubt about how the court would rule, especially since the crime was no longer treason but rather "undermining national defense." The verdict of one year in jail and a 50,000 francs penalty, as well as a state of "national indignity" upon Céline, was not particularly heavy.[142] The prison sentence, for one thing, would be vacated, as he had already been interned in Denmark for longer than one year. What stung was the order to seize half of Céline's goods in the future: any income he would make from writing would be taken by the French state. Remaining a fugitive in Denmark, under the provisional liberty that that state accorded him, in the isolated farmhouse of his lawyer's country home, was not going to be given up if the return to France meant financial ruin. He would rather, Céline told his lawyers, publish abroad and have his work circulate clandestinely in France than shell out a single cent to the *fisc*, which could "go to hell ONCE AND FOR ALL."[143]

The final gambit of the Céline case has made itself into literary history lore: he was amnestied a year later by lodging an application in a military tribunal under his given name, Destouches, with the military judges supposedly unaware that they were freeing the writer Céline. There is something delicious in the quote attributed to the presiding judge of the military tribunal pleading total ignorance of Céline's literary production, reportedly telling the minister of justice, "in literature, I've gone no further than Flaubert."[144] This story has been widely reprinted in any number of biographies and seems to show the legal ambiguities of authorship. It is, though, perhaps too good to be true. The basics of the case are the following: after the condemnation in absentia, Céline's lawyers attempted to benefit from a 1947 amnesty that allowed for convicted war veterans to be freed if their prison sentence was minor (less than three years). One year on from his condemnation, in late April 1951, a military tribunal declared an amnesty for Dr. Destouches, a war veteran of the First World War. Five days after the sentence, the press was let in on the secret: the tribunal had amnestied Céline without being aware of his identity.

The first problem with the story is a legal one: while there was a noticeable move to amnesty and rehabilitate war criminals by 1951 (most countries by this point had passed amnesty laws, but that did not stop the incongruous situation of purge courts still in operation), Céline could not have benefited from the 1947 law. There was a special provision for First-World-War veterans in that amnesty law, but there was also an explicit notice that "in no case" could individuals convicted for collaboration or designated with national indignity benefit from an amnesty.[145] The amnesty law did include a provision concerning convictions for speech and writings: propagandists for Vichy (which was "contrary to the interests of the French people" but effected by individuals who maintained "their duty of attachment to France") could be amnestied, with the implication being that individuals who had pushed pro-German propaganda could not.[146] If this distinction required the wisdom of Solon to discern, it was unclear if Céline's case would have fallen under it, as he had despised Vichy but had shown no great love for the Germans either. It would be unlikely to see Céline as maintaining his "duty of attachment to France" when he had abandoned the country in 1944.

If, legally, Céline should not have been amnestied, what happened? The fiction that the convictions for Céline the writer were unknown to the military tribunal treating the Destouches dossier are belied by the dossier transmitted to the court, which included the "Declaration of the Court of Justice in the trial against the named Destouches Louis-Ferdinand known as Louis-Ferdinand Céline."[147] No trained judge—and the court had military and civilian judges—could miss that "Destouches" had been convicted of collaboration and sentenced to national indignity. The military tribunal, furthermore, did not formally consider the amnesty law in its hearing but reaffirmed the earlier 1950 ruling. Rather than giving credit to Céline's inveterate paranoia, in which he saw himself as the victim of devilish plots, the archive shows Céline benefiting from machinations in his favor. Handwritten on the judicial judgment is a note granting Céline amnesty on the basis of the acts being committed before January 16, 1947, and Céline being a war veteran—but Anne Simonin argues that nothing in the tribunal hearing allowed for this to be added to the court judgment, as the amnesty was never discussed. That handwritten addition was nothing other than "a false statement on an official document" (a heavy crime in France, with a maximum penalty of forced labor for life).[148] How this could have happened can be explained by the widespread and well-organized movement within the military tribunals to undermine the purge sentences that many felt had been abusive.[149] The politics of the times had changed: the anti-communist collaborators condemned by the red wave in 1945 were, a half-dozen years later, on the right side of history. Even resistance figures like the serving Minister of Justice René Mayer were keen to wrap up the purge and put a definitive end to the continued martyrdom that it brought to figures like Pétain and Maurras. As Simonin points out, in late 1949 Mayer had signed the conditional liberty of the former minister of Jewish affairs, Xavier Vallat, so it was no surprise that there was a push to suspend the purge. When the Ministry of Justice was informed of the legal error made by the tribunal, it made a *pro forma* declaration that the judgment should be reversed, in the interests of the law itself (so it would not serve as a precedent for other fraudulent decisions), but that the individual who had benefited from the judicial error would not be tried again. It was not so much an authorial pseudonym that saved Céline but a written falsification on an official document.

Céline returned to France a few weeks after the amnesty. The exile in Denmark came to a bitter end, albeit with a whimper by this time, as the French government had stopped putting pressure on Copenhagen to extradite Céline by the late 1940s. The case nonetheless showed how the domestic purge was ensconced in a wider international system, with competing national and international interests playing off each other. Copenhagen's refusal to honor France's extradition request also demonstrated that the purge had come to be seen as a political process. For countries keen to restore a liberal legal tradition, pursuing a "trial of opinion" was not a step forward but a retreat back to fascist repression. As time passed, the political necessity of punishing collaborators diminished while the distance between a political trial and the rule of law grew. Céline also benefited from an act of misidentification to be amnestied, although his official name did not provide cover for his more famous pseudonym, as literary lore has it. Rather, it was the unauthorized, and probably illegal, use of writing on an official document which amnestied Céline. That, too, was driven by politics, but by the early 1950s an entirely different political order had come into being.

Conclusion

One fictional recreation of the postwar trials probably went too far in having newsies hawking hot sheets in courtrooms (there was a paper shortage, after all), but that was how Philippe Saint-Germain felt postwar justice had been like, with everyone, from judge to jury to accused, knowing that the trials were just for show.[150] While Saint-Germain's book appealed to fellow "victims" of the purge (he was Inmate 3407, the cover page announced; a veritable cottage genre of prison and postwar justice memoirs, premised on the martyrdom of the suffering inmate, with nary a word on the war's indisputably innocent victims, began to appear in the 1950s), Marcel Aymé's 1952 play *La tête des autres* recreated the chaos, and, as its title points out, the inherent cruelty, of the period. The opening scene is a bourgeois comedy of the purge, with young prosecutor Maillard relating how hard he had to work in court for a guilty sentence (even if there was no "decisive proof" that the condemned had committed the crime): "Twenty times I thought that the accused would save his head. I felt him getting away from me, slipping through my fingers. Each time I managed to hit back so that he went back into the cage." His wife swoons upon hearing that the accused would be executed: "My dear! I am so happy! You can't know what joy it brings me!"[151] Another prosecutor, though, is jealous: "Think of it, my friend. Your third head. At thirty-seven years of age, that's remarkable [*c'est joli*]." "You're forgetting," Maillard responds, "the four guys who I had shot in '45." They really don't count, though: "Those four rifled down, they were sitting ducks … Be reasonable, Maillard, the deck was stacked back then. Your arguments were just for show (*que pour la forme*)."[152] With its *plus ça change* careerism, Aymé's play questions what justice could mean when everyone was swept up in hatred and a desire for blind vengeance. If Saint-Germain and Aymé were aligned to the conservative right, and thus predictably played up the horrors of the purge, even Simone de Beauvoir bemoaned how "a revenge so eagerly desired" had turned sour, leaving a "taste of ashes in our mouths."[153]

Writers had the cards stacked against them. The slate had to be wiped clean to restore France's literary prestige, which had suffered so much during the war.[154] The signed paper trail supplied ready evidence for their crimes (even if, at times, the police could not procure copies of the incriminating texts, as Vichy decrees to ban certain writers or authors had the unintended effect of destroying the evidence the prosecutors needed). The glib surface reading of all wartime literary production, with no interest in plumbing the writer's intentions or discerning the particular context driving a text, also eased the prosecutor's task. Whatever structural factors might have conditioned a text (editorial directives, strict censorship, etc.) were dismissed as irrelevant when compared to the complicity of even appearing in print when the literary field was under the full control of the Germans. The defense that writers could muster was feeble in comparison. The exceptional courts dismissed out of hand any suggestion that the trials were illegitimate or that the writing in question had been legal at the time of its printing. The defense that most political and economic collaborators used to great success—that they were playing a *double jeu*—was not well-suited for the pen. A civil servant or factory owner could claim that executing German policies or supplying the German military allowed for the protection of others or kept French workers in a job (and thus stopped them from being sent to Germany as forced laborers). For writers, though, the *double jeu* would have had to have occurred in their private lives, which was hard to document and often unpersuasive when coming from an individual whose attitude toward the occupation seemed, in print, to be fixed.

The high-profile trials of authors reoriented the French literary field. After four years of servility, writers were back in control, playing leading parts in the trials of those who had dishonored the pen and French culture more broadly. The corporatist purge of the literary field proved to be a mixed blessing, though, as writers were less than competent administrators and prosecutors. What proved more lasting was the way in which authorial responsibility was refashioned by the postwar trials. The process of assigning moral value to the positions a writer took had already begun during the war, upending years of blithe, Belle Époque aestheticism, but it was given a legal form in the postwar as writers were called to task for the positions they took. That every act or word under occupation could spell death loaded meaning into every choice. Sartre's *écrivain engagé* reversed traditional literary values by seeing public engagement as a duty; it was impossible to remain an ostrich in the sand, unconcerned with a wider society. That engagement, though, came with a price: the right to error was no longer given.

Notes

1 Paul Éluard, *Au rendez-vouz allemand* (Paris: Éditions de Minuit, 2012), 9, 10–11, 12, 28, 53.
2 "La haine, devoir nationale," *L'Humanité*, January 10, 1945, 1.
3 "Le devoir de tuer," *Défense de la France* 44 (March 15, 1944), 1.
4 Peter Novick, *The Resistance Versus Vichy: The Purge of Collaborators in Liberated France* (New York: Columbia University Press, 1968), 28.
5 Marcel Jouhandeau, *Journal sous l'Occupation* (Paris: Gallimard, 1980), 132.
6 Quoted in Jean-Louis Crémieux-Brilhac, "Avant la Libération: La politique de la Justice à Alger et le procès Pucheu (1943–1944)," in *La justice de l'épuration: À la fin de la Seconde Guerre mondiale*, ed. Pierre Truche and Denis Salas (Paris: La Documentation française, 2008), 27–34, at 27.
7 Jean Galtier-Broissière, *Mon journal depuis la libération* (Paris: La Jeune Parque, 1945), 46.
8 Indomitus, *Nous sommes les rebelles* (Paris: Collection Défense de l'homme, 1945), 47.
9 "Épuration," *Esprit*, 30 NS, no. 1 (December 1944): 153.
10 Simone de Beauvoir, "An Eye for an Eye," in *Philosophical Writings*, ed. Margaret A. Simons (Urbana: University of Illinois Press, 2004), 237–60, at 246.
11 Herbert Lottmann, *The People's Anger: Justice and Revenge in Post-Liberation France* (London: Hutchinson, 1986), 33.

12 Ibid., 56.
13 *Résistance* 24 (June 25, 1944), 1.
14 Novick, *Resistance Versus Vichy*, 71.
15 Agnès Poirier, *Left Bank: Art, Passion, and the Rebirth of Paris, 1940–1950* (New York: Henry Holt, 2018), 75.
16 Charles de Gaulle, *Discours et Messages*, 5 vols. (Paris: Plon 1970), 1: 394.
17 Ibid., 1: 493.
18 The same was true for the art world, with every gallery or salon requiring official approval from the Propaganda Abteilung and no show able to open until a German *referat* inspected the exposed works. This did not strangle the art world: from May 1941 until autumn 1943, the number of galleries in Paris doubled; see Michèle Cone, *Artists Under Vichy: A Case of Prejudice and Persecution* (Princeton: Princeton University Press, 1992), 12.
19 Pascal Ory, *Les collaborateurs, 1940–1945* (Paris: Éditions du Seuil, 1976), 217; Bruno Goyet and Philippe Olivera, "Les mondes intellectuels dans la tourmente des conflits," in *La vie intellectuelle en France*, ed. Christophe Charle and Laurent Jeanpierre, vol. 2: *De 1914 à nos jours* (Paris: Seuil, 2016), 19–41, at 20.
20 Quoted in Jeanyves Guérin, *Les listes noirs de 1944: Pour une histoire littéraire de l'épuration* (Paris: Presses Sorbonne Nouvelle, 2016), 23.
21 "Les Sequestres de presse," n.d., ANF, 72AJ/383.
22 The number of official, German-licensed publications can be contrasted to the number of clandestine publications; the *Catalogue des périodiques clandestins* of the Bibliothèque nationale lists 1,106 venues that appeared clandestinely during the war. The difference was that many of these were no more than mimeographed one-page pamphlets, one-person jobs that appeared irregularly or only once, but others, like *Défense de la France*, had massive print runs (150,000) that required a vast secret network of contributors, producers, and distributors.
23 Pascal Fouché, *L'Édition française sous l'occupation, 1940–1944* (Paris: Bibliothèque de Littérature française contemporaine de l'Université Paris 7, 1987), 2: 193–5. See "Circulaire Hachette No. 1 – Mars 1945," ANF, 72AJ/383.
24 Ministry of Interior circular to Commissaires Regionaux, Prefets, and Police Prefets, November 3, 1944, ANF, 72AJ/383.
25 Quoted in Guérin, *Listes noirs*, 25.
26 Quoted in Lottman, *People's Anger*, 141.
27 Quoted in Lottman, *People's Anger*, 158.
28 CDG, *Mémoires de Guerre* (Paris: Plon, 1999), 711.
29 See Novick, *Resistance Versus Vichy*; Robert Aron, *Histoire de l'épuration*, vol. 2: *Le monde de la presse, des arts, des lettres, 1944–1953* (Paris: Fayard, 1976); Lottmann, *People's Anger*; Philip Watts, *Allegories of the Purge: How Literature Responded to the Postwar Trials of Writers and Intellectuals in France* (Stanford: Stanford University Press, 1998); Gisèle Sapiro, *La guerre des écrivains: 1940–1953* (Paris: Fayard, 1999); Alice Kaplan, *The Collaborator: The Trial and Execution of Robert Brasillach* (Chicago: University of Chicago Press, 2000); and Guérin, *Listes noires*.
30 "Epurons l'épuration," *Esprit* 30 NS, no. 2 (January 1945): 290–2, at 290.
31 See Alya Aglan and Emmanuelle Loyer, "Épuration, histoire d'un mot," in *Une poignée de misérables: L'épuration de la société française après la Seconde Guerre mondiale*, ed. Marc Olivier Baruch (Paris: Fayard, 2003), 19–34, at 21–3.
32 Sylvain Boulouque and Pascal Girard, "Introduction," in *Traîtres et trahisons: Guerres, imaginaires sociaux et constructions politiques*, ed. Sylvain Boulouque and Pascal Girard (Paris: Seli Arslan, 2007), 11–24, at 16.
33 Article 75.3, *JO*, July 30, 1939, 9631.

34 Quoted in Gérard Loiseaux, *La littérature de la défaite et de la collaboration* (Paris: Fayard, 1995), 158.
35 Maurice Betz, *Dialogue des prisonniers 1940* (Paris: Editions Émile-Paul Frères, 1940), 44.
36 *Aujourd'hui*, September 2, 1942, 1.
37 CDG, *Discours*, 1: 39; Schumann quoted in Lottman, *People's Anger*, 28.
38 Bernard Vosges, *Défense de l'occident* (Paris: Les Sept Couleurs, 1957), 9.
39 Novick, *Resistance Versus Vichy*, 141.
40 *JO*, July 6, 1944, 536. The same understanding of allegiance had been employed by Vichy, which promulgated a decree in February 1941 to allow for the denationalization of anyone from the colonies who "betray[ed] by his actions, speeches, or writings the duties incumbent upon him as a member of the national community." See Patrick Weil, *How To Be French: Nationality in the Making Since 1870*, trans. Catherine Porter (Durham: Duke University Press, 2008 [2002]), 87.
41 See Anne Simonin, *Le déshonneur dans la République: Une histoire de l'indignité 1791–1958* (Paris: Bernard Grasset, 2008).
42 Article 10, ordonnance June 26, 1944.
43 Jean Paulhan, *Lettre aux directeurs de la Résistance* (1952), in *Œuvres complètes*, vol. 5: *La tache aveugle* (Paris: Cercle du Livre Précieux, 1970), 440.
44 Quoted in Jean-Paul Cointet, *Expier Vichy: L'épuration en France (1943–1958)* (Paris: Perrin, 2008), 270.
45 Julian Jackson, *A Certain Idea of France: The Life of Charles De Gaulle* (London: Allen Lane, 2018), 338.
46 Pascal Girard, "La cinquième colonne en France, 1944–1946," in *Traîtres et trahisons*, ed. Boulouque and Girard, 65–89.
47 Virginie Sansico, "La cour de justice de Lyon, section du Rhône (septembre 1944–juillet 1949)," in *La justice de l'épuration*, ed. Truche and Salas, 45–57, at 50–1.
48 Éric Conan and Henry Rousso, *Vichy, un passé qui ne passe pas* (Paris: Fayard, 1994), 17.
49 Cointet, *Expier Vichy*, 190.
50 Ibid., 10–11.
51 Marc Olivier Baruch, "Une histoire sociale de l'épuration en France," in *Une poignée de misérables*, ed. Baruch, 7–15, at 10. See also Aron, *Histoire de l'épuration*, 2: 2.
52 Sapiro, *Guerre des écrivains*, 564.
53 That, at least, was the view of Edith Thomas, who had been on the CNE's organizing committee until resigning in 1947 when the CNE was, in her eyes, effectively run by Louis Aragon and his wife, Elsa Triolet, for their own political ends. See her memoir *Le Témoin compromise* (Paris: Éditions Viviane Hamy, 1995 [1952]).
54 This is how François Mauriac put it in a 1944 letter to Jean Paulhan, in Mauriac, *Lettres d'une vie (1904–1969)* (Paris: Grasset, 1981), 281.
55 Jean Paulhan to Marcel Jouhandeau, 7 September 1944, in Jean Paulhan, *Choix de lettres*, ed. Dominique Aury, Jean-Claude Zylberstein, and Bernard Leuilliot, vol. 2: *1937–1945, Traité des jours sombres* (Paris: Gallimard, 1992), 374.
56 *JO*, May 31, 1945, 3108.
57 Georges Lecomte to Gérard Frèche, November 7, 1945, ANF, F/21/8114, dossier 3.
58 Gabriel Timmory to Gérard Frèche, November 7, 1945, ANF, F/21/8114, dossier 3.
59 Ministre de l'Education Nationale to Gérard Frèche, January 25, 1946, ANF, F/21/8114.
60 Dossier Jean Cocteau, ANF, F/21/8124, dossier 1.
61 Dossier Henri Georges Clouzot, ANF, F/21/8124, dossier 1.
62 ANF, F/21/802.
63 ANF, F/21/8114.

64 Suarez was editor-in-chief of *Notre Temps* during 1938 and until the review ceased publishing in April 1939. When it resumed publication in May 1940, still spearheaded by Luchaire but with an anti-German position (Luchaire spoke of Hitler as the "successor of Attila" and one article spoke of "The German Cancer"), Suarez was no longer a contributor to *Notre Temps*.
65 Georges Suarez, "Pétain ou la démocratie? Il faut choisir," *Aujourd'hui*, December 3, 1940, 1.
66 Georges Suarez, "Y a-t-il deux devoirs?", *Aujourd'hui*, December 10, 1940, 1.
67 "Où sont les libérateurs?", *Aujourd'hui*, June 8, 1944, 1.
68 "La 'collaboration' de Georges Suarez sera payée plus cher que jamais," *L'Aurore*, October 20, 1944, 1.
69 Many inmates at Fresnes later wrote about the human comedy there; see Henri Béraud, *Quinze jours avec la mort: La chasse au lampiste* (Roanne: Éditions Horvath, 1987 [1952]), 79–80.
70 Report, Inspectors Cantot and Daulin, n.d. (October 1944), Fonds Robert Aron F Delta 1832/1/2.
71 *L'Aurore*, September 27, 1944, 1.
72 Helen I. Cowan, "France: Wage Trends and Wage Policies, 1938–1947," *Monthly Labor Review* 65.2 (August 1947): 149–57.
73 Archives de la Prefecture de Police, 77 W art. 1495-31769 (file Bernard Grasset).
74 *Franc-Tireur*, November 28, 1945.
75 Procès-verbal, October 4, 1944, Fonds Robert Aron F Delta 1832/1/2.
76 S.R. Report, October 30, 1941, Fonds Robert Aron F Delta 1832/1/2.
77 Maurice Garçon, *Journal 1939–1945* (Paris: Fayard, 2015), 636.
78 Suarez Trial, October 23, 1944, Fonds Robert Aron F Delta 1832/1/2, 2. All further citations from Suarez trial in parenthetical citation in text (there are pagination gaps in the archive, though).
79 Pierre Bénard, "Georges Suarez s'est cherché des excuses mais n'a pas eu un cri sincère," *France-soir*, October 25, 1944, 1–2, at 1.
80 "La Justice Passe: Georges Suarez condamné à mort," *L'Aurore*, October 24, 1944, 1–2, at 1.
81 Requisitoire de M. Raphaël, Suarez Trial, October 23, 1944, Fonds Robert Aron F Delta 1832/1/2, n.p.
82 Ibid.
83 Plaidoirie of Maître Boiteau, Suarez Trial, October 23, 1944, Fonds Robert Aron F Delta 1832/1/2, n.p.
84 Ibid.
85 Pierre Bénard, "Alors, graciez Georges Suarez!", *France-soir*, November 1, 1944, 1–2, at 1.
86 *Franc-tireur*, January 28, 1945, 1.
87 Jacques Isorni, *Le procès de Robert Brasillach (19 janvier 1945)* (Paris: Flammarion, 1946), 125.
88 Archives Départementales du Rhône (Lyon), 394W/1.
89 *Le Procès de Charles Maurras* (Paris: Albin Michel, 1946), 311.
90 Report, January 16–31, 1945, Archives Départementales du Rhône (Lyon), 283/W/22.
91 Philippe Bilger, *Vingt minutes pour la mort: Robert Brasillach: le procès expédié* (Paris: Éditions du Rocher, 2010), 69.
92 Jacques Isorni, *Les cas de conscience de l'avocat* (Paris: Librairie Académique Perrin, 1965), 220.
93 *Procès Brasillach*, 38.
94 Gilles Antonowicz, *Jacques Isorni: L'avocat de tous les combats* (Paris: Éditions France-Empire, 2007), 159, 186.
95 "Notes de Me Isorni pour assurer la défense de R. Brasillach," ANF, AB/XIX/5185.
96 Ibid.
97 *Procès Brasillach*, 50.
98 On the links between treason and homosexuality, see Erin Carlston, *Double Agents: Espionage, Literature, and Liminal Citizens* (New York: Columbia University Press, 2013).

99 Note on Action Française, June 29, 1946, Archives Départementales du Rhône (Lyon), 394/W/75.
100 Ibid.
101 *Combat*, January 25, 1945, 1.
102 Procès Maurras, 39–46.
103 *Franc-Tireur*, January 28, 1945, 1.
104 Louis-Ferdinand Céline, *Bagatelles pour un massacre* (Paris: Denoël, 1937), 56, 51.
105 Céline, *Bagatelles*, 194; Damian Catani, *Louis-Ferdinand Céline: Journeys to the Extreme* (London: Reaktion Books, 2021), 168.
106 Louis-Ferdinand Céline, *Les beaux draps* (Paris: Nouvelles Éditions Françaises, 1941), 44. On its sales, see the advertisement in *La Gerbe*, March 20, 1941, 7. In his March 1946 letter presenting his defense, Céline changed his tune and called the book "harmless," a "book of pacifism, poetry and philosophy." See Céline to Thorvald Mikkelsen, March 5, 1946, in Louis-Ferdinand Céline, *Lettres de prison à Lucette Destouches et à Maître Mikkelsen, 1945–1947*, ed. François Gibault (Paris: Gallimard, 1998), 52.
107 Resident permit request, June 1, 1945, in Helga Pedersen, *Le Danemark a-t-il sauvé Céline? (1945–1951)*, trans. François Marchetti (Paris: Plon, 1975), 44.
108 See Archives Diplomatiques, 186QOSUP (Direction d'Europe, Danemark, Anciens dossiers réservés 1944–55).
109 LFC to Thorvald Mikkelsen, December 25, 1945, *Lettres prison*, 35.
110 LFC to Erik V. Hansen, February 12, 1946, *Lettres prison*, 43.
111 Quoted in *L'affaire Louis-Ferdinand Céline: Les archives de l'ambassade de France à Copenhague, 1945–1951*, ed. David Alliott (Paris: Éditions Horay, 2007), 20.
112 Charbonnière to Georges Bidault, May 29, 1946, *Archives ambassade*, 52.
113 Charbonnière to Georges Bidault, September 21, 1946, *Archives ambassade*, 88.
114 Henrik Lundtofte, "Purges, Patriotism, and Political Violence: The Danish Case 1944–1945," in *Collective Identities and Post-War Violence in Europe, 1944–48: Reshaping the Nation*, ed. Ota Konrád, Boris Barth, and Jaromir Mrňka (Cham: Palgrave Macmillan, 2022), 129–64. See also Ditlev Tamm, *Retsopjøret efter besættelsen*, 2 vols. (Copenhagen: Gyldendal, 1997).
115 David Alliott and François Marchetti, *Céline au Danemark, 1945–1951* (Monaco: Éditions de Rocher, 2008), 36.
116 Pedersen, *Danemark*, 65.
117 LFC to Lucie Destouches, January 13/20, 1946, *Lettres prison*, 40. On Mikkelsen, see his memoir *Mit Liv I Kravlegården* (Copenhagen, 1960).
118 LFC to Thorvald Mikkelsen, March 30, 1946, *Lettres prison*, 87.
119 LFC to Thorvald Mikkelsen, June 12, 1946, *Lettres prison*, 135–6.
120 Commission rogatoire, May 5, 1945, in *"Toujours l'article 75 au cul!": Le procès de Céline, 1944–1951: Dossiers de la Cour de justice de la Seine et du Tribunal militaire de Paris*, ed. Gaël Richard (Tusson: Du Lérot, 2011), 81, note 2.
121 Commissaire Charrasse, exposé, December 3, 1949, *"Toujours article 75,"* 168–9.
122 LFC to Thorvald Mikkelsen, March 26, 1946, *Lettres prison*, 82.
123 LFC to Thorvald Mikkelsen, March 5, 1946, *Lettres prison*, 55.
124 LFC to Albert Naud, May 25, 1947, *Lettres à son avocat: 118 lettres inédites à Maître Albert Naud*, ed. Frédéric Monnier (Paris: La Flute de Pan, 1984), 27.
125 LFC to Thorvald Mikkelsen, March 5, 1946, *Lettres prison*, 59.
126 Henry Miller to Maurice Naudeau, February 16, 1950, *"Toujours article 75,"* 254.
127 Maurice Vanino, *L'affaire Céline: L'école d'un cadavre* (Paris: Editions Créator, 1952), 60.
128 See IMEC, Céline file, Dossier de presse de langue française, 1950–2.
129 "Aujourd'hui ouverture du procès Céline," *Combat*, February 21, 1950, 1, 5, at 5.
130 LFC to Albert Naud, January 24, 1950, *Lettres à son avocat*, 117.

131 LFC to Albert Naud, April 19, 1947, *Lettres à son avocat*, 15.
132 LFC to Charles Deloncle, December 16, 1949, Céline, *Lettres*, ed. Henri Godard and Jean-Paul Louis (Paris: Gallimard, 2009), 1261.
133 Anne Simonin, “A Distance: Céline et ses juges (1949–1951),” Colloque *Procès politiques: tremplin ou tribune pour l’opposition*, Université d’Orleans, November 2021, 11, at halshs-03658011.
134 Naud to Céline, n.d., *Lettres à son avocat*, 96.
135 LFC to Thorvald Mikkelsen, May 1945, *Lettres prison*, 25; LFC to Lucie Destouches, January 13/20, 1946, *Lettres prison*, 39; LFC to Thorvald Mikkelsen, March 5, 1946, *Lettres prison*, 55–6 (emphasis original).
136 LFC to Thorvald Mikkelsen, March 5, 1946, *Lettres prison*, 53.
137 LFC to Thorvald Mikkelsen, *Lettres prison*, June 28, 1946, 153.
138 LFC to Lucie Destouches, *Lettres prison*, August 13, 1946, 218.
139 LFC to Thorvald Mikkelsen, July 12, 1946, *Lettres prison*, 166.
140 LFC to Lucie Destouches, July 14, 1946, *Lettres prison*, 171.
141 LFC to Thorvald Mikkelsen, July 31, 1946, *Lettres prison*, 193.
142 See Report, February 22, 1950, Archives Prefecture de Police (Paris), GA art. 57-44845.
143 LFC to Albert Naud, January 5, *Lettres à son avocat*, 102.
144 Quoted in *Archives Ambassade*, 22.
145 *JO*, August 17, 1947, 8058.
146 Ibid., 8057.
147 Simonin, “A Distance,” 16.
148 Ibid., 17.
149 Éric Mazet and Pierre Pécastaing, *Images d’exil: Louis-Ferdinand Céline 1945–1951 (Copenhague-Korsor)* (Tusson: Du Lérot, 2004), 343–5.
150 Philippe Saint-Germain, *Article 75* (Paris: Bureau d’Études et de Publications Sociales, 1951).
151 Marcel Aymé, *La tête des autres* (Paris: Bernard Grasset, 1952), 14.
152 Ibid., 21–2.
153 De Beauvoir, *Philosophical Writings*, 246.
154 Watts, *Allegories of the Purge*, 32–3.

CHAPTER 4
KNUT HAMSUN'S OUTWORN PATHS

"It was in those days when I wandered about hungry in Kristiana, that strange city which no one leaves before it has set its mark upon him": no line in Norwegian literature is more famous than the opening of Knut Hamsun's *Hunger* (1890), save what that same author penned over a half century later:

> Hitler was a warrior, a warrior for humankind and a preacher of the gospel of justice for all nations. ...
>
> Thus may the ordinary Western European look at Adolf Hitler. And we, his close followers, bow our heads at his death.[1]

It would be easy to read Hamsun's obituary for the Führer, Oslo daily *Aftenposten*'s lead article on May 7, 1945, as the product of the "strange whimsies, moods, caprices of my restless brain," which is how *Hunger*'s nameless protagonist presents his literary output.[2] That was, in fact, the official verdict of the two psychiatrists who evaluated Hamsun: the old, deaf and infirm author, who had crowned Norwegian literature and culture with glory by winning the Nobel Prize for Literature in 1920, was no longer in full possession of his mental faculties during the war years. But the obituary can also be seen as the culmination of Hamsun's *volte-face* from championing outsiders and unbounded freedom to extolling the violent attractions of a blood-and-soil ideology whose apotheosis was National Socialism in its German and Norwegian variants.

Hamsun was no stranger to controversy. From his debut in print—a takedown of the choirs of two village churches that attracted months of angry rebuttals—to his final published work—*On Overgrown Paths* (1949), a strange mix of memoir and novel that upended the psychiatric diagnosis of "permanently impaired mental faculties"—Hamsun reveled in being "the man who stands most alone," to borrow a phrase from Ibsen's *An Enemy of the People*.[3] After shooting to fame with *Hunger*, Hamsun embarked on a lecture tour in which he sought to be, as he warned audiences, "*as aggressive, as destructive ... as possible*" in his demolition of literary predecessors, making it out as if he alone, a poor country boy with less than one year of schooling, would be the country's cultural awakening and beginning (Figure 4.1).[4] Provocation for Hamsun was not so much a sin as a talent, and one he had in spades. Even though those provocations led onto dark political paths, Hamsun remains a major figure in Norwegian and world literature; he is, as Ståle Dingstad notes, "like no one else" in the country's literary canon.[5] For many critics, Hamsun's politics were "ugly blots ... but did not directly affect his art."[6]

Figure 4.1 Portrait of the author Knut Hamsun by Alfredo Anderson, 1891. Oil on canvas, 85cm x 127cm. Courtesy of the Nasjonalmuseet for kunst, arkitektur og design, The Fine Art Collections, Oslo. Photo by Jacques Lathion.

This chapter looks at Hamsun's emblematic case in the Norwegian post-war reckoning, an affair that continues to function as a "collective trauma" in the country's culture.[7] At a wider level, the Second World War remains "ever-present" in narratives of contemporary Norwegian national identity.[8] Two recent formal apologies—in 2012 for its role in the Holocaust, and then six years later, for the harsh treatment meted out to "horizontal collaborators" (women who had relationships with German soldiers and officers)—demonstrate the tangled historical legacy of the war. No other country in Europe had a more comprehensive postwar purge, with over ninety thousand individuals, out of a country of three million, investigated. The death penalty, abolished decades earlier, was brought back for traitors. Norway's imprisonment rate, on a per capita basis, was 50 percent higher than in the Netherlands, 70 percent higher than in Denmark, and over seven times the rate in France.[9] As a country under occupation for over five years, with a domestic fascist party, Vidkun Quisling's Nasjonal Samling (NS), elevated to a position of power, there was ample scope for economic, ideological and political collaboration. Even if the literary purge was limited—sixteen writers were convicted of treason after the war—it included Norway's leading modernists, Hamsun and poet Rolf Jacobsen.[10] For the postwar government seeking to re-establish legitimacy, and for the Norwegian public clamoring for justice, though, Hamsun stood out as the major cultural figure whose wartime actions required punishment. While a number of recent books—most notably Tore Rem's *Knut Hamsun: Reisen til Hitler* (2014) and Ståle Dingstad's *Knut Hamsun og det norske Holocaust* (2021)—have offered deep dives into Hamsun's politics, they have had much less to say about his court case (Rem's book discusses the trial in a short chapter that appears after the epilogue—the coda to a coda, in other words). But the Hamsun case, even with his wartime writing in support of the Third Reich's New Order and personal meetings with Goebbels and Hitler, was not cut and dry. What stung most for Hamsun was that he never had a chance to establish his innocence; denied his day in court by a psychiatric assessment, he sought to rebut the charges against him in *On Overgrown Paths*, making his case truly unique in how postwar literary authorship navigated the charge of treason.

Norwegian States of Treason

The national question was a primordial one in Norway, which, after more than five centuries of foreign domination (by Denmark and, since 1814, Sweden), only became a sovereign nation in 1905. The nineteenth-century independence movement was united on the need for statehood, but the larger project of creating a national culture remained a pressing issue in the early twentieth century. In many respects Norway was a cultural laggard; at the time Ibsen was born, the country did not have a single art gallery.[11] Around one-quarter of the population had emigrated abroad; and despite a relatively homogeneous population, the country had two languages, Bokmål, developed from Danish, and Nynorsk, based on Norwegian dialects (Bokmål dominated in literary circles). As a legal matter, treason was codified in the Penal Code of 1902 to consist of bearing arms against Norway or aiding and abetting a foreign power "in advice or deeds" (Section 86). Norway had few such cases to try, as the country had secured independence peacefully, had no colonial possessions, and had remained removed from foreign wars through its state policy of neutrality. Seeking its place in the international system, Norway was a prominent backer of the League of Nations. Its Labor Party made unilateral disarmament a key plank in its party platform.

The era of tranquility came crashing down with the German invasion on April 9, 1940. While Oslo was captured that first day, with Quisling declaring himself prime minister and calling for the laying down of arms, it would be another two months before the Norwegian military capitulated. That was enough time for King Haakon VII, Prime Minister Johan Nygaardsvold and leading members of the Storting, the Norwegian Parliament, to flee to London, where they established a government-in-exile. The occupation of Norway was an economic, strategic, and cultural imperative for Berlin, which desired access to Scandinavian iron ore, control of Norway's long Atlantic coast, and the fusion of the healthy Norwegian people with the master race of the Germanic empire. Several hundred thousand German troops would end up garrisoned in the country. After the fighting ended in June 1940, those soldiers encountered minimal resistance, a point of shame for the government-in-exile, which undertook a major PR campaign to show that not all Norwegians were "quislings," the new moniker for treason in the period.[12] While all political parties save the NS were banned and civil servants who were not NS members could be summarily dismissed, efforts to create an occupation government similar to the Danish model never succeeded. Although instructed by Hitler to make "a friend of these people," Reichskommisar Josef Terboven ruled by fiat, and at a certain point in autumn 1942, in the interests of creating the impression of active Norwegian participation in the occupation, appointed Quisling as prime minister.[13] The NS was thus thrust into power, even if the Germans retained full control of the country's instruments of violence.

Although the end goal was the Germanization of Norway, the occupation was marked by economic exploitation, political terror, and cultural hegemony. Norwegians who resisted Nazification measures, from priests to schoolteachers, were interned, with around 40,000 coming to be arrested or imprisoned.[14] The presence of Jews on Norwegian soil was made illegal. Villages sheltering resistance Home Front or British spies were burned down, their men deported to forced labor. Around 400 Norwegians were executed, around one-quarter summarily.[15] NS members could retaliate with impunity to insults, legalizing assault.[16] Listening to foreign radio was punishable by death; so, too, was reading a clandestine newspaper. Forced laborers and POWs were sent to Germany to be worked to the ground.

Alongside this policy of terror there was an active effort to Germanize Norway. Unlike other occupied peoples, the Norwegians were not considered culturally inferior or racially impure; as the *Völkischer Beobachter* noted in 1935, "Hamsun's people live and act from the sound instincts of the Nordic races."[17] After the NS assumed power it distributed spoils like mayoralties and local council seats to loyalists and opportunists. Factories producing goods or extracting resources for the Axis war machine employed

150,000 "Germany workers." The SS's *Regiment Nordland*, inaugurated on Hitler's birthday in April 1940, enlisted Danes and Norwegians who wished to fight alongside their Germanic brothers. The NS established a Norwegian Legion to combat Bolshevism; in the end, around 5,000 Norwegians, including Hamsun's youngest son, Arild, became "frontfighters."[18] In the cultural sphere, German films and literature flooded the country through institutional channels like the German Institute, the German Theatre, and propaganda sheets like *Wacht im Norden* (Northern Watch) and *Deutsche Monatshefte in Norwegen* (German Monthly in Norway). A 1 percent tax levied on the gross turnover of Norwegian publishers was siphoned to the Nazi publishers' association.[19] Writers who had espoused left-wing, anti-fascist, and pacifist views in the 1930s, like Rolf Jacobsen and Åsmund Sveen, followed the new winds after being offered plum positions in NS broadsheets and cultural organizations. The Publishers' Association was Nazified in autumn 1941, with NS members taking over the country's largest publishing houses (Tore, Knut's eldest son, became managing director at Gyldendal, his father's publisher). Books considered damaging to the Norwegian people were banned, all films had to be cleared by the National Film Directorate, and the National Gallery cleared its collection of "degenerate" modern art.

While these repressive measures were enacted to ensure subservience and loyalty to the occupying power, the Norwegian government-in-exile responded with its own set of legal measures on treason. In the anomalous situation of two Norways—one in the country, run by the Germans; the other outside its borders, its legitimacy based on a moral continuity with the country's free past—treason necessarily became a contested term. To complicate matters, the resistance was also fractured, with a split between the Home Front (*Hjemmefronten*) and the London exiles. It was in London, in January 1941, that the first plans were proposed for "The Legal Reckoning with the Norwegian Traitors and Semi-Traitors." That document called for collaborators to be put on trial as soon as the war ended. Doing so required modifying the existing criminal law to include "crimes against the Fatherland in wartime under hostile occupation."[20] The exile government reintroduced the death penalty, which had been abolished four decades earlier, for treason. A working committee on the postwar purge liaised closely with the other exile governments in London and participated in the joint planning for the prosecution of German war criminals. On January 22, 1942, about ten days after the Allies announced that German war criminals would be tried for war crimes, the Norwegian government-in-exile issued what came to be known as the "Quisling Decree." All membership after that date in the "party of traitors" was criminalized, regardless of intent, motivation or level of activity.[21] Mindful of the scale of the task, the exile government also introduced alternatives to prison time for treason convictions (fines and/or the loss of civil rights). The *Norsk Lovtidend* (Norwegian Law Gazette) published the decree, with the exile justice minister declaring on air that "all members of the Nasjonal Samling are traitors."[22]

The various decrees issued by the government-in-exile equated treason with NS party membership, effectively turning the political party into an armed conspiracy or gang. That was a seemingly simple solution to the knotty problem of collaboration. As a senior civil servant laid out in a 1946 memo, "the occupation lasted for five years. The

Germans got full power over the entire Norwegian industry. One has to look the truth in the eyes that practically speaking the entire population worked for German interests."[23] The establishment paper *Dagbladet* had announced on June 10, 1940, immediately after the military capitulation, that a new order had come to the country: "The entirety of the population must now accept the consequences of the new situation, namely active cooperation [*samarbeid*] with the German authorities."[24] This was in line with what international law recognized when it came to foreign occupation. Even the exile justice minister conceded that public servants had to maintain "a certain connection" with the German authorities but warned against anyone becoming a "tool" of the Nazis.[25] But the thorny questions of collaboration and tacit support for the occupier were occluded when the sole test of treason was a party membership card.

From the perspective of the Home Front, the exiles were overly mindful of legal scruples. The introduction of alternative punishments for treason called into question how tough the postwar purge would be. Courting much greater risks and witnessing the destruction wrought by the occupation, the Home Front wanted tougher measures, in line with the "strong sense of retribution" among the populace.[26] Its legal committee, whose members came to fill key roles in the postwar purge, pushed for traitors (and their spouses) to pay reparations (to be administered through a newly-created office, the *Erstatningsdirektoratet* [Compensation Directorate]), and argued that anyone who had been an NS member from April 8, 1940 (that is, from the eve of the German invasion) was guilty of treason. The government-in-exile objected to both measures, especially the introduction of a retroactive crime, but it had little moral authority. What came to be known as the "Treason Decree" was issued on December 15, 1944. It held that NS membership after April 8, 1940, whether active or passive (and around 60,000 individuals had been NS members during the war), was a crime punishable by death, imprisonment, the forfeiture of civil rights, or an economic fine.[27] One sign of the hardening toward traitors was the decision to not publicize the decree so that potential traitors would not destroy evidence. A secret, retroactive law was hardly consonant with the rule-of-law tradition—"Borrowing from Hitler. Borrowing twice from Hitler," as a popular postwar novel put it—but the Supreme Court later approved this approach on the grounds that prior decrees had already given notice on how to behave during the war.[28]

When Norway was liberated in May 1945, the immensity of the task before the new government became evident. The freedom of liberation—"Fritt land. Fri tanke. Fritt ord" (Free land. Free thoughts. Free speech), as *Aftenposten* proclaimed in its first post-liberation issue—required, paradoxically, putting political beliefs on trial.[29] The primary purpose of the purge was to re-instill legitimacy in the new government and to show that the guiding principles of the Norwegian state, after five years of Nazi oppression, were justice and the rule of law. There was relatively little vigilante justice, as had occurred in some occupied countries, but the Norwegian public expected, and the government promised, a quick, thorough, and harsh justice. Traitors would be "met with a tough hand," announced Sven Arntzen, of the Home Front's law committee and newly appointed as *Riksadvokaten* (Director of Public Prosecutions), but "we will strive to conduct this reckoning in a way that is worthy of Norway, one of Europe's oldest legal communities, so that this reckoning can stand before the judgment of history."[30] Yet it was unprecedented, as the Bishop of Oslo noted, to have thousands of individuals on trial at the same time for the same crime; it was even more bewildering since this crime had almost no legal or historical precedents to guide the courts.[31] Equating NS membership with treason meant incarcerating and putting on trial about 2 percent of the population. In the first days of the occupation, the Oslo police chief pleaded with the public to understand that it did not have enough agents or prison cells to round up all NS traitors. A "Treason Police" section was created, but since many police officers had been NS members, an internal purge was also needed. For the courts, the prospect of handling tens of thousands of treason cases was unthinkable when in a typical year at most five thousand criminal cases, for much less severe offences, were tried.

There was a strong push from the public, egged on by the press, to continue hard and fast. The earliest press editorials called for "evil forces" to be punished, for "the quisling and their helpers" to receive "the most stringent treatment possible."[32] One intellectual who suggested staying the hand of vengeance was fiercely rebuked in the pages of *Arbeiderbladet*, the Labor Party paper: "You eradicate rats. These human beings are worse than rats. They must be eradicated, quickly and simply. This has nothing to do with hatred or revenge, it is a simple process of restoration."[33] Even within Parliament, there was a feeling that while the death penalty had no place in a civilized society, times were such that criminal law had to consider *folkeopinionen*, the opinion of the people. Oslo's bishop said as much in an influential tract urging the government to satisfy the primal needs of the people.[34] Some law professors and jurists saw this accommodation of public opinion as fatal to the rule-of-law tradition. Re-instilling faith in the government and the legal system required, paradoxically, the use of questionable legal maneuvers—a process that at first brooked no dissent but which eventually became open to criticism.

The first high-profile treason case, against an NS member who was a police officer, Gestapo collaborator, and former Norske Legion fighter, took place in mid-July 1945. Because it would set a precedent, the Supreme Court's opinion in the eventual appeal against the death sentence was critical. The first major point concerned the legal validity of the government-in-exile's treason decrees, an issue that also impacted the French postwar *épuration*—who constituted the legal government of Norway during the war years, the exiles in London or the German occupiers and their NS helpers? If the latter, then the treason decrees issued in London were not law in any meaningful sense. The Supreme Court ruled that the war had not ended when the military capitulated, the king and prime minister fled abroad, and the Germans assumed the functions of state (collecting taxes, administering state offices, etc.). Rather, a condition of war underlay the entire occupation, and it was led by the government-in-exile, which thus retained the power to issue laws. The second major decision of the Supreme Court's review of Reider Haaland's case concerned whether NS membership was a treasonable offence. Even though four of the eleven justices ruled that NS membership by itself, without further evidence, did not constitute treason, the legal precedent that carried the day was the majority decision that the government-in-exile's treason decrees had the force of law.

The Quisling trial, which opened on August 20, 1945, solidified these views. That same day around 30,000 workers assembled in Youngstorget, in the heart of Oslo's government district, to protest a perceived leniency against traitors: "La stormen komme" (The Storm Will Come) warned *Friheten* if the government continued to release traitors from detention or not punish them to the fullest.[35] The Quisling trial, extensively covered in the national and international press, allowed the government to stave off those growing criticisms. Presiding judge Erik Solem, a Home Front jurist who had authored the 1944 Treason Decree and had earlier that summer condemned Quisling's treason, employed undeniably aggressive language toward the accused throughout the three-week trial.[36] The final verdict of death was widely applauded, with a distinctly self-congratulatory tone, even if much in the way of judicial propriety was not followed.[37]

After Quisling, the problem remained: what about the others? By January 1946 over 90 percent of the cases against traitors had not made their way to court. There were moves to reintegrate traitors within society (a working committee on the subject was appointed in November 1945). While other countries had set up special courts or used professional associations, these approaches were rejected in Norway. Having promised a comprehensive, full purge, but at the same time one following the rule of law, something had to give: either more individuals would have to be put on trial, more quickly, with fewer legal protections, or the scope of the purge would have to be reduced. The formal simplicity of treason as membership in a political party could have led to convictions being handed down like administrative decisions, but that would have robbed the proceedings of the symbolic weight of a criminal trial and undermined the presumed legal probity of the purge. Public trials were necessary, as the Bishop of Oslo noted: "the first purpose of the punishment is for everyone to see."[38] Speeding up the trials by waiving prosecution for lesser forms of treason, like passive NS membership, begged the question of what "insignificant" or "minor" treason might mean. As historian Anika Seemann points out, the trials began to feel like a "burden" rather than a liberation from the past.[39]

Criticism of the trials soon came from various directions. Legal theorists, like Johannes Andenæs and University of Oslo Law Professor Jon Skeie, were highly critical of what they saw as vengeance draped in the cloak of justice and high-minded populism. Andenæs, who later wrote one of the key works of legal history on the postwar reckoning, had worked closely with the government but grew exasperated by what he saw as coddling to public opinion. Over time it emerged that the equality of law was undermined because those who were put in the dock first were punished more severely than those who managed to delay their trials (a Pardons Committee was eventually set up in the Ministry of Justice in early 1948 to equilibrate sentences). The former head of the Oslo military resistance, Oliver Langeland, argued in *Dømmer ikke* (Judge Not) that the purge tackled small fry in "*bagatellsaker*" (bagatelle cases) and was unfairly applied.[40] Reducing treason to an offence of the "kartotek" (filing cabinet) and punishing it with a minor fine made the term meaningless; the real traitors were those who had weakened Norway in the run-up to the war.[41] (The popularity of Langeland's book, which sold 25,000 copies, and his follow-up a year later, *Forat – i ikke skal dømmes*, led to a special counsel investigation and libel charges against the author, a sign of how touchy the authorities were about criticism and how writing continued to be perceived as a social act even in peacetime.) For NS sympathizers, the treatment of internees in inhumane detention centers and the arbitrary nature of the judicial proceedings became a major talking point. A gadfly cartoonist, Odd Einarson, made the postwar trials the central issue of his critical magazine, *Trollspeilet* (The Troll's Mirror), which eventually numbered 20,000 subscribers, until the major press distributors, probably bowing to state pressure, refused to carry the title (he relaunched it as *§100*, a reference to the section of the Norwegian constitution granting the right to free speech). And those convicted of treason came out with prison memoirs, whose basic point, as a genre, was that as anti-Bolshevists they only had Norway's best interests at heart. And, finally, there was a growing sense that a small country could not lock up tens of thousands of potentially productive workers, whose reintegration into society would be that much harder the longer they stayed in prison. "We are a small nation," a character in Sigurd Hoel's *Meeting at the Milestone* (1947) noted, "Do we have the right to make ourselves even smaller?"[42] The post-liberation consensus that had motored the trials began to break down. By January 1948, with no end in sight for the treason trials, the Parliament began releasing convicted traitors, passing a Halftime Act which allowed for those who had served half of their custodial sentence to be eligible for release. A "Christmas Pardon" in late 1949 whittled down the number of traitors remaining in jail to under 600. A series of scandals, like prison breaks of convicted traitors who took to the high seas (the *Solbris* affair in summer 1947) or the revelation that Oslo City's "Treason Police" employed former Gestapo agents, further called into question the legitimacy of the trials. But throughout all these changes, the one constant that remained was the equivocal treatment of Norway's great living writer.

Hamsun's New Orders

For a writer who insisted on the primacy and cultural calling of the vocation of authorship, Knut Pedersen's pen name—Hamsun—came about after a printer lopped off the final "d" from the young man's home village, Hamsund. Even more curious for someone "obsessed by fame and the desire to imprint his name on the world" was the insistence on publishing the first excerpts from *Hunger* anonymously.[43] Appearing in the Danish magazine *Ny Jord*, *Hunger*'s anonymous publication kick-started Hamsun's career, as furious speculation about the identity of the author heightened interest in the radical, formally innovative and seemingly nihilist work that came to be hailed as "Norway's first modernistic novel."[44] As soon as he was unmasked, the young author—who had none of the trappings of literary nobility, as he was born in a poor family in rural Norway—took it upon himself to spread his message about the modern novel, which in his hands, as he famously announced, would be shorn of lavish weddings and fancy-dress balls and lazy picnics. Fame brought its own misfortunes, as Hamsun quickly realized that he would never be part of the fraternity of letters; having attacked pretty much the entirety of the Norwegian establishment for producing works of plodding realism devoid of reality, he found himself isolated, as one 1893 letter put it: "Surely it has never before happened that an author can be attacked in this extreme way. It's almost as though I were not a person anymore ... It is no longer simply *one* man, *one* paper, *one* party that condemns me, but *everybody*."[45] From the start of his career, Hamsun made it his mission to speak "as hot as hate" toward the establishment.[46]

That hot hate accelerated Hamsun's literary standing. His early novels *Hunger* and *Mysteries* were key texts for the Scandinavian "breakthrough" and were quickly translated into the leading European languages.[47] When, in 1910, his fiftieth birthday neared, numerous articles dubbed him the *forer* (leader), the *Dikterkonge* (poet king), after the death of *de fire store* (the four greats: Ibsen, Lie, Kielland, and Bjørnson). It was a crown that Hamsun wore with both pride and discomfort; he deserved to be heard, as he had struggled and knew better, but his natural instincts were to undermine authority and power, to push the limits of propriety and decency, such as calling for the death penalty to be reintroduced in the case of an infanticide committed by a young mother ("Hang them!" his articles on the case ended, infuriating liberal opinion).

Although Hamsun seemed to be closing up shop when it came to fiction, as the title *Ringen sluttet* (The Ring Is Closed) announced in 1936, his desire to *épater la gauche* reached new heights. At a time when the prevailing ideology of most writers was vocally anti-fascist, Hamsun declared his unabashed support for Quisling: "Had I *ten* votes," he wrote in Nasjonal Samling's party organ *Fritt Folk*, "he would get them all."[48] Quisling's party in the early 1930s was modeled on the fascist movements sweeping the continent, with particularly close links to the Nazi Party. At around the time Hamsun called himself "Quislings mann" (Quisling's man), the NS had become pronouncedly anti-Semitic.[49] While other intellectuals were sounding the warning about what was happening in Germany and the danger that the NS posed locally, Hamsun trotted out a canard about Weimar decadence ("when the communists, the Jews, and [Heinrich] Brüning ruled in this Nordic country") to justify fascism's "ethical regeneration."[50] Hamsun also shattered the liberal consensus around the jailed German dissident Carl von Ossietzsky, who was awarded the Nobel Peace Prize in 1935 but was not allowed to travel to Oslo for the ceremony. While others saw a courageous truth-teller, Hamsun branded Ossietzsky a traitor who deserved his prison cell. A surprising number of Norwegian authors defended Hamsun's provocative statements on the grounds of free speech or because of Hamsun's special status as an author apart. The literary left unwittingly found itself agreeing with Goebbels's view that Hamsun was "beyond good and evil."[51] If not excused because of his daemonic genius, "a very old man's tiredness and anguish" explained his political views, as a diplomat-in-exile stated in May 1940.[52] Even clandestine resistance sheets like *V-posten* distinguished the "major poet" from the "propaganda figure" who the Germans used for their own ends, seemingly removing any responsibility on Hamsun's part for his political beliefs.[53]

In both cases, it was Hamsun's "blind and unconditional *love*" for Germany that was decisive.[54] Norway's nationalist awakening came at the same time as the rise of the German state, with the cultural prestige of Germany shaping Norwegian cultural and educational institutions. Norwegian literature entered the stream of world letters through German translation. Hamsun's career was no exception. One month after *Hunger*'s release, a Berlin publisher commissioned a translation, setting the stage for a steady German interest in his work. Although he never learned the language (but did speak, after his sojourns in America, English), Hamsun considered his a "Germanic heart and head."[55] This affinity with Germany appeared as early as 1886, when Hamsun, then just another poor immigrant in America, wore a black ribbon in sympathy for the four German anarchists sentenced to death for the Haymarket bombing.[56] Like many things with Hamsun, this identification was taken to extremes. During the First World War he told his German publishers that his pro-German sympathies were instinctive ("because I am German") and aligned with his Norwegian patriotism ("My pro-German attitude during the war is my way of trying to serve my country with all my heart").[57] Writing in Munich weekly *Simplicissimus* in 1914, Hamsun spoke of the "absolute necessity" that "Germany will one day triumph over England." It was a biological question: "The Germans, as the healthy and flourishing nation they are, have a mighty surplus of births. Germany needs colonial land, England and France have more colonial land than they need."[58] Hamsun trotted out this *Lebensraum* justification for German territorial aggrandizement decades later when Hitler invaded Poland.[59] Throughout his fiction, in fact, the trope of "den gode tyskeren, den onde engelskmannen" (the good German, the evil Englishman) was hard to miss.[60] Hamsun's support of Germany stressed "*Volk* and race more than *Kultur* and Goethe."[61] This interest in "racial hygiene" first surfaced in the 1880s, when Hamsun bemoaned the "diseased and degenerate human race material" that the "shiploads" and "flood of mean and sickly European immigrants" brought to America.[62] This thinking was very much in line with ideas of "racial hygiene" that became exceedingly popular in Norway in the early twentieth century (the country was a leading center for eugenics research, most notably through Jon Alfred Mjøen, whose *Racehygiene* [1914] Hamsun appreciated; Mjøen's wife translated Hamsun's work into German) and which infected National Socialist ideology.

There were good reasons for the Germans to see Hamsun as a kindred spirit. Although his early fiction espoused a new modernist style, replete with fragmentary consciousness and complex psychology, his 1917 *Markens grøde* (*Growth of the Soil*) was appropriated by nativist thinkers in Germany as a call for a simpler way of life, rooted in healthy thinking and racial purity. That novel not only resulted in Hamsun winning the Nobel Prize for Literature (in its citation, the Swedish Academy did not speak of the entirety of Hamsun's career but singled out just this novel) but also led to him being touted as a visionary by Goebbels (who referred to Hamsun in his diaries more than any other writer) and the leader of the Hitler Youth. The message of "Heimatboden," literally the notion that every human being was intimately connected with his or her "home soil," was music to the ears of those ideologues. To say "Jar er fra Jorden" (I am of the earth), as Hamsun did in 1910, called into question the status of those eternal wanderers, the Jews, who did not have a homeland and thus could never belong anywhere. "I am surrounded by Jews," Hamsun wrote around that time, "I work in every land against a wall of Jews."[63] In the 1920s he contributed to *Nationalt Tidsskrift*, an anti-Semitic sheet that backed Hitler as early as 1924 (its editor had written *Hvem er hvem i jødeverdenen* [Who's Who in the Jewish

World], whose intent was none other than doxing "hidden" Jews). Ideologically, as the Frankfurt School critic Leo Löwenthal highlighted in the mid-1930s, Hamsun was in lockstep with fascist "anti-intellectualism" and the cult of "blood and race."[64]

All of this formed the cultural and political baggage that Hamsun carried with him at the outbreak of the war: as Harald Grieg, his publisher at Gyldendal put it, "there could not be any doubt where he stood."[65] In late March 1940, Hamsun congratulated the NS's mouthpiece *Fritt Folk* on becoming a daily, praised it as a "clean" venue uncorrupted by Anglophilia, and expressed his "hope for Germany" to keep Norway safe.[66] When the German invasion came a few days later, Hamsun not only said good riddance to the ruling government—Prime Minister Carl Joachim Hambro, in an allusion to his Jewish roots, "is not Norwegian in his soul"—but also blamed Britain for provoking Germany.[67] A few weeks later, he called on the country's soldiers to lay down their arms: "NORDMENN! … The Germans are fighting for all of us and are now breaking England's tyranny against us and all neutrals."[68] Hamsun's call for the military to cease combat was not exceptional. Barely a week into the German invasion the Bishop of Oslo exhorted the public to not engage in resistance or sabotage.[69] Hamsun later insisted that he was trying to avoid "hopeless resistance and useless bloodshed."[70] His lawyer blamed his isolation, old age, and deafness ("he could not follow what was going on, he could not hear the radio," etc.).[71] Whatever his motivations, Hamsun, at a time when the Norwegian military was lawfully fighting the German invaders, was calling for soldiers to abandon their posts. He defended this call for desertion by saying that the law could never come before life, that "it's life that changes the laws."[72] These calls for order were perhaps realistic assessments of what resistance might accomplish and how overmatched the Norwegians were, but they dismissed the symbolic value of continuing the fight even when it was doomed. Members of the public sent scathing letters addressing Hamsun as "*Forræder og svin*" (traitor and swine).[73]

"Vi er alle germanere" (We are all Germanic): Hamsun's support of the NS and the German occupation was unreserved and highly visible, appearing not only in NS venues like *Fritt Folk* or Nazi propaganda sheets like *Berlin—Rom—Tokio* but also major dailies like *Aftenposten*.[74] He called on Norway's sons to join the Norwegian Legion and fight alongside their German blood-brothers, as his younger son was doing.[75] Norway's future would be resplendent under the "confederation of European states under German National Socialist leadership"—the "New Order" the Third Reich promised, he exclaimed, would usher in a new era of peace and mutually beneficial trade and exchange of ideas.[76] Hamsun ended up contributing over thirty articles during the war, all with the same message, that collaboration with the Germans was in Norway's best interest. The most callous lines were toward resistance fighters, who deserved their fate (torture and execution) because they endangered Norway's safety. Hamsun wrote enthusiastically about Hitler—"it is Hitler who has spoken to my heart"—while calling FDR "a Jew in the pay of the Jews."[77] He invited *Fritt Folk* into his home at Nørholm, with picture of his palatial grounds splashed like a celebrity spread.[78]

The German press never stopped praising Hamsun, with Goebbels ordering 100,000 reprints of his works to be published and distributed to soldiers (as Front and Wehrmacht editions) and the public. A German edition of *On the Cultural Life of Modern America*, Hamsun's account of his time in a land in thrall to Mammon, was reprinted as anti-American propaganda. Berlin radio broadcast Hamsun's "great joy" at his son joining the fight with the Germans.[79] To commemorate Hamsun's eighty-fifth birthday in 1944, the European Writers' Union, a Nazi cultural organization, announced the creation of the Knut Hamsun Fund that would award scholarships (worth 60,000 Reichsmarks) for five Norwegian authors to spend a year in Germany (in 1944!). The Norwegian literary establishment also rallied around Hamsun. In the collection of lectures *Nasjonalsosialister i norsk dikting*, the novelist, literary critic and translator Finn Halvorsen called Hamsun "the greatest writer of the twentieth century" whose works would create "the land of the future" by fusing Norwegian and German culture.[80] Hamsun's wife, Marie, a former actress who was a celebrity in her own right in Germany, was an enlisted supporter of the NS and an unreserved supporter of the Germans. As her husband's "literary and political messenger," she was put on local boards in Norway and toured Germany to lecture audiences about her husband's literature—with the obvious implication that he was fully behind their cause.[81]

Hamsun's engagement included several major propaganda coups for the Third Reich (see Figure 4.2). The first was the symbolic gifting of his Nobel Prize medal to Goebbels. In the letter accompanying the gifted medal, which was widely reprinted in the press, Hamsun lauded Goebbels as the most tireless idealist in Europe. That was then followed by a keynote speech—"England må i kne!" (England on its knees!)—at the Second International Congress of the Union of National Journalists in Vienna in the summer of

Figure 4.2 Knut Hamsun en route to an authors' congress in Vienna, June 22, 1943. Unknown author, Wikimedia Commons.

Figure 4.3 Hamsun welcomed in Germany: "Wir grüssen Knut Hamsun den grossen Dichter des Nordens" (We greet Knut Hamsun, the greatest poet of Scandinavia). Unidentified author. Courtesy of Nasjonalbiblioteket (Oslo).

1943 (see Figure 4.3). Addressing hundreds of delegates from German-occupied lands, Hamsun proudly called himself "deeply and fervently anti-Anglomaniac, anti-British" and an admirer of Hitler, a "crusader and reformer" of a "new era" for Europe.[82] Although scheduled to return home, the wild cheers for Hamsun's speech led to a summons from Hitler, who organized a private plane to bring Hamsun to Berchtesgaden. Hamsun later claimed that he had done nothing to seek out this audience, that he had played no part in it occurring, but his wife later indicated that Hamsun accepted the invitation to Vienna because he sensed that it could lead to a meeting with the Führer. Weeks before the trip, according to Marie, Hamsun played out imaginary conversations with Hitler, going through all the possible permutations and gambits of a possible talk.[83] But the meeting with Hitler did not go as planned, as the deaf author and the irritated dictator could not find common ground. Hitler wanted to speak about writing and art with a Nordic genius; Hamsun wanted to air his private grievances about Germany's heavy-handed occupation, which he felt allowed the Norwegians no freedom to organize their own affairs. An audience with Hitler, Hamsun told his interpreter, who wisely let the comment go untranslated, was like talking to a wall; Hitler, too, found Hamsun's demands outrageous, as he had no interest in allowing Norwegian autonomy.[84] That meeting with Hitler changed Hamsun's private beliefs about the German occupation,

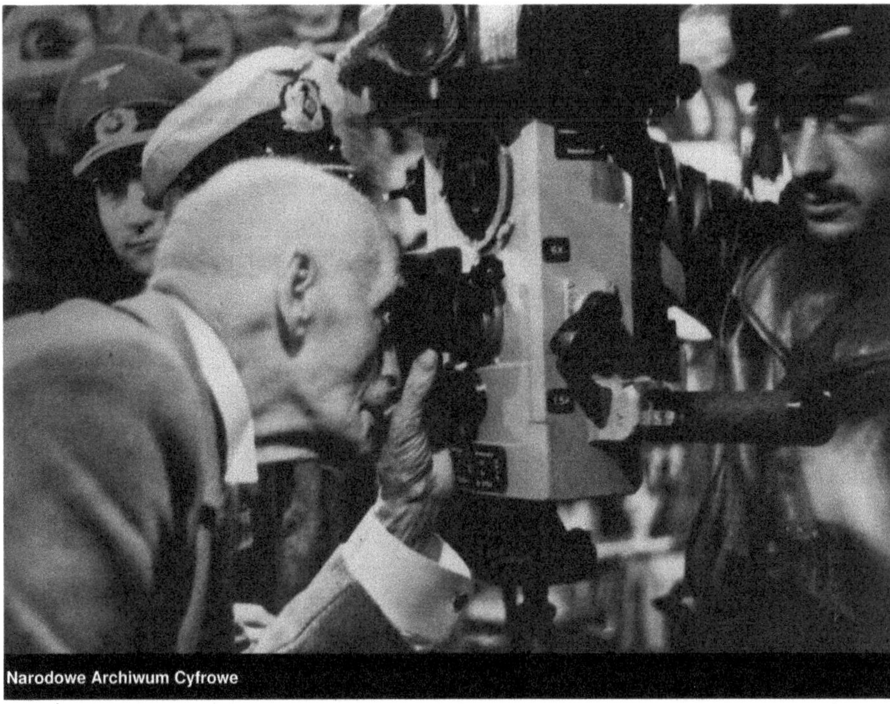

Figure 4.4 "Norwegian writer Knut Hamsun peers through a periscope aboard WWII Kriegsmarine submarine U 479 in Arendal, German-occupied Norway." June 27, 1944. Nazi war propaganda Narodowe Archiwum Cyfrowe 3 2 0 – 16208. Licensed under CC By 4.0.

which he increasingly saw as repressive and hostile. But, in public, under the mantle of Knut Hamsun, author, cultural visionary, *forer* of poets, there was no change (see Figure 4.4). In March 1944 he went on the radio to ask Norwegian seamen on Allied ships to come home, and even after D-Day he re-affirmed his faith in the German army and the wider cultural renewal that would come from Berlin—and then there was that obituary for Hitler, in which Hamsun penned perhaps the most infamous lines in Norwegian literary history.

On the Trail of Multiple Trials

In mid-April 1945, with the German army on its last legs and with Norwegians thinking about the coming liberation, the writer Olav Hauge worried that the war would come to be mythologized in terms of patriots and traitors, with no shade of gray or nuance. "We have not all been as good Norwegians as we should have been," he wrote in his diary, "either in word or deed."[85] Politics in the liberated land, he observed a dozen days after Oslo was freed, was "a mess of intrigue and hatred and envy."[86] As "Norges mest forhatte personer" (Norway's most hated person), Hamsun was, alongside Quisling, the most egregious case of collaboration.[87] For the three generations of Norwegians raised in the shadow of Hamsun's cultural pre-eminence and literary genius, there was bitterness toward the fallen idol, with the obituary for Hitler, appearing the day before Oslo's liberation, as the last act in this Wagnerian dramaturgy of betrayal.

Even though Hamsun was the country's most visible literary collaborator, there was no real rush to hunt down a "senile old man who once had a great name."[88] The Justice Ministry did not press matters when it needed time to prepare what would be one of the most important (and publicized) cases of the reckoning. There were also some mitigating circumstances that softened the rancor toward Hamsun. *Aftenposten*, just one week after the liberation, speculated that old age had made him an easy mark for the Germans. On the flip side, the public, after decades of Hamsun taking extreme positions, was inured to his outbursts; his political and social views were cast as unfortunate by-products of his "genius," unrelated to his artistic and cultural contributions.

About three weeks after the liberation Hamsun and his wife were placed under house arrest. A fortnight later Marie, a vocal NS member, was jailed in Arendal, about 20 kilometers away, but due to his age and medical condition (a cerebral hemorrhage in April 1942, and yet another one in early 1945), Hamsun was taken to the local hospital, where he stayed for a few months until a polio outbreak led to his transfer to an elderly care facility. The local police interrogated him on June 20, with constable Finn Kristensen detailing that Hamsun denied being an NS member but admitted to having been "led" by the party. Hamsun was convinced "in his mind and conscience" that "he has acted in the best interests of Norway."[89] The next day Hamsun was charged with having "consented" to being a member of the NS.[90] Two days later, a preliminary arraignment was held in local court against Hamsun for having "provided the enemy with advice and action, by writing a number of newspaper articles containing propaganda."[91] Hamsun was pointedly asked—and pointedly refused to answer—if he would have supported Germany had he known about the atrocities the Third Reich had committed (he needed "time to think" about this "rather complicated" question); he did, though, admit to having "slipped" into NS membership.[92]

That summer and early autumn the local police interrogated Hamsun several times, confirming his authorship of a number of articles in the fascist Norwegian or German press. Hamsun was questioned about his contacts with German officials and his meeting with Hitler in 1943, and his private correspondence was read. The local police concluded its enquiries by noting two acts of collaboration during the war: firstly, Hamsun had "consented" to NS membership and wore the NS badge on his lapel; and, secondly, he had "engaged in persistent written propaganda for Nasjonal Samling and the Germans."[93] A local district doctor who examined Hamsun concluded that he was in good health for his age and in full possession of his mental faculties and thus "fully liable under criminal law for his actions."[94]

Everything was thus ready for Hamsun to be put on trial: evidence had been processed and Hamsun was cleared both medically and psychiatrically. As a criminal matter, being a member of the NS, as Hamsun was considered, was de facto treason under the Treason Act of December 15, 1944. Propaganda was also a criminal offence under Section 140 of the Penal Code. As the courts reasoned in one case, "[in] modern warfare, where all means are used, the war correspondent's efforts are no less significant than armed combat."[95] But three days after the local officials cleared Hamsun for criminal trial, Gabriel Langfeldt, one of the country's most famous and powerful psychiatrists, called up the prosecutor's office in Oslo and asked for Hamsun to be put in his care for a thorough psychiatric assessment. Whether Langfeldt had been prompted to make this request remains an open question: the government may well have wanted to avoid the unseemly spectacle of an 87-year-old Nobel Prize winner convicted of treason, and in a private letter Langfeldt later told Hamsun's wife that the decision to put Hamsun under psychiatric observation "was part of an attempt to save him from being punished."[96] While Langfeldt had no first-hand knowledge of Hamsun's mental state which could have prompted the request, he had felt that Quisling's psychiatric examination had been rushed (he protested officially and, two decades later, wrote a book about the case) and may well have wanted to avoid the same fate befalling Hamsun.[97] In his September 1945 presidential address to the Norwegian Psychiatric Association, Langfeldt singled out "scientific investigations of the traitors" as the "most pressing" work for the profession, "a task *that we must not neglect under any circumstances*."[98] It helped that research money would flow for such studies—and having a Nobel Prize winner in the pool added cachet (if not scientific rigor). The decision to transfer Hamsun to Langfeldt's psychiatric clinic in Oslo was highly irregular; not only had Hamsun been examined by a medical professional, but if there were questions about that diagnosis, normal practice would dictate a local examination, not a 300-kilometer transfer to Oslo. In the end, Langfeldt's prestige and standing carried the day (that he had hid Jews and other refugees insulated him from charges of being soft on collaborators). Within a few weeks Langfeldt reported that Hamsun was "rather reduced," a "mental weakening" that made him "extremely easily influenced" and required further psychiatric observation.[99] Hamsun stayed in the psychiatric clinic for nearly four months (due to his deafness, he had to write down answers to the psychiatrists' questions, but even that was complicated, as he had difficulty holding a pen and his handwriting was very shaky). In mid-February 1946, Hamsun was determined to not be insane but to suffer from "permanently impaired mental faculties" (coincidentally enough, Ezra Pound in the Unites States was judged mentally impaired around the same time).

The psychiatric assessment put a stop to any criminal charge. The Attorney General quickly announced that "the public good will not be served by proceeding with a case against the accused, who will soon be eighty-seven years old and is to all intents and purposes deaf."[100] The outcry against this decision came from the public and press—Hamsun was "the country's greatest poet," *Dagbladet* reminded its readers, and his wartime output was not a mystery to anybody—and from Hamsun himself, who stated that he was "deeply embittered and furious" that he would not have his day in court to prove his innocence.[101] While any corporeal punishment to the aged and physically weak author was ruled out, the government decided to engage a civil case that would punish Hamsun financially by trying him for the damage he did to the country as an NS member. This would have its own rewards; the burden of proof for financial damages was lower than in a criminal trial, and Hamsun, who owned a large villa with expansive grounds, would, in the period's resounding metaphor, "pay" for selling out. After full inventories were made of his residence (the cows and hens counted, the artwork appraised, his writing desk valued at 150 NOK, the same as his bed) and financial holdings (his 200 shares in Gyldendal and the future value of his royalties), Hamsun was determined to be very wealthy indeed, so the government would not only get much-needed capital but also score a publicity coup when a tantalizingly large fine could be splashed in headlines. When it first filed charges against Hamsun in mid-May 1946, the Compensation Directorate sought 500,000 NOK in damages—a huge sum, representing around 70 percent of his total wealth. To put that figure in perspective: the psychiatrists who evaluated Hamsun were paid 7.5 kroners per hour, so the total sum Hamsun was asked to pay would take a highly educated professional 35 years to earn.

The financial case against Hamsun hinged on his being an NS member. On the face of it, the case was simple since he was listed as member number 26000 in the NS directory. The problem was that, although he had filled out and signed a members' questionnaire, he had never paid his *medlemavgift*, his membership dues. Or perhaps his wife had paid them on his behalf (could one become a member by proxy?). When questioned, NS members who knew Hamsun stated that they considered him as one of their own but could not be certain that he was, formally, a member. In most cases of criminal conspiracy associating with individuals known to be part of a criminal enterprise would suffice to prove guilt, but in postwar Norway it was formal membership in the NS that mattered. And the NS, like a garden cooperative or a tennis club, had its own bylaws determining membership. Whether Hamsun considered himself a member or was considered by others one was irrelevant. Treason would be determined not on what Hamsun had done or written but on whether the right form was properly filled out.

The compensation proceedings against Hamsun dragged on for over two years. In Hamsun's eyes, the government kept delaying and postponing the proceedings in the hope that he would die (he joked that he was too stubborn to commit suicide); from the government's point of view, Hamsun's guilt was obvious but the evidence hard to gather. The prosecutors knew early on that Hamsun had never paid his NS membership dues; it knew, too, that his NS membership form was incomplete. The way the charges were framed against Knut and Marie showed this: he was charged with having "consented" to being an NS member, while she was charged with being one. But it was inconceivable that Hamsun could have signed an article "Hvorfor jeg er medlem av N.S." ("This Is Why I Am an NS Member") and not have been a member. Throughout the war years, as an internal memo from the Compensation Directorate noted, Hamsun had "supported the NS and contributed greatly to the authority of this organization by placing his world-famous author's name in solidarity with the organization." Hamsun's literary fame was a critical prop for the NS: "When the world-famous author Knut Hamsun carried out, as an outspoken NS member, this propaganda for the occupying power, it must have been highly likely to strengthen the occupying power's confidence in the party and also the party's ability to carry out its unlawful and damaging activities."[102]

The question of Hamsun's membership was never resolved. In the first ruling against Hamsun, by the Sand District Court in December 1947, the question was cast aside on the doubtful claim that a great artist like Hamsun could not possibly be concerned with such a pedestrian matter as paperwork.[103] What mattered was that his "world-famous author's name" supported the party: "the greatest emphasis must be placed on his position as a world-renowned poet and one of the leaders of the Norwegian intellectual life," the court ruled: "Due to his cultural, social and also economic position and due to the authority of Hamsun's words, his behavior was to the highest degree suitable as an example for others, which Hamsun himself must have understood."[104] The defense countered by showing that Hamsun's opinions during the war were the same ones he had advocated for years, thus stressing his continuity of thought (and dismissing the possibility that he could be, like so many other collaborators, an opportunist). In that trial, held in a small room on the second floor of a local savings bank, the sitting magistrate found that there was no evidence in the 213-page prosecutorial brief for Hamsun's NS membership, but the two lay judges voted to convict and fined Hamsun 425,000 NOK. The conflict here was between the rule of law, which invalidated the proceedings against Hamsun, and popular justice, which found it a mockery that someone who wholeheartedly supported the NS, and continued to proclaim, as Hamsun had done in a thirty-five-minute rambling speech to the court, that Norway would have been better off in a German-led New Order, could be let off (see Figure 4.5). The editor of *Dagbladet*, who had previously written a fawning biography of the great Knut, said that the law would be a hollow shell if it could not find a way to convict. Although the sentiment behind this position undermined the autonomous liberal construction of the rule of law, it expressed the view that the law needed to adapt itself to prevailing conditions, a position that also animated the thinking behind postwar international tribunals.

Hamsun's lawyer promptly appealed. Two months later, the director of the NS membership department noted that four specific conditions were required for someone to become an NS member: a completed membership form, the payment of fees, an answered questionnaire, and a submitted photograph. Hamsun, he stated, had only completed the questionnaire, but never paid dues, never sent in a complete membership form, and never supplied a photograph. As an organization, the NS had been keen to get Hamsun on board, but even with his wife's enthusiastic participation it could not get him to become a member. The Supreme Court ruled otherwise:

> It is certainly the case that, as far as it seems clear, he has not applied to the party to become a member and that it is not at all clear how he joined the NS. However, according to what is available, this lack of clarity relates only to the question of how membership was established, not also to the question of whether he became a member. The evidence in the case leaves, as far as I can see, no doubt that Hamsun has actually been a member for at least more than the last three years of the occupation … Hamsun was listed in the NS membership card index and had a membership number, that he constantly wore an NS badge, that he himself filled out, signed and sent in to the party organization a tracing form that in its printed text expressly states that it is an appendix to the application for admission to the NS, that he publicly stated clearly that he was "Quisling's man" and, finally, that

Figure 4.5 "Knut Hamsun at court." Photograph by Sverre Heiberg. Courtesy of Oslo Museum.

he in the interrogation in court on 23 June 1945 stated that he "gradually became fond of this association [NS], so he must admit that he has considered himself to be a member." I also mention that as early as April 1940, he conducted extensive and intense propaganda for NS and the Germans … His conduct during the occupation does not at all seem to have left any reasonable doubt that membership had been established.[105]

Given the sophistry in this accumulation of circumstantial conjecture, it is perhaps not surprising that the Supreme Court judgment was not published in the Official Gazette, as would typically happen.[106] Wearing a party badge and mouthing that party's slogans could reasonably be taken to mean that a person supported a particular party, but those acts have nothing to do with the question of whether one was a member. The problem here was analogous to what happened in the Joyce trial in London: the factual question of whether Joyce was a British subject got obfuscated to the question of whether he thought he was, or whether he was treated by others as one; but whatever he or others thought was entirely irrelevant to the material fact in question. So, too, in the Hamsun case. The judge was right in stating that Hamsun very much acted like an NS member. But acting like an NS member was not an offence under law; being one was. By removing all questions of intent from its understanding of treason, Norway had made the most serious crime under the law a bureaucratic question, yet one that, in Hamsun's case, was treated unscrupulously.

Outworn Paths

For Hamsun, the greatest tragedy of the postwar reckoning was not that the fine imposed on him was economically calamitous—it was, but, at his age, money no longer meant much—but that he never had a chance to defend himself. The legal proceedings took on a formal administrative character, with no interest in determining the content of his actions or the intent animating his wartime behavior and writings. His physical limitations made the few courtroom experiences trying affairs; he could barely hear the proceedings, read the documents, or stand up to speak. The legal reckoning was synonymous with him being silenced: "jeg finder ikke ord," I do not find the words, he lamented to his close friend Christian Gierløff in 1946.[107] He was shut up in hospitals and psychiatric wards and elderly care homes where the nurses "refused to engage in conversation with me."[108] The official diagnosis of "permanently impaired mental faculties" undermined any validity to his words. His reply to this silencing came in *On Overgrown Paths* (1949), a memoir of his arrest, trials, and psychiatric examination that blended fact with fiction to present his truth of his confinement and postwar handling.

Few people in the late 1940s would have expected another Hamsun book. Not only had he claimed *Ringen sluttet*—the ring is closed, as the title of his last novel, from 1936, announced—but he had escaped criminal charges on the grounds that he was permanently mentally impaired. It also seemed unlikely that postwar publishers would take a risk with such an infamous writer: "I am truly a dead man in Norway and the world," he admitted to his publisher in 1946.[109] Through 1948 and the first six months of 1949 his book sales amassed only 700 NOK in royalties.[110] It was thus no surprise that Gyldendal kept pushing back a decision on the manuscript. Editor Harald Grieg had been publishing Hamsun since the 1920s (see Figure 4.6), but "*de onde år*" (the evil years) had fissured their relationship.[111] "You wonder 'what has come between you and me,'" Grieg wrote candidly, "The answer is very simple. In a life and death struggle we

Figure 4.6 Portrait of Harald Grieg and Knut Hamsun, 1936. By Anders Beer Wilse. Courtesy of Nasjonalbiblioteket (Oslo).

stood on opposite sides—and still do."[112] During the war Grieg had been interned, and to make matters worse, Hamsun's son Tore, an NS member, had been installed at the head of the firm. Although refusing a text from "forlagets storste dikter" (the country's best writer) was unthinkable, Grieg thought that Hamsun's manuscript was essentially German propaganda.[113] The book did not show any change in Hamsun's thinking or that he had any regrets. It also was potentially libelous in attacking, by name, respectable figures like Langfeldt. Were it to come out, Grieg warned, all of Hamsun's wartime writings would resurface, further turning people against him.[114] All this made the book go against the grain—a spate of publications in the immediate postwar period, such as *Friheten*, the bestselling posthumous poetry collection of resistance legend Nordahl Grieg (1945), Harald's brother, spoke to the glories of the resistance. These works helped shape a patriotic memory culture in which a united front of good, solid Norwegians stoically endured the occupation.[115] There were dissenters to this myth, such as Oliver Langeland, the head of the military resistance of Oslo, who noted in 1949 that the country's liberation was due to others: "We must not lie to ourselves … the Norwegian people did not engage in any united struggle."[116] But Langeland had the moral authority to take an unpopular stance; Hamsun did not.

The negotiations to publish *On Overgrown Paths* consumed Hamsun, who considered it a "life or death matter" for the book to come out.[117] For one thing, he needed the money; he also wanted to reshape his historical legacy, to justify his actions, while he was still alive (in the same way that Céline and Wodehouse wanted to "correct" the public's understanding of their cases). Hamsun's lawyer, Sigurd Stray, was told to cut all ties with Gyldendal and to seek out foreign publishers for the book, but the Swedish, Danish, and Finnish publishers who were approached did not bite. Publishers in Brussels, London and New York also rejected the book; at one point, Hamsun floated the idea of having it published in Germany, but export restrictions made that a self-defeating proposition. In the end, Swedish publisher Bonnier offered Hamsun a contract (as did a Zurich publisher). *On Overgrown Paths* eventually came out in late September 1949 (Figure 4.7), with Grieg bowing to the pressures of the foreign editions that would undercut domestic sales if Gyldendal stalled too long. The full print run of the Norwegian first edition, 7,000 copies, sold out in a matter of days.[118]

On Overgrown Paths is firmly situated, as its first two lines show, as a postwar work about Hamsun's political and legal troubles: "It's the year 1945. On the 26th of May the Arendal chief of police came to Nørholm and proclaimed house arrest for my wife and myself for thirty days."[119] The book is framed by the legal case, as the opening lines of many of the short sections show: "On the 14th of June I was taken by car from my home and brought to the hospital in Grimstad" (5); "On June 23rd I was brought before the examining magistrate" (10); "September 2. A policeman comes into my room and says without any introduction, 'You're going to move'" (35); "Today, September 22, summoned once again before the examining magistrate" (42); "It is 1946, February 11. I'm no longer in the institution" (68). The entirety of Hamsun's July 23, 1946, letter to the Attorney General, running several thousand words, is reproduced, as is his address to the court in December 1947. And then there are the book's final words: "Midsummer

KNUT HAMSUN

PAA GJENGRODDE STIER

GYLDENDAL NORSK FORLAG

OSLO 1949

Figure 4.7 Title page of *Paa gjengrodde Stier* (Oslo: Gyldendal, 1949). By Asav – own work, CC BY-SA 4.0.

Day 1948. Today the Supreme Court has handed down its verdict, and I end my writing" (231). The memoir is formally structured by the legal trial; without it, there would be no writing. By reducing the memoir's chronology to the legal investigation and court dates and police interrogations and psychiatric diagnoses, Hamsun turns it into a legal saga.

With Hamsun subject to the force of the carceral state apparatus, the book is also a kind of prison memoir since, as Hamsun details early on, "we now have political prisoners in Norway" (16). Even in "czarist Russia" (42), he opines, the condemned had more rights. The counterpoint to this confinement is Hamsun as wanderer seeking out "home and homeland" (107): "I wander about the hospital grounds" the third entry begins (6); "I wander about day after day" the next one adds (7). Mobilizing historic tropes of peripatetic philosophers like the Sophists or Rousseau's *Les Rêveries du promeneur solitaire*, this wandering reframes the writing away from the formal structure of the legal case. As Hamsun roams the earth—and the memoir takes a great delight in place names across the globe, a Dutch woman who sends him cigars from Indonesia, galoshes bought in Serbia and worn in Vienna, a Russian he met in Finland, showing the French, in France, just what *politesse* means—he discovers truths that would have remained closed were he locked up and confined as everyone wants. Perhaps the most important secondary figure in the memoir is the shoeless wanderer Martin, who hails from Hamsun's hometown and has the unique gift of being understood by the deaf author. "I've often thought of you," Hamsun tells Martin when they meet for the second time, "you are a true wanderer, you require so little, you just wander. That's your way" (146). Not attached to anyone or any institution, Martin survives by the good grace of people who shower kindness upon him; he lives close to the word of God. In "his simplicity, his childishness" (149), Martin is both Hamsun's *doppelgänger* and opposite, what he could have been had he not chosen the path of authorship and fame.

The truths discovered while wandering demonstrate the poverty of the formal legalism that ostensibly structures the work. Most of the book consists of short sections (mostly a few paragraphs, rarely longer than a page), making it a collection of occasional jottings, scraps that could be composed on a park bench. Several times Hamsun mentions being out on his wanderings and "making notes, scribbling" (28). If "I'm quite accustomed to throwing away my scraps of paper" (160), *On Overgrown Paths* collates these texts. There is something incongruous about this occasional, dreamlike writing fitting within the chronological strictures of a legal case, and as the text goes forward, time begins to drift: "Three months, that is. I read, ramble, and play solitaire" (12); "Another two months—good, it makes no difference to me one way or the other" (43); "The days go by, the months go by, and I'm not getting much better" (71); "The summer is going by. I don't feel any great difference between the seasons … the time is timeless and the summer is lost to me" (81). Legal time is also undermined by the mention of alternate temporalities, such as seasons, ecological time, or events from Hamsun's childhood. And then there is cosmic time, which is no time at all: "They are all will-o'-the wisps: they come, shine for a moment, and are gone. Come and go, as I came and went" (85).

Among these competing epistemologies, Hamsun shows the emptiness of the legal one. Here is what happens when his case is finally heard in court:

> The day arrives. The court is in session. As I do not hear and my eyesight has been greatly impaired this last year, I'm rather confused; entering a dark courtroom, I can only make out something here and there and have to be instructed. Then the prosecutor speaks, and my defense attorney, appointed on the spot, responds. Then there is a recess. I have neither heard nor seen what has taken place. (181)

What should be memoir's climax turns out to be muted and sad; there is something pathetic about the scene. The legal order, and legal time, are denuded of any deep meaning or value. So, too, is scientific truth, as represented by the psychiatric investigation. What it destroyed in him, he says, "cannot be measured. It has nothing to do with weights and measures. It was a slow, slow tearing up by the roots" (120). As he puts it, the entire system is to blame: "Lording it over living life, regulations without intuition and heart, a psychology of squares and rubrics, an entire spite founded on spite" (120). The system is thus analogous to the law—and its products are equally foreign to Hamsun. The chief psychiatrist—and here Hamsun got into trouble with his publishers, as he mentioned Gabriel Langfeldt by name—struck Hamsun

> as a typical college graduate, one who has come back from college with all the book learning he has picked up from schoolbooks and learned tomes, and which he has of course brought up to date through later studies ... He is so secure in his knowledge. But that is not the same as being secure in the old wisdom: nothing can be known for certain! (127–8)

Psychiatry as a science and the law as a system work together to create false knowledge. When the police question Hamsun, or the psychiatrists examine him, they do not find any truth; but when he ruminates on his walks or meets people in town or watches children and recounts how they treat him, those events are encounters in a deep sense, with a self-reflexive human truth emerging. Judgments of law will, paradoxically, be forgotten, even though they are written down, while fleeting encounters between two strangers reveal deeper truths. The very form of the book thus subtly plays up Hamsun's innocence, or attempts to prove it, by taking away from the law its epistemological sovereignty.

These various epistemological frames single out how truth and history are configured. *On Overgrown Paths* goes further on this point via its intense rumination on reading and texts. On one level there are the newspapers, the archetypal form of "fact" in the modern world. Because of Hamsun's disability—he could no longer hear much, with voices sounding like a continual buzzing—his only access to the outside world was through newspapers. As he stated in his address to the court, during the war years "I had nothing to go by except my two newspapers, *Aftenposten* and *Fritt Folk*, and those two papers never said there was anything wrong with what I wrote. On the contrary" (187). There is a sense, then, that he could not be guilty of treason if his worldview mirrored the period's establishment papers. During the investigation, Hamsun is told by the police that he can longer have access to newspapers. His family send clippings in with the laundry, making the newspaper contraband in Hamsun's prisoner world. Even so, he remains adrift: "I still do not understand much of what is happening in the world; I read the papers and study the dispatches, but I fall short" (100). On one level, Hamsun is denied entry into that epistemological world of facts, and the memoir conveys his frustration at not being able to stay up to date. The other implication here is that the papers provide false knowledge; one paper says his case will come up in September, another paper three days later says it will not (162). From his point of view, the papers work up prejudice against him, while the deep truth of the individual encounter, like what he experiences among the public when he visits Oslo, is what should really matter.

The contemporaneous reviews of *On Overgrown Paths* were full of praise, marveling at how the "wizard of poetry, the master of masters," as the press dubbed Hamsun, had not lost it.[120] In *Dagbladet* Philip Houm created a parallel between Hamsun's ties to Nazism and the current inability to see Soviet abuses (a view that also vindicated Hamsun's anti-Bolshevik stance); most of the reviews, in fact, hammered home the split between the "poetic genius and the political idiot."[121] This view continues to inform opinion of Hamsun. Thorkild Hansen's three-volume *Processen mot Hamsun* (1978) and Jan Troell's feature film *Hamsun* (1996) were largely indebted to *On Overgrown Paths*, with Troell's film beginning with an elegiac voiceover, "As I walk down the overgrown path through the forest." In that film, famously, it is Marie, the enthusiastic NS member, who is blamed for leading Knut astray. (In the 1950s, Marie wrote two best-selling memoirs, *Regnbuen* [The Rainbow, 1953], which recounted events to the late 1930s, and *Under gullregnen* [Under the Laburnum Tree, 1959], which treated the war years and the postwar, although without much discussion of her or her husband's collaboration with the Germans). If, "with the passage of time," as Monika Žagar notes, "Hamsun is indeed winning his case," that is partly due to *On Overgrown Paths*, which helped solidify the case for Hamsun's artistry and stylistic mastery.[122] For a book framed by politics and the law in an intensely political postwar moment, there is almost nothing about the war save for an off-hand reference to his galoshes transporting him "to Hitler on a famous occasion."[123] For someone accused of treason, the longing for "home and homeland" (107) is largely metaphorical, elegiac and nostalgic. By not really offering a defense of his actions—"So many things crowd in on me at this moment, things I could say in my defense, but I shall keep quiet about them" (41)—Hamsun elevates himself above questions of guilt. Foregrounding his physical debility but showcasing his mental acuity, the memoir creates a sympathetic portrait of a harmless old man ("I hadn't killed anyone, stolen anything, or set fire to a house" [25]) seeking to live out his numbered days in peace, ambling through the fresh Norwegian earth in the gentle company of his compatriots.

If we resist *On Overgrown Paths*'s portrait of Hamsun as a "a political prisoner within a postwar police state maintained by the victors," it is nonetheless the case that the ham-fisted legal proceedings against him contributed to a residual sympathy.[124] Those whom Hamsun harmed—and his writings during the war raised the animus of hatred against Jews and enjoined his fellow countrymen to support, wholeheartedly and materially, the German occupation—remain spectral abstractions, out of sight, while the author's old body subject to the whims of the police and courts and doctors is very much present. Despite having Europe's most comprehensive purge, Norway found it difficult to deal with Hamsun, who had helped establish his country's literature on the global stage and embodied the country's values and national identity. Knocking down this totemic symbol of Norway was hard enough; doing so given his advanced age seemed gratuitous. While reducing treason to a formal question of NS membership facilitated the processing of the tens of thousands of cases, it proved ill-suited to the ambiguity of wartime collaboration (what was morally permissible in 1940 may not have been in 1944) and to the complexities of Hamsun's case. Dragging out the case for years, as political configurations and public opinion changed, undermined the purported neutrality of the law, and, like in the Pound case, spawned conspiracy theories and claims of persecution or leniency, depending on one's point of view.

Conclusion

The Norwegian postwar purge was one of the most comprehensive in Europe, but it was also one of the most rigid, with a formal understanding of collaboration as membership in a political party, the fascist Nasjonal Samling. Although there was a spirited resistance, both inside the country's borders and outside, in the exile government based in London, five years of German occupation had made collaboration unavoidable. With his dozens of articles in the fascist press, birthday greetings to Goebbels, headliner status at a Nazi-sponsored conference on the New Europe, a personal meeting with Hitler and then a eulogy upon his death, there was little doubt that Hamsun was ideologically aligned with the NS and the Third Reich. What was missing was evidence to convincingly prove that he was, formally, an NS member.

As the preeminent writer not only of his generation but of his entire country's independent existence, Hamsun could not so easily be put on trial. His writings had put Norway on the world's cultural map and had created a new, modern style for the country while also honoring its ancient past. The psychiatric diagnosis of mental illness was a convenient out, driven more by politics (and the politics of science) than science. That Hamsun was able to pen such an elegant rebuttal of his diminished mental capacities in *On Overgrown Paths*, without so much in the form of apology or regret for his political stance, revealed the difficulty of purging major cultural figures (as the Wodehouse case also reveals). If authorship rarely gave special rights under the law, cultural prestige, especially by figures whose writings were synonymous with the cultural self-definition of the nation, did.

Notes

1 Knut Hamsun, *Hunger*, trans. Sverre Luyngstad (Harmdonsworth: Penguin, 1998), 3; *Aftenposten*, May 7, 1945, 1.

2 Hamsun, *Hunger*, 4.
3 Robert Ferguson, *Enigma: The Life of Knut Hamsun* (London: Hutchinson, 1987), 30–1; Gabriel Langfeldt and Ørnulv Ødegård, *Den rettspsykiatriske erklæring om Knut Hamsun* (Oslo: Gyldendal, 1978), 101.
4 Quoted in Leonard F. Lisi, *Marginal Modernity: The Aesthetics of Dependency from Kierkegaard to Joyce* (New York: Fordham University Press, 2013), 188 (emphasis original).
5 Ståle Dingstad, *Knut Hamsun og det norske Holocaust* (Oslo: Dreyers, 2021), 431.
6 Sverre Lyngstad, *Knut Hamsun, Novelist: A Critical Reassessment* (Bern: Peter Lang, 2005), 327.
7 Atle Kittang, "Knut Hamsen og nazismen," in *Nazismen og norsk litteratur*, 2nd ed. (Oslo: Universitetsforlaget, 1995), 254–67, at 254–6.
8 Gunnar Iversen, "From Trauma to Heroism: Cultural Memory and Remembrance in Norwegian Occupation Dramas, 1946–2009," *Journal of Scandinavian Cinema* 2.3 (2012): 237–48, at 237.
9 Anika Seemann, *The Quislings: The Trials of Norwegian Wartime Collaborators, 1941–1964* (Cambridge: Cambridge University Press, 2024), 21.
10 Bjarte Birkeland, "Forfattarmiljø og nazisme i trettiåra," in *Nazismen og norsk litteratur*, ed. Bjarte Birkeland and Stein Ugelvik Larsen (Bergen: Universitetsforlaget, 1975), 21–31. On Jacobsen, see Dean Krouk, *Fascism and Modernist Literature in Norway* (Seattle: University of Washington Press, 2017), 14.
11 Toril Moi, *Henrik Ibsen and the Birth of Modernism: Art, Theater, Philosophy* (Oxford: Oxford University Press, 2006), 43.
12 C. J. Hambro, *I Saw It Happen in Norway* (New York: Appleton-Century, 1940).
13 Quoted in Despina Stratigakos, *Hitler's Northern Utopia: Building the New Order in Occupied Norway* (Princeton: Princeton University Press, 2020), 8.
14 Johannes Andenæs, *Det vanskelige oppgjøret: Rettsoppgjøret etter okkupasjonen*, 3rd ed. (Oslo: Aschehoug, 1998), 63.
15 Ole Kristian Grimnes, *Norway in the Second World War: Politics, Society and Conflict*, trans. Frank Stewart (London: Bloomsbury Academic, 2022), 85.
16 Andenæs, *Vanskelige oppgjøret*, 61.
17 Quoted in Tore Rem, *Knut Hamsun och resan till Hitler*, trans. Ulrika Junker Miranda (Stockholm: Atlantis, 2015), 65.
18 Terje Emberland and Matthew Kott, *Himmlers Norge: nordmenn i det storgermaske prosjekt* (Oslo: Aschehoug, 2012) and Sigurd Sorlie, *Soldkors eller hakekors: nordmenn i Waffen-SS 1941–1945* (Oslo: Dreyers Forlag, 2015).
19 Alex Brinchmann and Sigurd Evensmo, *Norske forfattere in krig og fred* (Oslo: Gyldendal, 1968), 89.
20 Ot. prp. nr. 92 (1945–6), 70.
21 Ot. prp. nr. 92 (1945–6), 73.
22 Justis- og politidepartementet, *Om landssvikoppgjøret: Innstilling fra et utvalg nedsatt for å skaffe tilveie materiale til en innberetning fra Justisdepartementet til Stortinget* (1962), 41–2, at https://www.stortinget.no/no/Saker-og-publikasjoner/Stortingsforhandlinger/Lesevisning/?p=1962-63&paid=3&wid=b&psid=DIVL62&pgid=b_0009&vt=b&did=DIVL66&s=True. Last accessed: January 22, 2026.
23 Quoted in Seemann, *Quislings*, 207.
24 Quoted in O. H. Langeland, *Dømmer ikke* (Oslo: Heim and Samfund, 1948), 78.
25 Ø. Hetland, N. Karcher, and K. B. Simonsen, "Navigating Troubled Waters: Collaboration and Resistance in State Institutions in Nazi-Occupied Norway," *Scandinavian Journal of History* 46.1 (2021): 84–104, at 84.

26 Richard Overy, "Scandinavia in the Second World War," in *Hitler's Scandinavian Legacy: The Consequences of the German Invasion for the Scandinavian Countries, Then and Now*, ed. John Gilmour and Jill Stephenson (London: Bloomsbury, 2013), 13–37, at 31.
27 Andenæs, *Vanskelige oppgjøret*, 49.
28 Sigurd Hoel, *Meeting at the Milestone*, trans. Sverre Lyngstad (Copenhagen: Green Integer, 2002 [1947]), 36.
29 *Aftenposten*, May 14, 1945, 1.
30 *Aftenposten*, May 22, 1945, quoted in Seemann, *Quislings*, 87.
31 Eiving Berggrav, "Folkedommen over NS Menneskelig og moralsk: Hva vil være rett av oss?" *Kirke og Kultur* 50 (1945): 6–44, at 6.
32 Quoted in Seemann, *Quislings*, 95.
33 *Arbeiderbladet*, May 28, 1945, quoted in Seemann, *Quislings*, 102.
34 Berggrav, "Folkedommen over NS."
35 *Friheten*, August 17, 1945, 1.
36 Hans Fredrik Dahl, *Quisling: A Study in Treachery*, trans. Anne-Marie Stanton-Ife (Cambridge: Cambridge University Press, 1999), 378. See also Erik Solem, "Rettsoppgjøret," *Vedens Gang*, June 27, 28, and 30, 1945.
37 See "Dommen" (editorial), *Aftenposten*, September 11, 1945, 2.
38 Berggrav, "Folkedommen over NS," 43.
39 Seemann, *Quislings*, 146.
40 Langeland, *Dømmer ikke*, 291.
41 Ibid., 259, 15.
42 Hoel, *Meeting*, 32.
43 Ferguson, *Enigma*, 98.
44 John Brumo and Sissel Furuseth, *Norsk litterær modernism* (Bergen: Fagbokforlaget, 2005), 17.
45 Quoted in Ferguson, *Enigma*, 146–7.
46 Quoted in Ferguson, *Enigma*, 137.
47 Arnold Weinstein, *Northern Arts: The Breakthrough of Scandinavian Literature and Art, from Ibsen to Bergman* (Princeton: Princeton University Press, 2008).
48 Knut Hamsun, *Hamsuns polemiske skrifter*, ed. Gunvald Hermundstad (Oslo: Gyldendal, 1998), 236. Hereafter cited *PS*.
49 Gunvald Hermundstad, "Innledning," in *PS*, 7–18, at 13; Dahl, *Quisling*, 118–21.
50 Hamsun, *PS*, 234.
51 Quoted in Ferguson, *Enigma*, 369.
52 *NYT*, May 5, 1940, 32. The diplomat in question, Wilhelm Munthe de Morgenstierne, went on to become Norway's ambassador to the United States.
53 Quoted in Rem, *Resan*, 317.
54 Ferguson, *Enigma*, 345.
55 Hamsun, *PS*, 201.
56 Richard Nelson Current, "Introduction," in *Knut Hamsun Remembers America: Essays and Stories, 1885–1949*, ed. and trans. Richard Nelson Current (Columbia: University of Missouri Press, 2003), 1–13, at 9.
57 Quoted in Ferguson, *Enigma*, 233, 239.
58 Hamsun, *PS*, 198, 200.
59 Ingar Sletten Kolloen, *Hamsun: Erobreren* (Oslo: Gyldendal, 2004), 213.
60 Ibid., 222.
61 Tore Rem, "Out of the Ruins: Knut Hamsun's 'Idealism' and the Inheritance of World War I," *Journal of European Studies* 51.3–4 (2021): 262–72, at 266.
62 Hamsun, *Hamsun Remembers America*, 17, 18.

63 Quoted in Dingstad, *Hamsun og det norske Holocaust*, 169.
64 Leo Löwenthal, "Knut Hamsun," in *The Essential Frankfurt School Reader*, ed. Andrew Arato and Eike Gebhardt (New York: Continuum, 1998), 319–45, at 322.
65 Harald Grieg, *En forleggers erindringer: Ny, øket utgave* (Oslo: Gyldendal, 1971), 531.
66 Hamsun, *PS*, 239.
67 Ibid., 241.
68 Ibid., 242.
69 Arne Hassing, *Church Resistance to Nazism in Norway, 1940–1945* (Seattle: University of Washington Press, 2014), 44.
70 Hamsun, *PS*, 244.
71 Sigurd Stray, *Min klient Knut Hamsun* (Oslo: H. Aschehoug, 1979), 88.
72 Hamsun, *PS*, 248.
73 Ibid., 245.
74 Ibid., 250.
75 Ibid., 253.
76 Ibid., 252.
77 Quoted in Ferguson, *Enigma*, 362, 365.
78 *Fritt Folk*, June 10, 1944, in National Archives Norway (NAN), Aa 7168/3.
79 *New York Herald-Tribune*, May 18, 1943, in NAN, Aa 7168/3.
80 Quoted in Dean Krouk, "Prophet of Regeneration: On Two Fascist Readings of Knut Hamsun," *Nordlit* 25 (2009): 29–40, at 34.
81 Kolloen, *Erobreren*, 220.
82 Hamsun, *PS*, 267.
83 Kolloen, *Erobreren*, 271.
84 Hamsun, *PS*, 270.
85 Olav H. Hauge, *Dagbok 1924–1994*, vol. 1 (Oslo: Norske Samlaget, 2000), April 12, 1945, 227.
86 Ibid., May 19, 1945, 227.
87 Kolloen, *Erobreren*, 454.
88 *Aftenposten*, May 14, 1945, 9.
89 L SAK, Police Report, June 20, 1945.
90 L SAK, June 21, 1945.
91 Quoted in Stray, *Min klient*, 101.
92 L SAK, Report for Sand District Court, June 23, 1945.
93 L SAK, Police Report, September 25, 1945.
94 L SAK, October 9, 1945.
95 Quoted in Seemann, *Quislings*, 168.
96 Quoted in Anine Kierulf and Cato Schiøtz, *Høyesterett og Knut Hamsun: En nærmere fremstilling of vurdering av erstatningssaken mot Knut Hamsun* (Oslo: Gyldendal, 2004), 42.
97 Robert M. Kaplan, "Norwegian Psychiatry and the Trial of Vidkun Quisling," *Nordic Journal of Psychiatry* 66.3 (2012): 155–8.
98 Quoted in Øyvind Giæver, "The Psychiatry of Quislingism: Norwegian Psychiatric Research on the Collaborators of World War II," *Science in Context* 17.3 (2004): 267–92, at 269.
99 L SAK, Langfeldt to Riksadvocaten, November 1, 1945.
100 Quoted in Ferguson, *Enigma*, 402.
101 *Dagbladet*, February 23, 1946; Hamsun to Gierløff, March 25, 1946, quoted in Stray, *Min klient*, 111.
102 L SAK, Note, Compensation Directorate, September 3, 1946.
103 L SAK, Sand District Court judgment, December 16, 1947.
104 Sand District Court ruling, December 19, 1947, in Stray, 183–91.
105 L SAK, Supreme Court decision, June 23, 1948.

106 Kierulf and Schiøtz, *Høyesterett og Knut Hamsun*, 10.
107 Quoted in Kolloen, *Erobreren*, 376.
108 Knut Hamsun, *On Overgrown Paths*, trans. Sverre Lyngstad (Copenhagen: Green Integer, 1999), 3.
109 Quoted in Grieg, *En forleggers erindringer*, 533.
110 Kolloen, *Erobreren*, 443.
111 Grieg, *En forleggers erindringer*, 530.
112 Quoted in Kolloen, *Erobreren*, 410.
113 Grieg, *En forleggers erindringer*, 532.
114 Stray, *Min klient*, 146.
115 Synne Corell, "The Solidarity of a National Narrative: The German Occupation in Norwegian History Culture," in *Nordic Narratives of the Second World War: National Historiographies Revisited*, ed. Henrik Stenius, Mirja Österberg, and Johan Östling. (Lund: Nordic Academic Press, 2011) 101–26; Tom Kristiansen, "The Norwegian War Experience: Occupied and Allied," in *Nordic War Stories: World War II as History, Fiction, Media, and Memory*, ed. Marianne Stecher-Hansen (Oxford: Berghahn, 2021), 49–64, at 52.
116 Langeland, *Dømmer ikke*, 8.
117 Stray, *Min klient*, 143.
118 Grieg, *En forleggers erindringer*, 554.
119 Hamsun, *Paths*, 5.
120 Quoted in Stray, *Min klient*, 170.
121 Kolloen, *Erobreren*, 445.
122 Monika Žagar, *Knut Hamsun: The Dark Side of Literary Brilliance* (Seattle: University of Washington Press, 2009), 225.
123 Hamsun, *Paths*, 84.
124 Arne Lunde, "Politics, Aesthetics, and Afterlife in *På gjengrodde stier:* Retracing Knut Hamsun's 'Overgrown Paths' Toward Nazism," *Scandinavica* 47.2 (2008): 175–90, at 183.

CHAPTER 5
EASTERN FRONTIERS AND PEOPLE'S JUSTICE: THE LITERARY PURGE IN ROMANIA

"Suspicions, denunciations, black lists, arrests": the general contours of the Romanian literary field in the postwar period were, even by the standards of mass upheaval characterizing European letters at the time, extreme.[1] That seemed unlikely given the country's wartime experience. Since there had been almost no popular resistance to Marshal Ion Antonescu's fascist regime, which was toppled by a coup d'état in late August 1944, the appetite for vengeance, with everyone's hands dirty, was limited. Reviewing war crimes trials across Eastern Europe, *Pravda* unfavorably contrasted the "empty words" and lack of "concrete measures" in Romania to the energetic people's justice in Bulgaria and Hungary.[2] But a few years later, the literary purge had become a harbinger of the communist system of ideological control and press censorship. The avant-garde energies of Romanian prewar modernism—the country had incubated Constantin Brancuşi's abstract formalism, Tristan Tzara's Dada, Isidore Isou's Lettrism, Eugène Ionesco's theater of the absurd, and Emil Cioran's nihilism—were not simply dismissed as meaningless aesthetic escapades but came to be seen as reactionary, fascist-imbued provocations; better for authors to pre-emptively confess "Am fost un poet decadent" [I was a decadent poet], as Nina Cassian, a close friend of Paul Celan in postwar Bucharest, did in her first published poem. In secret police files on authors, the hermeneutics of suspicion was no theoretical fancy but a tangible instrument of state violence.

The Romanian postwar stands out from the others treated in this book in a number of ways. First, the political organization of the country was entirely upended by external forces. The Antonescu regime was removed from power by a coup d'état; several months later, the Soviets—granted by a napkin in Yalta a 90 percent sphere of influence in the country—forcibly intervened to install a communist front government. The wheels of postwar Romania ran not toward reconstruction but Stalinization. Second, Romania's home-grown fascist movement, the Garda de Fer (Iron Guard), flourished without external support and captured the spirits of the country's students and leading intellectuals.[3] While the Iron Guard was outlawed because of the violence it spawned, its influence over state policy and elite culture was undeniable. Third, the postwar trials for collaboration and war crimes were initially limited in scope and relatively clement, but they became a model for repression, which, paradoxically, intensified over time. The People's Tribunals in Bucharest and Cluj found just over 1,000 individuals guilty of war crimes, a shockingly low figure given the number and nature of atrocities committed, with only four executions as a result (in Bulgaria, capital sentences accounted for around 26 percent of the nearly 10,000 convictions).[4] Despite its limited scope, the system of postwar people's justice had a lasting legacy, serving as the institutional basis for the communist reform of the legal system. Finally, Romania's war crimes trials centered on specific groups or social classes: the first brought together officials involved in the occupation of Odessa, the second concerned writers and journalists, and subsequent trials involved wider groups like those carrying out the Jewish genocide or the Antonescu regime *tout court* (the Marshal stood accused alongside several dozen associates). One trial before the People's Tribunal in Cluj grouped together 185 defendants in a single indictment! A crude Marxism seemed to be at play in making specific social categories living symbols of what needed to be cleansed away on the road to history's end.

This chapter details the various political pressures, both domestic and foreign, on Romania's postwar literary purge through an extended reading of the "journalists' trial." After a four-day trial in late May 1945, fourteen defendants (seven *in absentia*) were found guilty. The convicted included press moguls Stelian Popescu and Pamfil Şeicaru, the owners of the two largest Romanian newspapers, *Universul* and *Curentul*; some editors and journalists from the right-wing press; officials from the wartime Propaganda Ministry, including essayist Nichifor Crainic; and the poet and balladeer of the Iron Guard, Radu Gyr. My reading of this trial comes from a previously undiscovered transcript prepared by the Ministry of Propaganda, not the contemporary newspaper reports that prior scholarship has relied on.[5] Even though this transcript provides a fuller account of the trial, it is not a full stenographic record. While every word of the prosecution is recorded for posterity, large chunks of the defense are paraphrased or simply glossed over, and several pages of the transcript are missing. (The pointed use of archives and the distortion of documentary records for political ends was not a one-off in postwar Romania, as other postwar trials were also historically doctored for immediate political ends.[6]) The transcript of the journalists' trial was distributed to newspapers, with the Propaganda Ministry even spotlighting how it could be amended to reflect what history should have been. Despite these limitations, the transcript is a rare archival find since, as dissident Silviu Brucan (whose wife was involved in the trial) later noted, communists preferred "to operate by leaving no trace."[7] The trial transcript remained undiscovered for so long because access to archives was limited in the communist period and, then, in the post-1989 context, the lack of reckoning with the Romanian Holocaust and diffuse anti-Semitism contributed to making the postwar purge problematic.[8] This only goes to show that the politics of the postwar did not end in 1945, as the convictions in the journalists' trial were overturned in 1995 when Romania, finding itself in another moment of transitional justice, was still grappling over how to deal with war crimes. While it is illegal to rehabilitate war criminals, public memorials and streets remain named after them; efforts to change that are widely resisted because of widespread discomfort over how "communist justice"—which four decades of dictatorship turned into an oxymoron—was used to settle scores. While working at the newly-built National Library in Bucharest, I passed by a conference room named after Mircea Vulcănescu, a prominent intellectual from the 1930s who was sentenced to eight years of hard labor for war crimes committed while a sub-secretary of state in the Ministry of Finances. And there was his name, without any further commentary.[9]

Romanian States of Treason

If geography dictates existence for nations, it created propitious conditions for treason throughout Romania's history. Foreign occupations by Ottoman Turks, Russians, and Austro-Hungarians constantly shifted allegiances and belonging. Upon independence in the mid-nineteenth century, a foreign king was summoned, and the 1866 constitution copied models abroad (Belgium and France). The law on treason mimicked, almost word for word, the French penal code: high treason meant siding with a foreign power or working with foreign agents to undermine the territorial integrity or military security of the state.[10] The nationalist dream of unifying the Romanian people *de la Nistru pân-la Tisa* [from the Nistru (River) to the Tisza (River)] was realized after the First World War when Transylvania, the Banat, Bukovina, and Bessarabia were incorporated into *România Mare* [Greater Romania]. These new territories doubled the country's size and population but also contained substantial national minority groups (Hungarians, Germans, Serbs) and religions (Jews, Greek Catholics, and Protestants).

Citizenship took on a modern, liberal form when the 1923 Constitution used the formula "without regard to ethnic origin, language, or religion" to affirm the universal character of rights. Yet the history of the interwar period's two defining political ideologies—communism and fascism—pointed to the fraught imaginary of national belonging and treason. The Romanian Communist Party (*Partidul Comunist Român*, or PCR) was outlawed in 1924 not because it called for revolution but because its platform called for Bessarabia and parts of Bukovina to be ceded back to Moscow. With over three-quarters of the PCR's membership drawn from minority groups (Hungarians, Jews, Bulgarians, Russians, and Ukrainians), the party had fewer than one thousand members, and few sympathizers.[11] Although communism stood almost no chance of gaining power in free elections, the fears it raised resulted in the formation of fascist groups.[12] Political violence flourished as prime ministers—plural, no less—were assassinated by fascists, who were in turn hunted down by state security agencies. In the name of a pre-modern, mystical "ethnocratic state" with a "homogeneity of blood," ethnic nationalism committed treason by excess.[13] To give *Totul pentru Ţara* (Everything for the Country), as the Iron Guard's political party was called, could also be treason.

From the late 1930s until the instauration of the communist people's republic in late 1947, no fewer than seven governing regimes held power. The longest-lasting one was led by army officer Marshal Ion Antonescu (Figure 5.1).[14] He came to power, in September 1940, after a disastrous summer in which Transylvania, Bukovina and Bessarabia were seized by foreign powers. To minimize the severity of an inevitable German occupation and to recover those lost lands, Antonescu opted for an alliance with the Axis. The widespread distrust of Stalin and Bolshevism, deeply anchored in the country because of past occupations and recently inflamed by the annexation of Bessarabia, led even

Figure 5.1 Romania's entry into the Axis, 1941. Ion Antonescu, Horia Sima, and King Mihai are in attendance. Courtesy of National Digital Archive, Poland.

committed leftists to support war against the Red Army. Antonescu's politics—fascist in spirit, if not in name—were also no stumbling block to an alliance with the Third Reich. Antonescu invited the Iron Guard into a governing coalition built around the policy of "Romanization," but that cohabitation lasted only a few months, culminating in a failed January 1941 revolt by the Legionnaires (who wanted even harsher ethnic policies implemented, more quickly). Antonescu's liquidation of the Iron Guard was a welcome balm for intellectuals who longed for democracy, even if the overall climate was one of repression. A February 1941 decree made it a capital crime to author "manuscripts, manifestos, drafts and drawings" that challenged state power. Singing revolutionary songs was punishable with five to fifteen years of hard labor. All student political activity was banned. Penalties for crimes of a seditious nature were doubled when committed by Jews, communists, or non-ethnic Romanians.[15] Another decree, aiming for "the nationalization of the 'Romanian printed word,'" excluded Jews from the literary field.[16]

In late August 1944, Antonescu was deposed (and taken into Soviet custody) by King Mihai and a few politicians. The Romanian army promptly switched sides and found itself not only fighting the retreating Germans but also racing to occupy national territory before it could be "liberated" by the Soviets, who came to occupy Bucharest (see Figure 5.2).[17] Suing for peace, Romania was treated as one of the vanquished. It was "forced to pay through the nose for its past transgressions," George Kennan observed,

Figure 5.2 Entry of the Soviet Army in Bucharest, August 1944. Arhiva Institutului de Istorie al PMR, 56/1944, Photograph #C056. Courtesy of Fototeca online a comunismului românesc.

surrendering treasure (economic reparations), soil (Bessarabia and northern Bukovina were ceded to the Soviet Union), sovereign power (to the Soviet-run Allied Control Commission), and blood (over 100,000 Romanians of ethnic German origin were deported to Soviet work camps).[18] The Armistice Convention outlawed fascist political groupings and formalized the obligation to punish war criminals, a major Soviet demand given the barbarous Romanian occupation of Odessa. The Soviets had a ready helper in Lucrețiu Pătrășcanu, the minister of justice who had been a PCR member since the 1920s and key figure in the August coup.

On paper, the national unity government set up in August 1944 promised to haul war criminals before an unspecified "Special Court"; in reality, other matters pressed. The army, led by the same figures who had served Antonescu, was trying to regain territory in Transylvania, so a purge would have decapitated it at a crucial time. Entrenched bureaucrats were loath to clean house and could not imagine how executing legal commands could be turned into a crime. The first decree on purging bureaucrats, from September 1944, specified the need to respect constitutional protections. "Nothing in the State apparatus has moved," one leading communist bemoaned.[19] In October the Council of Ministers sanctioned preventive arrests of war criminals and also called for three prominent editors and journalists to be arrested—but these directives were never executed.[20] Six weeks after the August coup, with not a single high-profile war criminal punished, the Soviets sent a list of forty-seven individuals, including two serving cabinet ministers, to be tried. The Romanians stalled, with the excuse that there was no legal instrument to punish or even arrest war criminals.[21] This did not impress the Soviets, who had been prosecuting war criminals for over two years.

It was only in the third government after the August coup—three national unity cabinets in 150 days says everything about the political instability of the time—that war crimes legislation finally got in the books. Laws 50 and 51 of January 1945 defined war crimes and war profiteering (law 50) and created the new crime of "those responsible for the country's disaster" (*celor vinovați de dezastrul țării*, law 51). These crimes were to be tried by "public accusers" in Special Tribunals. War crimes mainly concerned *jus in bello* (inhuman treatment and torture, but also setting up ghettos or organizing deportations), but there was a political element in including acts perpetrated against "political internees" or those "opposed to the war or the dictatorial regime." It was also a war crime to desert the national territory and then attack "through writing, speech or any other medium." Working for German propaganda organs had a maximum sentence of forced labor for life. The retroactive crime of "those responsible for the country's disaster" covered those who had set up the "dictatorial regime" or supported the alliance with the Axis.[22]

On paper, these two laws violated the 1923 Constitution, which prohibited retroactive legislation and special courts, but nothing, as two seen-it-all politicos told a visiting journalist, was cheaper in Bucharest than the paper on which laws were written.[23] It was par for the course for a communist justice minister who thought that "bourgeois law" was an "instrument for oppressing the working class" to press for exceptionally severe war crimes laws, but other cabinet ministers were not keen on the new laws.[24] The communists accused Prime Minister Nicolae Rădescu, a career army officer who spent two years in jail for opposing Antonescu's pro-German policies, of "sabotage." A mass protest outside the Parliament, with its major theme the inaction toward war criminals, spiraled into violence when the police opened fire (others claimed communist provocateurs fired first). Rădescu took to the airwaves to call the communists foreigners "without God or nation"; Pătrășcanu gracelessly replied, "Death to the Fascists."[25] So much for national unity!

The Soviets maneuvered to replace the sitting government by a "democratic front" headed by Petru Groza. Vowing to put war crimes trials at the top of its agenda, the Groza government decreed an even harsher war crimes law. Law 312 ordered the creation of a People's Tribunal to judge "those responsible for the country's disaster." Severity was a virtue, Pătrășcanu told the Council of Ministers:

> We are drafting a law of swift repression. Unfortunately, we are doing this now in April, when it should have been done in September. Our problems would have been solved already had this been done earlier. But there is no reason at all, and it is in no one's interest, to endlessly prolong these trials with appeals. The law, in its very essence, is a law of political repression—and nothing else—in order to satisfy the demands of the people, the Allies, and what we in Romania believe to be important today.[26]

To have put in place "Hitlerism or fascism," in whatever mode, was now a war crime.[27] The public accusers were granted unchecked investigative powers. The property of accused war criminals could be seized while their cases were brought to the People's Tribunals, whose juries would be drawn from magistrates and jurors on party-approved lists. The new law also stipulated that trial transcripts would be "summary," no doubt because a complete transcript would slow down the swift justice the People's Tribunal was called to deliver (dispensing with an historical record of what many knew would be questionable legal proceedings was a bonus). This exceptional law was supposed to remain in force for less than five months, but it remained on the books for nearly two years, with its reach extended to establishing a tribunal in Cluj.

As this new war crimes law came into effect, Groza called for a purge of fascists from public life and state institutions. Removing one bureaucrat allowed the party to slot in another who would remain indebted to the party. Programs of "re-education" were implemented for civil servants to imbibe the "spirit of a democratic Romania."[28] The Ministry of Interior Teohari Georgescu, a former typesetter, announced in April 1945 that those who now sided with the "people" would be judged leniently for their past affiliations.[29] Some ministries were more important to purge, such as the Ministry of Justice, where a central committee examined the wartime conduct of judges, state prosecutors and auxiliary judicial personnel. Reports of arbitrary arrests, preventive detentions, and false accusations sent ripples of fear throughout the judicial apparatus, which had heard that Andrei Vyshinsky, the leading Soviet official in the country and the chief figure behind the Moscow show trials in the 1930s, had given orders for the dismissal of more than 1,000 magistrates.[30] Pătrăşcanu had to navigate between communist hardliners and liberal lawyers, and with leadership ambitions that he did not disguise, he acted harsher than his natural inclinations might have prompted (Figure 5.3). (It was a bitter irony that the system he set up came to be his undoing: in the early 1950s, he was found guilty of betraying the party and hauled before a firing squad. His secret police archive runs to 204 volumes.[31])

The new war crimes push was by no stretch too little, but it was too late. From August 1944, when the Antonescu regime was deposed, to March 1945, when the communists took control of the cabinet, was a long period of time to dither. South of the border the people's tribunals in Bulgaria had been busy at work for months before even the semblance of a plan appeared in Romania (the two countries were liberated at roughly the same time). Could it have been hard to arrest ministers from Antonescu's cabinet? Their names were not unknown, and around forty such souls were still on Romanian soil. This lack of decisive action after the coup d'état made it far too easy for individuals to flee, either abroad or internally, or to work the system so that one's ducks were in a row: an alibi for this, an explanation for that, one witness bought, that paper trail destroyed. In every other country in Europe, there had been public explosions of fury that made even the most biased and perverse legal proceedings seem like textbook expositions of the rule of law. In Romania there had been none of that, and now the courts were playing catch-up to bring people's justice to a people who had not shown much inclination to act.

The communist idea of "people's justice" was drawn from the Soviet view that the legal system was a political tool to advance instrumental ends; "law's empire" as an

Figure 5.3 Lucrețiu Pătrășcanu (with legs crossed) watching a May Day parade in Bucharest with PCR cadres (including future leader Gheorghe Gheorgiu-Dej). Printed in *Scânteia*, the official PCR organ. #FA007. Courtesy of Fototeca online a comunismului românesc.

autonomous sphere was dismissed out of hand as a liberal fable. As Vyshinsky had put it, "The specific mark of Soviet law, distinguishing it, radically and in principle, from the law of all other societies and epochs, is that it serves, in the true and actual sense of the word, the people—society—which for the first time in history comes into its own."[32] Soviet courts, in his view, existed to "destroy[] without pity all the foes of the people in whatsoever form they manifest their criminal encroachments upon socialism."[33] Elevating Pătrășcanu to Justice Minister—a position he held across the various cabinets formed after the coup—would radically upend the "old apparatus of justice" to "the people's way of seeing, the true beliefs of the people."[34] The "political law" setting up the People's Tribunal, Pătrășcanu readily admitted, served as "the example according to which we will transform the country's whole justice system."[35] Not only were "the people" the ostensible beneficiaries of this justice, but a notion of collective guilt permeated the postwar Romanian legal system. Individual trials were bourgeois luxuries, slow and cumbersome; the lessons they taught were limited compared to the easily assimilable narrative of a wider class that was incorrigibly guilty. The paean to this people's justice during the trial of Antonescu makes for melodramatic reading today: the People's Tribunal was "born from the immense sufferings that the Romanian people had endured, was created from waves of blood, waves of pain, from the tears of mothers … from the tears and pains of orphans."[36]

The inquisitorial criminal system in the People's Tribunals was channeled exclusively through the presiding judge, who had the sole right to pose questions. The chief magistrate in Bucharest was Alexandru Voitinovici, a thirty-year old Jewish lawyer from Iaşi with little experience at the bar. His interests were, in fact, literary (under the pseudonym Al. Voitin, he debuted with his first volume of poetry in 1934, at the age of 19, and was close to the group around *Însemnări ieşene*, a salon from the northern city of Iaşi). It was from this literary circle that he was recruited to the PCR, eventually becoming close to Pătrăşcanu, who pressed for his appointment as head of the People's Tribunal. While maintaining his literary career (he wrote a number of plays with legal themes), Voitinovici later became the President of the Supreme Tribunal from 1954 to 1967. One of the other magistrates was Alexandru Iancu Petrescu, a military lawyer whose wartime record was zealous, possibly murderous—but he had pledged himself to the communists. This transfer of allegiance was accepted without qualms because the party was in no position to impose purity tests upon capable, efficient, and useful individuals (the PCR welcomed into its fold former fascists, who tended to have messianic mindsets and, importantly, tended to be ethnic Romanians).[37]

The main actors in the postwar trials were not the judges, though, but the public accusers. Around ten examining cabinets, each with two public accusers, investigated war crimes, assembled evidence, interrogated defendants, and brought cases before the People's Tribunal. Most of the public accusers were PCR members with no illusions about whose interests they served. Their daily actions were chronicled in the press: months before any cases would come to the courts, PCR organ *Scânteia* informed its readers what witnesses had been telling the public prosecutors in ongoing investigations. *România liberă* "unmasked" the "crypto-fascists" in its "Portraits of Traitors" column.[38] Fittingly enough for representatives of the people, public accusers were presented in mass dailies with portraits and short bios. The public accusers played the game, telling the press that certain accused, who were called out by name, offered up ridiculous defenses—so much for the presumption of innocence. That calculated collaboration with the press not only moved public opinion but also maintained pressure on the accusers, who were not uniformly zealous in the execution of their duties (future Interior Minister Alexandru Drăghici noted that some public accusers were in office for nearly two years without managing to secure a single conviction).[39]

The chief public accuser, Avram Bunaciu, had defended the communists in 1930s political trials. He had been interned alongside fellow PCR members and even harbored the printing press for *România liberă* at his home; he became justice minister in 1948 (after having turned on his mentor Patraşcanu). Another public accuser with a legal background was Constantin Vicol, a law professor who delivered the government's requisition at the journalists' trial; in his scholarly assessment, a political trial had to offer "the appearance of legality," not the thing itself.[40] Vasile Stoican later served as General Secretary in the Ministry of Justice and then worked as a legal advisor for the Securitate. Some zealous PCR members with no legal training were also public accusers. Alexandru Drăghici was a worker who rose to become Minister of Interior and was instrumental in arranging the Pătrăşcanu show trial and clamping down on dissidents in the 1950s and 1960s (before being branded a dissident himself by Nicolae Ceauşescu); Dumitru Săracu had been a waiter at Casa Capşa, a Belle Epoque Bucharest locale famous for backroom deals, political gossip and overpriced fare; the engineer Alexandra Sidorivici was married to Silviu Brucan, the managing editor of *Scânteia*.

What distinguished Romania from other systems of "people's justice" set up elsewhere in Eastern Europe was the centralization of the People's Tribunals. Hungary's people's tribunals (*nébíróságok*) consisted of lower trial courts in county seats and a National Council in Budapest that heard appeals. In Poland "special penal courts" (*specjalne sądy karne*) were first established in Lublin, Kraków, and Siedlce in October 1944, with six more courts later formed in other districts. But in Romania the People's Tribunal had, at first, only a single court, in Bucharest (a second court eventually opened in Cluj, but plans to open courts in Iaşi and Galaţi never materialized). Few war crimes, though, had been committed on the capital's busy roads, or even on Romanian territory, so it was not easy to assemble evidence, question witnesses, or even formally identify the guilty from 92 Boulevard Ferdinand. It did not help that several key government agencies, among them the Secret Police or the Ministry of War, were loath to cooperate.[41] The Soviets were no better, refusing to release captured war criminals out of fear that the Romanians would bungle the proceedings. A single public accuser had anywhere from 250 to 300 open case files, an unmanageable load in the best of circumstances. And because trials had grave political implications, simply establishing guilt was not enough—the guilt had to serve that moment's political needs. Often enough—around one hundred times, according to one exasperated public accuser—some higher-up would put a stop to a slam-dunk case in order to protect the guilty party (out of friendship, avarice, or ambition, the reasons to do so were plenty).[42] Despite all these obstacles, the war crimes trials that did take place were models of quick justice: the first war crimes trial, on the occupation of Odessa, lasted eight days; the journalists' trial, four. Even the Antonescu trial, with nearly forty defendants and major political questions hanging in the air, was done and dusted in ten days.

The People's Press

In early 1945, the media landscape in Romania was radically restructured with communist political interests in mind. Two attitudes had found ready expression in the interwar and wartime press: an undisguised anti-Semitism and a pronounced hatred of Bolshevism. The communists believed that the press had fostered a deep "hatred of the Soviet Union" throughout the country which it now had to extirpate as part of the larger mission of "removing fascism from the minds of the people."[43] To that end, the armistice convention granted the Soviet High Command control over the "printing, importation and distribution … of periodical and non-periodical literature, the presentation of theatrical performances and films, the work of wireless stations, telegraph and telephone" (Art. 16). Every news article touching upon political matters required a "ready-for-print" authorization; failure to secure one could result in the seizure and destruction of a full print run, while repeated offenses led to publication bans. The censorship regime was formalized in February 1945 with a law targeting "journalists, publicist and press collaborators" who had "put into action Hitlerism or fascism" or "prepared public opinion for the entrance in the Axis Powers and ... persuaded the public to support the unjust war against the Soviet Union."[44] A five-person commission was granted wide powers to investigate "dangerous vipers" who supported "fascist jackals," as Miron Constantinescu, commission member and editor-in-chief of *Scânteia*, put it.[45] The commission's judgment was final; it also did not have to respect any legal norms ("The commission can inform itself however it desires and is not obliged to show how it arrived at its final determination") when sentencing the guilty.[46] A few days after the press law was passed, the National Liberty Party's paper, *Viitorul*, was shut down. Other papers were told to not bother approaching the censor, which effectively forced them to cease publication.[47] One of the first acts of the communists after seizing power in early March 1945 was the creation of a Ministry of Propaganda whose remit was to "manage and lead all propaganda and information actions in the country."[48] As Groza remarked upon its creation, "We are for the freedom of the press, but for the freedom of the press and propaganda when it comes to democratic ideas. We are in no way ready to open the doors to an enemy that will destroy our young democratic state."[49] The Ministry's first minister, Petre Constantinescu-Iaşi, who had been sentenced in 1936 to thirty months of hard labor for writing anti-fascist articles, boasted that "lagers for those who conducted criminal fascist propaganda have been opened."[50] Foreign journalists whose reporting was "not objective" were harassed or deported.[51]

Besides censorship, control over the material production and distribution of print also contributed to the communist restructuring of the media landscape. With the paper stock limited, opposition sheets had their paper ration decreased, which limited the size and circulation of each issue, while communist papers, with low readerships, had paper to burn (better, though, to sell it on the black market to fill up party coffers and enrich cadres). On the production side, typesetters and printers refused to handle "reactionary" attacks on the new regime; on the distribution side, delivery vans for independent papers were attacked and kiosks stocking non-communist sheets were vandalized, their sellers roughed up, with the police pointedly told to not intervene.[52] (*Plus ça change*: in the 1930s fascists and leftists regularly battled around newspaper stands.) In short, "the multiple-wired sieve of Communist-led typesetters, Communist-controlled paper distributors, Communist-thought police, Rumanian censors and Soviet censors" had a noticeable impact on what the public read; as one American journalist put it, the system ensured that "the Rumanian papers write Russian thoughts and Russian commands in Rumanian (Latin) letters."[53]

While the communists were most interested in newspapers and cinema newsreels, books were also targeted. If every sentence was a "fact," which could be either "a good fact or a bad fact," Prime Minister Groza deduced before a writers' congress in August 1945, then it was incumbent upon communists to protect only good ones.[54] Several months earlier, the Romanian Commission for the Application of the Armistice gave booksellers and publishers fifteen days to hand in books that damaged "good relations with the Soviet Union." Receipts issued for books to be pulped indicated the title, number of copies, and even the weight of the volumes. (Predictably enough, a brisk trade in banned books ensued.)[55] In late March 1945 the Ministry of Propaganda released a list of 167 banned books. A few weeks later, book censorship was expanded to include any print matter, appearing from January 1, 1917, to August 23, 1944, with "legionary, fascist, Hitlerite, chauvinist, or racist ideas" or containing "passages undermining good relations" with the Soviet Union.[56] Going so far back in time was a clear way to ensure that anti-Bolshevik texts (no coincidence with 1917!) could be removed from circulation. The remit of the censorship commission was not just to punish crimes from the recent war but to control opinion in the future. Every publisher or typesetter had two months to send in a list of every book it had published over a nearly thirty-year period. Politically suspect works were pulled from sale, even from second-hand bookshops or sidewalk *bouquinistes*. Agents conducted sweeps to seize banned items: in the final two weeks of May 1945, over 500 such raids were conducted on booksellers or private collectors in Bucharest.[57] What was politically suspect was an open question, but, mindful to err on the side of caution, the chief Romanian censor sent over 400 books to the Soviet legation for final judgment.[58] From March 1945 to January 1946, the Ministry of Propaganda released over twenty separate lists of censored books. The multilingual censorship—of the nearly 1500 books censored, more than half were in foreign tongues (630 in Magyar, 254 in Italian, 84 in German, 71 in French)—included not only openly pro-fascist works but also classic Romanian writers like Mihai Eminescu (the national poet, toward whom the communists had very conflicted feelings in 1945 because of his nationalist and anti-Semitic beliefs) and intellectuals like Ovid Densusianu, a literary critic who championed modernist ideas, Nae Ionescu, the charismatic philosophy professor whose conservative ideas spearheaded the 1927 Generation, and Nicolae Iorga, a nationalist historian whose academic laurels were as lengthy as his anti-Semitism was deep. The banned books included ostensible fascist titles, but the wide remit of the commission led to some curious decisions, such as banning a two-volume biography of Immanuel Kant, guidebooks issued by the National Office of Tourism (*Romania's Beaches, Hunting in Romania*, etc.), or farmer's almanacs. One children's storybook co-authored by Radu Gyr was to be "partially purged"—by eliminating Gyr's name as a co-author (the text remained)! The list of banned books, by June 1948, swelled to nearly 8,000 titles.[59]

Suppressing anti-communist newspapers or books was one side of the communist propaganda coin; the other was actively creating a communist print culture. In its first public issue in late September 1944, *Scânteia* rhapsodized: "After two years of deep illegality, after two decades of terrorization … the arrests of editors, collaborators and distributors, of tortures, of heavy punishments, and killings, *Scânteia* now appears."[60] The press, PCR comrade Ilie Zaharia noted, was "the sharpest weapon" in the political struggle: "As an agitator, the newspaper needs to know how to mobilize the masses to action, to bring to light certain facts, and to train the masses for the political fight and for professional revendications."[61] Yet there were few communist intellectuals or journalists around. There had been theoretical instruction about agitprop in Moscow but, with most members abroad or in jail, little on-the-ground training. At a three-day conference on communist propaganda in late January 1945, multiple editors from provincial communist papers admitted to insufficient "professional training": "Not a single one of us who began to write the paper," said an editor from *Inainte* [Forward], "was prepared, either politically or professionally."[62] The chief editor of *Scânteia* "needed a scribe and a grammarian to make his articles intelligible"; the journalists on staff "knew Hungarian better than Romanian" or, alternately, "knew Russian better than Romanian."[63] The voice of those frustrations was Silviu Brucan, the managing editor, who at least had a significant body of experience in the leftist press. (*Scânteia*'s staff also included, for a short while, an eighteen-year-old Isidore Isou, who later founded Lettrism in Paris.) The aptly named *Tribuna Poporului* was run by literary critic George Călinescu, who, *faute de mieux*, was left-leaning but not an ideologue (he also collaborated with the Antonescu regime).[64] *Scânteia* struggled to draw readers away from more established papers; it was only starting in spring 1945, when active suppression of other papers and press diktats were issued, that readers turned to the sheet, which copied the visual layout, formatting, and columns of the country's most popular paper, *Universul*.[65] On the book publishing front, the Editura de Partid (The Party Publishing House) was set up immediately after the August coup to distribute political pamphlets, mostly translations of Soviet works. While some of the print runs were massive—over 500,000 copies shifted in six months—only about five booksellers in Bucharest stocked its series. At some point the Red Army was corralled into the propaganda battle, its soldiers distributing pamphlets on the streets and its planes dropping leaflets. Soviet literary culture also spread through translations. Paul Celan, after two years in a work camp, first worked at *Bucovina Sovietică* in his native Czernowitz and then, in Bucharest, translated Soviet political speeches for *Scânteia* and worked at Cartea Rusă [Russia House], where Mihail Sadoveanu, the favored writer of the communists, also worked.[66] All this was enshrined in the 1948 Constitution, whose article on free expression put the "means of printing" at "the disposal of the working people," thus limiting the right to whatever the state sanctioned.

These official, state-sponsored measures targeting the daily press and the book trade were reinforced and supplemented by professional associations working in the same direction. In late September 1944 the Society of Romanian Writers elected Victor Eftimiu as its new president. He had run a heavily politicized campaign promising to remove fascist writers from its ranks and turn the organization into a communist body to bring literature "down to the villages."[67] Because of the sheer impossibility of earning a living as a professional writer in Romania without regular journalism work, almost every member had questionable wartime associations: a complete purge would have left the Writers' Union empty. In the end, the writers with the least pull found themselves unceremoniously removed, and membership requirements were lowered so that several "worker writers" could join. The press syndicate and journalists' union set up purge commissions in October 1944, drawing up lists of members to be purged that included many of the same individuals who would eventually be put on trial for war crimes.[68] But a new press purge commission was only created months later, as too many individuals slipped through the cracks or found unlikely mercy. In the end, after all, a state trial was a much harsher, and much more public, sentence than a boardroom purge by committee. When it came to the rights of the accused, though, the differences were not so marked.

The Word on Trial

To bring to account all the guilty writers in Romania—"We will search out everything that has been written in the past six years in order to denounce before the public all those responsible for our disaster," one journalist vowed in September 1944—was an impossible task when the wartime literary field had been structured by strict censorship, a repressive state, and German occupation.[69] There was no conceivable way in which a writer published from September 1940 to August 1944 could avoid complicity with the Antonescu regime. Yet writers who "had done nothing but to write for money, to earn their daily bread," Petru Groza told his ministers, were better off being re-educated:

> I do not want to see anyone in the dock in this big trial except those responsible, the moral authors. The only ones to be purged should be the heads of the list; if we do otherwise, I don't know what the lists to come will contain. If we continue with everyone, I don't know when we'll ever end.[70]

In late January 1945, ten of the sixty-four individuals (15 percent) that the Council of Ministers ordered to be preventively arrested for being "responsible for the country's disaster" were writers. In mid-May, twenty-nine "leading propagators of fascism and Hitlerism" were banned from print for life and another fifteen received two- to five-year suspensions. The punishments handed down by the country's highest political body were, unsurprisingly, politically inflected: the financier and owner of *Viața*, a paper that "clearly contributed to preparing public opinion to accept and consolidate the politics of Antonescu's dictatorship," received the same five-year ban as a cartoonist who caricatured Uncle Joe.[71]

But simply banning writers from publishing in the future was not enough to discipline the word—there also had to be a reckoning with the past. On the morning of May 30, 1945, the first major trial of war criminals of the pen opened. There was more than a hint of sadness in the air as the day before, the Romanian-Jewish novelist, playwright, and attorney Mihail Sebastian was crossing Bulevardul Regina Maria when a bus driven by a drunk Soviet soldier rammed into him at full speed. Having lived through wartime anti-Semitism and German occupation, with the specter of deportation to death camps or a pogrom never far distant, and then having survived the German aerial bombardment of the capital at war's close, in which his house was completely destroyed, Sebastian met his end crossing the street. There were a few ironies floating around: Sebastian was convening a course on French letters for the communist-run Free Democratic University, an adult education center established a few months earlier, but he was privately critical of the communist takeover of the literary field (which he had helped into being, having worked all night to put out the first issue of *România liberă* in late

August 1944). The involvement of a Red Army soldier remained unreported—the press blamed the bus's faulty brakes and did not mention alcohol—to not impugn the Soviet "liberation." As a lawyer, Sebastian would have had a special interest in the upcoming journalists' trial, but he did not hold out much hope for justice when the new institutions being created were overrun by "a mixture of desperate failures and mediocrities seeking revenge": writers were agile leopards changing spots, emitting loud professions of faith in the "new democracy" to better camouflage fascist pasts.[72] It's not that Sebastian was against retribution—let the shoe go on the other foot was his feeling after hundreds of thousands of the country's Jews were sent to death camps and hundreds of thousands of others were denied the right to work and had their homes and businesses confiscated—but he was morally divided on what form that revenge would take and who should mete it out.

The journalists' trial was presided by Ilie Ţabrea, a councillor for the Bucharest Court of Appeals (with a spotty war past: he had headed a commission in Transnistria during the Romanian occupation), alongside Alexandru Voitinovici. The three public accusers running the show were Constantin Vicol, Ion D. Ion and Alexandra Sidorivici. The seven-person jury mainly consisted of workers (one juror, the teacher Constantin Lăpuşneanu, had served on the jury of the first war crimes trial that had wrapped up a few days earlier; another juror, the lawyer Stelian Niţulescu, would go on to serve as minister of justice from 1949 to 1952). The writers and editors on trial were a motley bunch: press magnates (Stelian Popescu and Pamfil Şeicaru owned the two largest Bucharest dailies, *Universul* and *Curentul*); a handful of editors and journalists from the fascist press (most of whom had been banned during the war years); officials from the Propaganda Ministry; and the poet and balladeer of the Iron Guard, Radu Gyr. Most of the accused had already been blacklisted for life by the Council of Ministers, and quite a few of them had also been banned for writing or had been imprisoned during the Antonescu regime, when the Iron Guard and its press outlets were banned in 1941, or even earlier, in the crackdown on the Iron Guard in the 1930s, so it was not simply a case of double but of triple jeopardy in some cases! Not a single publisher was put on trial, and several major literary figures with concrete ties to fascism (Mircea Eliade and Emil Cioran supported the Iron Guard and held cultural diplomacy posts for the Antonescu regime; philosopher Constantin Noica edited an Iron Guard paper and worked at the Romanian Institute in Berlin) were overlooked.

If anything held the defendants together, it was a marked antipathy toward communism. Ilie Rădulescu had founded "Anticommunist Romania" in 1936 and set up *Porunca Vremii* to counter Bolshevism. The major press dailies owned by Popescu and Şeicaru were vocal in their distrust of the Soviets. In the new reality of forced communization, showing writers what could happen when one stepped out of line was critical. Punishing writers also placated the Soviets. After Romanian atrocities in Odessa were tried, it made sense to move on to questions of free expression, which was inimical to the proper development of a communist utopia (why have free expression when one can express the truth?). Finally, there was an economic motive. When the first investigations of the accused were opened months earlier, complete inventories of property to be seized, down to the last spoon, were taken. The seized factories, machinery, paper stocks, and office spaces of indicted press magnates propped up the nascent communist press and publishing houses while the three horses and one cow at a summer house, the two wooden beds, the flower-patterned crystal vase, the Blüthner pianola *und so weiter und so fort* could grease the palms of cadres. The immense holdings of the press magnates—Pamfil Şeicaru's fortune was estimated at 1.5 billion lei, and Stelian Popescu's *Universul* was even more profitable—were tantalizing for the new regime.[73]

The main charge in the *actul de acuzare* (indictment) was that the accused had created a climate of opinion favorable to fascism: "In our country, a whole series of writers and publicists, some of whom attained fame through their writings, had developed and systematically supported for years on end the fundamental racialist, fascist and thus anti-democratic, warlike, and imperialist tenets of Hitlerist propaganda." A "weapon of war like any other," propaganda had led the country into the abyss by manipulating the people, whose opinion was the basis upon which a society was governed ("A political action cannot be realized without a favorable, or at least neutral, public opinion"). The indictment was heavy on rhetoric ("How many of the torturers, thieves and assassins from the camps on the other side of the Nistru River had not been faithful readers and fervent admirers of the prose style of Ilie Rădulescu or Pamfil Şeicaru?"), but the overall thrust of the charges was confused. The accused supposedly intoxicated the Romanian public through their writings, but not one was considered an independent thinker. Were the accused spreading an ideology or could "their nationalism and patriotism … be exclusively reduced to their wallets"?[74] That the majority of the accused held noxious, prejudicial ideas—about the supremacy of Romanians, the degeneracy of Jews, the spiritual leadership of Hitler, and so on—was not in dispute, but that those ideas were criminal was less than obvious when the language and form of texts by "nationalist" and "anti-Semitic" writers had permeated the entire literary field since the infancy of the Romanian state and were part and parcel of "state policy" as well.[75]

Although most of the indicted writers had been investigated for months, the trial proceedings were rushed, with the indictment appearing two weeks earlier and some of the accused charged only a few days before the trial opened. Only seven of the accused were physically in the dock (Ilie Rădulescu had been apprehended only a few weeks earlier); the other seven were tried *in absentia* (most had fled abroad, but Nichifor Crainic remained in hiding, in Romania, hidden by a priest, for over two years!). Only one, Alexandru Hodoş, a press propagandist in Berlin (who had been an intimate of the fascist poet-prime minister Octavian Goga before the war and as a deputy minister drafted a bill to restrict journalism to ethnic Romanians), had an attorney present. Four days before the trial started some attorneys had been assigned to the accused, but some of those attorneys were being purged by the bar association and thus could not enter the courtroom. One defendant asked to see the files against him, only to be told to wait until his interrogation was finished; another asked to see the full print run of his wartime articles—again, patience. The first morning of the trial was spent reading out the criminal indictment and a resolution from the Council of Ministers on fascist propaganda. Behind the scenes, there was a scramble to find defense attorneys, a difficult task since "Death to the Defenders of War Criminals" had been chanted during the first trial at the People's Tribunal a week earlier. Somehow three attorneys, two of them quite junior female attorneys, were rustled up for the afternoon session; each was given two clients to defend but no time to meet those clients, familiarize themselves with the charges, or go through any documents.

The most pressing issue for the court was not supplying the accused with a chance to conduct a reasonable defense but rather eliciting their clear guilt through highly scripted interrogations. No more than eight to ten questions were directed to each accused; there was no desire to go into a full history or enter into much detail when all that had to be done was to establish the accused's authorship of a set of incriminating articles. Questions beginning with a rote formula of "Is it true," "Is it the case," "Do you acknowledge" were followed by an incriminating act: "Do you recognize that through these subjects public opinion was moved to support Hitler's war?" Subtle explanations of how a text took on different meanings in different contexts, or could have been prompted by wartime propaganda directives, or might have been altered by censors or editors, were dismissed as irrelevant and not even recorded for posterity: "The [defendant] tries to negate the charge and stumbles over his explanations."[76] Several defendants argued that they tried to undermine propaganda directives by writing "between the lines," flooding their texts "in an enormous bath of literature that hid … antifascist beliefs"—but the court had no desire to decode subtle literary meanings.

The interrogations of the seven accused took up the afternoon and evening session on the first day. A series of prosecution witnesses, mostly journalists from the communist press (two of whom were embroiled in defamation lawsuits against the accused), were then called. Their "evidence" was little more than hearsay or opinion: "Personally I do not know, but the entire city said it, the entire country said it" is how one witness described the nefarious blackmail supposedly conducted by Ilie Rădulescu, the editor of the far-right *Porunca Vremii*: "as the proverb has it," the public accuser agreed, "there is no smoke without fire." When asked if Romulus Dianu took money from the Germans, a journalist from Bacău spoke sophistically of alchemists hiding their tracks before saying, with a straight face, "In this sense I am not able to say on my conscience that I know, but I can say with an untroubled conscience that I know it. I do not know that the accused Romulus Dianu received money from the Germans, but I believe it." The Romanian public "believed word for word whatever was written" in the press, explained Zaharia Stancu, a press purge commission member (and future president of the Union of Writers). The public accusers took all these conjectures as evidence: "We are in front of the People's Tribunal, and what we affirm is proof. The defense might try to prove the contrary, but as we base ourselves on public opinion, what was known by the entire public is for the People's Tribunal proof." The most serious credible evidence of a crime came from a woman who claimed that Ilie Rădulescu had kidnapped and raped her—but that serious charge was not followed up by the prosecutors, who preferred to focus on how Rădulescu had supposedly stolen some of her jewelry (evidence of his greed and avarice fit the narrative of traitors as sell-outs).[77]

The one issue the court had to settle was whether writing during the war years conveyed personal convictions or was the product of a "triple framework of control," as the accused Romulus Dianu called the system of press owners, fascist editors, and censorship regime.[78] There could be no criminal responsibility for writing in a rigid system of totalitarian control when both writers and the public knew that everything printed was controlled by the State. This was a version of the *Befehl ist Befehl* line of defense for writing: only those at the very top could be judged guilty when everyone else had no choice but to execute orders. The alliance with the Axis was a geopolitical version of the same line of defense: there was simply no other choice. There was also an economic motive underpinning wartime writing, as Dianu pointed out. He had started his career at the left-wing *Rampa* and had collaborated with Jewish modernist Sergiu Dan (whose 1945 *Unde Începe Noapte* [Where Night Begins] was one of the first personal accounts of concentration camps to appear in Europe) but found himself out of a job in the late 1930s when the political climate shifted—the only way he could avoid starving was to supply right-wing, pro-German, anti-Semitic copy. Then, formal control over writing was instituted during the war with press directives that dictated what could be printed. Ion Dimitrescu's frontline dispatches from 1943 were commissioned by the military: "Not a single piece of reportage existed that was not revised and modified … All of the documents here were second, third, sometimes even fourth drafts" with the military cabinet and even Antonescu personally commenting on drafts.[79] (Dimitrescu refused to sign the first four articles and then signed the final pieces with his military title ostentatiously displayed to indicate that the articles were institutional products.) The prosecutors freely admitted that Dianu was a socialist, not a fascist, and that Dimitrescu was personally against the Antonescu regime, but this "duplicity" was neither here nor there: "The accused is not on trial for his thoughts, but for what he wrote … He is on trial for the destructive beliefs he brought into the public opinion."[80]

On paper, these arguments about economic necessity or the censorship system undermining aesthetic autonomy could have been taken straight from Marx. The public accusers argued that the mere fact that the Romanian wartime state acted brutally showed that the beliefs expressed in writing had an impact—but did the ideas reflect a contemporary reality or bring it into being? The communists had no problem forgiving many writers who had flirted with fascism so long as they signed up for "re-education." But a blanket amnesty was not on the cards; some writers had to be declared guilty so that the others could get on with their new tasks of exhorting the workers to build paradise. The specious claim was made that the propaganda directives by the Antonescu regime were optional, that "only traitors respected the decrees."[81] Some papers were known to be less scrupulous than others when it came to reproducing the fascist word, but the wiggle room afforded was hardly expansive. Dianu was indicted not because of his writings—which during the war years were mainly on music and books—but because he had chaired a press commission during the war. Even if that commission had weeded out fascists and Legionaries from the Romanian press, it had also targeted communists.

The one defendant who most closely resembled the other writers discussed in this book was Radu Demetrescu-Gyr, a poet who became the Iron Guard's unofficial balladeer. An intellectual blue blood with an uncanny resemblance to Robert Brasillach, Gyr held a doctorate in literature and taught at the University of Bucharest. He had been kicked out of high school "for collaborating on democratic, progressive, Jewish, and Bolshevik journals," but in the 1930s became politically radicalized to the far right, serving as the chief commander for the Iron Guard in his native region of Oltenia.[82] During the few months of the Iron Guard and Antonescu regime cohabitation in late 1940, Gyr directed the National Theater, banning Jews from the Romanian stage (but also creating an all-Jewish theater company that regularly performed in Bucharest). Gyr's poems were regularly sung at Iron Guard demonstrations and assemblies, with the public accusers stating that torturers and executioners regularly hummed his ballads when committing their bestial acts. Their loaded meaning did not come about through their language—"Evening wind, evening wind | wandering cherry tree wind | Take away my bitter sadness | Evening wind, wandering wind" hardly rises to a level of loaded political meaning—but rather in how they had become appropriated by the movement.[83] Gyr had already been condemned to prison twice, first in the late 1930s and then again during the war, for incitement to violence (for speeches made to a mob), and during the trial he argued that he was being punished twice for the same crime. (In 1956 he reframed his 1940 "Rise Up, Gheorghe, Rise Up, Ioana!" as an anti-communist poem, leading to more years of detention.)[84] For the public accusers, there was little doubt that Gyr had more to answer than the others because of his academic pedigree and high intellectual standing. He was a "proper" intellectual, a poet of indisputable talent and fame who lent his moral support to the fascists.

When Constantin Vicol, a law professor and the lead public accuser, began his closing argument, he noted that for over twenty years he had been a defense attorney. Supporting the powerless now meant thinking about widows and orphans, soldiers mangled at the front, the tens of thousands of nameless victims in unmarked graves, and, above all, in Vicol's political arithmetic of suffering, the true victims of the war, the democrats who opposed the regime and found themselves in prisons or camps. The "crimes and politics of treason" flourished in the country because of the fascist literary field, where countless writers succumbed to the venal desire for recognition and pay. The massacres and atrocities judged during the first war crimes trial before the People's Tribunal would not have been possible without writers creating "the necessary mental climate" that normalized such actions: "one was born of the other, one was the parent and legitimate father of the other." Writing had been a "narcotic" that "deranged" the minds of the people and pushed them toward "the most barbaric" doctrines and acts. Confusingly, though, this propaganda was camouflaged, because the Romanian people—who remained honorable, upright, and by no means fascist as they now clamored *en masse* for a communist future—would have "attacked with stones" anyone suggesting that Romania should be subordinate to Germany. Looking at the accusation now, the contradiction between simultaneously arguing that the naïve Romanian public believed every word printed in the papers while also rebelling against pro-German propaganda is too obvious. If it was "impossible" for a "gazette of ideas" to survive financially in Romania, as Vicol claimed, what were the accused, who trafficked in "commonplace ideas," guilty of? If "belief is one thing and treason is another," and "not everything written, not every phrase, constitutes a belief," how could the two be disentangled? For the court, it was important to set itself above the fray. If one believed that "there is no fascist ideology or belief" worthy of the name, that fascism's followers were all "sellouts" and "scoundrels," then one was not punishing a belief or idea—but rather a criminal enterprise. Throughout Vicol's closing statement, what really came under attack was the entire mode of operation of the "gangster gazetteers" that ruled the Romanian literary field since the 1930s.[85] What was put on trial, in short, was what brought about fascism, not its crimes when in power. This made sense politically, as the trial showed how the old way of doing things was fundamentally corrupt; by implication, the communist restructuring of the literary field would put an end to such abuses.

The just punishment of such crimes, Vicol stressed, was confiscating the gains of venal profiteers and putting their assets to the service of the new state. This should be paired with "civic degradation," a Romanian version of *indignité nationale*: no right to vote or publish. But the court had to do more than find this first batch of writers guilty; it had to make its sentence resound through the land: "The punishment that you will give should be a way to satisfy the public opinion, becoming a way to grow belief in this country in popular justice, which, from now on, will be this country's true justice." In this trial over the symbolic order, then, the court could not neglect its function within the new regime. The people crying for justice had to be satisfied (even if they were bused in and paid for their trouble); the intellectuals following events had to understand that their role was no longer truth or free creation or self-expression but rather "to guide, to orient … to lead the people on its proper line."[86]

The defendants had the final word, but there was little space for a proper defense (see Figure 5.4). The Ministry of Propaganda preferred to comment on how "the entire hall broke out in hilarious laughter" when one defendant called himself "anti-fascist." There were reasonable arguments about how writers, and journalists especially, did not create reality but represented it in language; to believe that government policy could be the creation of the press or a wider literary milieu exaggerated the power of the daily squabble; "incitement" had a precise legal meaning that the texts in question never satisfied. The only reason he was on trial, Rădulescu believed, was because he was an anti-Semite—but in that he was hardly alone. This feeling of being made out to be a scapegoat was also felt by Ilie Popescu-Prundeni:

> We here are only a few. In the last few days, probably at least ten thousand individuals in their capacity as journalists, or occasional publicists, or authors of books and pamphlets had added their signatures to written opinions. There are fourteen of us accused in the dock but, as you can see, only seven of us present in the courtroom. Those of us here represent yesterday's press and are being called to pay for yesterday's press.

When "everything in Romanian society vibrated powerfully to the magic calling of the national idea," he added, when "everything valuable in Romanian history, in our political

Figure 5.4 A war crimes trial in Romania. Fond CC al PCR, Albume foto Gheorghe Gheorghiu-Dej, album A3, foto 22. Courtesy of Fototeca online a comunismului românesc.

rhetoric, in Romanian literature, in poetry, even in music and art, revolved around the national idea," how could articulating nationalist beliefs make one guilty of treason? He had been nothing but the "thermometer registering the temperature of opinions in my time."[87]

All these "defense arguments quickly turned into indictments," *Scânteia* told its readers.[88] Some of the accused had, indeed, stumbled into Damascene conversions. "I do not ask for this freedom and do not even want to convince you of my innocence. If I cannot be of use to this country with my worthless mind, at least my arms, still strong," could be put to work, pleaded Alexandru Hodoş; "in prison I will be able to purify my beliefs," intoned Ilie Rădulescu, who quoted Stalin several times; "since the ideals that I have believed in have been destroyed," Popescu-Prundeni noted, he no longer represented a danger to society and as "an honest man of good faith, as a man willing to work," he could now serve the new society.[89] With these self-confessions, the show trial was now complete. Since some of the accused had submitted written defenses, the judges dismissed the court on June 2 and announced that they would deliver a verdict in two days. In the meantime, the "democratic press" filled up with telegrams, declarations, and motions from unions, factories, and shops calling for the severest punishment: "We, typographer workers, will never forget what these gangsters of writing and traitors of the people have done—they were among the biggest enemies of the working class."[90] These paeans to revenge—"The People will not forget, the People will not forgive!"—were meant to maintain pressure on the court as it deliberated, but in a way there was little doubt about the final verdict. Handed down on June 4, the People's Tribunal sentenced press magnate Pamfil Şeicaru to death (a largely symbolic sentence since he was abroad, in Spain) and punished most of the ones in the dock with ten- to twenty-year sentences while those not in custody received (again, symbolic) life sentences. All of the guilty would suffer "civic degradation" for ten years and lose the entirety of their property.

The same day that the People's Tribunal handed down its sentences, the Society of Romanian Writers was reorganized so as to put itself on a "new path, wide, full of light," alongside the people: "through their organization writers have to cultivate progressive writing, in concordance with the most noble traditions of the past and the future aspirations of the people."[91] A few days later, the Council of Ministers purged another twenty-two individuals from print for life. Two of the individuals just condemned by the People's Tribunal were included in the list of the permanently excluded. A journalist who had stopped writing fascist articles in 1939 was also banned, as was Ion Vinea, Tristan Tzara's closest childhood friend and a key figure in Romanian avant-garde circles in the 1920s and 1930s. Despite his "notorious democratic activities" in the past, Vinea was handed a five-year suspension for having "changed his political convictions" during the war years by taking a hostile stance toward the Soviet Union. But some journalists who had engaged in "intense propaganda" for Antonescu or "an intense propaganda campaign characterized by fascist and anti-Semite beliefs" only had one-year terms, while others were reprieved for wartime articles because they had quickly changed sides after the August coup d'état.[92] In early July, the Council of Ministers condemned a further sixty-four journalists. All of these bans were summary, without any trial or formal procedure.[93]

The literary field was being reorganized, through the law and institutional reforms, to support the new political reality. Venerable institutions like the Romanian Academy or the Society of Romanian Writers were abolished or radically purged so as to break any continuity with the past. A few days after the journalists' trial ended, Iuliu Maniu, the leader of the National Peasants' Party, was under no illusions: Romania was "no longer a sovereign state," he told the highest-ranking American military officer in the country, since its government "consists almost entirely of Russian Quislings."[94] But while the "journalists' trial" was meant to be the opening salvo against fascist writers, the hope that all the guilty would face their reckoning became an empty promise in the immediate postwar. The People's Tribunal did not have the institutional resources for that—and there was little political desire to do so, either, when the main issue was controlling the message now and for the future. The Communist Party needed writers and propagandists in the present, and the country simply did not have enough trained pens and intellectuals to afford a comprehensive purge. The wind was also taken out of retributive sails when it became clear that severe punishment was not really on the cards. The public accusers became demoralized when they saw harsh sentences reduced or commuted. It was an inauspicious start for the journalists' trial, for instance, to hear the king (who would be dethroned soon enough) tell the accusers that the judgments in the first trial before the People's Tribunal had been overzealous.[95]

In early February 1946, the People's Tribunal brought forth a case against eleven writers, intellectuals, and former ministers, including a series of writers linked to *Sfarmă Piatră*, an anti-Semitic daily, that included future Prix Goncourt winner Horia Vintilă. These individuals were said to be part of a "German Fifth Column" whose "nefarious, deceitful propaganda supporting fascism and Hitlerism … induced the public opinion into error, narcotizing the public into lethargy and making it impossible for it to react against the instauration of the Antonescu regime and the fascist dictatorship." Their writings were "an act of auto-incrimination"; their guilt "was sufficiently established and could not be reduced through any witnesses or any other evidence."[96] The problem for the court was thus not establishing the guilt of the indicted but rather the fact that only four of the eleven were physically in the dock—the other seven were, in terminology with unfortunate overtones in a totalitarian system, "today disappeared." This was also the case with the German- and Hungarian-language writers that the People's Tribunal in Cluj put on trial. Of the twenty-eight ethnic minority writers indicted for supporting and spreading fascism in March 1946, only two were in custody.[97] A good number had fled to Germany or Hungary, where they hoped that the postwar chaos would make it difficult for them to be found or that those foreign governments would offer protection. The Hungarians accused of war crimes had written anti-Soviet and anti-Semitic screeds but had also penned anti-Romanian propaganda—and in this way, their politics was closer to the communists, who also objected to the wartime Romanian state. Judging writing after the fact, on the politics of the day, turned out to be very messy, especially when the Hungarians and Romanians were both working to overcome their traditional enmity in the interests of a "socialist brotherhood."

Conclusion

The postwar targeting of writers in Romania was not a radical departure from the unstable interwar years when writing was surveilled by the secret police and the politics of print was closely monitored. Some of the writers found guilty in the journalists' trial, like Radu Gyr and Nichifor Crainic, had already served jail time in the 1930s for their writings; others, like Alexandru Hodoş, knew what it meant to have an apartment searched in the middle of night, with manuscripts and drafts bundled away as incriminating evidence. There was, in other words, an easy assumption that writing had political consequences and that intellectuals were the "moral authors" of the sorry state of affairs characterizing the country. "Writers must show," the purge committee of the Society of Romanian Writers announced during the journalists' trial, "more character and more clairvoyance than the rest of the people."[98] This clichéd idea of the intellectual as the guiding light of society existed alongside mass illiteracy and heady contempt for honesty or truth in public life. The problem with this view was that causality was very difficult to establish between a written text and a social reality. How could any writer be guilty of things decided "above the head of the accused, above our heads, above the country's head"?[99]

The interwar Romanian literary field had been marked by excess. Radical, avant-garde little reviews vied for space in the same mediascape as anti-Semitic dailies that openly applauded mass violence. Invective and polemics were well-established genres, with writers adopting a series of pseudonyms or cloaking themselves in anonymity so as to press forward whatever side the daily mood favored. The written word was surveilled by the internal police, which in a monarchic and weakly democratic (that is, highly corrupt) state was encouraged to be heavy-handed with troublemakers who pushed for communist, radical, or fascist beliefs. The postwar period created an anomalous situation whereby the former victims—the communists, who had been banished from the public sphere since 1924—were in charge of prosecuting another group that had been excluded from public life, the radical fascists. The campaign against writers had become formalized and repressive to a previously unknown degree with a "moral obligation," as *Scânteia* put it, to punish erroneous beliefs. In expectation of the verdict in the journalists' trial, the communist mouthpiece published a symposium on the role of intellectuals in society, which it prefaced with the following: "Fascist journalists will be harshly punished so that this kind of crime will not be repeated and these kinds of false intellectuals will no longer have any place in our society." The famed linguist Alexandru Rosetti knew the party line: "The journalist's duty is to guide the people onto the right path."[100] In other words, all roads lead to Moscow. If the guiding motif of the traitor as a sellout was widespread in the postwar period, there was some heavy irony in communists cashing in: most of the respondents to *Scânteia*'s survey were slated to be delegates to a writers' junket to the Russian capital.

In a way, the Romanian example inverts the "treason of the intellectuals": it was not being in politics that betrayed the role of intellectuals, but for the PCR it was writers staying out of politics that betrayed the people.[101] The mission of the writer was very much to further the interest of the people—in a way, the communists simply replaced the ethnic understanding of the "people" under fascism with a class-based one. However it was diced, the function of the writer remained the same, just the allegiance had shifted. It was thus easy to go from the wartime fascist literary field to the new communist one: if the jargon had to change, the underlying ideological structure of fascism could be easily applied to the new history being written by the communists in arms. The prevailing cliches of the period—the "writer-fighter," the "writer-worker"—and one can add, the "writer-politician": the communist Democratic Front brought into elected office a number of prominent writers and critics. Much was made of moving writers out of their ivory towers and bringing them down to the level of the people—to the street, to the villages, to the land. The contemporary writer, to build a new society, had to be thrust in the midst of social life, among the masses. In this way the writer could be at the head of the social revolution, noted Victor Eftimiu, whose remit as president of the Society of Romanian Writers was to advance the professional standing of workers of the pen, which, for him, meant political alignment with the communists.[102] "Instead of creating," the chief critic of the Peasant Party paper, *Dreptatea*, Nicolae Carandino, later rued, "our intellectuals adhere."[103]

Notes

1 Ana Selejean, *Trădarea intelectualilor / Reeducare și prigoană* (Bucharest: Cartea Românească), 17.
2 Quoted in Iulia Crăcană, *Dreptul în slujba puterii: justiția în regimul comunist din România, 1944–1958* (Bucharest: Institutul Național pentru Studiul Totalitarismului, 2015), 84.
3 Tom Gallagher, *Modern Romania: The End of Communism, the Failure of Democratic Reform, and the Theft of a Nation* (New York: New York University Press, 2005), 33–5.
4 Nadège Ragaru, "The Prosecution of Anti-Jewish Crimes in Bulgaria: Fashioning a Master Narrative of the Second World War (1944–1945)," *East European Politics and Societies and Cultures* 33.4 (November 2019): 941–75, at 948.
5 National Archives of Romania (Bucharest), Inv. 2904 (Ministry of Propaganda), Study and Documentation part, dossier 322. Hereafter cited as NAR, Transcript Journalists' Trial. The published compendium of archival documents on the journalists' trial lacks any trial transcript; see Emil Rus, ed., *Delictul de opinie: Procesul ziariștilor, 1945* (Bucharest: Instititul Național pentru Studiul Totalitarismului, 2012).
6 In 1946 the published transcript of the Antonescu trial did not include his closing statement. It is unclear what "historical documentary value" there could be in an "in extenso stenographic trial record" (of a 1948 trial against "conspirators, spies and saboteurs") that omitted or provided only summaries of the defense of the accused; see *Procesul grupului de complotiști, spioni, și sabotori: Textul complect al desbaterilor care au avut loc în fața Tribunalului Militar din București dela 27 Octombrie la 2 Noembrie 1948* (Bucharest: Editura de Stat, 1949).
7 Silviu Brucan, *The Wasted Generation: Memoirs of the Romanian Journey from Capitalism to Socialism and Back* (Boulder: Westview Press, 1993), xii.
8 Andrei Muraru, "Legislation and the War Criminals' Trial in Romania," *New Europe College—Stefan Odobleja Program, Yearbook 2009–2010* (Bucharest: NEC, 2010): 111–76, at 111.
9 A Bucharest high school is also named after Vulcănescu; protests to change the name in 2017 to commemorate instead a mayor of Czernowitz who tried to shield Jews from slaughter were defeated by a sizeable neo-fascist, neo-Christian defense of Vulcănescu's legacy and cultural standing.
10 See Eleodor Focșeneanu, *Istoria Constituțională a României (1859–2003)*, ed. Anca Focșeneanu (Bucharest: Eikon, 2018).
11 Dennis Deletant, *Communist Terror in Romania: Gheorghiu-Dej and the Police State, 1948–1965* (New York: St. Martin's Press, 1999), 14; Corneliu Coposu, *Mărturisiri* (Bucharest: Humanitas, 1996), 15.
12 Ludmila Rotari, *Mișcarea subversivă din Basarabia în anii 1918–1924* (Bucharest: Editura Enciclopedică, 2004).
13 Nichifor Crainic, "Programul statului etnocratic," *Sfarmă Piatră*, 20 May 1937, quoted in Radu Ioanid, *The Sword of the Archangel: Fascist Ideology in Romania*, trans. Peter Heinegg (Boulder: East European Monographs, 1990), 93.
14 See Dennis Deletant, *Hitler's Forgotten Ally: Ion Antonescu and His Regime, Romania 1940–44* (New York: Palgrave Macmillan, 2006).
15 Decree no. 236, February 5, 1941.
16 Quoted in Jean Ancel, *The History of the Holocaust in Romania*, trans. Yaffah Murciano, ed. Leon Volovici (Lincoln: University of Nebraska Press, 2011), 101.
17 Liliana Saiu, *The Great Powers and Rumania, 1944–1946: A Study of the Early Cold War Era* (Boulder: East European Monographs, 1992).
18 George Kennan, Telegram from Moscow to Washington, D.C., November 11, 1944, in *Foreign Relations of the United States, Diplomatic Papers, 1945, vol. IV: Europe* (Washington, D.C.: GPO, 1966), 259.

19 Meeting, 23–24 September 1944, in *Stenogramele Ședințelor conducerii P.C.R.: 23 septembrie 1944–26 martie 1945*, eds. Radu Ciuceanu, Corneliu Mihail Lungu, Florin Constantiniu, and Sever Catalan (Bucharest: Institutul Național pentru Studiul Totalitarismului, 2003), 57. Hereafter cited as *Stenogramele PCR.*

20 CNSAS D77, vol. 1, f. 7.

21 December 14, 1944, in *Stenogramele Ședințelor Consiliuliu de Miniștri: Guvernarea Generalului Nicolae Rădescu (6 decembre 1944 - 28 februarie 1945)*, ed. Marcel-Dumitru Ciucă (Bucharest: Saeculum, 2013), 39. See also CNSAS D16369, f. 5.

22 *Monitorul Oficial* (*MO*), January 21, 1945, 415–17.

23 R. G. Waldeck, *Athene Palace* (Iași: Center for Romanian Studies, 1998), 100.

24 Lucrețiu Pătrășcanu, "Despre reformă justiție," *Contimporanul*, September 12, 1947, 3.

25 Quoted in Burton Y. Berry, *Romanian Diaries, 1944–1947*, ed. Cornelia Bodea (Iași: The Center for Romanian Studies, 2000), 84.

26 March 31, 1945, in *Stenogramele Ședințelor Consiliului de Miniștri: Guvernarea Dr. Petru Groza: Instaurarea regimului pro-comunist, vol. 1 (7 martie–27 iulie 1945)*, ed. Marcel-Dumitru Ciucă (Pitești: Editura Ordessos, 2014), 177. Hereafter cited as *Stenogramele Groza.*

27 Law 312, *MO*, April 25, 1945, at https://legislatie.just.ro/Public/DetaliiDocumentAfis/36. Accessed: January 22, 2026.

28 Lucrețiu Pătrășcanu, "Cuvîntare rostită in fața funcționarilor publici din Capitală in ziua de 17 decembrie 1944," in *Scrieri, articolege, cuvîntări, 1944–1947* (Bucharest: Editura Politică, 1983), 28.

29 Interview, *Timpul*, April 21, 1945, 4.

30 Dennis Deletant, *Romania under Communist Rule* (Iași: The Center for Romanian Studies, 1999), 44.

31 See Lavinia Betea, *Lucrețiu Pătrășcanu: Moartea unui lider comunist*, 4th ed. (Bucharest: Curtea Veche, 2018).

32 Andrei Y. Vyshinsky, *The Law of the Soviet State*, trans. Hugh W. Babb (New York: Macmillan, 1948), 75. See also Arkady Vaksberg, *The Prosecutor and the Prey: Vyshinsky and the 1930s' Moscow Show Trials*, trans. Jan Butler (London: Weidenfeld and Nicolson, 1990).

33 Vyshinsky, *Law Soviet State*, 498.

34 Lucrețiu Pătrășcanu, *Spre o justiție populară* (Bucharest: Editura Partidului Comunist Român, 1948), 5, 11.

35 Lucrețiu Pătrășcanu, "Legea criminalilor de razboiu și legea epurației aparatului de stat," in *Democratizarea Armatei* (Bucharest: Ministerul de Război, 1945), 100–11, at 107.

36 *Procesul lui Ion Antonescu*, ed. Ioana Cracă (Bucharest: Editura Eminescu, 1995), 307.

37 In October 1945 this was formalized in a "nonaggression" pact between the communist and the Iron Guard; the main targets of communist violence would now be members of the historic political parties who stubbornly clung to liberal ideals. Bottoni estimates that around 15 to 20 percent of the PCR total membership was made up of former legionaries; see Stefano Bottoni, "Reassessing the Communist Takeover in Romania: Violence, Institutional Continuity, and Ethnic Conflict Management," *East European Politics and Societies and Cultures* 24.1 (2010): 59–89, at 77.

38 *România liberă*, September 26, 1944, 3. Other papers got in on the act: *Democrația* had a column entitled "Profiluri negre" (Black Profiles) and *Orizont* "Morți la 23 August 1944" (Dead on August 23, 1944).

39 "Sedința cu foștii acuzatori publici," March 27, 1947, in Andreea Andreescu, Luciana Nastasă, and Andrea Varga, eds., *Minorități Ethnoculturale mărturii documentare: Evreii din România (1945–1965)* (Cluj: Centrul de Resurse pentru Diversitate Etnoculturală, 2003), 312.

40 Constantin Vicol, *Procesul lui Socrate: Studiu juridic și istoric* (Bucharest: Animnator, 1947), 8.

41 CNSAS, Fond 8686 / D20563.

42 Dumitru Săracu, in "Sedința cu foștii acuzatori publici," March 27, 1947, in *Minorități Ethnoculturale mărturii documentare*, 320.
43 PCR Central Committee meeting, December 14, 1944, in *Stenogramele PCR*, 192.
44 Law 102, *MO*, February 12, 1945.
45 Miron Constantinescu, "Viperele," *Scânteia*, May 31, 1945, 1.
46 Law 102, *MO*, February 12, 1945.
47 There are numerous testimonials from editors and journalists in Department of State, *Evidence of Violations of Human Rights Provisions of the Treaties of Peace by Rumania, Bulgaria, and Hungary*, vol. 1: Violations by the Rumanian Government Freedoms of Expression and of Press and Publication (Washington, D.C.: GPO, 1951).
48 March 19, 1945, decree, in NAR, Inv. 2904, Study and Documentation part, dossier 320.
49 "Textul cuvîntării președintelui Consiliului de Miniștri, dr. Petru Groza, cu ocazia instalării ministrului propagandei naționale," in *23 August 44: Documente, vol. IV: 1944–1945*, eds. Ion Ardeleanu, Vasile Arimia, and Mircea Mușat (Bucharest: Editura Stiințifică și Enciclopedică, 1984), 4: 263.
50 Petre Constantinescu-Iași, "Sarcinile Guvernului de largă concentrare democratică Dr. Petru Groza," in *Democratizarea Armatei*, 54–70, at 67.
51 Berry, *Romanian Diaries*, 51.
52 See the motions and petitions in *23 August 44*, 4: 7–10.
53 Reuben H. Markham, *Rumania under the Soviet Yoke* (Boston: Meador, 1949), 14–15.
54 Tiberiu Troncotă, *România comunistă: Propagandă și cenzură* (Bucharest: Tritonic, 2006), 61.
55 NAR, Inv. 2904, Information part, file 1098.
56 See Ion Zainea, *Politică și Administrație în România (6 martie 1945 - 1 martie 1946): Epurarea* (Oradea: Editura Universității din Oradea, 2004), 26.
57 NAR, Inv. 2904, Study and Documentation part, file 1027.
58 NAR, Inv. 2904 (Ministry of Propaganda), Study and Documentation part, file 1018.
59 See the 1948 brochure released by the Ministry of Art and Information, *Publicații interzise până la 1 mai 1948*, excerpted in Department of State, *Evidence of Violations*, 175–9.
60 *Scânteia*, September 21, 1944, 1.
61 PCR Conference on Propaganda, January 28, 1945, in *Stenogramele PCR*, 292–3.
62 Ibid., 254.
63 Brucan, *Wasted Generation*, 34.
64 Călinescu considered his *Istoria literaturii române de la origini până în prezent* (History of Romanian Literature from Its Origins to the Present) "an act of propaganda," as he told Antonescu in a 1943 memo; see George Neagoe, *Mizantropul optimist: G. Călinescu și (de) stalinizarea României* (Bucharest: Cartea Românească, 2015), 34.
65 Victor Frunză, *Istoria stalinismului în România* (Bucharest: Humanitas, 1990), 246.
66 On Celan in postwar Bucharest, see Petre Solomon, *Paul Celan: The Romanian Dimension*, trans. Emanuela Tegla (Syracuse: Syracuse University Press, 2019).
67 Selejean, *Trădarea intelectualilor*, 52.
68 CNSAS, D12678, vol. 2.
69 *Dreptatea*, September 2, 1944, quoted in Selejean, *Trădarea intelectualilor*, 33.
70 Meeting, May 17, 1945, in *Stenogramele Groza*, 295.
71 *MO*, May 17, 1945, 23–5, in Zainea, *Politică și Administrație*, 323.
72 Mihail Sebastian, September 1, 1944, September 5, 1944, in *Jurnal 1935–1944* (Bucharest: Humanitas, 2016), 561, 563.
73 Report, April 24, 1945, CNSAS, D77, vol. 5, f. 171.
74 "Actul de acuzare al lotului de 12 ziariști întocmit de Constantin Vicol și Ion D. Ion, acuzatori publici," CNSAS, D77, vol. 10, part I, ff. 21–55.

75 In a 1942 book, Rădulescu looked back at his main political beliefs since the early 1930s ("anti-Judaism" internally and a pro-German foreign policy) and noted that both are now "state policy" (7). See Ilie Rădulescu, *Pentru un imperialism românesc* (Bucharest: Editura ziarului Porunca Vremii, 1942).
76 NAR, Transcript Journalists' Trial, f. 8.
77 Ibid.
78 Memo, April 1945, in CNSAS, D77, vol. 4, ff. 82–98.
79 Ion Dimitrescu, "Documentele manuscrise reţinute dela Cabinetul Militar cu modificarile autografe ale Mareşalului sau ale Colonelului-Şef," n.d., CNSAS, D77, vol. 1, f. 244.
80 NAR, Transcript Journalists' Trial, f. 71.
81 Ibid., f. 79.
82 Petre Pandrea, *Memoriile Mandarinului Valah* (Bucharest: Editura Albatros, 2000), 101.
83 This came from the 1940 song "Vânt de seara" [Evening Wind], which, as a Ministry of Interior report noted, had become a cult hit among fascists for its nostalgic, wistful tone. The Antonescu regime investigated Gyr for that song, and the communists continued investigating, too. See CNSAS, P7208, vol. 1.
84 CNSAS, P276, vol. 5.
85 NAR, Transcript Journalists' Trial, ff. 177–8.
86 Ibid.
87 In Rus, *Delictul de opinie*, 184–90.
88 *Scânteia*, June 4, 1945, 1.
89 In Rus, *Delictul de opinie*, 190.
90 *Scânteia*, June 3, 1945, 3.
91 *Scânteia*, June 6, 1945, 2.
92 Council of Ministers, June 4, 1945, in Zainea, *Politică şi Administraţie*, 333–5.
93 Zainea, *Politică şi Administraţie*, 61–2.
94 Cortland Schuyler to War Department, June 8, 1945, *FRUS 1945*, V: 553.
95 Note, May 28, 1945, CNSAS, Fond 8686 / D20563 (Tribunal Poporului, 1943–5).
96 NAR, Tribunal Poporului, Act de acuzare, February 9, 1946.
97 CNSAS, D16354, D16355.
98 *Scânteia*, May 30, 1945, p. 2.
99 NAR, Tribunal Poporului, Trial of Gheorghe A. Cuza et al., February 20, 1946.
100 Alexandru Rosetti, "Intelectualii şi răspunderea îndrumătorilor de opinie publică," *Scânteia*, June 3, 1945, 1–2.
101 Selejean, *Trădarea intelectualilor*, 74.
102 Victor Eftimiu, "Menirea scriitorului," *Democraţia*, January 14, 1945, 1, 4, at 1.
103 Quoted in Selejean, *Trădarea intelectualilor*, 118.

CHAPTER 6
THE MORAL TRIALS OF NEUTRALITY: FRANCIS STUART AND THE CAVE OF IRISH DARKNESS

In the eyes of the Allies, the "so-called neutrality of the so-called Eire" (as Churchill put it) showed its true face on the evening of May 2, 1945, when Éamon de Valera paid a visit to the German Minister to Dublin to offer official condolences upon Hitler's death.[1] Not following diplomatic protocol upon the death of a head of state would have heaped "absolute contempt" upon Éire, de Valera later rationalized, but what he wished to avoid quickly surfaced in the world's press.[2] Raising neutrality "to the dignity of a national principle" was not morally equivalent that early May, and, over time, has fared even worse.[3] Louis MacNeice's 1942 poem on the subject castigated his brethren in the South:

> But then look eastward from your heart, there bulks
> A continent, close, dark, as archetypical sin,
> While to the west off your own shores the mackerel
> Are fat—on the flesh of your kin.[4]

Complicity in evil was a charge de Valera slaked off when both sides were at fault, and, of course, the British had occupied their lands (and continued to do so in the Six Counties) for several centuries. There was no need to be entangled in foreign wars, or ways, when Éire's future was as a country "bright with cosy homesteads, whose fields and villages would be joyous with the sound of industry, with the romping of sturdy children, the contests of athletic youths, and the laughter of happy maidens."[5] That pastoral fantasy, spun by de Valera in a St. Patrick's Day radio address in 1943, was a jarring contrast to the fierce fighting then taking place over Kharkov or the savagery in the Pacific, battles whose outcomes would determine, even if those on the island refused to acknowledge it publicly, whether Éire would remain independent (Figure 6.1).

The moral trials of Irish neutrality can be fruitfully examined by looking at the long career of Francis Stuart. Born in 1902 in Australia, to Ulster Protestant stock, educated at Rugby School, Stuart was jailed for his IRA activities in the early 1920s, penned a volume of verse in prison that was awarded a major prize by W. B. Yeats, co-founded a little magazine, *To-Morrow*, in the mid-1920s, and wrote a series of dazzling modernist novels in the 1930s. In 1933 Harold Nicolson called Stuart "one of the most remarkable authors of our time"; a dozen years later, he was being de-Nazified in internment camps after having broadcast from Berlin during the war.[6] "What became of Francis Sable,

Figure 6.1 "Neutrality." Caricature of Eamon de Valera by Bernard Partridge (1942). Copyright National Portrait Gallery, London.

I wonder?" asked Ethel Mannin in her thinly-disguised fictionalization of her ex-lover in *Late Have I Loved Thee* (1948): "No one seems to know whether he is alive or dead."[7] As Stuart put it of his postwar travails, "I came under suspicion not because I was a Nazi, which God knows I never was, but because I was not on any side."[8] Leaving aside his tendentious understanding of neutrality, Stuart's case spotlights whether writers, or nations, could ever be above the fray.

The debate over "the oddest voice in modern Irish writing," as Damien Keane calls Stuart, has never been resolved.[9] Stuart positioned himself as an eternal outsider, what he diagnosed, in his mid-life memoir *Things to Live For* (1934), as the longing to be with

> those on the coastline, the frontiers. With gamblers, wanderers, fighters, geniuses, martyrs and mystics. With the champions of wild loves and lost causes, the storm troopers of life. With all those who live dangerously though not necessarily spectacularly, on the knife edge between triumph and defeat.[10]

Joining the "storm troopers of life" held a particular meaning in the mid-1930s, which makes it all the more surprising that Stuart was convinced, and able to convince others in a series of postwar retellings, especially his novel-cum-apologia *Black List, Section H* (1971), that his sojourn in wartime Berlin was a purely personal adventure and that his talks on German radio were of a "literary" and "artistic" character.[11] Toward the end of his life Stuart was conferred the golden torc of the Saoi ("Wise one"), the highest Irish state recognition for a living artist, which seemed to validate how his artistry had risen above noxious politics, which never entirely subsided (in a 1990s television documentary, Stuart stated that "the Jew was always the worm that got into the rose and sickened it").[12] Yet the entanglement of literature with politics in Stuart's career, from the Irish Civil War in 1922 to the fractious debates over Stuart being named a Saoi in the 1990s, showcases the pull of competing national, political and cultural pressures upon the literary space, even in a "neutral" sphere that for many years resisted any serious discussion of its wartime past.

Irish States of Treason

Henry Green's 1945 comic novel *Loving*, which details the lives and romantic dalliances of servants in an Anglo-Irish country house, was set in a fairytale "Eire where there is no blackout."[13] While the curtains were not drawn and tea was unrationed (the servants in Green's novel delight in bottomless cuppers), the "Emergency," as the Second World War was called in Ireland, was a challenging period. The threat of invasion, either from the Germans or the British, was real due to the country's strategic military position. The risk that any such invasion would succeed was high. Though forged in battle one generation earlier, the country's military was under-armed, under-resourced, and under-manned; curiously enough for an island, its coastal defenses, navy or air service were near non-existent (the British had always ensured the territorial integrity of its coasts); and its post-colonial economy remained heavily dependent upon the export of agricultural foodstuffs to its former occupier.[14] At the same time, the war presented an enormous opportunity. Crude Machiavellian logic—"The enemies of England are … the friends of Ireland," an internal IRA document noted—meant that a British defeat would hasten the realization of the great patriotic dream, the end of partition, which the 1937 Constitution had haughtily ignored when asserting sovereignty over the entire island.[15]

That constitution also noted that "fidelity to the nation and loyalty to the state are fundamental political duties of all citizens" (Art. 9.3). Within Irish history, the colonial struggle had freighted treason with a heavy symbolic value: "for generations in this country," a parliamentarian (TD) noted, "treason has been regarded as a virtue."[16] Patriots like Roger Casement ("I should be glad to die a thousand times for the name of Ireland") were charged with treason by the occupiers while those who followed the law and sided with the British were traitors.[17] Even after the 1922 founding of the Free State, debates over who was genuinely Irish and who was a *fealltóir* continued. For the Irish Republican Army (IRA), all those from de Valera on down who refused to take the fight to the British were traitors. On the flip side, the IRA challenged the state's monopoly of violence, risking instability, if not civil war.

As a legal matter, the 1925 Treasonable and Seditious Offences Act defined treason along familiar lines, namely, levying war against the state (either inside or outside Éire's territorial borders). The punishment was death, with the trial requiring the testimony of two witnesses but otherwise following the procedure of a homicide trial. The 1937 Constitution, following the American model, explicitly defined treason:

> Treason shall consist only in levying war against the State, or assisting any State or person or inciting or conspiring with any person to levy war against the State, or attempting by force of arms or other violent means to overthrow the organs of government established by this Constitution, or taking part or being concerned in or inciting or conspiring with any person to make or to take part or be concerned in any such attempt.[18]

This definition is more limited than the "aid and comfort to the enemy" in the American one. Continuing contestation over democratic legitimacy, mainly due to the unsolved tensions of partition and lingering divisions over the 1922 treaty, made the Irish state anxious about armed uprisings. That is why treason was primarily defined as an act of physical violence through arms; the elements of conspiracy and incitement within the definition pertained to those who organized that armed violence (such as the IRA). Two years later, the 1939 Treason Bill was passed, but not as a response to the coming war (the fraught international climate was, of course, a contributory factor as the bill was debated that spring), but to the S-Plan, the IRA bombing campaign to force the British out of Ulster. Over one hundred incidents from January 1939 to March 1940 targeted British elites and cities, the deadliest a bomb attack in Coventry in late August 1939 that killed five. While the IRA targeted the occupier—"I came over here [to England] to fight … for a full and free life, for my countrymen, North and South, and for the removal of the baneful influence of British Imperialism from Irish affairs," Brendan Behan affirmed to the police—it also wreaked havoc inside the state, such as when the IRA made off with more than one million rounds of ammunition from a military depot.[19] While treason in other countries consisted of siding with a foreign state, the threat to the Irish state came from fighting the avowed enemy; too much patriotism, over-identification with the national interests, spilled over into treason by precipitating armed conflict. "There can be no democracy and no liberty," the thinking went, "unless violent methods by groups within the State are prevented."[20] As "a free community, sovereign, able to mould its own institutions in its own ways," de Valera told the Dáil, the state could not allow rogue groups to contest its power.[21]

Not everyone was happy with the proposed change, or the timing, of the 1939 Treason Bill. If vigorous treason laws were most needed in moments of crisis, "repressive legislation" could "beget protests and annoyance" due to what one parliamentarian descriptively called "a feeling of yeastiness and commotion."[22] Another TD called treason "a very indefinite sort of offence, a very vague type of offence," especially in comparison to what he knew from his years in the Gardaí, the state police: "In murder you have something solid, something substantial. At least you have the corpse to start with." With treason, though, "you have nothing substantial. A group of excited boys might seize a public building and issue a proclamation. These boys would be guilty of treason under this Bill." Could "the plain people of this country" distinguish between the freedom fighters of the recent past—now commemorated in memorials and statues and schoolbooks—and the offences that the new act forbade? Treason was truly a matter of dates when "many years should be allowed to elapse before we enact a law making treason an offence."[23] More political interventions focused on how the law was an explicitly repressive measure against "political opponents," which everyone understood to mean the IRA. For de Valera, though, an effective treason law was a mark of statehood: "Every State in the world, unfortunately, needs force to defend itself. If we do not protect the State, having got our freedom, we will soon lose that freedom."[24]

After six months of debate, the Treason Bill was passed in late May 1939 while the IRA was still bombing targets in the North and throughout Britain. But one truly difficult question remained: who exactly was an Irish subject, and what did that mean in law? Even though the 1922 Constitution made everyone resident within Ireland an Irish citizen (art. 3), it also confusingly spoke of "the common citizenship of Ireland with Great Britain" (art. 17), as the twenty-six counties held Dominion status within the British Commonwealth. Parliamentarians, until the passage of the Irish Nationality and Citizenship Act (1935), took an oath to the king. That legislation clarified who could be a natural-born citizen, but it did not resolve the problem that holders of Irish passports were formally treated as British subjects and that Irish diplomats were credentialed through the Court of St. James's in London. The Irish Neutrality League railed against this incomprehensible situation: "In Ireland, we are told that we owe allegiance to no king, but when we leave Ireland, we become subjects of the same king the English have … Are we, when we go abroad, Irishmen or not? Just what are we?"[25] Only in 1949, after the passage of the British Nationality Act and the Ireland Act, did this confused state of affairs cease (with some quirks: even today, Irish citizens in the United Kingdom are treated as non-foreigners, with the right to vote and stand for Parliament, while residents of Northern Ireland are automatically eligible to be citizens of Éire). Adding to the confusion, residents of Northern Ireland were not citizens under Irish law but the 1937 Constitution treated the Six Counties as an integral part of the sovereign state. The misalignments between affect and law jarred.

Wartime, and especially neutrality, exacerbated these tensions. Just days after war broke out, the Emergency Powers Act gave the state sweeping powers to control and censor the press, to limit the movement of people, and to detain or arrest without a warrant—all this in the interests of "public safety and the preservation of the state in time of war."[26] The next summer the act was expanded to allow the police to seize, without a warrant or prior authorization, any document or text deemed "prejudicial to the public safety or the preservation of the State or the maintenance of public order."[27] Avoiding war required, paradoxically, an absolute war footing, with the state given "full and plenary powers, enormous powers" while the people were "stripped … of all our constitutional liberties."[28] Neutrality, as the highest good, was considered a way for Ireland to assert its sovereignty and to avert a civil war. The country would not be a staging ground for British ships or follow its former occupier into battle; Éire would resist whatever "weapons of coercion" Churchill used against them.[29] It also would not allow the IRA to arrogate the executive power of the state by "waging war" in Ulster.[30] (Around 800 IRA internees spent the war years in camps.) At the same time, there was, as Elizabeth Bowen noted in one of her MI5 intelligence reports, a marked "pro-British feeling and sympathy" in the country.[31] Due to family ties and cultural affinities, a huge number of Irish men and women sided with Britain, not only in spirit but also in arms (over 150,000 young Irish men enlisted in the British services) or by emigrating to work in war factories.[32] Others, seeing a spate of "anti-Irish cartoons, anti-Eire neutrality articles, and attacks on de Valera, Irish Catholics and Eire generally" in the British press, considered that "the same old John Bull" remained the enemy.[33]

Given the inevitable contestation surrounding neutrality, the state was anxious to control the flow of information. Frank Aiken, the former IRA Chief of Staff who was named Minister for the Co-ordination of Defensive Measures in September 1939, oversaw a censorship that he claimed was necessary to maintain neutrality.[34] The Censor's office studied how neutral countries like Portugal, Spain, Sweden, and Switzerland enacted censorship, justifying tough measures at home as in line with the international climate.[35] These comparative studies did not teach Dublin many new tricks, as the censorship card had been played since the state's inception. One of the first legislative measures passed by the Free State was a Censorship of Films Act, and the name given to a working group in the Ministry of Justice, the "Committee on Evil Literature," showed just how strongly the state felt about the matter. The Censorship of Publications Act (1929) allowed concerned citizens to send in "marked passages" to the Censorship Board, which ruled on their morality in isolation. Any mention of sex or abortion, or mockery of religion, pricked Irish sensitivities. Declan Kilberd called this act one of "self-harm, even self-mutilation," because it undermined the cultural foundations of Irish nationhood.[36] It certainly stung

Irish writers, who were systematically targeted by the censor: the list of prohibited items in March 1941 ran to over 1,300 books and 117 periodicals.[37]

If censorship was for *The Bell*, the most vibrant Irish wartime literary periodical, "a wholly negative and destructive piece of machinery" ("We are not really wide-awake at all"), those in power were convinced that it was essential to keep the peace.[38] The logic behind censorship was simple: if little information filtered down, if the people were plunged into the darkness of Plato's cave, to take up one famous metaphor for the war years, there would be no agitation for one side or another.[39] "A small and relatively defenceless people such as we are," a parliamentarian noted, could not be entrusted to make up its mind on distant events, so the state had to protect the people from being "pushed hither and thither by every kind of pressure, or by every economic or political breeze that blows."[40] That such a statement could be made without thinking about its implications for what freedom and independence might mean, or why it had been fought for, shows just how scared the state had become of existing social divisions.

The problem was that shutting the island off from propaganda was impossible. With bombing raids on Northern Ireland's war factories and the occasional accidental explosion in Éire, the war was not that distant; more critically for Dublin's perspective was the easy circulation of print matter from Belfast to the South. Radio waves smoothly crossed borders. The Germans first began broadcasting in Gaelic in December 1939 (a fifteen-minute show on Sunday night, just after Haw-Haw's transmission) and then ramped up efforts with the creation of Irland-Redaktion in 1942, which broadcast in both Gaelic and English.[41] (The initial reaction to those broadcasts in Gaelic—pleasure at the "first international recognition" of the language—spoke volumes about Dublin Castle's naiveté.)[42] The BBC, although heavily criticized at home for its uninspiring fare, was downright dramatic and exciting compared to Radio Éireann (RE), which everyone agreed was amateurish. RE had a miniscule budget (around £70,000 in FY 1940–1, compared to the nearly £10 million the BBC was spending), was chockful of unpopular programs (folk music, not jazz hits, on the turntable, and loads of Gaelic dramas despite only 100,000 individuals understanding the language), and could barely be heard on the island, much less further afield (the short-wave from Athlone gave out "a continuous din" in Wexford, while German, British and other stations came in loud and clear).[43] Irish writers preferred the BBC, which paid over three times RE's going rate; the speakers on Irish radio were specialists in mumbling; and some programs were downright batty, such as an earnest description of a ballet ("Now they are moving to the left, now they are moving to the right, now they are coming down the centre, now something else is happening").[44] That Radio Éireann failed miserably to get "the Irish point of view" across, while "in every other country in the world radio propaganda is carried on morning, noon and night," was readily conceded.[45] Even more harmful was the fact that other peoples formed their views of Irish culture from RE's "amateur concert hall."[46] "What a joke it is to think that Radio Éireann is the expression of the national consciousness," a TD observed: "What is the opinion of the world? Go into any country in Europe, and they look on Radio Éireann simply as a joke. Go to adjacent countries and it is regarded as a joke—when you can hear it."[47] Censorship worked to not only prevent news from coming in but also seemed to prevent anything of interest from going out!

Invariably, those targeted by the censor were not well pleased. The Germans often complained that their war news did not receive typographic equality with British reports (a small font size, misleading headlines); the British felt that censorship went against the rights of free speech (framing material interests in terms of rights being, for outsiders, the essence of perfidy).[48] For Irish writers, censorship was its own sort of disaster. To be modern without tackling sex or religion was impossible. Censorship was another dagger to the viability of the Irish literary space, which had a witch's brew of a tiny and parochial reading public, impoverished domestic publishers, and a hostile state. Throw in the fact that a huge literary market existed across the sea, in the same language and with long-standing cultural ties, and it was obvious that Ireland struggled to support native artists. In this analysis, Irish literature was for export, but that made it, paradoxically enough, parochial: foreign readers or the Irish diaspora wanted their preconceptions confirmed, not critical perspectives or art that rose above the national. (The reception of Joyce's *Dubliners* is the obvious confirmation of this.) For the few Irish writers who did not publish in London or New York, and who resented their colleagues who did, the obvious recourse was an "extreme self-preoccupation" that traded in "hyper-nationalism."[49] "Ourselves alone!" MacNeice mocked, "Let the round tower stand aloof | In a world of bursting mortar!"[50] Francis Stuart felt, too, that Ireland had to be connected to the world, but his choices were at odds with those of his contemporaries.

On the Town, In the Air: Stuart in Berlin

In early 1939, Stuart was by all accounts still a young writer, but he felt washed up and depleted (Figure 6.2). Having made his literary debut over fifteen years earlier, he had already published a lifetime's body of work—a collection of poetry, a memoir, eleven novels—before turning forty. He had won literary prizes and had been fêted in the *New York Times*, but his earnings from literature were so meager his main incoming most months (and, more frequently, his major losses) came from the horses. His marriage to Irish literary-political royalty (to Iseult Stuart, the daughter of Maud Gonne) had proven disastrous: they married when he was a clumsy, inexperienced seventeen-year-old, and she was cold and aloof. Money troubles wore them down, as did raising two young children in an isolated country house in Laragh, County Wicklow. So when he received an invitation in spring 1939 to tour Germany to promote *The Great Squire*, he jumped at the opportunity. He was welcomed in Berlin by the head of the English Faculty at the Deutsche Akademie (and later deputy head of the Broadcasting Department of the German Foreign Office) and then sent off for lectures in Munich, Hamburg, Bonn, and Cologne. After years of eking out a threadbare existence, luxury hotels, chauffeurs, interpreters, and parties in one's honor could turn a head. Stuart was impressed by the Third Reich, telling Iseult that it was "extraordinary ... to see the busy, fashionable streets of a big city without Jewish faces."[51]

Figure 6.2 Portrait of Francis Stuart by Werner & Son. Courtesy of National Library of Ireland.

Stuart's stay in Germany lasted a few months, but before his departure he agreed to come back that fall to take up a teaching post at Berlin University: "we are glad," the secretary there said, that "you want to come to Germany."[52] The outbreak of the war halted those plans, but Stuart's close ties to Eduard Hempel, the German Minister to Dublin, ensured that a solution would be found. Already that August, MI5 was informed that Hempel was trying to set up an "Irish Legion" led by Stuart and his brother-in-law Séan MacBride (future Irish foreign minister and Nobel Peace Prize recipient). Hempel was a frequent visitor to Laragh Castle and knew Stuart's politics well. A German official looking to cultivate sympathetic Irishmen could do worse than a "genuine friend of contemporary Germany" who railed against "democratic clap-trap" and the iniquity of British imperial rule ("I know that there is much in the German case to interest the average Irishman").[53] One of Stuart's earliest print pieces was a Sinn Fein pamphlet, "Nationality and Culture," which swiped at "the money-mad, sterile civilization" Britain's cultural hegemony imposed upon Ireland, and his early 1930s novel *Try the Sky* rhapsodized about Viennese brownshirts taking control of that Judaized city.[54] The Irish police took note of Hempel's visits to Laragh and how they coincided with changes in Stuart's behavior (calling Thomas Cook to enquire about flights to Switzerland the day after Hempel visited, etc.).[55] IRA contacts got wind of Stuart's planned travels and summoned him to re-establish contacts with the Abwehr (the IRA's secret radio transmitter had just been seized). Stuart applied for a visa to Switzerland on medical grounds; the Gardaì found it inconceivable that a fellow "in excellent health," often seen taking long, robust walks, needed Alpine air.[56] The surveillance operations were both meticulously detailed and farcically inept. It took several years for Stuart's name to be spelled correctly; he was incorrectly identified as "a native of England"; and details about his career were written in a speculative tone (even in late 1944, G2 admitted, "We have no definite information regarding the date of birth, birthplace, or parentage of Francis Stuart").[57] Yet these security agents closely tracked comings and goings, logging visitors and deviations from routines: "During the past few weeks Stewart [*sic*] and his wife have been working at papers in the house till the small hours of the morning and during this period the maid was let off early, this being unusual."[58] The Irish security services knew which boat Stuart took for London in January 1940, the hotel he stayed at (Garland's, Suffolk Place, W1), and even how much money he had on him (£30), but did nothing to prevent the trip (or to inform MI5).[59] The Irish state knew that many individuals traveling to belligerent countries were clearly bent on engaging in "unneutral activities"—but stopping those trips would have been even worse for Irish neutrality.[60]

Stuart arrived in Berlin in January 1940. Without a ration card or a place to stay, he went to the university and found himself the lucky recipient of back pay (the term had started in October) and the keys to a three-bedroom flat. Stuart quickly settled into the routine of teaching and writing, and his social calendar filled up despite his German never getting up to scratch (he could read the language but could do no more than hold a "superficial conversation" in it).[61] He was a frequent visitor to the Irish Legation (until it was bombed out in 1943), where he listened to the wireless, read the Irish papers (which arrived a few weeks late), and consorted with IRA hangers-ons, among them

Frank Ryan, who had been repatriated from Spain, and John Francis O'Reilly, from County Clare (who was later employed at the Propaganda Ministry before joining the SS espionage service). "I must not become too involved," Stuart warned himself in his diary about these men's wide-eyed plans for using German might to deliver to the Irish their island free of Britons, but "it is right for me to do something."[62] Having smuggled guns out of Brussels in the early 1920s, Stuart was not averse to getting his hands dirty and at one point agreed to sail back to Ireland aboard a Breton fishing boat to re-establish contacts with the IRA.[63] Nothing came of this scheming, but Stuart was more involved when it came to Hermann Görtz's mission. A Luftwaffe reserve lieutenant with excellent English (a three-year spell in a British prison for spying proved better than Berlitz), Görtz frequently met with Stuart as he planned his mission—he would parachute into Éire in May 1940 to liaise with the IRA to pave the way for a German invasion. Stuart told Görtz that his home, Laragh Castle, could be used as a safe house since Iseult would agree to any plan that struck at the British (Iseult came to be put on trial under the Offences Against the State Act for aiding a foreign agent).[64] For St. Patrick's Day Stuart threw a party where he met Phyllis Ursula James, the adopted daughter of General Sir Ian Hamilton, who went by the name Rosaleen James. The two soon moved in together even though Rosaleen was already pregnant, and Stuart eventually secured work for her at the Propaganda Ministry, where she translated and also went on air. The couple also visited POW camps to drum up Irish recruits; after the war, Rosaleen reinvented herself as Róisin Ní Mheara (her Gaelic-language memoir featured Holocaust denial).[65]

The more local haunts Stuart frequented included the Cantina Romana, on Rankestrasse, just off the Kurfürstendamm, and the Auslandspress Klub. At the Presseklub in Leipziger Platz he met with Ruth Weiland, who had worked as an agent for Maud Gonne's 1938 autobiography. Weiland was editing *Irishe Freiheitskämpfer* (Irish Freedom Fighters), for which Stuart wrote an introduction which noted that throughout the country's history it had always been a "small group" that kept "the ideal of Irish freedom alive."[66] Weiland was instrumental in getting Stuart a contract for *Das Leben Sir Roger Casements* (1940). The Germans had wanted to translate William Maloney's *The Forged Casement Diaries* (1936), but he refused to sell the rights, so Stuart was asked to bring out, and update, the main points of that book. The rhetorical concluding flourish, which Stuart later disowned as not a product of his own authorship, shows why Maloney was wary of dealing with the Germans: "Perhaps one day, no longer lying far away, Irish and German soldiers will stand together before his [Casement's] unmarked grave … to honor the great patriot who has done so much to further friendship between the two nations."[67] That work paved the way for further commissions, including articles for *Die Woche*, a mass-circulation illustrated weekly. The German translations of *The Great Squire* and *The Bridge* "sold a lot" and *The Colored Dome* was serialized.[68] Stuart boasted that he was "becoming quite international" as translations in Czech, Dutch, Italian, Romanian, Spanish, and Swedish came out.[69] There was genuine interest among the German public about Ireland, with two feature films in 1940 depicting the Irish struggle for freedom, books on Ireland selling "very well," and numerous popular lectures attracting large audiences.[70]

"What a blessing it is that these days in the midst of war," Stuart noted in mid-May 1943, when nightly air raids punctured Berlin, "I have so much time for my own life and its needs."[71] Stuart had few demands at the university, teaching only a few hours per week on modern Irish literature. It was in a seminar room that he met Madeleine Meissner, who became his second wife (her memoir *Manna in the Morning* details their early meeting and also her admiration for Lord Haw-Haw, whose scripts she helped prepare). His colleagues at the university introduced him to the world of radio propaganda. Professor Walter Schirmer was deputy head of foreign language transmissions at the Foreign Office, where he worked alongside Reinhard Haferkorn. Celtic specialists like Franz Fromme, the right-wing, anti-Semitic author of *Irlands Kampf um die Freiheit* (1933), and Hans Hartmann, a linguist who led the Gaelic section at the Rundfunkhaus, were also in demand. Within weeks of arriving in the German capital Stuart was writing broadcasts for William Joyce about "historic acts of aggression on the part of the United Kingdom."[72] This ghost-writing for Haw-Haw lasted half a year. In June 1940 Stuart debuted on Berlin Radio with a broadcast to America, "The Modern Novel and Society," speaking about how the novel form could only be revived through "the new social and spiritual order being created in Europe" by Germany.[73]

Stuart's literary fortunes were not completely dashed by his foray into Axis broadcasting—the Abbey Theatre premiered *Strange Guest* (a strange play, indeed, with a nun who bets on the horses as the lead) in December 1940, and Irish national radio even beamed a recording of that play abroad. The second edition of *An Anthology of Modern Irish Poetry*, which came out for the Christmas season in 1945, included poems by Stuart. It was perhaps not such a surprise that a Protestant Unionist boy turned Catholic IRA man would straddle two sides. Finding that neutral space was how Stuart later rationalized his broadcasting for Irland-Redaktion, which began, with some regularity, in February 1942:

> The broadcasts usually didn't deal with politics; they dealt very often with literature, both English and Irish, and even with other literature. When they were political, they concentrated on the internal situation in Ireland ... I'd always, I should stress, had Irish neutrality at heart, and I never for a moment wished the Irish to enter the war on one side or the other.[74]

Stuart also claimed that no one really listened, saying that when he came back to Ireland that "I hardly ever met anyone who heard me. I don't think anyone really listened."[75] For sure the security services sometimes didn't get in clean hearings—"Whole broadcast extremely noisy—very difficult to hear"—but with around 160,000 radio receivers in the land, and not much worth listening to save the BBC and German stations, Stuart got this bit wrong.[76]

The purported neutrality and "literary" bent of Stuart's one-hundred-plus radio broadcasts can be called into question. His first talk, in which he dismissed any intent "to add to this mass of propaganda," perfectly dovetailed with German official policy by stressing the wisdom of Ireland's "strict and fearless neutrality" and denouncing the "large number of foreign troops" occupying Ulster. Those two ideas repeated official Irish policy, but the fact that the message was coming from Berlin changed the tune for those hearing it in Dublin. Stuart also reneged on his promise of no propaganda when he argued that "complete isolation" was a mistaken course when Éire had to be "linked with the future of Europe," which required recognizing the "alien" nature of the "god of money" ruling over American and British civilization.[77] Those arguments, given Nazi plans for the "European New Order" and their unmistakable anti-Semitic overtones, fell squarely in with Berlin's wider goals. If that talk was a test of Stuart's suitability for broadcasting, on the level of content he passed.

When it came to delivery, though, his broadcasts lacked the naturalness of the rambling, man-in-the-pub effect Stuart was going for: "I do not yet know how to control my voice. It was not properly spoken. That is a matter of practice and next time I reckon I can do that better."[78] The problem with his delivery persisted, as Stuart would get distracted with all the commotion in the studio or his voice would become affected, falling at the end of sentences.[79] Other times he bemoaned how he always sounded "flat and monotonous"; it was better to be "a bit angry, that is in attack," he told himself in his diary.[80]

Stuart had to put out broadcasts with very little information to go on: newspapers came in weeks late, and were censored; Radio Éireann was hard to catch, and dull; and even the German Foreign Office could not get much from its minister in Dublin since all communication passed through London. Lacking the material for topical broadcasts, Stuart indulged in nostalgia for the "struggle," picked on old scabs of Irish nationalism, and traded in tropes about the "the rule of money camouflaged as democracy."[81] In one of his diary injunctions, Stuart told himself that his broadcasts, like a poem, had to "flow out of … one emotional mood," with "no abstract arguments, not too many 'ideas.'"[82] That there were few concrete ideas to be had was the unstated underbelly of this view.

This retreat from the news of the day in Stuart's broadcasts did not make them less political. Propaganda toward Ireland did not require commentary on the present state of affairs—which was settled and censored, anyway—but could work by passing through the many gates of historical grievance, for which partition afforded many entries. Talks about Easter 1916, Parnell, or readings from the Wolfe Tone diaries were displaced in time but effective emotional pushes. Old *Punch* numbers showcased "the whole nasty business" of London as "international gangster and policeman … imposing its ideas on the rest of the world."[83] The colonial struggle predated the war:

> There are millions of people in the world today who want one thing from England and America, and that is to be left alone. That is what the people of India want, the people of Burma, of the Philippines, of Iceland, of the Azores, most of the people of South America, the Liberian Negroes, the Arabs of Palestine, the peoples of Iran and Iraq, not to speak of our own people in the Six Counties.[84]

The fact that there was a global war on did not have to mean anything to the Irish people:

> I have no aim in these talks except the one in which you can all share, that is to keep our thoughts fixed on a free and united Ireland in the midst of all the chaos, hostile propaganda and attempts at internal sabotage. There is only one supreme important aim for us Irish now: while Irish people are being hounded, imprisoned and persecuted in the north-eastern [counties] we outside them must do all in power to end that intolerable situation as soon as possible.[85]

It was obvious, though, that "a decisive victory for England and America would … mean the last chance of winning the lost province in the North would greatly recede."[86]

Stuart did have more information on one subject than his fellow countrymen, and that was conditions in Germany, a country "at the hub of Europe" ushering in "a world revolution, the great dividing line in history, a vital change upon the face of life."[87] Having come of his own free will to witness this great transformation, he hoped that his privileged position would give the Irish people an unbiased account of the Third Reich. What he transmitted was hardly apolitical, or literary, or neutral:

> Here in Germany I have had the opportunity to see how a great leader can inspire a whole nation. Whatever propaganda you may hear, one thing I will tell you: Germany is today an inspired nation. That is the main secret of her victorious armies; the source of that inspiration is rooted in one man, Hitler.[88]

In another instance, he noted that he had always thought that Hitler's dictatorship was preferable to the invisible tentacles of financiers:

> Our lives were dominated by a group of financial dictators and it seemed to me at least preferable to be ruled by one man whose sincerity for the welfare of his people could not be doubted than by a gang whose only concern was the market price of various commodities in the world markets.[89]

He was no sellout but spoke the truth as he saw it:

> There are none of you who need have the slightest fear that you will ever hear from me words that I am paid to speak or that I speak in order to in some way improve my own immediate position. This may be the case with only too many of the writers who have given their services to the British and American broadcasting programmes, but that is no concern of ours. Those of you who have read my books can see that my belief has not changed … I admired Hitler from the first days of power in Germany. In another [book] of mine … written in 1932 and published in New York and London in 1933, I described a clash between brownshirts and government forces in Munich, in which I did not hide my sympathies for the revolutionaries, as they were then.[90]

And while he dismissed any suggestion that he was "the mouthpiece of official German views," there was "one German view that I recognise the truth of more and more clearly: it is that which declares that Mr Roosevelt is warmonger number one."[91]

In August 1943, Allied air raids forced Irland-Redaktion to decamp to Luxembourg. Stuart moved, too; freed of his teaching at the university and confronted with a staff shortage in the Irish section, he agreed to deliver two weekly talks. His talk from mid-October disguised the fact that he was no longer in Berlin; they also proclaimed a "freedom of the air" that undermined his purported desire "to avoid all politics":

> Here from Germany I can say what no Irishman would be allowed to say anywhere else, neither in England, America, nor in Ireland itself. I can speak to you here from Germany and tell you the truth about this war, and I shall go on doing so as long as the hospitality of the German wireless is given me, even though there may be a group at home who would do whatever they can to stop me speaking to you and to impute to me motives of personal gain or ambition.[92]

"I as an Irishman have no axe to grind," he told his listeners on another occasion, "and will tell you the truth as far as I know." "And because of this," he added, in a curious defensive admission, "I feel a deep sense of responsibility and shall always avoid saying anything that I do not fully believe." But the rope was thin for neutrality when he subsequently praised the "qualities of endurance and tenacity" that Germany had shown after military setbacks.[93] As these continued, Stuart tried to marry its likely fate ("national subjection and ignominy") with the long Irish struggle.[94] The outcome of the war was a historical fork in the road: "Either this war will end with a victory for power politics and money politics, and humanity will be plunged into another dark age, or there will be the beginning of a new conception of social and national life."[95]

As his talks slid deeper into propaganda, especially when actively calling for the desertion of Irishmen in Allied armies ("you have only to wait for a suitable opportunity and go over to the Germans … And I can promise you that you will be received as friends and well treated"), concerns about Stuart's broadcasts grew.[96] After Stuart vigorously objected to the prosecution for high treason of three IRA members, the Department of External Affairs summoned the German minister to object to provocative remarks "aiding and abetting the IRA against the Government."[97] The censorship system enforcing neutrality had made Dublin sensitive to how individual opinion could be construed as representative of a wider policy, and it applied that understanding of diffuse responsibility to Stuart's case. There was also a feeling that Stuart's talks had become "steadily and openly pro-German."[98] The eulogy for the bravery of German soldiers fallen at Stalingrad—"If I were a German I should be filled with the deepest pride; as it is, I am glad to be living among such people—glad to be here in a country that can produce such men, men who still can overcome all human limitations … This is an affair of human beings, a triumph of flesh and blood"—was one confirmation of this shift.[99] The other was Stuart's series of radio talks on the Irish general election. Stuart's view that the only issue which mattered was ending partition, that Fine Gael stymied the IRA while seeking closer ties with Britain and America, was "an unwarrantable interference in our internal affairs," the Irish formally protested.[100] If Wilhelmstrasse was able to defuse the situation, Stuart was less protected when it came to the fallout, which most drastically involved the non-renewal of his Irish passport. In the summer of 1942, Frank Aiken, who had been jailed alongside Stuart in the early 1920s, had blocked Stuart's passport renewal, on the rather hysterical grounds that the Irish state had no reason to extend its diplomatic protection "now with the enemy at the gates of the city!"[101] Stuart did no favors for his cause when he refused to guarantee to "conduct himself as a neutral citizen should."[102] In June 1944 the Department of External Affairs was firm: "Stuart's passport should not be renewed STOP For yourself he is regarded as having forfeited any claims to our diplomatic protection by unneutral and disloyal behaviour."[103]

For its part, G2 had been keeping track of Stuart's whereabouts through intercepted mail. The correspondence Stuart maintained with his wife, children, and mother was regularly opened. Stuart knew that he was being surveilled—"There is not very much that one can say in these letters," he admits—by both the Germans and the Irish.[104] The security services also followed the money. A July 1943 G2 memo noted that Stuart had three probable sources of income: his salary as a lecturer, his employment in the Propaganda Ministry, and "literary earnings, irregular and probably now much reduced." Stuart's salary was estimated as "only moderate," with his wife receiving twenty pounds every two or three months. That Stuart was still trying to "sell stuff on the comparatively unremunerative Irish market" suggested that he was "trying everything to make money"; it also suggested that his propaganda job "is not very highly paid."[105] The remittances Stuart sent (at first via America), and the royalties he turned over, barely covered Iseult's expenses ("We are very hard up and badly in debt"); at one point she had to cut the telephone line to save money.[106] If she really needed more money, Francis told her, she should explicitly ask for a certain sum—and he would then take the letter to the German authorities to get permission to send more.[107] There were also suggestions that Iseult was being given money by the Germans; despite constant complaints of being "very short of money," after Hempel visited she was observed paying "a number of bills and appears to be in funds."[108] When it came to Stuart's radio broadcasts, G2 at first thought that they were entirely predictable, "what one might expect from an exile with acute nostalgia and an inherent dislike of partition." While noting that Stuart's appearance on the microphone coincided with more vigorous German propaganda, he was "not sufficiently violent" to create trouble. It was only when he gave his talk on Stalingrad that Stuart "more or less identif[ied] himself with pro-German propaganda." From that day forward, the security services noted, "Stuart has been steadily and openly pro-German."[109]

The one issue Stuart deviated from Berlin involved the Soviet Union. While most German propaganda harped on about the threat posed by "atheistic communism," Stuart refused to engage in that line of attack. On some level he might have felt immune from that pressure—he was the sole remaining Irishman in the section and had consistently produced pro-republican, anti-British copy. The wider German propaganda machine, though, was moving toward making the anti-Bolshevik line the central tenet of its message—it correctly calculated that in the choice of two devils, most peoples would choose Nazism over communism—and Stuart's obstinacy on this score stuck out. When Francis and Madeleine left Luxembourg in February 1944, he was instructed to report back to the Rundfunkhaus in Berlin, but he refused, finding himself the subject of late-night phone calls, unexpected visits, and thinly-veiled threats. Luckily Stuart had several friends high up in the German Foreign Office who petitioned for the return of his passport and ensured that he was protected from further reprisals (unlike some other announcers, who found that leaving the viper's nest resulted in forced labor camps). With no suitable replacements for Stuart (he tried to recruit a POW to take his place, but otherwise the pickings were slim for the Germans, with fewer than 100 Irish citizens in all of Germany when the war broke out), and with the war going the wrong way, German propaganda to Ireland became inconsistent, no longer appearing several times per night, as it had in its heyday, but once or twice per month. The Allied landings in Normandy and consequent push eastward made it necessary to abandon the Luxembourg station, but in Berlin things were catastrophic by the end of 1944. Broadcasting some words in Gaelic or according any importance to Ireland staying neutral—after four years of war, and with the end in sight—was no longer a priority. Trying to survive was.

Among the Ruins

As the war was coming to an end, Stuart and Madeleine went on the run, leaving Berlin in September 1944 on a two-day pass, taking advantage of the chaotic times to scramble for housing and food in the hope of reaching Switzerland. One month here, another there; sleeping rough in the forest; foraging—anything to avoid staying in one place for too long to attract attention or allow for questions about their lack of papers. In early August 1945 Stuart made it to Paris, telling the Irish officials that he had "never done anti British propaganda but agreed they could take it as such," which was the main reason "he did not want to fall into British hands."[110] All the Irish officials were willing to do was give him some money Iseult had forwarded. Stuart returned to Germany, where he and Madeleine managed to stay free until November 1945, when they were both arrested by French military security. Six months later he was transferred to Freiburg, where he was interrogated by French military officers on his activities as an "agent for German intelligence."[111] Stuart had spent fifteen months in jail during the 1921–2 civil war, but those had been different times, different places. Now, with Francis among the forgotten and the hunted, Iseult feared the worst: "A French jail possibly under the control of left-wing elements," she began rather dramatically,

> it isn't nice to think of. And Heaven knows how long he may have been in already! I read how my old friend, Ezra Pound, was driven insane; yet he always seemed so well balanced [!!!] but like Francis, a writer and a poet. For such people jail conditions are particularly dangerous.[112]

Those fears were overblown, though, as the French soon agreed to a conditional release. Stuart then began a rather peripatetic postwar, shuttling between Paris and the occupied military zones where Madeleine was held. Irish officials were amazed at Stuart's ability to get around, as if border controls and military occupations meant nothing.

There was little discussion in Dublin about prosecuting Stuart, who was probably guilty of overstepping the boundaries of neutrality, but that would only have led to internment during the war. Other countries, though, would be less forgiving toward the main broadcaster on Irland-Redaktion, who could be considered a British subject given that he was born in Australia (then a British territory) in a family hailing from Northern Ireland (still British territory) and had been educated in England (at Rugby). Calling for Northern Irishmen serving in the British armed forces to desert made Stuart a person of interest. Some "quite influential people," among them Liddell Hart, the esteemed military strategist, lobbied for Stuart to be treated lightly, but that, the Principal Secretary at the Dominions Office noted internally in February 1946, made a mockery of British efforts to bring suspected war criminals to justice.[113] Stuart's name was on the "stop list" because "this case looks pretty bad," noted one official who rifled off the list of possible transgressions that included a fraudulent visa to enter Germany, the years on the air, and possible undercover acts for closer German-IRA ties.[114]

Stuart wanted to return to Ireland, but not on any terms. He insisted that Madeleine be allowed to accompany him, but there was little hope of her receiving a visa to leave Germany (she had worked for the Propaganda Ministry) or one to enter Ireland (the Catholic country had little interest in aiding and abetting adultery). The Irish Foreign Office had irregular contacts with Stuart, fronting him money and trying to figure out how, if at all, to repatriate him. There was the diplomatic problem that "Stuart's return would certainly lead to publicity … attention would thereby be drawn to any immunity granted, and British would be unlikely to agree to anything so apt to occasion criticism in Parliament."[115] Then there was the logistical problem that all travel to Dublin from the continent had to pass through England. In Stuart's case that was "inadvisable" since the British Foreign Office would not allow for the transit of a known collaborator.[116] For his part, Stuart made it clear that "I do not wish to return there [Ireland] at present."[117] Trying to get him back against his wishes would likely drive him "underground," where he would "get into more trouble"—so the best thing to do was simply ride out the time.[118] It was even wiser to stop all communications so that Allied postal censors did not catch wind of his whereabouts or plans.

Stuart's radio silence did not extend to his fiction, which used his time in internment camps and among the continent's "apatriates" as source material for a remarkable postwar trilogy. Never, he fictionalized, had he ever "felt the sweet intensity of living; the miracle of life" as he had when scrambling for bread among the ruins; "these three years in Germany," he journaled, "have been the most fruitful of my life."[119] Renting out a flat in Freiburg, writing nearly 6,000 words per day, Stuart completed *The Pillar of Cloud* in October 1947 and sent it to Victor Gollancz, the leftwing publisher who had brought out Stuart's work in the 1930s and was now advocating reconciliation with Germany. The problem, for Gollancz, was that *Pillar of Cloud* was unbearably bleak, as the title of its first chapter—"Hunger and Cold"—baldly announced. Set in a "place and time of famine and desolation [where] every man was an enemy," the novel's holy trinity are bread, a bunk, and papers. For all this harsh exterior, though, the novel is otherwise conventional in following the artistic and sentimental-romantic exploits of Irish poet Dominic Malone, who befriends and falls in love with, and tries to protect, two sisters scarred by the war. Even if the ceaseless interrogations never reveal much about Dominic's purported war crimes, the final moral abjures any judgment over "men capable of repentance": "No one is really fit to deal with the great criminals but the innocent … We others, in judging and punishing them, become corrupted by our power over them."[120]

"I am no judge of such things," the Irish priest states at the beginning of *Redemption*, a novel that Gollancz received soon after from Stuart. While *Pillar* surveyed the continent's ruins, *Redemption* had the familiarity of the sleepy Irish town confronting the uncanny, the returning native son trying to efface the memories of the war: "All that's over and done with. You're among friends now, eh, Ezra, me boy?"[121] Yet for Ezra Arrigho (whose name showcased foreignness; one could also read the nod to Ezra Pound), the memories of war are not easy to disentangle, the return problematic. Gollancz seized on both works, bringing out *The Pillar of Cloud* in 1948 (it went through two editions that year, and then a third the next year, when *Redemption* was published). From his new residence in Paris, where he settled in July 1949, Stuart completed the postwar trilogy with *The Flowering Cross* (1950), which took as its central figure a sculptor in love with a blind orphan jailed for theft. The story, again, is one of a mitigated triumph, both artistic and personal, over the prison walls, hunger, and the world's indifference.

Throughout his postwar trilogy, Stuart rarely touched on the central problem of his war experience, his collaboration with the German propaganda machine. The artist-protagonists are all enjoined to keep the "faith," to create art in a world denuded of meaning, but the war past is always obscure. That famously changed with *Black List, Section H*, which came out in 1971. In the intervening period Stuart had managed to leave France, settling in London in June 1951 with Madeleine (whose entry visa was sponsored by Ethel Mannin), the two of them taking on menial jobs and struggling in obscurity. After Iseult died, Stuart was able to marry Madeleine (in 1954), and on their four-year anniversary they emigrated to Dublin. Stuart's postwar dream—of setting up an independent publishing house to escape the clutches of commercial fiction—was never realized. Finding publishers became more challenging, but not because Stuart was somehow "tainted" by his wartime associations—in 1950s Ireland, the less one said about the war, the better (and, more broadly, former collaborators were being rehabilitated across Europe). The problem was that Stuart had had plenty of chances to prove his (financial) viability as an author, and in most cases had disappointed; publishers could bank on artistic potential for only so long (a Gollancz editor told Stuart in 1951 that another "minor work," by which she meant one with poor sales, would be "quite fatal to your future as a writer").[122] A new work that was very long (over 150,000 words) and potentially libelous (written in the first person, with the real names of people for the characters) was a tough sell. After shopping around "We the Condemned," the working title for *Black List, Section H,* to every London publisher, from the established players to the back-room operators, Stuart had to settle, in the end, for a tiny advance from Southern Illinois University Press. The editorial director there was persuaded to take a chance on this neglected Irish author whose "few radio broadcasts from Germany to Ireland," as the preface to the first edition put it in a case of obvious misinformation, were "more in the manner of P. G. Wodehouse than of Ezra Pound."[123] The work would be in print, even if its initial sales—an average of around 200 copies per year—hardly marked it out as a magnum opus.

Black List, Section H was a work of a lifetime—and about a lifetime, Stuart's. It was initially drafted in the first person, with Stuart's real name for the protagonist, but it was no playful autofiction *avant la lettre* but rather an earnest *Künstlerbildungsroman*, based on Stuart's life but with a liberal imaginative transformation of the facts to make sense of, and justify, his wartime collaboration. ("The imaginative writer can invent his facts," Stuart later noted.)[124] To be on a black list is a mark of honor for an artist and is the calling card for "H," the protagonist of the novel with only an initial for a name: "Dishonour is what becomes a poet, not titles or acclaim."[125] The entire work is shrouded in the trope of the outcast battling against the strictures of society: "nothing short of the near despair of being utterly cast off from society and its principles could create the inner condition conducive to the new insights that it was the task of the poet to reveal." This realization comes to H in the same place where he tells Iseult that a poet needs dishonor, a term whose full meaning he could not grasp until he saw a group of girls tied to a church railing, their heads shaved and the word "Traitors" pinned on them (the IRA meted out this punishment in the early 1920s for women who consorted with the British). H sees himself in these girls; a poet must be "exposed and condemned" for refusing the "closed judgments" of society and the "categorical divisions into right and wrong that prevailed" (41). By implication, terms like "treason" or "traitor" were misplaced when it came to the artist, who had a higher calling than fidelity to a nation or an idea—or even to another life, as that chapter ends with the death of a child that H "hadn't loved, had hardly taken … in" (43).

In this *apologia pro vita sua*, Stuart begins by detailing H's early career and the difficulties—mainly sexual—of his marriage. In one harrowing scene, rage at his wife, named as Iseult Gonne in the text, results in him burning her dresses and setting fire to the garden, only for them to spend the rest of the day "in a moist, healing glow of reconciliation" (31). This scene encapsulates the extremes of Stuart's moral universe, the uncontrolled violence followed by rapturous forgiveness. But morality is a difficult term in *Black List, Section H*; there are acts, but they do not need to be justified so long as they are deeply and personally intentioned. The entire framework of morality, its division into right and wrong, is called into question for stifling the search for new ways of thinking and feeling. While Hugo Hamilton is right in saying that Stuart "never made any attempt to stage-manage his past," *Black List, Section H* was an exercise in shifting the frames of judgment.[126] For the reader immersed in H's consciousness and his struggles to find himself as an artist, there is no place for judgment and "formal guilt," anyway, was only society's judgment. The only guilt for a writer was "sharing in universal attitudes for the sake of easing imagination's lonely ache" (305). As Kevin Kiely, who was close friends with Stuart for over two decades, remarked, Stuart was "fundamentally artistically driven; no other consideration was ever of as much importance to him."[127]

If Stuart managed to remain true to himself, then, how could he be a traitor? Disregard for morality in this Nietzschean universe of the artist as *übermensch* is its own politics, of course. Conventional pieties are mocked—"Pee, piss, pock" take the place of "church, family, nation" (180)—as H seeks only his own self-realization as an artist.[128] But that has to happen in the world, and his move to Germany is undergirded by the hope that Berlin will lead a "possible inner revolution … a psychic earthquake" (263). That this never comes about—the Germans he meets dream of cottages in Somerset and admire Jane Austen—is a great disappointment, but H rationalizes his time in Berlin as an artistic choice to side with the guilty and moral outcasts. That Germany would suffer immensely in a few years after fire bombings turned its cities into ruins of rubble was not something that could have been in anyone's mind in 1940 or 1941, though, so Stuart's claim, repeated throughout the years, that he had sided with the Germans so as to experience absolute defeat rings false (and makes a mockery of Nazism's helpless victims). The book ends with H coming to understand that he was now among "the community of the just" when imprisoned in a cell, and that his transformation into a true artistry, whose words he could only dimly hear, was about to begin, largely because of his wartime experiences.

The Wisdom of State Honors

After years in the literary wilderness, *Black List, Section H* relaunched Stuart's career, first leading to a half-hour RTÉ show chronicling his impressions of contemporary Berlin (with no mention of his propaganda past, the program allows Stuart to frame Germany as a nation of tragic victims: "two disastrous wars, invasions from east and west, saturation bombings, long periods of cold and starvation, always in a normal lifetime").[129] More acclaim came after Penguin picked up the UK rights to *Black List, Section H* in 1982 and re-issued it in paperback. If the *Observer* review spoke of "A Portrait of the Artist as a Young Nazi," most critics passed over the book's politics and centered on its technical accomplishments and imaginative energies. It helped Stuart's case that few people actually knew what he said on the air, and *Black List, Section H* did not fill in the gaps, either, with its chapters on his radio broadcasting focusing mainly on his relationships with his superiors and his doubts about any ideology being correct. The Irish literary establishment took up Stuart as a forgotten voice of the great Irish modernist experiment, and he became a regular at small press events, university symposia, and literary journals (see Figure 6.3). *Books Ireland* showed him clutching a pet rabbit on its cover; *Hibernia* gave him column space for a fortnightly ramble. His work came out by small, independent Irish presses (like Raven Arts, founded by a seventeen-year-old Dermot Bulger in Dublin in 1971). The crowning achievement of all this was the 1996 induction of Stuart, by Taoiseach Mary Robinson, as one of the five *saoi* of the Aosdána,

Figure 6.3 Portrait of Francis Stuart, 1983. Photo by Thierry Martinot. Copyright Bridgeman Images.

joining such illustrious company as Samuel Beckett and Seamus Heaney (only five living artists could be a *saoi* at any time).

Like many other national arts bodies across Europe, the Irish Arts Council was first established in the postwar period (1951), though without much enthusiasm or funding given "officialdom … and the general philistinism in the country."[130] In 1983 the Arts Council established a body of artists, Aosdána, whose membership was by application "for the top 150 artists" in the country.[131] (Unsurprisingly, very few female artists were selected, and the Arts Council favored artists whose reputations had been made decades earlier.)[132] Stuart was among the first members, and he received the body's main perk, a five-year stipend (*cnuas*) of £4,000 per annum. These bursaries were set up, as Taoiseach Charlie Haughey put it, to "ensure that Irish artists of distinction will be enabled to pursue their art without too much pressure from those economic circumstances that have so often impeded their genius in the past."[133] The members of the Aosdána considered new membership applications, went through bursary requests, and proposed names to be honored with the title of Saoi. That process was bureaucratically laid out in the Aosdána's general regulations: at least fifteen members had to propose a member to be named a *Saoi*; that proposal then went to the ten-member Toscairi (a supervisory board of Aosdána members), which had to approve the name; and then a vote was put to the entire membership, with a simple majority needed. One of the first *Saoi* was Samuel Beckett, who received the golden torc in 1986.

Stuart's induction a decade later was more controversial. Máire Cruise O'Brien (Maire Mhac an tSaoi) was incensed that the body had awarded "its highest distinction to someone who unrepentantly chuckles over his role as wartime propagandist for Nazi Germany."[134] The distinguished Gaelic poet, later named a *Saoi* herself, had heard Stuart's broadcasts during the war (her father was a pro-Ally Minister of Finance, and she had studied in Paris from 1945 to 1947) and was also aghast at how, in a recent Channel 4 documentary on the Holocaust, Stuart had said that "the Jew was always the worm that got into the rose and sickened it" (repeating a line from *Black List, Section H* which said that a "Jewish idea" would always be a "contradiction … a worm that could get into a lot of fine-looking fruit").[135] She filed a motion to strip Stuart of his title—"What we are doing," she told the membership, "is not merely forgiving Mr Stuart's past, we are exalting it"—but only a few members concurred.[136] There was little interest in dredging up old wounds, especially wartime and its moral ambiguities, as the booming Celtic Tiger economy made Ireland a proverbial "ship of fools" (as Fintan O'Toole later chronicled those years) with no interest in disruptive history or moral ruminations.[137] A lingering feeling that Stuart had done nothing more in Berlin than push for Irish interests—he was an advocate of neutrality, after all, which was official policy—also made it hard to see what the fuss could be. It was only with the release of Brendan Barrington's edition of Stuart's wartime broadcasts in 2000, and then wider historical re-assessments of Ireland's wartime past, such as Clair Wills's *That Neutral Island*, in 2007, that Stuart's authorship could be more seriously examined.

Conclusion

Although Francis Stuart was never charged with the crime of treason, his case is included in this book because it spotlights how neutral countries navigated the complicated questions of wartime allegiance. Ireland was not alone in this; throughout Europe, countries like Portugal, Spain, Sweden, and Switzerland also had to consider the boundaries of opinion in a neutral space. While Portugal and Spain as fascist regimes had pronounced sympathies with the Axis powers, Ireland was a country both closer to Great Britain but also, in its own way, at war with the occupier of the North. Stuart's case shows the complexities of allegiance for the ostensibly neutral writer. Stuart was surveilled by the security services of numerous states (Ireland's G2, Britain's MI5, France's DGSI) and interned in the postwar period. Given the uncertain status of Irish citizenship, he could have been charged with high treason in an English court, but the diplomatic fallout of that would have been high. But even in an Irish court a case could have been made that Stuart overstepped the boundaries of neutrality by pushing for closer ties between Éire and the Axis powers; neutrality as an official state policy did not give individual citizens *carte blanche* to pick a preferred side. Neutrality, in fact, involved a very strict policing of opinion, to the point that favoring one side in any manner went against the interests of the state. That the Irish state did not prosecute Stuart for these breaches of wartime neutrality law came down to his postwar stay in occupied Germany and then France, but there was also little interest in Ireland to dreck up the past via postwar trials. Neutrality had gotten Ireland through the war, and the least said about it afterwards, the prevailing belief went, the better.

Stuart's postwar authorship—his trilogy of books about the postwar chaos, and then his radical rewriting of his time in Berlin radio in *Black List, Section H*—brought him back to public attention and eventually led to him receiving the highest state honors in Ireland. Remarkably, these books did not occlude his wartime past but spoke directly about his involvement, although in a way that reframed his authorial responsibility and choices: the true artist, in these books, is the one who goes against the grain, who chooses the side of suffering, who becomes an ascetic, a hunger artist, a prisoner. This reframing, as well as the general ignorance of what Stuart had said on the air from Berlin, was exceptionally successful. Stuart appealed to a long-standing belief of authors as social visionaries above moral judgment (they were exclusively the beneficiaries of moral sympathy as victims of society's prejudices). Over time, though, with the opening of archives and interest in revisiting the war years, Stuart's case, with its experimental anti-modernism and an exaggerated, mystical faith in the artist figure, shows that even neutrality comes with a price for authorship.

Notes

1 Quoted in Eunan O'Halpin, *Spying on Ireland: British Intelligence and Irish Neutrality During the Second World War* (Oxford: Oxford University Press, 2008), 1; IEMA, G2/X/0002/03 (German Legation file).

2 Dáil Éireann, July 19, 1945. See https://www.oireachtas.ie/en/debates/ for Irish parliamentary records. Last accessed: January 22, 2026.
3 R. M. Smyllie, "Unnatural Neutral Eire," *Foreign Affairs* 24.2 (January 1946): 317–26, at 317. The clearest picture of wartime Ireland and debates over the morality of neutrality can be found in Clair Wills, *That Neutral Ireland: A History of Ireland During the Second World War* (London: Faber and Faber, 2007).
4 Louis MacNeice, "Neutrality," in *Collected Poems of Louis MacNeice* (London: Faber and Faber, 1966), 202.
5 St. Patrick's Day Radio Address (March 17, 1943), at https://www.rte.ie/archives/exhibitions/eamon-de-valera/719124-address-by-mr-de-valera/. Accessed: January 22, 2026.
6 Review of Francis Stuart, *Glory*, in *Daily Telegraph*, September 1, 1933.
7 Ethel Mannin, *Late Have I Loved Thee* (London: Jarrolds, 1948), 9.
8 Quoted in Anne McCartney, *Francis Stuart Face to Face: A Critical Study* (Belfast: Institute of Irish Studies, 2000), 158.
9 Damien Keane, *Ireland and the Problem of Information: Irish Writing, Radio, Late Modernist Communication* (University Park: Pennsylvania State University Press, 2014), 108.
10 Francis Stuart (FS), *Things To Live For: Notes for an Autobiography* (London: Jonathan Cape, 1934), 144.
11 Jerry H. Natterstad, *Francis Stuart* (Lewisburg, PA: Bucknell University Press, 1974), 64.
12 Quoted in Andreas Roth, "Francis Stuart's Broadcasts from Germany, 1942–4: Some New Evidence," *Irish Historical Studies* 32.127 (May 2001): 408–22, at 408.
13 Henry Green, *Loving*, in *Loving Living Party Going* (Harmondsworth: Penguin, 1993), 18.
14 See Eunan O'Halpin, *Defending Ireland: The Irish State and Its Enemies Since 1922* (Oxford: Oxford University Press, 1999), 144–9.
15 Quoted in Brian Girvin, *The Emergency: Ireland 1939–45* (London: Macmillan, 2006), 54.
16 TD Cogan, Dáil debate, March 30, 1939.
17 Quoted in H. Montgomery Hyde, ed., *Famous Trials 9: Roger Casement* (Harmondsworth: Penguin, 1964), 55.
18 Article 39.
19 Brendan Behan, *Borstal Boy* (London: Arrow Books, 1990), 4.
20 Cablegram, February 24, 1939, INA, DFA 247/2.
21 The Taoiseach, Dáil Debate, February 23, 1939.
22 TD Norton, Dáil Debate, February 23, 1939.
23 TD Cogan, Dáil Debate, February 23, 1939.
24 The Taoiseach, Dáil Debate, February 23, 1939.
25 Irish Neutrality League, *Bulletin*, May 15, 1940, 2.
26 Emergency Powers Act, September 3, 1939.
27 Emergency Powers Order No. 36, July 12, 1940.
28 TD John Lymbrick Esmonde, Dáil debate, September 28, 1939.
29 Quoted in Paul Bew, *Churchill and Ireland* (Oxford: Oxford University Press, 2016), 141.
30 Seanad Eireann Debate, January 4, 1940.
31 Elizabeth Bowen, "Note on Eire, 9 November 1940," in Elizabeth Bowen, *"Notes on Eire": Espionage Reports to Winston Churchill, 1940–2* (Cork: Aubane Historical Society, 1999), 11.
32 Bryce Evans, *Ireland During the Second World War: Farewell to Plato's Cave* (Manchester: Manchester University Press, 2014).
33 Robert Cole, *Propaganda, Censorship and Irish Neutrality in the Second World War* (Edinburgh: Edinburgh University Press, 2006), 20; Irish Neutrality League, *Bulletin*, May 15, 1940, 1.

34 Donal Ó Drisceoil, *Censorship in Ireland, 1939–1945: Neutrality, Politics and Society* (Cork: Cork University Press, 1996).
35 INA, DFA 214/66.
36 Declan Kiberd, *After Ireland: Writing the Nation from Beckett to the Present* (Cambridge: Harvard University Press, 2017), 6.
37 Henry Bellew, "Censorship, Law, and Conscience," *The Bell* 3.2 (November 1942): 140–8, at 145.
38 "The Mart of Ideas," *The Bell* 4.3 (June 1942): 153–7, at 153; "Silent Ireland," *The Bell* 6.6 (September 1943): 457–66, at 465.
39 F. S. L. Lyons, *Ireland Since the Famine* (London: Weidenfeld and Nicolson, 1971).
40 TD Norton, Dáil Debate, March 5, 1942.
41 G2 memo, January 21, 1943, INA, DFA 4/205/108.
42 Eduard Hempel telegram to Berlin Foreign Office, December 13, 1939, quoted in David O'Donoghue, *Hitler's Irish Voices: The Story of German Radio's Wartime Irish Service* (Belfast: Beyond the Pale, 1998), 36.
43 See debate on Radio Eireann in the Dáil, May 1, 1940.
44 TD Daniel Morrissey, Dáil Debate, June 4, 1941.
45 TD Esmonde, Dáil Debate, June 17, 1942; TD Larkin, Dáil Debate, November 9, 1943.
46 TD McCann, Dáil Debate, November 26, 1942.
47 TD Larkin, Dáil Debate, November 9, 1943.
48 The German minister complained that German military communiqués were usually reported in "very small or even the smallest letter types," chopped up across articles as well, which undercut "the original conception and unity" of the reports. Memo, n.d., INA, DFA 216/303. At other times, the "unfriendly and prejudiced tone of the newspaper headlines" caused disappointment (Memo, October 9, 1943, INA, DFA 216/303).
49 "Ireland and the Modern World," *The Bell* 5.6 (March 1943): 423–8, at 423, 424.
50 Louis MacNeice, *Autumn Journal* (London: Faber and Faber, 2012 [1939]), 53.
51 Quoted in Kevin Kiely, *Francis Stuart: Artist and Outcast* (Dublin: Liffey Press, 2007), 121.
52 Isolde Krafft to Francis Stuart, November 2, 1939, in Francis Stuart Archive, Coleraine.
53 Hempel's characterization of Stuart quoted in Roth, "Francis Stuart's Broadcasts from Germany," 411; FS, "Ireland a Democracy? The Real State of Affairs: Freedom Defined," *The Young Observer*, December 1, 1939, 3; FS, Letter-to-the-Editor, *Irish Independent*, October 5, 1939.
54 FS, *Lecture on Nationality and Culture* (Dublin: Sinn Fein, 1924), 4, 12.
55 Garda Report, December 11, 1939, IEMA, G2/0214.
56 Garda Report, November 11, 1939, IEMA, G2/0214.
57 G2 to DFA, October 6, 1944, IEMA, G2/0214.
58 Police report, April 27, 1939, IEMA, G2/0214.
59 IEMA, G2/0214.
60 See letters by J. P. Walshe to G2 and Liam Archer, Department of Defence, autumn 1939, in IEMA, G2/0214.
61 Diary entry, September 18, 1942, Coleraine.
62 Diary entry, September 17, 1942, Coleraine.
63 FS, "A Berlin Diary," in *States of Mind: Selected Short Prose, 1936–1983* (Dublin: Raven Arts Press, 1984), 31–45, at 34.
64 Mark M. Hull and Vera Moynes, *Masquerade: Treason, the Holocaust, and an Irish Imposter* (Norman: University of Oklahoma Press, 2017), 48.
65 Geoffrey Elborn, *Francis Stuart: A Life* (Dublin: Raven Arts, 1990), 135; on James, see Hull and Moynes, *Masquerade*.
66 *Irische Freiheitskämpfer* (Berlin: 1940), 6.

67 Quoted in Natterstad, *Francis Stuart*, 61.
68 FS to Iseult Stuart, March 25, 1943, IEMA, G2/0214.
69 FS to Aunt Janet, February 20, 1943, IEMA, G2/0214.
70 Extract from the Annual Report of the Irish Legation in Germany for 1941, *Documents on Irish Foreign Policy* [*DIFP*], vol. 7, no. 227, at https://www.difp.ie. Accessed: January 22, 2026.
71 FS, diary, May 15, 1943, Coleraine.
72 FS, "Extracts from a Berlin Diary," February 18, 1940.
73 Quoted in Keane, *Ireland and the Problem of Information*, 115.
74 Jerry H. Natterstad, "Interview with Francis Stuart," *The Journal of Irish Literature* 5.1 (January 1976): 16–31, at 27.
75 Quoted in Robert Fisk, *In Time of War: Ireland, Ulster, and the Price of Neutrality, 1939–45* (London: André Deutsch, 1983), 351.
76 Memo, n.d. (early 1942), INA, DFA/4/205/108.
77 FS, broadcast, March 17, 1942, in *The Wartime Broadcasts of Francis Stuart, 1942–1944*, ed. Brendan Barrington (Dublin: Lilliput Press, 2000), 69, 70.
78 FS, diary, August 6, 1942, Coleraine.
79 Ibid., August 25, 1942.
80 Ibid., August 26, 1942.
81 FS, January 6, 1943, *Wartime Broadcasts*, 108.
82 FS, diary, August 6, 1942, Coleraine.
83 FS, March 27, 1943, *Wartime Broadcasts*, 123.
84 Ibid., October 19, 1943, 166.
85 Ibid., September 23, 1942, 88.
86 Ibid., August 21, 1943, 143.
87 Ibid., March 29, 1942, 71.
88 Ibid., October 7, 1942, 90.
89 Ibid., December 16, 1942, 99.
90 Ibid., November 13, 1943, 175.
91 Ibid., January 13, 1943, 110.
92 Ibid., October 16, 1943, 164.
93 Ibid., February 20, 1943, 117–18.
94 Ibid., September 4, 1943, 146.
95 Ibid., November 20, 1943, 178.
96 Ibid., May 15, 1943, 128.
97 Frederick Bolan, memo, December 30, 1942, INA, DFA/4/205/108.
98 Quoted in O'Donoghue, *Hitler's Irish Voices*, 107.
99 FS, February 6, 1943, *Wartime Broadcasts*, 113–14.
100 DFA to Berlin, May 27, 1943, IEMA, G2/0214.
101 INA, DFA/10/113–14.
102 Note, May 19, 1944, INA, DFA/10/113–14.
103 Telegram, June 1, 1944, INA, DFA/DE/2/64.
104 FS to Iseult Stuart, July 14, 1942, IEMA, G2/0214.
105 "Francis & Iseult Stuart—Money Affairs," memo, July 5, 1943, IEMA, G2/0214.
106 Iseult Stuart to FS, June 12, 1942, IEMA, G2/0214.
107 FS to Iseult Stuart, March 25, 1943, IEMA, G2/0214.
108 IEMA, G2/0214.
109 Ibid.
110 Telegram from Paris to Dublin, August 29, 1945, INA, DFA/10/113–14.
111 Seán Murphy to F. H. Boland, September 11, 1946, INA, DFA/10/113–14.
112 Iseult Stuart to F. H. Boland, May 15, 1946, INA, DFA/10/113–14.

113 Internal note, February 14, 1946, Kew, DO 130/73.
114 J. L. Maffey to Liddell Hart, October 29, 1946, Kew, DO 130/73.
115 Telegram to Paris, September 25, 1945, INA, DFA/10/113–14.
116 INA, DFA/10/113–14.
117 FS, letter, September 19, 1946, INA, DFA/10/113–14.
118 F. H. Boland to Seán Murphy, August 30, 1946, INA, DFA/10/113–14.
119 FS, "The Destroying Angel," in *States of Mind*, 46–52, at 51; FS, diary, November 20, 1948, Coleraine.
120 FS, *The Pillar of Cloud* (Dublin: New Island Books, 1994 [1948]), 225.
121 FS, *Redemption* (Dublin: New Island Books, 1994 [1949]), 79.
122 Sheila Hodges to FS, September 28, 1950, Coleraine.
123 Quoted in Kiely, *Francis Stuart*, 311.
124 FS, "Novelists on the Novel: Ronan Sheehan Talks to John Banville and Francis Stuart," *Crane Bag* 3.1 (1979): 76–84, at 83.
125 FS, *Black List, Section H* (Harmondsworth: Penguin, 1982 [1971]), 20.
126 Hugo Hamilton, "Understanding Francis Stuart," *Writing Ulster* 4 (1996): 69–76, at 73.
127 Kiely, *Francis Stuart*, 151.
128 FS, *Black List, Section H*, 180.
129 "Francis Stuart Revisits Berlin," at https://www.rte.ie/archives/2017/1205/925167-francis-stuart-in-germany/. Last accessed: January 22, 2026.
130 Kevin Rafter, *Taoisigh and the Arts* (Dublin: Martello, 2022), 76.
131 Memo, October 20, 1981, INA, AHG/2018/184/32.
132 See Eamonn O'Doherty, "Aosdana," *Irish Times*, May 26, 1986, in INA, AHG/2018/184/34.
133 Speech by the Taoiseach, Mr. Charles J. Haughey, at the Royal Irish Academy, March 5, 1981, INA, AHG/2018/184/32.
134 Maire Cruise O'Brien, *The Same Age as the State* (Madison: University of Wisconsin Press, 2004), 333.
135 FS, *Black List, Section H*, 58.
136 O'Brien, *Same Age as the State*, 335.
137 Fintan O'Toole, *Ship of Fools* (London: Public Affairs, 2010).

CONCLUSION

Writing this conclusion in March 2025, almost eighty years after the end of the Second World War, I am struck by how the historical issues described in this book resound in the present. The polarized political landscape in America, the resurgence of populism in Europe, a major land war in the heart of that continent, repressive sedition laws abutting unfettered free-speech absolutism, cancel culture progressives: the volatile cocktail of forces that I had thought locked in the past when I first began writing this book seem to be inescapable elements of our political present. Freedom and censorship seem to be growing together. The expansion of open media platforms has removed so many constraints to distributing a text, but these platforms are also subject to fierce debates over the regulation of online speech.[1] My hope is that this book, by bringing out the entanglement of writing, politics, and the law in the postwar, will shed some light on how writing can be corralled and limited, sometimes for necessary, just ends, but often with questionable methods.

When the most destructive war in human history came to a close in 1945, the hunt was on for those who, as the Romanian war crimes law put it, were the authors of the nation's destruction. Even the high apostle of free speech in the Anglo-American world, George Orwell, compiled "lists" of unreliable writers that he passed on to state authorities and intelligence services.[2] States could be excused for believing that writing had a wide social and political impact (even if those beliefs were often exaggerated).[3] The ubiquity of wartime propaganda had seared in the collective memory a hatred of print and audio collaboration. Its authors were easy prey, their signed articles tantamount to confessions. For writers who remained silent or courted great risks by publishing in the clandestine press—as Halik Kochanski reminds us, one of the first acts of resistance in countries "almost immediately after the occupation had begun" was the appearance of an underground press—those writers who received honors and pay from the Axis were reviled intensely.[4]

But the arc of history had been moving toward free expression, the marketplace of ideas, not censorship boards or books put on trial. That abruptly changed course during the war when even the most liberal regimes began putting limits on what could be said, and where. Purely "literary" topics that appeared in hostile venues came to be considered instances of propaganda. In every single country treated in this book the laws on the circulation of ideas and on treason were drastically revised during wartime, either pre-emptively, before the war started, or by exile governments or resistance forces. In unoccupied countries fears of fifth columns and enemy propaganda contributing to a defeatist attitude led governments to redraft treason laws to make postwar prosecution simpler, with fewer protections for the accused and less pomp and circumstance for a crime that had become banal.

"It is obvious that we are in the century of treason," French literary critic André Thérive noted, "never before have we spoken so much about traitors."[5] Treason was a disease, like gangrene, that the country had contracted and could not rid itself of. But there were also more traitors because there were more laws and an expansion of the term's meaning: the term no longer had a sure legal footing when it came to mean, colloquially, a political opponent, someone who thought differently than you. But the legal framework itself had lost its legitimacy: after the wartime years of unjust laws, the postwar purge brought in their stead "retroactive laws, popular tribunals, exceptional 'decrees' … this could not be called law," Thérive added, "but the application of force."[6] Listen to one of Knut Hamsun's compatriots: "The Norwegian people, which in this battle of fate showed composure and honor under the regime of horrors of traitors and their henchmen, demand that the reckoning with society's rotten animals be seen to consistently and swiftly. All unnecessary procedure must be set aside, their crimes do not deserve mitigating circumstances."[7] Or a Russian observer at the Belsen trial: "To us it seems more like a game than a trial. Anyone who was on the staff at either Belsen or Auschwitz should be shot on the spot."[8] That happened often enough, with "savage" purges taking place in any number of countries. But lawless times could not persist simply because they satisfied the people's primordial urge for revenge. Law had to be called in, as one Italian *partigiano* recognized: "in war you shoot, but when the war is finished, you can't shoot anymore."[9]

The law could still supply bullets, but it had to be selective about which chambers to fill. In *The Judicial Imagination*, Lyndsey Stonebridge notes that "the law was at its most audacious and creative in the immediate postwar period."[10] This book has shown both the promises and the dangers of that audacity and creativity. The balancing act required of postwar governments—to purge the past but also reconstruct the future—was a tight one. The law was oftentimes too blunt a tool to that end. It was easy to target writers and authors because their acts were signed, their names known. But was it fair to do so? As the postwar French saying had it, the fellows who had built the Atlantic Wall were strolling down the boulevards as millionaires, while the journalists who had praised its construction, at one franc per line, found themselves in jail.[11] But since "you cannot reconstruct on the basis of hatred," a Belgian prime minister noted, the most egregious cases of collaboration were in many cases passed over, as the trials would have been too complicated and the defendants too important to be jailed.[12]

When authors were put on trial, the reading of texts within the various trials was for the most part reductive and unsophisticated, often relying on isolated passages or quotations (which in many instances were wrongly transcribed). The long experience of the propaganda war had cut language into bits and pieces. As a legal matter, isolating passages was standard practice in obscenity cases (the marked-up passages in *Lady Chatterley's Lover* that a servant should not be allowed to read, etc.). There was little consideration for how any number of structural elements—the political intentions of an author, the wider historical context, editorial interventions, direct censorship directives, self-censorship—impacted the composition of a text or radio program. And while very few of the figures treated in this book could honestly claim that they were writing "between the lines," using ambiguity and double meanings to subvert the ostensible meaning of a text, a tactic Leo Strauss foregrounded in *Persecution and the Art of Writing* (1941), it was still doubtful that a text could have only one meaning as prosecutors often claimed.[13] Just as the line between collaboration and resistance had been drawn sharply for the benefit of postwar reconstruction and national myths, so, too, did language have to become fixed and invariable, one thing and one thing only.

The Janus-faced quality of the postwar, which looked back to the war but also to the future to be built, contributed to the moral morass of the present. "Few moments in world history," Leela Gandhi and Deborah Nelson argued, "have had such far-reaching impact, temporally and geographically, in terms of intellectual developments and lived experience," as the postwar.[14] The new nation-states and global institutions created in this period fundamentally reshaped the world, with many countries coming to experience unprecedented prosperity in the decades that followed. In the moment, though, there was only uncertainty. Shifting political alliances and continued material hardships made every day a rude voyage into the unknown. What could "the right of the creative artist to create and inhabit his own moral universe" mean in 1945?[15] For many peoples recovering from war and occupation, Knut Hamsun's grandiose remit for artists meant very little at all, and the numerous examples of authors who had used freedom for pernicious ends, Hamsun included, only solidified that antagonism toward the pen.

The law can never be perfect, and less so when it comes to political trials. The ideal of law as a civilized response to violence had prompted the proliferation of legal forms in the postwar period.[16] But engaging in "destructive" political trials—that is, "the use of legal procedure for the purpose of defeating a real or imagined enemy"—undermined confidence in the purge in almost every country studied.[17] Even in a country like Norway where the legal definition of collaboration was a simple exercise in determining membership in a political party, the variety of punishments meted out, the inconsistencies in sentencing, the slowness of the general procedure coupled with great haste in individual trials, chipped away at the legitimacy of the purge. Countries with a less sure legal footing were, understandably, even more muddled. Rather than restoring law's empire, these trials harkened back to the pointed political repression of the fascist past that was meant to be extirpated, creating martyrs and victims. But inaction was not an option. In a broken world, complete justice did not exist.

Creating martyrs was a foreseeable but regrettable consequence of the literary trials undertaken in the wake of the Second World War; so, too, was wider state control over expression and speech. The most obvious instance of that were the loyalty tests and investigations of "un-American activities" during the Red Scare. Applauding freedom while hammering down the gavel on penniless revolutionaries or dissolute anarchists was par for the course in the period. For all the Congress for Cultural Freedom talk of free expression, the kind of speech that was encouraged and subsidized had to be ideologically aligned to a certain system of belief; an artist had to "fall in with our platoon" and be "a good citizen" before being considered a good artist.[18] Over one hundred years of the artist gradually dissociating from the outside world (Baudelaire, the *poète maudit*) was upturned by the war and its aftermath. The reaction to that—in the form of New Critics drowning politics out of literary baths, intention being called a fallacy, and then authors being eviscerated, so all that remained was pure text—was not without its own failings. The tribunals in the postwar period showed how unstable a supposed *ur*-text was, how impossible it was to isolate meaning without considering intention or context.

The trials of authorship in the wake of the Second World War threw in sharp relief the sovereign claims of the political, legal, and aesthetic domains. The sovereignty of the body politic; law's empire; aesthetic autonomy: all three domains claim, in various ways, to be complete and unto themselves. If the three universalist claims could be accommodated in times of social unity and generalized peace, wartime and postwar reconstruction placed impossible pressures upon them. In most cases, politics prevailed, using law in novel, unorthodox ways to silence art and free expression. If those postwar exigencies were bracketed off as exceptional, they had lasting impacts that continue to be felt to this day.

Notes

1 Nicole Moore, "Introduction," in *Censorship and the Limits of the Literary: A Global View*, ed. Nicole Moore (London: Bloomsbury Academic, 2015), 1–10.
2 Glenn Burgess, *George Orwell's Perverse Humanity: Socialism and Free Speech* (London: Bloomsbury Academic, 2023), 222–35.
3 See Peter J. Kalliney, *The Aesthetic Cold War: Decolonization and Global Literature* (Princeton: Princeton University Press, 2022).
4 Halik Kochanski, *Resistance: The Underground War Against Hitler, 1939–1945* (New York: Liveright, 2022), 40.
5 André Thérive, *Essai sur les trahisons* (Paris: Calmann-Lévy, 1951), xxxiii.
6 Ibid., 10.
7 Quoted in Seemann, *Quislings*, 136.
8 Quoted in Victoria Stewart, *Literature and Justice in Mid-Century Britain* (Oxford: Oxford University Press, 2023), 57.
9 Quoted in Lowe, *Savage Continent*, 151.
10 Lyndsey Stonebridge, *The Judicial Imagination: Writing After Nuremberg* (Edinburgh: Edinburgh University Press, 2011), 2.
11 Jean Paulhan, *De la paille et du grain* (Paris: Gallimard, 1948), 98.
12 Belgian Prime Minister Achille Van Acker, quoted in Philip Morgan, *Hitler's Collaborators: Choosing Between Bad and Worse in Nazi-Occupied Western Europe* (Oxford: Oxford University Press, 2018), 15.
13 Leo Strauss, *Persecution and the Art of Writing* (Glencoe: Free Press, 1952), 25.
14 Leela Gandhi and Deborah L. Nelson, "Editor's Introduction," *Critical Inquiry* 40.4 (Summer 2014): 285–97, at 286.
15 Knut Hamsun, quoted in Ferguson, *Enigma*, 405.
16 See Shoshana Felman, *The Juridical Unconscious: Trials and Traumas in the Twentieth Century* (Cambridge: Harvard University Press, 2002).
17 Jens Meierhenrich and Devin O. Pendas, "'The Justice of My Cause Is Clear, but There's Politics to Fear': Political Trials in Theory and History," in *Political Trials in Theory and History*, ed. Jens Meierhenrich and Devin O. Pendas (Cambridge: Cambridge University Press, 2016), 1–64, at 57.
18 Charles Morgan, "The Artist in the Community," *The Yale Review* 35.4 (January 1946): 594–613, at 611.

SELECT BIBLIOGRAPHY

Archives

Archives Départementales du Rhône et de la métropole de Lyon (Lyon).
Archives Nationales de France (Paris).
Les archives de la Préfecture de Police (Paris).
BBC Written Archives Centre (Reading).
Beinecke Rare Book and Manuscript Library, Yale University (New Haven, CT).
Booth Family Center for Special Collections, Georgetown University (Washington, D.C.).
British Library (London).
Centre des Archives diplomatiques de La Courneuve (Paris).
Consiliul Național pentru Studierea Arhivelor Securității (Bucharest).
La Contemporaine (Nanterre).
Department of Justice (Washington, D.C.).
Franklin Delano Roosevelt Presidential Library (Hyde Park, NY).
FBI Archives (Washington, D.C.).
FOIA Request 1415563-000, Frank L. Amprim File.
Harry Ransom Center, University of Texas at Austin (Austin, TX).
Henry W. and Albert A. Berg Collection of English and American Literature, New York Public Library (New York, NY).
Houghton Library, Harvard University (Cambridge, MA).
Institut Mémoires de l'édition contemporaine (Caen).
Irish National Arhives (Dublin).
Kislak Center, University of Pennsylvania (Philadelphia, PA).
Library of Congress (Washington, D.C.).
Lilly Library, Indiana University (Bloomington, IN).
Mass Observation Archive, University of Sussex (Brighton).
McFarlin Library, Department of Special Collections and University Archives, University of Tulsa (Tulsa, OK).
The Military Archives (Dublin).
National Archives (College Park, MD, and Washington D.C.).
National Archives of Romania (Bucharest).
The National Archives, United Kingdom (Richmond).
Norwegian National Archives (Oslo).
Princeton University Library, Department of Special Collections, Manuscript Division (Princeton, NJ).
Seeley G. Mudd Manuscript Library, Princeton University (Princeton, NJ).
Swarthmore College Archives (Swarthmore, PA).
Swarthmore College Peace Collection (Swarthmore, PA).
University Archives, University of Ulster (Coleraine, Northern Ireland).

Select Bibliography

Adorno, T. W. *Current of Music: Elements of a Radio Theory*. Ed. Robert Hullot-Kentor. Cambridge: Polity Press, 2009.

Aglan, Alya, and Emmanuelle Loyer. "Épuration, histoire d'un mot." In *Une poignée de misérables: L'épuration de la société française après la Seconde Guerre mondiale*. Ed. Marc Olivier Baruch. Paris: Fayard, 2003. 19–34.

Alleman, Michael J. "A Pound of Flesh: Ezra Pound at St. Elizabeths." Unpublished PhD dissertation, University of Dallas, 2007.

Alliott, David, ed. *L'affaire Louis-Ferdinand Céline: Les archives de l'ambassade de France à Copenhague, 1945–1951*. Paris: Éditions Horay, 2007.

Alliott, David, and François Marchetti. *Céline au Danemark, 1945–1951*. Monaco: Éditions de Rocher, 2008.

Ancel, Jean. *The History of the Holocaust in Romania*. Trans. Yaffah Murciano. Ed. Leon Volovici. Lincoln: University of Nebraska Press, 2011.

Andenæs, Johannes. *Det vanskelige oppgjøret: Rettsoppgjøret etter okkupasjonen*. 3rd ed. Oslo: Aschehoug, 1998.

Andreescu, Andreea, Luciana Nastasă, and Andrea Varga, eds. *Minorități Ethnoculturale mărturii documentare: Evreii din România (1945–1965)*. Cluj: Centrul de Resurse pentru Diversitate Etnoculturală, 2003.

Antonowicz, Gilles. *Jacques Isorni: L'avocat de tous les combats*. Paris: Éditions France-Empire, 2007.

Ardeleanu, Ion, Vasile Arimia, and Mircea Mușat, eds. *23 August 44: Documente, vol. IV: 1944–1945*. Bucharest: Editura Stiințifică și Enciclopedică, 1984.

Arjomand, Minou. *Staged: Show Trials, Political Theater, and the Aesthetics of Judgment*. New York: Columbia University Press, 2018.

Arnold, Thurman. *Fair Fights and Foul: A Dissenting Lawyer's Life*. New York: Harcourt, Brace & World, 1965.

Aron, Raymond. *Chroniques de guerre: La France libre, 1940–1945*. Ed. Christian Bachelier. Paris: Gallimard, 1990.

Aron, Robert. *Histoire de l'épuration*. Vol. 2: *Le monde de la presse, des arts, des lettres, 1944–1953*. Paris: Fayard, 1976.

The Arraignment, Tryal & Condemnation of Algernon Sydney, Esq. for High-Treason. London, 1683.

Aymé, Marcel. *La tête des autres*. Paris: Bernard Grasset, 1952.

Barnes, James Strachey. *A British Fascist in the Second World War: The Italian War Diary of James Strachey Barnes, 1943–45*. Ed. Claudia Baldoli and Brendan Fleming. London: Bloomsbury, 2014.

Barnhisel, Greg. *James Laughlin, New Directions, and the Remaking of Ezra Pound*. Amherst: University of Massachusetts Press, 2005.

Barrell, John. *Imagining the King's Death: Figurative Treason, Fantasies of Regicide, 1793–1796*. Oxford: Oxford University Press, 2000.

Barrett, William. "A Prize for Ezra Pound." *Partisan Review* 16.4 (April 1949): 344–7.

Barry, John Vincent. "Treason, Passports and the Ideal of Fair Trial." *Res Judicatae* 7.3 (1955): 276–303.

Barthes, Roland. *Image—Music—Text*. Trans. Stephen Heath. London: Fontana Press, 1977 [1968].

Baruch, Marc Olivier. "Une histoire sociale de l'épuration en France." In *Une poignée de misérables: L'épuration de la société française après la Seconde Guerre mondiale*. Ed. Marc Olivier Baruch. Paris: Fayard, 2003. 7–15.

Beauvoir, Simone de. *Philosophical Writings*. Ed. Margaret A. Simons. Urbana: University of Illinois Press, 2004.
Becker, Howard S. *Art Worlds*. 25th anniversary ed. Berkeley: University of California Press, 2008.
Behan, Brendan. *Borstal Boy*. London: Arrow Books, 1990.
Belgion, Montgomery. *Victors' Justice: A Letter Intended to Have Been Sent to a Friend Recently in Germany*. Chicago: Regnery, 1949.
Bellamy, John. *The Tudor Law of Treason: An Introduction*. London: Routledge and Kegan Paul, 1979.
Bellew, Henry. "Censorship, Law, and Conscience." *The Bell* 3.2 (November 1942): 140–8.
Ben-Yehuda, Nachman. *Betrayal and Treason: Violations of Trust and Loyalty*. Boulder: Westview, 2001.
Béraud, Henri. *Quinze jours avec la mort: La chasse au lampiste*. Roanne: Éditions Horvath, 1987 [1952].
Berggrav, Eiving. "Folkedommen over NS Menneskelig og moralsk: Hva vil være rett av oss?" *Kirke og Kultur* 50 (1945): 6–44.
Bergmeier, Horst J. P., and Rainer E. Lotz. *Hitler's Airwaves: The Inside Story of Radio Broadcasting and Propaganda Swing*. New Haven: Yale University Press, 1997.
Berry, Burton Y. *Romanian Diaries, 1944–1947*. Ed. Cornelia Bodea. Iaşi: The Center for Romanian Studies, 2000.
Betea, Lavinia. *Lucreţiu Pătrăşcanu: Moartea unui lider comunist*. 4th ed. Bucharest: Curtea Veche, 2018.
Betz, Maurice. *Dialogue des prisonniers 1940*. Paris: Editions Émile-Paul Frères, 1940.
Bew, Paul. *Churchill and Ireland*. Oxford: Oxford University Press, 2016.
Biddle, Francis. *In Brief Authority*. Garden City, NY: Doubleday, 1962.
Bilger, Philippe. *Vingt minutes pour la mort: Robert Brasillach: le procès expédié*. Paris: Éditions du Rocher, 2010.
Birkeland, Bjarte. "Forfattarmiljø og nazisme i trettiåra." In *Nazismen og norsk litteratur*. Ed. Bjarte Birkeland and Stein Ugelvik Larsen. Bergen: Universitetsforlaget, 1975. 21–31.
Blackstone, William. *Commentaries on the Laws of England in Four Books*. 2 vols. Philadelphia: J. B. Lippincott, 1893 [1753].
Bodet, Gerald P. "Sir Edward Coke's Third Institutes: A Primer for Treason Defendants." *The University of Toronto Law Journal* 20.4 (Autumn 1970): 469–77.
Booth, Marcella [Spann]. "Through the Smoke Hole: Ezra Pound's Last Year at St. Elizabeths." *Paideuma* 3 (Winter 1974): 329–34.
Borchard, Edwin. *The Diplomatic Protection of Citizens Abroad, or the Law of International Claims*. New York: Banks Law, 1916.
Bosworth, R. J. B. *Mussolini's Italy: Life Under the Dictatorship, 1915–1945*. New York: Penguin, 2006.
Bottoni, Stefano. "Reassessing the Communist Takeover in Romania: Violence, Institutional Continuity, and Ethnic Conflict Management." *East European Politics and Societies and Cultures* 24.1 (2010): 59–89.
Boulouque, Sylvain, and Pascal Girard. "Introduction." In *Traîtres et trahisons: Guerres, imaginaires sociaux et constructions politiques*. Ed. Sylvain Boulouque and Pascal Girard. Paris: Seli Arslan, 2007. 11–24.
Boveri, Margret. *Treason in the Twentieth Century*. Trans. Jonathan Steinberg. London: Macdonald, 1961.
Bowen, Elizabeth. *"Notes on Eire": Espionage Reports to Winston Churchill, 1940–2*. Cork: Aubane Historical Society, 1999.
Bowen, Elizabeth. *The Heat of the Day*. London: Vintage, 1998 [1948].

Bowen, Elizabeth, Graham Greene, and V. S. Pritchett. *Why Do I Write? An Exchange of Views Between Elizabeth Bowen, Graham Greene, and V. S. Pritchett.* London: Percival Marshall, 1948.

Brinchmann, Alex, and Sigurd Evensmo. *Norske forfattere in krig og fred.* Oslo: Gyldendal, 1968.

Brophy, John. *Britain Needs Books.* London: National Book Council, 1941.

Brucan, Silviu. *The Wasted Generation: Memoirs of the Romanian Journey from Capitalism to Socialism and Back.* Boulder: Westview Press, 1993.

Brumo, John, and Sissel Furuseth. *Norsk litterær modernism.* Bergen: Fagbokforlaget, 2005.

Bulloch, John. *Akin to Treason.* London: Arthur Barker, 1966.

Bunting, Madeleine. *The Model Occupation: The Channel Islands Under German Rule, 1940–1945.* New York: Harper Collins, 1995.

Burgess, Glenn. *George Orwell's Perverse Humanity: Socialism and Free Speech.* London: Bloomsbury Academic, 2023.

Burgwyn, H. James. *Mussolini and the Salò Republic, 1943–1945: The Failure of a Puppet Regime.* London: Palgrave Macmillan, 2018.

Buruma, Ian. *Year Zero: A History of 1945.* New York: Atlantic Books, 2013.

Cantril, Hadley, and Gordon W. Allport. *The Psychology of Radio.* New York: Harper & Brothers, 1935.

Carlson, John Roy. *Under Cover: My Four Years in the Nazi Underworld of America.* New York: E. P. Dutton, 1943.

Carlston, Erin. *Double Agents: Espionage, Literature, and Liminal Citizens.* New York: Columbia University Press, 2013.

Carpenter, Humphrey. *A Serious Character: The Life of Ezra Pound.* London: Faber and Faber, 1988.

Carr, E. H. *Nationalism and After.* New York: Macmillan, 1945.

Casanova, Pascale. *The World Republic of Letters.* Trans. M. B. Debevoise. Cambridge: Harvard University Press, 2004 [1999].

Catani, Damian. *Louis-Ferdinand Céline: Journeys to the Extreme.* London: Reaktion Books, 2021.

Cavarocchi, Francesca. *Avanguardie dello spirit: Il fascismo e la propaganda culturale all'estero.* Rome: Carocci, 2010.

Céline, Louis-Ferdinand. *Bagatelles pour un massacre.* Paris: Denoël, 1937.

Céline, Louis-Ferdinand. *Les beaux draps.* Paris: Nouvelles Éditions Françaises, 1941.

Céline, Louis-Ferdinand. *Lettres à son avocat: 118 lettres inédites à Maître Albert Naud.* Ed. Frédéric Monnier. Paris: La Flute de Pan, 1984.

Céline, Louis-Ferdinand. *Lettres de prison à Lucette Destouches et à Maître Mikkelsen, 1945–1947.* Ed. François Gibault. Paris: Gallimard, 1998.

Céline, Louis-Ferdinand. *Lettres.* Ed. Henri Godard and Jean-Paul Louis. Paris: Gallimard, 2009.

Cerf, Bennett. *At Random: The Reminiscences of Bennett Cerf.* New York: Random House, 1977.

Chadwick, Kay. "Our Enemy's Enemy: Selling Britain to Occupied France on the BBC French Service." *Media History* 21.4 (2015): 426–42.

Chapin, Bradley. *The American Law of Treason: Revolutionary and Early National Origins.* Seattle: University of Washington Press, 1964.

Cointet, Jean-Paul. *Expier Vichy: L'épuration en France (1943–1958).* Paris: Perrin, 2008.

Coke, Edward. *Institutes of the Laws of England,* part III: *Concerning High Treason and Other Pleases of the Crown, and Criminal Causes.* London: Brooke, 1797.

Cole, Robert. *Propaganda, Censorship and Irish Neutrality in the Second World War.* Edinburgh: Edinburgh University Press, 2006.

Conan, Éric, and Henry Rousso. *Vichy, un passé qui ne passe pas.* Paris: Fayard, 1994.

Cone, Michèle. *Artists Under Vichy: A Case of Prejudice and Persecution.* Princeton: Princeton University Press, 1992.

Constantinescu-Iaşi, Petre. "Sarcinile Guvernului de largă concentrare democratică Dr. Petru Groza." In *Democratizarea Armatei*. Bucharest: Ministerul de Război, 1945. 54–70.

Coposu, Corneliu. *Mărturisiri*. Bucharest: Humanitas, 1996.

Corell, Synne. "The Solidarity of a National Narrative: The German Occupation in Norwegian History Culture." In *Nordic Narratives of the Second World War: National Historiographies Revisited*. Ed. Henrik Stenius, Mirja Österberg, and Johan Östling. Lund: Nordic Academic Press, 2011. 101–26.

Cornell, Julien. *Conscience and the State: Legal and Administrative Problems of Conscientious Objectors, 1943–1944*. New York: John Day, 1944.

Cornell, Julien. *The Conscientious Objector and the Law*. New York: John Day, 1943.

Cornell, Julien. *Lexcetera*. Central Valley, NY: n.p., 1971.

Cornell, Julien. *New World Primer*. New York: New Directions, 1947.

Cornell, Julien. *The Trial of Ezra Pound*. New York: John Day, 1966.

Corrigan, Robert. "Literature and Politics: The Case of Ezra Pound Reconsidered." *Prospects* 2 (1976): 463–82.

Corwin, Edward S. *Total War and the Constitution*. New York: Alfred A. Knopf, 1947.

Cowan, Helen I. "France: Wage Trends and Wage Policies, 1938–1947." *Monthly Labor Review* 65.2 (August 1947): 149–57.

Coyle, Michae, and Roxana Preda. *Ezra Pound and the Career of Modern Criticism: Professional Attention*. Rochester: Camden House, 2018.

Crăcană, Iulia. *Dreptul în slujba puterii: justiția în regimul comunist din România, 1944–1958*. Bucharest: Institutul Național pentru Studiul Totalitarismului, 2015.

Crane, Paul T. "Did the Court Kill the Treason Charge: Reassessing *Cramer v. United States* and Its Significance." *Florida State University Law Review* 36 (2009): 635–96.

Crémieux-Brilhac, Jean-Louis. "Avant la Libération: La politique de la Justice à Alger et le procès Pucheu (1943–1944)." In *La justice de l'épuration: À la fin de la Seconde Guerre mondiale*. Ed. Pierre Truche and Denis Salas. Paris: La Documentation française, 2008. 27–34.

Current, Richard Nelson. "Introduction." In *Knut Hamsun Remembers America: Essays and Stories, 1885–1949*. Ed. and trans. Richard Nelson Current. Columbia: University of Missouri Press, 2003. 1–13.

Dahl, Hans Fredrik. *Quisling: A Study in Treachery*. Trans. Anne-Marie Stanton-Ife. Cambridge: Cambridge University Press, 1999.

Darnton, Robert. *Censors at Work: How States Shaped Literature*. New York: Norton, 2014.

Deák, István. *Europe on Trial: The Story of Collaboration, Resistance, and Retribution During World War II*. Boulder: Westview Press, 2015.

Déak, István. "Introduction." In *The Politics of Retribution in Europe: World War II and Its Aftermath*. Ed. István Déak, Jan T. Gross, and Tony Judt. Princeton: Princeton University Press, 2000. 3–14.

De Gaulle, Charles. *Discours et Messages*. 5 vols. Paris: Plon, 1970.

De Gaulle, Charles. *Mémoires de guerre*. Paris: Plon, 1999.

Deletant, Dennis. *Communist Terror in Romania: Gheorghiu-Dej and the Police State, 1948–1965*. New York: St. Martin's Press, 1999.

Deletant, Dennis. *Hitler's Forgotten Ally: Ion Antonescu and His Regime, Romania 1940–44*. New York: Palgrave Macmillan, 2006.

Deletant, Dennis. *Romania Under Communist Rule*. Iaşi: The Center for Romanian Studies, 1999.

Department of State. *Evidence of Violations of Human Rights Provisions of the Treaties of Peace by Rumania, Bulgaria, and Hungary*. Vol. 1: *Violations by the Rumanian Government Freedoms of Expression and of Press and Publication*. Washington, D.C.: GPO, 1951.

Department of State. *Germany 1947–1949: The Story in Documents*. Washington, D.C.: GPO, 1950.

Dingstad, Ståle. *Knut Hamsun og det norske Holocaust*. Oslo: Dreyers, 2021.
Dinsman, Melissa. *Modernism at the Microphone: Radio, Propaganda, and Literary Aesthetics During World War II*. London: Bloomsbury Academic, 2015.
Diplock, Kenneth. "Passports and Protection in International Law." *Transactions for the Year* 32 (1946): 42–59.
Doherty, M. A. *Nazi Wireless Propaganda: Lord Haw-Haw and British Public Opinion in the Second World War*. Edinburgh: Edinburgh University Press, 2000.
Domenico, Roy Palmer. *Italian Fascists on Trial, 1943–1948*. Chapel Hill: University of North Carolina Press, 1991.
Donaldson, Frances. *P. G. Wodehouse: A Biography*. London: Weidenfeld and Nicolson, 1982.
Doob, Leonard W. "Introduction." In *"Ezra Pound Speaking": Radio Speeches of World War II*. Ed. Leonard W. Doob. Westport, CT: Greenwood Press, 1978. xi–xv.
Dudziak, Mary L. *War Time: An Idea, Its History, Its Consequences*. New York: Oxford University Press, 2012.
Edwards, John Carver. *Berlin Calling: American Broadcasters in Service to the Third Reich*. New York: Praeger, 1991.
Elborn, Geoffrey. *Francis Stuart: A Life*. Dublin: Raven Arts, 1990.
Éluard, Paul. *Au rendez-vouz allemand*. Paris: Éditions de Minuit, 2012.
Emberland, Terje, and Matthew Kott. *Himmlers Norge: nordmenn i det storgermaske prosjekt*. Oslo: Aschehoug, 2012.
Evans, Bryce. *Ireland During the Second World War: Farewell to Plato's Cave*. Manchester: Manchester University Press, 2014.
Evans, Frederic. "The Re-Education of Germany." *Political Quarterly* 16.1 (January-March 1945): 21–30.
Feldman, Matthew. *Ezra Pound's Fascist Propaganda, 1933–1945*. London: Palgrave Macmillan, 2013.
Felman, Shoshana. *The Juridical Unconscious: Trials and Traumas in the Twentieth Century*. Cambridge: Harvard University Press, 2002.
Ferguson, Robert. *Enigma: The Life of Knut Hamsun*. London: Hutchinson, 1987.
Filreis, Alan. *Counter-Revolution of the Word: The Conservative Attack on Modern Poetry, 1945–1960*. Chapel Hill: Univeristy of North Carolina Press, 2008.
Fisk, Robert. *In Time of War: Ireland, Ulster, and the Price of Neutrality, 1939–45*. London: André Deutsch, 1983.
Flannery, Harry W. *Assignment to Berlin*. London: Michael Joseph, 1942.
Fletcher, George P. *Loyalty: An Essay on the Morality of Relationships*. New York: Oxford University Press, 1993.
Flournoy, Jr., Richard W. "The Proposed Pan American Convention for Preventing Dual Nationality, Drafted at Lima by the American Institute of International Law." *Proceedings of the American Society of International Law at Its Annual Meeting (1921–1969)* 19 (23–25 April 1925): 69–94.
Focşeneanu, Eleodor. *Istoria Constituţională a României (1859-2003)*. Ed. Anca Focşeneanu. Bucharest: Eikon, 2018.
Fouché, Pascal. *L'Édition française sous l'occupation, 1940–1944*. Paris: Bibliothèque de Littérature française contemporaine de l'Université Paris 7, 1987.
Friedrich, Carl J. *The Pathology of Politics: Violence, Betrayal, Corruption, Secrecy, and Propaganda*. New York: Harper & Row, 1972.
Frunză, Victor. *Istoria stalinismului în România*. Bucharest: Humanitas, 1990.
Gallagher, Tom. *Modern Romania: The End of Communism, the Failure of Democratic Reform, and the Theft of a Nation*. New York: New York University Press, 2005.

Galtier-Broissière, Jean. *Mon journal depuis la libération*. Paris: La Jeune Parque, 1945.
Gandhi, Leela, and Deborah L. Nelson. "Editor's Introduction." *Critical Inquiry* 40.4 (Summer 2014): 285–97.
Gary, Brett. *The Nervous Liberals: Propaganda Anxieties from World War I to the Cold War*. New York: Columbia University Press, 1999.
Giæver, Øyvind. "The Psychiatry of Quislingism: Norwegian Psychiatric Research on the Collaborators of World War II." *Science in Context* 17.3 (2004): 267–92.
Girard, Pascal. "La cinquième colonne en France, 1944–1946." In *Traîtres et trahisons: Guerres, imaginaires sociaux et constructions politiques*. Ed. Sylvain Boulouque and Pascal Girard. Paris: Seli Arslan, 2007. 65–89.
Girvin, Brian. *The Emergency: Ireland 1939–45*. London: Macmillan, 2006.
Gollancz, Victor. *Our Threatened Values*. London: Victor Gollancz, 1946.
Goyet, Bruno, and Philippe Olivera. "Les mondes intellectuels dans la tourmente des conflits." In *La vie intellectuelle en France*. Ed. Christophe Charle and Laurent Jeanpierre. Vol. 2: *De 1914 à nos jours*. Paris: Seuil, 2016. 19–41.
Green, Henry. *Loving Living Party Going*. Harmondsworth: Penguin, 1993.
Greene, Graham. *A Life in Letters*. Ed. Richard Greene. London: Abacus, 2007.
Grieg, Harald. *En forleggers erindringer: Ny, øket utgave*. Oslo: Gyldendal, 1971.
Grimnes, Ole Kristian. *Norway in the Second World War: Politics, Society and Conflict*. Trans. Frank Stewart. London: Bloomsbury Academic, 2022.
Guérin, Jeanyves. *Les listes noirs de 1944: Pour une histoire littéraire de l'épuration*. Paris: Presses Sorbonne Nouvelle, 2016.
Hackaworth, Green Haywood. *Digest of International Law*. Vol. 3. Washington, D.C.: GPO, 1942.
Hall, Jr., Robert A. "The Persecution of P. G. Wodehouse." *Institute for Historical Review* 7.3 (Fall 1986): 345–51.
Hambro, C. J. *I Saw It Happen in Norway*. New York: Appleton-Century, 1940.
Hamilton, Hugo. "Understanding Francis Stuart." *Writing Ulster* 4 (1996): 69–76.
Hamsun, Knut. *Hamsuns polemiske skrifter*. Ed. Gunvald Hermundstad. Oslo: Gyldendal, 1998.
Hamsun, Knut. *Hunger*. Trans. Sverre Luyngstad. Harmdonsworth: Penguin, 1998.
Hamsun, Knut. *On Overgrown Paths*. Trans. Sverre Lyngstad. Copenhagen: Green Integer, 1999.
Harrison, Tom. "Who'll Win?" *Political Quarterly* 15.1 (January-March 1944): 21–32.
Hassing, Arne. *Church Resistance to Nazism in Norway, 1940–1945*. Seattle: University of Washington Press, 2014.
Hauge, Olav H. *Dagbok 1924–1994*. Vol. 1. Oslo: Norske Samlaget, 2000.
Hentea, Marius. "Hope for a New World Order: Postwar PEN and the Reconstruction of the Global Republic of Letters." *Comparative Literature* 77.4 (December 2025): 429–52.
Hentea, Marius. "Pound's *Four Pages*: 'Literary Camouflage' and Postwar Anonymous Propaganda." *PMLA* 137.3 (May 2022): 424–41.
Hetland, Ø., N. Karcher, and K. B. Simonsen. "Navigating Troubled Waters: Collaboration and Resistance in State Institutions in Nazi-Occupied Norway." *Scandinavian Journal of History* 46.1 (2021): 84–104.
Heymann, C. David. *Ezra Pound, The Last Rower: A Political Profile*. New York: Seaver Books, 1976.
Hillyer, Robert. *Collected Poems*. New York: Knopf, 1961.
Hillyer, Robert. *In Pursuit of Poetry*. New York: McGraw-Hill, 1960.
Hillyer, Robert. "Poetry's New Priesthood." *Saturday Review of Literature* 32.25 (June 18, 1949): 7–8.
Hillyer, Robert. "Treason's Strange Fruit: The Case of Ezra Pound and the Bollingen Award." *Saturday Review of Literature* 32.24 (June 11, 1949): 9–11.

Hobbes, Thomas. *Behemoth, or The Long Parliament*. Ed. Ferdinand Tönnies. Chicago: University of Chicago Press, 1990.

Hoel, Sigurd. *Meeting at the Milestone*. Trans. Sverre Lyngstad. Copenhagen: Green Integer, 2002 [1947].

Holman, Valerie. "Carefully Concealed Connections: The Ministry of Information and British Publishing, 1939–1946." *Book History* 8 (2005): 197–226.

Holmes, Colin. *Searching for Lord Haw-Haw: The Political Lives of William Joyce*. London: Routledge, 2016.

Hull, Mark M., and Vera Moynes. *Masquerade: Treason, the Holocaust, and an Irish Imposter*. Norman: University of Oklahoma Press, 2017.

Hurst, James Willard. *Law of Treason in the United States*. Westport: Greenwood, 1971.

Hurst, James Willard. "Treason in the United States: III. Under the Constitution." *Harvard Law Review* 58.6 (July 1945): 806–57.

Hyde, H. Montgomery, ed. *Famous Trials 9: Roger Casement*. Harmondsworth: Penguin, 1964.

Hynd, Alan. *Passport to Treason: The Inside Story of Spies in America*. New York: Robert M. McBridge, 1943.

Indomitus. *Nous sommes les rebelles*. Paris: Collection Défense de l'homme, 1945.

Ioanid, Radu. *The Sword of the Archangel: Fascist Ideology in Romania*. Trans. Peter Heinegg. Boulder: East European Monographs, 1990.

Isorni, Jacques. *Les cas de conscience de l'avocat*. Paris: Librairie Académique Perrin, 1965.

Isorni, Jacques. *Le procès de Robert Brasillach*. Paris: Flammarion, 1946.

Iversen, Gunnar. "From Trauma to Heroism: Cultural Memory and Remembrance in Norwegian Occupation Dramas, 1946–2009." *Journal of Scandinavian Cinema* 2.3 (2012): 237–48.

Jackson, Julian. *A Certain Idea of France: The Life of Charles De Gaulle*. London: Allen Lane, 2018.

Jähner, Harald. *Aftermath: Life in the Fallout of the Third Reich*. Trans. Shaun Whiteside. London: W.H. Allen, 2021.

Jasen, David A. *P. G. Wodehouse: A Portrait of a Master*. London: Garnstone Press, 1975.

Javadizadeh, Kamran. "The Institutionalization of the Postwar Poet." *Modernism/Modernity* 23.1 (January 2016): 113–39.

Jones, J. Mervyn. *British Nationality Law*. Rev. ed. Oxford: Clarendon Press, 1956.

Jouhandeau, Marcel. *Journal sous l'Occupation*. Paris: Gallimard, 1980.

Joyce, William. *Dicatorship*. London: BUF, 1933.

Joyce, William. *National Socialism Now*. London: The National Socialist League, 1937.

Joyce, William. *Twilight Over England*. London: Imperial War Museum, 1992 [1940].

Judt, Tony. *Postwar: A History of Europe Since 1945*. New York: Penguin, 2005.

Justis- og politidepartementet. *Om landssvikoppgjøret: Innstilling fra et utvalg nedsatt for å skaffe tilveie materiale til en innberetning fra Justisdepartementet til Stortinget*. 1962. At https://www.stortinget.no/no/Saker-og-publikasjoner/Stortingsforhandlinger/Lesevisning/?p=1962-63&paid=3&wid=b&psid=DIVL62&pgid=b_0009&vt=b&did=DIVL66&s=True. Last accessed: January 22, 2026.

Kalliney, Peter J. *The Aesthetic Cold War: Decolonization and Global Literature*. Princeton: Princeton University Press, 2022.

Kamuf, Peggy. *Signature Pieces: On the Institution of Authorship*. Ithaca: Cornell University Press, 1988.

Kaplan, Alice. *The Collaborator: The Trial and Execution of Robert Brasillach*. Chicago: University of Chicago Press, 2001.

Kaplan, Robert M. "Norwegian Psychiatry and the Trial of Vidkun Quisling." *Nordic Journal of Psychiatry* 66.3 (2012): 155–8.

Keane, Damien. *Ireland and the Problem of Information: Irish Writing, Radio, Late Modernist Communication*. University Park: Pennsylvania State University Press, 2014.

Keene, Judith. *Treason on the Airwaves: Three Allied Broadcasters on Axis Radio during World War II*. Lincoln: University of Nebraska Press, 2010 [2009].

Kenner, Hugh. "In the Caged Panther's Eyes." *Hudson Review* 1.4 (Winter 1949): 580–6.

Kiberd, Declan. *After Ireland: Writing the Nation from Beckett to the Present*. Cambridge: Harvard University Press, 2017.

Kiely, Kevin. *Francis Stuart: Artist and Outcast*. Dublin: Liffey Press, 2007.

Kierulf, Anine, and Cato Schiøtz. *Høyesterett og Knut Hamsun: En nærmere fremstilling of vurdering av erstatningssaken mot Knut Hamsun*. Oslo: Gyldendal, 2004.

Kimpel, Ben D., and T. C. Duncan Eaves. "More on Pound's Prison Experience." *American Literature* 53.3 (November 1981): 469–76.

Kirchheimer, Otto. *Political Justice: The Use of Legal Procedure for Political Ends*. Princeton: Princeton University Press, 1961.

Kittang, Atle. "Knut Hamsen og nazismen." In *Nazismen og norsk litteratur*. Rev. ed. Ed. Bjarte Birkeland and Stein Ugelvik Larsen. Oslo: Universitetsforlaget, 1995. 254–67.

Kochanski, Halik. *Resistance: The Underground War Against Hitler, 1939–1945*. New York: Liveright, 2022.

Koessler, Maximilian. "Subject, Citizen, National, and Permanent Allegiance." *Yale Law Journal* 56 (1946): 58–76.

Koestler, Arthur. *Darkness at Noon*. Trans. Daphne Hardy. London: Jonathan Cape, 1940.

Kolloen, Ingar Sletten. *Hamsun: Erobreren*. Oslo: Gyldendal, 2004.

Kristiansen, Tom. "The Norwegian War Experience: Occupied and Allied." In *Nordic War Stories: World War II as History, Fiction, Media, and Memory*. Ed. Marianne Stecher-Hansen. Oxford: Berghahn, 2021. 49–64.

Krouk, Dean. *Fascism and Modernist Literature in Norway*. Seattle: University of Washington Press, 2017.

Krouk, Dean. "Prophet of Regeneration: On Two Fascist Readings of Knut Hamsun." *Nordlit* 25 (2009): 29–40.

Kushner, Barak. "Treacherous Allies: The Cold War in East Asia and American Postwar Anxiety." *Journal of Contemporary History* 45.4 (2010): 812–43.

Lane, Anthony. "Beyond a Joke." *The New Yorker*, April 19, 2004. 138–49.

Langeland, O. H. *Dømmer ikke*. Oslo: Heim and Samfund, 1948.

Langfeldt, Gabriel, and Ørnulv Ødegård. *Den rettspsykiatriske erklæring om Knut Hamsun*. Oslo: Gyldendal, 1978.

Lauterpacht, H. "Allegiance, Diplomatic Protection and Criminal Jurisdiction Over Aliens." *The Cambridge Law Journal* 9.3 (1947): 330–48.

Law Reports of Trials of War Criminals, Selected and Prepared by the United Nations War Crimes Commission. Vol. 2: *The Belsen Trial*. London: HMSO, 1947.

Lawrence, W. H. "*Rex v. Lord Haw-Haw*." *Hastings Law Journal* 2 (1951): 73–9.

Lean, E. Tangye. *Voices in the Darkness: The Story of the European Radio War*. London: Secker and Warburg, 1943.

Lee, Youngjae. "Punishing Disloyalty? Treason, Espionage, and the Transgression of Political Boundaries." *Law and Philosophy* 31 (2012): 299–342.

Leek, J. H. "Treason and the Constitution." *The Journal of Politics* 13.4 (November 1951): 604–22.

Lehoulier, Jacques. "Chronique des salaires: Le mouvement des salaires en France depuis 1938." *Journal de la société statistique de Paris* 86 (1945): 172–6.

Leick, Karen. "Ezra Pound v. *The Saturday Review of Literature*." *Journal of Modern Literature* 25.2 (Winter 2001–2): 19–37.

Lisi, Leonard F. *Marginal Modernity: The Aesthetics of Dependency from Kierkegaard to Joyce.* New York: Fordham University Press, 2013.

Little, Marie-Noëlle. *The Knight and the Troubadour: Dag Hammarskjöld and Ezra Pound.* Uppsala: Dag Hammarskjöld Foundation, 2011.

Loiseaux, Gérard. *La littérature de la défaite et de la collaboration.* Paris: Fayard, 1995.

Lottmann, Herbert. *The People's Anger: Justice and Revenge in Post-Liberation France.* London: Hutchinson, 1986.

Lowe, Keith. *Savage Continent: Europe in the Aftermath of World War II.* New York: Viking Press, 2012.

Löwenthal, Leo. "Knut Hamsun." In *The Essential Frankfurt School Reader*. Ed. Andrew Arato and Eike Gebhardt. New York: Continuum, 1998. 319–45.

Lunde, Arne. "Politics, Aesthetics, and Afterlife in *På gjengrodde stier:* Retracing Knut Hamsun's 'Overgrown Paths' Toward Nazism." *Scandinavica* 47.2 (2008): 175–90.

Lundtofte, Henrik. "Purges, Patriotism, and Political Violence: The Danish Case 1944–1945." In *Collective Identities and Post-War Violence in Europe, 1944–1948: Reshaping the Nation.* Ed. Ota Konrád, Boris Barth, and Jaromir Mrňka. Cham: Palgrave Macmillan, 2022. 129–64.

Lyngstad, Sverre. *Knut Hamsun, Novelist: A Critical Reassessment.* Bern: Peter Lang, 2005.

Lyons, F. S. L. *Ireland Since the Famine.* London: Weidenfeld and Nicolson, 1971.

Macdonald, Dwight. "Homage to Twelve Judges." *Politics* 6.1 (Winter 1949): 1–2.

MacNaughton, Bill. "Pound, A Brief Memoir: 'Chi Lavora, Ora.'" *Paideuma* 3 (Winter 1974): 319–24.

MacNaughton, Bill. "The Secret History of St. Elizabeths." *Paideuma* 30.1/2 (Spring/Fall 2001): 69–96.

MacNeice, Louis. *Autumn Journal.* London: Faber and Faber, 2012 [1939].

MacNeice, Louis. *Collected Poems of Louis MacNeice.* London: Faber and Faber, 1966.

Mannin, Ethel. *Late Have I Loved Thee.* London: Jarrolds, 1948.

Manning, Roger B. "The Origins of the Doctrine of Sedition." *Albion* 12.2 (Summer 1980): 99–121.

Markham, Reuben H. *Rumania Under the Soviet Yoke.* Boston: Meador, 1949.

Marsh, Alec. *John Kasper and Ezra Pound: Saving the Republic.* London: Blooomsbury Academic, 2015.

Martland, Peter. *Lord Haw Haw: The English Voice of Nazi Germany.* Richmond: National Archives, 2003.

Mason, Henry. *The Purge of Dutch Quislings: Emergency Justice in the Netherlands.* The Hague: Martinus Nijhoff, 1952.

Mass-Observation. *War Begins at Home.* London: Chatto and Windus, 1940.

Mauriac, François. *Lettres d'une vie (1904–1969).* Paris: Grasset, 1981.

May, Larry. *After War Ends: A Philosophical Perspective.* Cambridge: Cambridge University Press, 2012.

Mazet, Éric, and Pierre Pécastaing. *Images d'exil: Louis-Ferdinand Céline 1945–1951 (Copenhague-Korsor).* Tusson: Du Lérot, 2004.

McCartney, Anne. *Francis Stuart Face to Face: A Critical Study.* Belfast: Institute of Irish Studies, 2000.

McCrum, Robert. *Wodehouse: A Life.* London: Penguin, 2005 [2004].

Meacham, Harry M. *The Caged Panther: Ezra Pound at Saint Elizabeths.* New York: Twayne, 1967.

Meerloo, A. M. *Aftermath of Peace: Psychological Essays.* New York: International Universities Press, 1946.

Meierhenrich, Jens, and Devin O. Pendas. "'The Justice of My Cause Is Clear, but There's Politics to Fear': Political Trials in Theory and History." In *Political Trials in Theory and History.*

Ed. Jens Meierhenrich and Devin O. Pendas. Cambridge: Cambridge University Press, 2016. 1–64.

Mikkelson, Thorvald. *Mit Liv I Kravlegården*. Copenhagen: n.p., 1960.

Moi, Toril. *Henrik Ibsen and the Birth of Modernism: Art, Theater, Philosophy*. Oxford: Oxford University Press, 2006.

Monteleone, Franco. *La Radio italiana nel periodo fascista: Studio e documenti: 1922–1945*. Venice: Marsilio, 1976.

Montherlant, Henry De. *Le Solstice de juin*. Paris: Grasset, 1941.

Montherlant, Henry De. *Mémoire*. Paris: Gallimard, 1976.

Monticone, Alberto. *Il Fascismo al Microfono: Radio e politica in Italia (1924–1945)*. Roma: Edizioni Studium, 1978.

Moody, A. David. *Ezra Pound: Poet: A Portrait of the Man and His Work*. Vol. 3: *The Tragic Years, 1939–1972*. Oxford: Oxford University Press, 2015.

Moore, Nicole. "Introduction." In *Censorship and the Limits of the Literary: A Global View*. Ed. Nicole Moore. London: Bloomsbury Academic, 2015. 1–10.

Morgan, Charles. "The Artist in the Community." *The Yale Review* 35.4 (January 1946): 594–613.

Morgan, Philip. *Hitler's Collaborators: Choosing Between Bad and Worse in Nazi-Occupied Western Europe*. Oxford: Oxford University Press, 2018.

Muggeridge, Malcolm. *Like It Was: The Diaries of Malcolm Muggeridge*. Ed. John Bright-Holmes. London: Collins, 1981.

Mullins, Eustace. *This Difficult Individual, Ezra Pound*. New York: Fleet, 1961.

Muraru, Andrei. "Legislation and the War Criminals' Trial in Romania." In *New Europe College—Stefan Odobleja Program, Yearbook 2009–2010*. Bucharest: NEC, 2010. 111–76.

Natterstad, Jerry H. *Francis Stuart*. Lewisburg, PA: Bucknell University Press, 1974.

Natterstad, Jerry H. "Interview with Francis Stuart." *The Journal of Irish Literature* 5.1 (January 1976): 16–31.

Neagoe, George. *Mizantropul optimist: G. Călinescu și (de)stalinizarea României*. Bucharest: Cartea Românească, 2015.

Novick, Peter. *The Resistance Versus Vichy: The Purge of Collaborators in Liberated France*. New York: Columbia University Press, 1968.

Ó Drisceoil, Donal. *Censorship in Ireland, 1939–1945: Neutrality, Politics and Society*. Cork: Cork University Press, 1996.

O'Brien, Maire Cruise. *The Same Age as the State*. Madison: University of Wisconsin Press, 2004.

O'Connor, William Van, and Edward Stone, eds. *A Casebook on Ezra Pound*. New York: Thomas Y. Crowell, 1959.

O'Donoghue, David. *Hitler's Irish Voices: The Story of German Radio's Wartime Irish Service*. Belfast: Beyond the Pale, 1998.

O'Halpin, Eunan. *Defending Ireland: The Irish State and Its Enemies Since 1922*. Oxford: Oxford University Press, 1999.

O'Halpin, Eunan. *Spying on Ireland: British Intelligence and Irish Neutrality During the Second World War*. Oxford: Oxford University Press, 2008.

Orwell, George. *Collected Essays, Journalism and Letters of George Orwell*. Volume 2. Ed. Sonia Orwell and Ian Angus. New York: Harcourt, Brace, Jovanovich, 1971.

Orwell, George. *The Complete Works of George Orwell*. Vol. 17: *I Belong to the Left, 1945*. Ed. Peter Davison. London: Secker & Warburg, 1998.

Ory, Pascal. *Les collaborateurs, 1940–1945*. Paris: Éditions du Seuil, 1976.

O'Toole, Fintan. *Ship of Fools*. London: Public Affairs, 2010.

Otto, Thomas. *St. Elizabeths Hospital: A History*. Washington, D.C.: U.S. General Services Administration, 2013.

Overy, Richard. "Scandinavia in the Second World War." In *Hitler's Scandinavian Legacy: The Consequences of the German Invasion for the Scandinavian Countries, Then and Now*. Ed. John Gilmour and Jill Stephenson. London: Bloomsbury, 2013. 13–37.

Pandrea, Petre. *Memoriile Mandarinului Valah*. Bucharest: Editura Albatros, 2000.

Papa, Antonio. *Storia politica della radio in Italia, Dalla Guerra d'Etiopia al crollo del fascismo, 1935–1943*. Naples: Guida Editori, 1978.

Pătrăşcanu, Lucreţiu. "Legea criminalilor de razboiu şi legea epuraţiei aparatului de stat." In *Democratizarea Armatei*. Bucharest: Ministerul de Război, 1945. 100–11.

Pătrăşcanu, Lucreţiu. *Scrieri, articolege, cuvîntâri, 1944–1947*. Bucharest: Editura Politică, 1983.

Pătrăşcanu, Lucreţiu. *Spre o justiţie populară*. Bucharest: Editura Partidului Comunist Român, 1948.

Paul, Catherine E. *Fascist Directive: Ezra Pound and Italian Cultural Nationalism*. Clemson, SC: Clemson University Press, 2016.

Paulhan, Jean. *Choix de lettres*. Ed. Dominique Aury, Jean-Claude Zylberstein and Bernard Leuilliot. Vol. 2: *1937–1945, Traité des jours sombres*. Paris: Gallimard, 1992.

Paulhan, Jean. *De la paille et du grain*. Paris: Gallimard, 1948.

Paulhan, Jean. *Œuvres complètes*. Vol. 5: *La tache aveugle*. Paris: Cercle du Livre Précieux, 1970.

Paxton, Robert O. *The Anatomy of Fascism*. London: Allen Lane, 2004.

Pedersen, Helga. *Le Danemark a-t-il sauvé Céline? (1945–1951)*. Trans. François Marchetti. Paris: Plon, 1975.

Petitjean, Armand. *Combats préliminaires*. Paris: Gallimard, 1941.

Petrella, Luigi. *Staging the Fascist War: The Ministry of Popular Culture and Italian Propaganda on the Home Front, 1938–1943*. Oxford: Peter Lang, 2016.

Piggott, Francis. *Nationality, Including Naturalization and English Law on the High Seas and Beyond the Realm*. 2 vols. London: William Clowes and Sons, 1907.

Plender, Richard. *International Migration Law*. 2nd rev. ed. Dordrecht: Martinus Nijhoff, 1988.

Poirier, Agnès. *Left Bank: Art, Passion, and the Rebirth of Paris, 1940–1950*. New York: Henry Holt, 2018.

Potter, Rachel. "International PEN and the Republic of Literature." In *Cultural Organizations, Networks and Mediators in Contemporary Ibero-America*. Ed. Diana Roig-Sanz and Jaume Subirana. London: Routledge, 2020. 108–26.

Pound, Ezra. *ABC of Economics*. London: Faber and Faber, 1933.

Pound, Ezra. *"Ezra Pound Speaking": Radio Speeches of World War II*. Ed. Leonard W. Doob. Westport, CT: Greenwood Press, 1978.

Pound, Ezra. *Ezra Pound's Poetry and Prose: Contributions to Periodicals*. Ed. Lea Baecherl, A. Walton Litz, and James Longenbach. 11 vols. New York: Garland, 1991.

Pound, Ezra. *Jefferson and/or Mussolini: L'Idea Statale, Fascism as I Have Seen It*. London: Stanley Nott, 1935.

Pound, Ezra, and Dorothy Pound. *Letters in Captivity, 1945–1946*. Ed. Omar Pound and Robert Spoo. Oxford: Oxford University Press, 1999.

Pound, Ezra, and James Laughlin. *Ezra Pound and James Laughlin: Selected Letters*. Ed. David M. Gordon. New York: Norton, 1994.

Pound, Ezra, and William Borah. *The Correspondence of Ezra Pound and Senator William Borah*. Ed. Sarah C. Holmes. Urbana: University of Illinois Press, 2001.

Pritt, D. N. "The Trial of War Criminals." *Political Quarterly* 16.3 (July-September 1945): 195–204.

Le Procès de Charles Maurras. Paris: Albin Michel, 1946.

Procesul grupului de complotişti, spioni, şi sabotori: Textul complect al desbaterilor care au avut loc în faţa Tribunalului Militar din Bucureşti dela 27 Octombrie la 2 Noembrie 1948. Bucharest: Editura de Stat, 1949.

Procesul lui Ion Antonescu. Ed. Ioana Cracă. Bucharest: Editura Eminescu, 1995.
Prusin, Alexander V. "Traitors or War Criminals: Collaboration on Trial in Soviet Courts in the 1940s." In *Stalin's Soviet Justice: "Show" Trials, War Crimes Trials, and Nuremberg*. Ed. David M. Crowe. London: Bloomsbury Academic, 2019. 879–903.
Quartermaine, Luisa. *Mussolini's Last Republic: Propaganda and Politics in the Italian Social Republic (R.S.I.), 1943–45*. Exeter: Elm Bank, 2000.
Rachewiltz, Mary de. "Fragments of an Atmosphere." *Agenda* 17.3 (1979/80): 157–70.
Rădulescu, Ilie. *Pentru un imperialism românesc*. Bucharest: Editura ziarului Porunca Vremii, 1942.
Rafter, Kevin. *Taoisigh and the Arts*. Dublin: Martello, 2022.
Ragaru, Nadège. "The Prosecution of Anti-Jewish Crimes in Bulgaria: Fashioning a Master Narrative of the Second World War (1944–1945)." *East European Politics and Societies and Cultures* 33.4 (November 2019): 941–75.
Reale, Egidio. "The Passport Question." *Foreign Affairs* 9.3 (April 1931): 506–9.
Redman, Tim. *Ezra Pound and Italian Fascism*. Cambridge: Cambridge University Press, 1991.
Redman, Tim. "The Repatriation of Pound, 1939–1942: A View from the Archives." *Paideuma* 8.3 (Winter 1979): 447–57.
Rem, Tore. *Knut Hamsun och resan till Hitler*. Trans. Ulrika Junker Miranda. Stockholm: Atlantis, 2015.
Rem, Tore. "Out of the Ruins: Knut Hamsun's 'Idealism' and the Inheritance of World War I." *Journal of European Studies* 51.3–4 (2021): 262–72.
Richard, Gaël, ed. *"Toujours l'article 75 au cul!": Le procès de Céline, 1944–1951: Dossiers de la Cour de justice de la Seine et du Tribunal militaire de Paris*. Tusson: Du Lérot, 2011.
Riding, Alan. *And the Show Went On: Cultural Life in Nazi-Occupied Paris*. New York: Knopf, 2010.
Roberts, C. E. Bechhofer, ed. *The Trial of William Joyce*. London: Jarrolds, 1946.
Rose, Sonya O. *Which People's War? National Identity and Citizenship in Wartime Britain, 1939–1945*. Oxford: Oxford University Press, 2004.
Rotari, Ludmila. *Mişcarea subversivă din Basarabia în anii 1918–1924*. Bucharest: Editura Enciclopedică, 2004.
Roth, Andreas. "Francis Stuart's Broadcasts from Germany, 1942–4: Some New Evidence." *Irish Historical Studies* 32.127 (May 2001): 408–22.
Rus, Emil, ed. *Delictul de opinie: Procesul ziariştilor, 1945*. Bucharest: Instititul Naţional pentru Studiul Totalitarismului, 2012.
Saint-Germain, Philippe. *Article 75*. Paris: Bureau d'Études et de Publications Sociales, 1951.
Saiu, Liliana. *The Great Powers and Rumania, 1944–1946: A Study of the Early Cold War Era*. Boulder: East European Monographs, 1992.
Sansico, Virginie. "La cour de justice de Lyon, section du Rhône (septembre 1944–juillet 1949)." In *La justice de l'épuration: À la fin de la Seconde Guerre mondiale*. Ed. Pierre Truche and Denis Salas. Paris: La Documentation française, 2008. 45–57.
Sapiro, Gisèle. *La guerre des écrivains: 1940–1953*. Paris: Fayard, 1999.
Sartre, Jean-Paul. *Situations II*. Paris: Gallimard, 1948.
Schmitt, Carl. *The Concept of the Political*. Trans. George Schwab. Chicago: University of Chicago Press, 1996.
Sebastian, Mihail. *Jurnal 1935–1944*. Bucharest: Humanitas, 2016.
Seemann, Anika. *The Quislings: The Trials of Norwegian Wartime Collaborators, 1941–1964*. Cambridge: Cambridge University Press, 2024.
Selejean, Ana. *Trădarea intelectualilor / Reeducare şi prigoană*. Bucharest: Cartea Românească.
Shawcross, Hartley. "The State and the Law." *The Modern Law Review* 11.1 (January 1948): 1–8.

Shirer, William. *Berlin Diary: The Journal of a Foreign Correspondent, 1934–1941.* New York: Knopf, 1941.

Shulman, Holly Cowan. *The Voice of America: Propaganda and Democracy, 1941–1945.* Madison: University of Wisconsin Press, 1990.

Simonin, Anne. "A Distance: Céline et ses juges (1949–1951)." Colloque *Procès politiques: tremplin ou tribune pour l'opposition*, Université d'Orleans, November 11, 2021. At halshs-03658011.

Simonin, Anne. *Le déshonneur dans la République: Une histoire de l'indignité 1791–1958.* Paris: Bernard Grasset, 2008.

Smyllie, R. M. "Unnatural Neutral Eire." *Foreign Affairs* 24.2 (January 1946): 317–26.

Sollors, Werner. *The Temptation of Despair: Tales of the 1940s.* Cambridge: Harvard University Press, 2014.

Solomon, Petre. *Paul Celan: The Romanian Dimension.* Trans. Emanuela Tegla. Syracuse: Syracuse University Press, 2019.

Sorlie, Sigurd. *Soldkors eller hakekors: nordmenn i Waffen-SS 1941–1945.* Oslo: Dreyers Forlag, 2015.

Sproat, Iain. *Wodehouse at War.* London: Ticknor and Fields, 1981.

Steffen, Lisa. *Defining a British State: Treason and National Identity, 1608–1820.* Basingstoke: Palgrave Macmillan, 2001.

Stenogramele Şedinţelor conducerii P.C.R.: 23 septembrie 1944–26 martie 1945. Ed. Radu Ciuceanu, Corneliu Mihail Lungu, Florin Constantiniu, and Sever Catalan. Bucharest: Institutul Naţional pentru Studiul Totalitarismului, 2003.

Stenogramele Şedinţelor Consiliului de Miniştri: Guvernarea Dr. Petru Groza: Instaurarea regimului pro-comunist, vol. 1 (7 martie–27 iulie 1945). Ed. Marcel-Dumitru Ciucă. Piteşti: Editura Ordessos, 2014.

Stenogramele Şedinţelor Consiliului de Miniştri: Guvernarea Generalului Nicolae Rădescu (6 decembre 1944–28 februarie 1945). Ed. Marcel-Dumitru Ciucă. Bucharest: Saeculum, 2013.

Stewart, Victoria. *Literature and Justice in Mid-Century Britain.* Oxford: Oxford University Press, 2023.

Stone, Geoffrey R. *Perilous Times: Free Speech in Wartime.* New York: W.W. Norton, 2004.

Stonebridge, Lyndsey. *The Judicial Imagination: Writing After Nuremberg.* Edinburgh: Edinburgh University Press, 2011.

Stratigakos, Despina. *Hitler's Northern Utopia: Building the New Order in Occupied Norway.* Princeton: Princeton University Press, 2020.

Strauss, Leo. *Persecution and the Art of Writing.* Glencoe, IL: Free Press, 1952.

Stray, Sigurd. *Min klient Knut Hamsun.* Oslo: H. Aschehoug, 1979.

Stuart, Francis. *Black List, Section H.* Harmondsworth: Penguin, 1982 [1971].

Stuart, Francis. *Lecture on Nationality and Culture.* Dublin: Sinn Fein, 1924.

Stuart, Francis. *The Pillar of Cloud.* Dublin: New Island Books, 1994 [1948].

Stuart, Francis. *Redemption.* Dublin: New Island Books, 1994 [1949].

Stuart, Francis. *States of Mind: Selected Short Prose, 1936–1983.* Dublin: Raven Arts Press, 1984.

Stuart, Francis. *Things to Live For: Notes for an Autobiography.* London: Jonathan Cape, 1934.

Stuart, Francis. *The Wartime Broadcasts of Francis Stuart, 1942–1944.* Ed. Brendan Barrington. Dublin: Lilliput Press, 2000.

Swift, Daniel. *The Bughouse: The Poetry, Politics and Madness of Ezra Pound.* New York: Farrar, Straus and Giroux, 2017.

Tamm, Ditlev. *Retsopjøret efter besættelsen.* 2 vols. Copenhagen: Gyldendal, 1997.

Thérive, André. *Essai sur les trahisons.* Paris: Calmann-Lévy, 1951.

Thiranagama, Sharika, and Tobias Kelly. "Introduction: Specters of Treason." In *Traitors: Suspicion, Intimacy, and the Ethics of State-Building*. Ed. Sharika Thiranagama and Tobias Kelly. Philadelphia: University of Pennsylvania Press, 2010. 1–23.

Thomas, Edith. *Le Témoin compromise*. Paris: Éditions Viviane Hamy, 1995 [1952].

Torrey, E. Fuller. *The Roots of Treason: Ezra Pound and the Secrets of St. Elizabeths*. London: Sidgwick & Jackson, 1984.

Tzara, Tristan. *Œuvres complètes*. Ed. Henri Béhar. 6 volumes. Paris: Flammarion, 1975–1991.

Usborne, Richard. *Wodehouse at Work to the End*. London: Barrie and Jenkins, 1976.

Vaksberg, Arkady. *The Prosecutor and the Prey: Vyshinsky and the 1930s' Moscow Show Trials*. Trans. Jan Butler. London: Weidenfeld and Nicolson, 1990.

Vanino, Maurice. *L'affaire Céline: L'école d'un cadavre*. Paris: Editions Créator, 1952.

Vasanthakumar, Ashwini. "Treason, Expatriation and "So-Called" Americans: Recovering the Role of Allegiance in Citizenship." *The Georgetown Journal of Law and Public Policy* 12 (2014): 187–224.

Vatulescu, Cristina. *Police Aesthetics: Literature, Film, and the Secret Police in Soviet Times*. Stanford: Stanford University Press, 2010.

Vicol, Constantin. *Procesul lui Socrate: Studiu juridic și istoric*. Bucharest: Animnator, 1947.

Vosges, Bernard. *Défense de l'occident*. Paris: Les Sept Couleurs, 1957.

Vyshinsky, Andrei Y. *The Law of the Soviet State*. Trans. Hugh W. Babb. New York: Macmillan, 1948.

Waldeck, R. G. *Athene Palace*. Iași: Center for Romanian Studies, 1998.

Washburn, Patrick S. *A Question of Sedition: The Federal Government's Investigation of the Black Press During World War II*. Oxford: Oxford University Press, 1986.

Watts, Philip. *Allegories of the Purge: How Literature Responded to the Postwar Trials of Writers and Intellectuals in France*. Stanford: Stanford University Press, 1998.

Weil, Patrick. *How to Be French: Nationality in the Making Since 1870*. Trans. Catherine Porter. Durham: Duke University Press, 2008 [2002].

Weinstein, Arnold. *Northern Arts: The Breakthrough of Scandinavian Literature and Art, from Ibsen to Bergman*. Princeton: Princeton University Press, 2008.

Wertham, Fredric. "The Road to Rapallo." *American Journal of Psychotherapy* 3.4 (October 1949): 585–600.

West, Rebecca. "The Crown Versus William Joyce." *New Yorker*, September 29, 1945. 30–42.

West, Rebecca. *The Meaning of Treason*. Harmondsworth: Penguin, 1965 [1949].

Wilkinson, James D. *The Intellectual Resistance in Europe*. Cambridge: Harvard University Press, 1981.

Williams, William Carlos. "Ezra Pound: Lord Ga-Ga!" *Decision* 1.3 (September 1941): 16–24.

Wills, Clair. *That Neutral Ireland: A History of Ireland During the Second World War*. London: Faber and Faber, 2007.

Wimsatt, Jr., W. K. and M. C. Beardsley. "The Intentional Fallacy." *The Sewanee Review* 54.3 (July-September 1946): 468–88.

Wodehouse, P. G. "The Art of Fiction LX." *The Paris Review* 64 (1975): 149–171.

Wodehouse, P. G. "Berlin Broadcasts (I)." *Encounter*, October 1954. 17–24.

Wodehouse, P. G. *Joy in the Morning*. Stockholm: Continental Book Company, 1947 [1946].

Wodehouse, P. G. *A Life in Letters*. Ed. Sophie Ratcliffe. London: Hutchinson, 2011.

Wodehouse, P. G. *Over Seventy*. In *Wodehouse on Wodehouse*. Harmondsworth: Penguin, 1981. 465–645.

Wodehouse, P. G. *Performing Flea: A Self-Portrait in Letters*. London: Wyman and Sons, 1954.

Wodehouse, P. G. *Uncle Fred: An Omnibus*. London: Penguin, 1992.

Woolston, Howard. “Free Speech in War Time.” *American Sociological Review* 7.2 (April 1942): 185–93.

Žagar, Monika. *Knut Hamsun: The Dark Side of Literary Brilliance*. Seattle: University of Washington Press, 2009.

Zainea, Ion. *Politică și Administrație în România (6 martie 1945–1 martie 1946): Epurarea*. Oradea: Editura Universității din Oradea, 2004.

INDEX